Dark Harbor

A Chesapeake Bay Mystery

Vivian Lawry
and
W. Lawrence Gulick

iUniverse, Inc.
New York Bloomington

Dark Harbor
A Chesapeake Bay Mystery

This is a work of fiction. All of the characters, names, incidents, organizations, businesses, locations, and dialogue in this novel are either the products of the authors' imaginations or are used fictitiously.

iUniverse books may be ordered through booksellers or by contacting:

iUniverse
1663 Liberty Drive
Bloomington, IN 47403
www.iuniverse.com
1-800-Authors (1-800-288-4677)

ISBN: 978-1-4401-6734-8 (sc)
ISBN: 978-1-4401-6736-2 (dj)
ISBN: 978-1-4401-6735-5 (ebk)

Printed in the United States of America

iUniverse rev. date: 9/18/2009

DEDICATION

To all the gods,
goddesses,
and spirits
of the Sea.

ACKNOWLEDGEMENTS

Among the many people who supported and encouraged us during the writing of this book, we are especially grateful to those who read earlier versions of the manuscript and offered helpful insights and opinions: Doris Chalfin, Pam D'Antonio, Lawrence Greenberg, Patty Grieb, Joan Hamilton, Doug Jones, Joseph O. Humphreys, Rosaleen Humphreys, Donald Makosky, Kate Payne, Bennett Shaver, Barbara Sholley, Bill Sites, Peg Sites, Madlyn Smith, and Chris Steele. Other people too numerous to mention commented on chapters, plot, or other aspects of the story. You know who you are and we thank you.

Many people gave generously of their time and knowledge to help us get it right, including Charles F. Crossley, Jr., Ann Egolf, Winifred Gulick, Glenn Hargas, Valerie Ruth, David McGill, and the staff of the Centreville Historical Society. If we've overlooked anyone, our sincere apologies. And if we didn't get it right, the fault is ours.

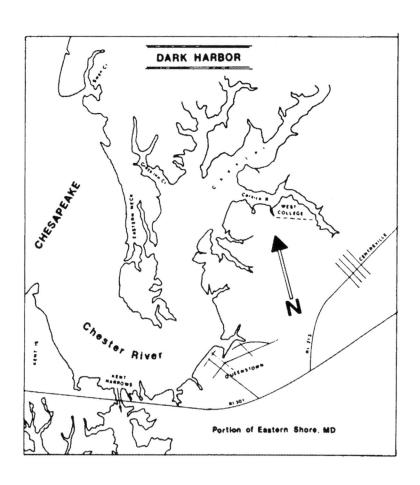

DARK HARBOR

CHESAPEAKE

Chester River

Portion of Eastern Shore, MD

CHAPTER ONE

Nora knocked on the patio door and waited, tapping her toe, her gaze gliding over lush vegetation and thick plantings marking the property line. Evergreens intermingled with oaks and maples in full fall plumage. "Never. I'll never leave my cell phone ashore again, no matter how short the sail." She glanced at her watch. "Ten-thirty. Surely he's up," she muttered. "Maybe he's out already." When her second knock went unanswered, she tried the sliding glass door. Unlocked. Opening it a crack, she called, "Ted? Hey. Anybody home?" She closed the door and waited.

Van said, "Damn. What about a public phone?"

"There isn't one within miles." Nora shaded her eyes against the glare of the morning sun and peered through the heavy glass. "There's a phone on the desk." She glanced at Van. "What the hell. I'm going in."

"You cannot just barge in."

"I most certainly can! And I will. What's the worst thing that could happen? I have to apologize to a colleague?"

Van retreated a step as Nora slid the door open. A feeling of invading someone else's space propelled her quickly across the floor. As she reached the desk, the smell engulfed her—dead and fetid. She gagged, clapped one hand over her mouth and nose, and whirled back toward the door. A body lay near the gas log fire, on its left side, curled into the fetal position. Stains, shiny and black, spattered the slate, smeared the floor, and clotted the hair. The skin was surreal—green and black. The bloated face, eyes and tongue protruding, looked like a Halloween mask. But the smell was real. And the hair. The hair moved. She recognized flies and maggots. She clamped her hand tighter over her mouth, muffling her "Oh, my God!" and pushed past Van in the open doorway. She made it outside just in time to vomit in the shrubbery. Van supported her as she retched, one arm around her waist, one hand on her forehead. Nora spit a couple of times and wiped her tongue on her sleeve. She felt light-headed.

He said, "What is it?"

"A body. Van, there's a body in there." Until now, her total experience with dead bodies had been the open-casket funerals of elderly relatives, seen only after the mortician had combed and rouged and puffed to the point that the bodies looked more like mannequins than people. "We've got to call the police. But . . ." She twisted the ring on her left hand, still queasy—and embarrassed for Van to see her acting such a ninny.

"I will call—if you like."

His formal phrases and solicitous tone put steel in Nora's spine. "No. I saw it. I'll call." She ran in, snatched the cordless phone from the desk, and rushed back outside without inhaling. Shaking, she closed the patio door. Fingers stiff, she had to dial 911 twice to get it right.

Less than ten minutes after the call, a petite blond with fluffy hair and freckles came around the corner of the house. "I'm Officer Barker. Are you the woman who called about a body?" Her piping, little girl voice struck Nora as comically inappropriate. Making people take her seriously would be an uphill climb, even wearing the gray-and-black uniform, the .40-caliber Beretta at her waist.

"Yes. I'm Nora Perry." Nora's five feet ten inches towered over the young officer.

"Are you sure this person is dead, not just injured?"

Nora swallowed hard and nodded. "Positive. The smell . . . And the bugs . . ."

"Did it look like an accident?"

Nora shook her head. "I couldn't . . . I didn't look that closely."

"Was there anyone else around when you got here?"

The question didn't register with Nora. Van stepped forward. "Not that we saw."

Barker turned to him. "And who are you? Did you go in the house?"

"Hendrick van Pelt. I stepped in briefly—a second or two."

"Did you touch anything? Move anything?" Her glance included both of them.

Van said, "No."

Nora shook her head, then frowned. "I mean, just the phone." She gestured in the direction of the instrument lying on the weathered picnic table. "It was on the desk."

"Okay. You two wait here. Don't go anywhere, don't touch anything." They nodded mutely in unison, and Nora thought they must look like a couple of bobble heads in yachting caps. Barker disappeared around the corner of the house. Van seemed to examine the vertical cedar siding and the Andersen sliding doors before he moved stiffly toward the chaise lounge. It was the first time Nora had seen him in pain. Thank goodness he wasn't one of those big, strong men who turn into whiny children when hurt. She hoped for the hundredth time that it was no more than a bruised back and a slight muscle strain.

Barker reappeared through the patio door, bringing the fetid smell with her. Nora swallowed her rising gorge and turned her face into the breeze from the harbor. Barker called the dispatcher—talking fast, nearly shouting. "I have a dead body, pretty rotten, probably male, in the living room. Massive head injuries. Not self-inflicted. Accidental is pretty much out of the question, too. No sign of a struggle, no sign of a break-in. The woman who called it in is here. Also a guy who says he only stepped inside for a few seconds. There's no one in the house. Send backup." Nora wondered whether she and Van should be overhearing such a call.

Nora had sagged against the patio table during the phone call. Now Barker got in her face and snapped, "Tell me about it." Nora blinked at her, trying to dispel the memory of the distorted face, trying to figure out what the officer wanted. Barker sucked in air and exhaled long, then spoke more slowly. "Tell me why you are here. Did you know the victim? Why did you go in the house? Tell me everything."

Nora's difficulty focusing upped her anxiety, and she struggled to be coherent. "Van and I anchored here last night." She waved toward *Duet*, swinging gently in the harbor. "We came up to the house this morning to use Ted's phone."

"Is the body him—Ted?"

"Yeah." Nora stopped. "I mean, I guess so. I didn't—We were colleagues—not really friends—I'm not sure who that is!"

"Back up a minute. Why did you need a phone?"

"A lightning strike fried my boat's electronics last night—including the radio. And we'd left our phones ashore." Nora gazed at her boat, thinking how much they'd expected to enjoy the sail, a day cut off from the outside world.

"Go on."

"What? Oh. He didn't answer when I knocked and called out, so I went in."

"You said you weren't friends, but you just walked in?" Barker vibrated with impatience.

"I had to! *Duet's* completely—inoperable. Sails ruined. No engine. I've got to get her towed—get a taxi home." Nora rubbed her forehead.

"You could have called from a neighbor's house."

"I didn't think about neighbors. And I saw the phone on the desk."

"Wasn't the door locked?"

"No. It was just the way I left it."

"So you charged in. Then what?"

"Nothing. I mean, I went in as far as the desk. And then I smelled it. And saw the hair move." Nora swallowed spittle and willed herself not to gag. "I ran out and threw up in the bushes." Heat surge into her face at the memory of Van holding her head, as if she were a sick child. "I made myself go back in for the phone."

"Did you see anyone else?" Nora shook her head. "Did you touch anything else?" Nora shook her head again.

Barker turned on Van. "And where were you when all of this was going on?"

Nora heard a distant siren. Before Van could answer, a patrol car rolled down Old Wharf Lane and Barker broke off questioning.

Nora remained propped against the table, sweaty hands clenched in her pockets. Police kept coming, apparently from nowhere. She wondered whether Frank Pierce would be among them. Probably. She looked at Van stretched out on a chaise lounge, eyes closed, and felt an almost overwhelming urge to say something, anything, to take her mind off what was in the house behind her. She knew her companion well enough to recognize his quiet repose for the mask it was. But not well enough to let herself just fall apart right before his eyes. She muttered "Get a grip" under her breath, marched to the low stone patio wall, and tried to find something to think about that would block out the sight and smell of the body.

CHAPTER TWO

Sunday morning, but Captain Franklin J. Pierce arrived at the scene barely an hour after the 911 call to the dispatcher. He'd left his wife and three-year-old twins on the church steps. Claire didn't protest, but her face settled into familiar lines of resignation.

Bystanders strolled up and down Old Wharf Lane and milled around the entrance to the driveway, straining to see. Even without bystanders, the area would have been crowded. Two white Queen Anne's County Sheriff's patrol cars blocked the drive, red, blue, and white lights flashing, black and gold letters sharp in the fall sunshine. A tan-on-brown State Police car hovered nearby, dark and threatening. Frank hoped the State Police weren't going to start a pissing contest over jurisdiction. The CID detectives' unmarked car stood behind Sheriff Bentley's gray Honda near the top of the driveway. Frank released a pent-up breath. Homicide in Queen Anne's County was a good news/bad news event. The good news was its rarity, not more than one a year. Last year and the year before that, none. The bad news was that when one came along, everyone with any excuse for being involved would be.

A reporter from the *Record Observer* pushed forward. "What can you tell us about the dead man? Was he murdered?"

Frank sidestepped deftly. He still had the slim build and quick grace that had defined his every move on the basketball court and earned him the nickname The Matador. "When there's a comment to be made, I'll make it," he said, ignoring questions from other bystanders.

As captain and chief deputy, Frank ranked second in command after the sheriff. He had more training and broader experience than anyone else on the force—including the sheriff—but there was no way in hell that the good people of rural Queen Anne's County would elect a black man sheriff. He'd known that when he came back twelve years ago. But he'd wanted out of Philadelphia—out of the politics, out of city life—and so was willing to be the top non-elected officer. He'd never regretted the trade-offs.

Officer Barker guarded the front door, rocking on the balls of her feet, giving the impression of a small missile about to be launched. Frank would know soon enough whether her training or her inexperience had carried the day. He stopped to speak to Sheriff Bentley. "Mornin', Jake. What do we have here?" It didn't hurt to give the sheriff his due when it cost no more than an unnecessary question.

"Mornin', Frank. I don't know any more than you do. It sounds like murder." The man with the flame-red hair and slightly soft middle had to look up to his tall, athletic captain. He never seemed to mind. Frank and Jake had different strengths and respected each other for them. The sheriff said, "Given your experience and all, we decided to wait for you to get a first look in the house."

Frank surveyed the officers standing around, tense and eager, and knew waiting had been Jake's decision. "Thanks." He suppressed any sign of irritation. Everyone should have stayed on the street. Any evidence in the driveway, the flagstone walk, or the yard might as well have been trampled by elephants.

"The CID men went in a while ago. I trust you trained them well the last time." Bentley smiled.

In theory, the Criminal Investigation Division was in charge. Mostly, the Queen Anne's County CID got forgeries, narcotics, thefts, B&Es during daylight hours, maybe half a dozen rapes a year—not much homicide experience, compared to Frank's thirteen years in the city. Joe Jamieson had eighteen years of police work, but all of it was in Queen Anne's County. So Joe and Sy Brown, along with everyone else from the patrol officers to the sheriff himself, knew Captain Pierce would be running this one.

"I guess I'd better get at it. I'll catch you later, Jake." Frank strode to the door.

"Morning, Frank. You want a rundown?" At Frank's nod, Barker launched into a detailed account of everything she had done since the call came in. "It looks like someone bashed his head in while he was fixing himself a drink. I didn't see any signs of a struggle or a search or anything. The body's pretty disgusting."

"Who's been in?"

"Just me and the woman who found the body. She said she didn't touch anything but the phone. The guy with her says he just stepped inside the door, didn't touch anything. Joe and Sy are in there now."

"Good work. Walk me through it." Cindy looked pleased but said nothing as she followed him into the house.

Frank paused in the oak-floored foyer. On the right, a door to the kitchen. The adjacent dining area with its wrought iron-and-brass railing along the far side overlooked a sunken living room, maybe 15 x 35 feet. Joe Jamieson stood at the bottom of the step-down. When Sy Brown saw Frank, he clasped his hands behind his back and joined Joe.

While Jamieson and Brown sketched the scene and took measurements, Frank concentrated on getting a feel for the place, and thus the man. It looked like a decorator's showroom in a high-end furniture store: Oriental rugs on expanses of hard-wood, large modern paintings and small abstract sculptures, furniture covered in leather and coordinated prints, and a wall on the harbor side nearly all glass.

Floor-to-ceiling bookcases surrounded a desk, desk chair, and wet bar in the left half of the sunken room. To the right, two- and three-seater sofas and two club chairs flanked three sides of a coffee table near the fireplace. Slate hearth. Gas fireplace logs, on low. To the right of the fireplace stood a set of wrought iron fireplace tools with brass handles, matching the railing that separated the two levels. The poker was missing. The body lay between the coffee table and the fireplace, half curled on its left side as if tackled carrying a football, head toward the two-seater, feet toward the sliding glass doors. Except for the body—and the blood—the only thing that appeared to be out of place was an overturned ice bucket.

Frank moved in for a closer look, careful not to step on stains. A white man, probably in his forties, generally fit under all the bloat. The hair not covered by dried blood or insects was dark brown. Frank suppressed his revulsion. The distorted features and putrid odor brought back countless similar bodies from his years in Philadelphia. This one wore silk pajama bottoms and an embroidered smoking jacket with velvet lapels, no shoes or socks. "A regular Hugh Hefner," he said. The visible parts of the body showed massive black and green discoloration. Breathing through his mouth to minimize the smell, Frank looked closely at the head wound. Flies, maggots, beetles. He reached to lift the right elbow to check rigor but stopped short, realizing he might pull off the skin. By the time a body had decomposed this much, rigor would have passed off. Blood had pooled and dried around the man's head. Splashes, all dried now, dotted the sofas, the club chairs, the floor, the fireplace, and the wall. Two bloody smears marred the larger sofa. A single sandstone coaster and a bowl of mixed nuts and dried fruit sat on the end of the coffee table. Near the overturned ice bucket stood an unopened bottle of tonic and a small bowl of shriveled lime wedges.

Frank turned to Joe and Sy. "Who is it?"

Joe answered. "Seems to be Theodore Slater, a teacher at West College." He slid a careful look at Frank. "Nora Perry made the 911 call." Now Frank understood the careful look. "She said she couldn't recognize the body, but according to her, Slater lives here." Frank paused to absorb the fact that his former lover had found the body. What was she doing here? Were she and the dead man involved? And who was the man Barker mentioned? Frank looked through the patio doors. Nora sat on the low stone wall, facing the harbor. No man was visible. When Frank tuned back in, Joe was saying, "There's a wallet on the dresser in the master bedroom with a driver's license for Theodore Slater. As best I can tell, this guy fits the description: brown hair, brown eyes, six-two, a hundred and eighty pounds, age forty-two. There's a car in the garage registered to Slater."

Frank thrust thoughts of Nora aside and focused on proceeding as usual. "What else have we got?"

"No sign of forced entry. But who'd need to? The patio door was unlocked when Barker got here, the curtains open like you see, and Nora says she found it that way. The garage door was locked, but the doors from the garage to the yard and the kitchen weren't. Barker says the front door was unlocked too." Joe gestured with his notebook. "There's no sign anyone else was living here, but we just got started."

Sy spoke for the first time, a little too loudly. "I think he was expecting a woman. Maybe her husband or her lover came instead and beat the shit out of him." He clamped his mouth shut and shot a glance toward Frank.

"Why's that?" Frank asked.

Sy raised his chin and spoke to a spot above Frank's right shoulder. "Everything. The way he's dressed. Everything all spic-and-span in the bathroom, the bed all smooth. He was a stud expecting a big night. But the bruises—no woman could've beat him up like that."

"Interesting idea. I'll take a look around, and then we'll talk about it." Frank started toward the bedroom door. "The state crime lab ought to have somebody out here from Pikesville any minute. You guys start taking pictures and measurements."

Joe took pictures, room by room, in the usual clockwise fashion, each frame overlapping the one before. Sy took notes. Following the big-view pictures, they took close-ups of the immediate area of the crime, measuring devices included in each shot.

Frank emerged from the bedroom. "Thanks for the walk-through, Barker. I expect the bystanders are getting antsy. Get back out there and help keep access under control." She looked disappointed but left without protest.

Joe spoke first. "So, what do you make of it?"

"I'd say he's been dead at least thirty-six hours, less than forty-eight. What Sy took for a beating is decomposition, advanced by heat from the fire." Frank glanced from one detective to the other. "He entertained a woman before he was killed. He knew and trusted the killer." Frank's thoughts flicked again to Nora Perry. "A woman could have done it. I'd say it was a spur-of-the-moment crime, probably an act of rage." He looked directly at Sy as he delivered this contrary version of the murder.

Joe seemed puzzled, Sy skeptical. "What makes you think that?" Sy demanded.

"Exactly what isn't clear?" Frank kept his tone mild, his gaze steady.

"Everything. How you can be so sure about time of death, that a woman had already been here—everything."

"First, there's the local fauna. Ten minutes after somebody's dead, flies arrive. After twelve hours you get maggots. Beetles arrive between twenty-four and thirty-six hours, and spiders at forty-eight. There are no spiders yet, and the rigor has passed off, which usually takes thirty hours or more." Frank flipped his hand toward the coffee table. "The scene doesn't fit with a death yesterday morning, so I place it the night before." Frank paused. "As for the rest of it—well, the murderer was able to get behind him and swing the weapon—probably the missing poker—while he was making a drink, which looks like someone he knew and trusted. He was hit at least three times. The first blow must have felled him, or he'd have turned around, struggled. More blows tell me the assailant was really ramped up. It might have been a drug high, I suppose. Or extreme panic or fear. But I'd opt for rage." Sy looked at him stonily, and Frank wondered whether Sy's problem was with him, with authority, or with blacks. "You were on the right track, in general. A woman's pretty definitely involved, but she'd already arrived—and maybe left—before he died." He glanced at Sy again. "Any woman he was entertaining in silk pajamas would probably have come in if he didn't answer the door, and nobody reported the body—*any* body—on Friday night."

"Maybe she was scared. Or stood him up."

"Maybe. But there was a condom wrapper on the bedside table—"

"Where?" Sy's face could have been chiseled in marble.

"Under the edge of the clock." Frank answered with more patience than he felt. "Not that everything fits. There are plenty of questions left."

Joe puckered his brow. "Like what? Besides who the dame was, I mean."

"Well, as Sy noticed, the towels are fresh, and the bed hasn't been slept in. Now, if it had nothing to do with the murder, why was everything tidied up after sex? There are no dirty towels or sheets that I could see. The lab technician needs to check the hamper. What's taking him so long anyhow?" Frank glanced toward the door and back to Joe. Joe shrugged. "I think things were cleaned up and taken away. If he was entertaining, why only one coaster? It looks like he was standing over the ice bucket when he got clobbered—probably fixing a drink. There's an empty gin bottle in the trash but no alcohol on the table. When the Pikesville technician gets here, I want the handles of the freezer and the dishwasher dusted for prints. We need to know what's inside."

Sy started to ask another question when Frank realized that they had been joined by a medium woman: medium height, medium weight, medium age, medium-brown hair. "It sounds like you've done my work for me." She wrinkled her nose. "Whew. We've got a ripe one. Sorry it took so long to get here. There was an accident on the Bay Bridge. I'm Madeline Goldberg." When no one responded she added, "From the state crime lab." Still no one spoke. She cast a disgusted look in their direction and removed a putrefaction mask from her bag.

Frank recovered first. "Sorry. We were expecting Charlie Long. He worked with us on the last one."

"Charlie's been retired for two years. I'm his replacement."

Frank cocked his head and grinned. "Guess that tells you something about the homicide rate in Queen Anne's County."

"Yes, well, give me some background."

Frank nodded to Joe. Officially, it was his baby. After the summary Frank added, "So we'd like to get a look in the dishwasher, the clothes hamper, and the closets as soon as you can clear them."

Madeline gestured toward the patio. "Is that disoriented-looking woman out there the one who found the body?"

Joe hit his forehead with the heel of his hand. "Jesus, I forgot. Sy, go get their statements. They can come in tomorrow and sign them."

Sy hesitated, scowling, and Frank guessed he was wondering whether he was being brushed aside or given a responsibility. Frank said, "I'll talk to them," and started toward the patio. He hadn't spoken to Nora in nearly ten years, but it had to happen sometime.

As he left, Madeline called after him. "I need their fingerprints and shoe treads before you let them go!"

"Hello, Nora."

She whirled to face him. Her yachting cap tilted at an incongruously jaunty angle. The breeze coaxed wisps of auburn hair from her single French braid, the curls glinting in the sun. "Hello, Frank. It's been a long time." She looked like a fiery-haired Diana, just back from the hunt. She would be fifty-one now—three years older than he—but she looked more like forty.

Frank masked the emotion that spurted through him under a cold glare and brusque tone. "You needed a telephone." Nora said nothing. "Was there some other reason you just happened to be here?"

"What do you mean?"

Frank turned to Van. "And who are you?"

Before Van could answer, Nora stepped between the two men. "This is Hendrick van Pelt, a faculty colleague of mine."

Why the hell be so protective? Were Nora and Slater lovers? If so, what was her relationship with van Pelt? He ignored Van's extended hand and barked at Nora: "What the hell were you doing here?"

Nora lifted her chin and threw back her shoulders in that old, familiar way. "Damn it, Frank, what's your problem?"

What indeed? He needed to calm down. Nora was not a woman to be bullied. He forced a more neutral tone. "The rep from the state crime lab needs fingerprints and shoe treads from both of you. I'll be back in a few minutes. Don't leave till I get your statements."

As he left he heard Nora say, "How the hell does he think we could leave?"

Inside the house, Frank glanced around the crime scene, ostensibly checking progress. He had to marshal his thoughts. He wouldn't get anywhere going off half-cocked. And he damn well couldn't let his history with Nora screw up the investigation.

Returning to the patio, he said, "I'll need to talk to each of you separately."

"That's silly. We were together the whole time. There's no need to hear it twice."

"That wasn't a request, Nora." She looked like a smoldering volcano. If he interviewed her first, maybe he could forestall an eruption. He glanced at Van, who had said nothing so far and seemed content with that. "Let's sit on that bench under the trees." He thought she might continue to argue, but after a long, hard look, she turned on her heel and stomped off toward the bench, French braid swinging.

Frank sat beside her, notebook in hand. "So, what were you doing here?"

Nora lifted her chin. "Are you actually going to let me answer this time?"

Her question was justified, but he admitted it only to himself. He cocked his head. "Not only will I let you answer, I want it in detail. Start with why you came to Queenstown harbor."

"We had only an overnight. This is a pretty little anchorage, and not too far from my mooring at the college."

Frank looked at the harbor, at lumps of milfoil on hummocks where the shore went marshy. The bright greens of the late-spring sea grasses had passed through the deep greens of summer to muted shades of brown. A pretty little anchorage. Only an overnight.

"But as a last sail of the season, it was more bust than boom." She stared across the water as if watching the events she described. "We had a hell of a blow coming down the Chester River. It swept in out of nowhere, sheets of rain racing toward us across the Chesapeake, pellets bouncing on the gray water as if they were rubber hitting concrete. We were trying to get anchored when I lost steerage, and *Duet* veered broadside to the wind and waves. Van pitched backward onto a corner of the forward hatch." Her tone turned defensive. "But that wasn't my fault! We found out later that the key had slipped out of the rudderpost."

Grateful for Nora's habit of long, detailed stories, Frank nodded encouragement as if he knew what she was talking about. Anything might be helpful. "So then what?"

"We came in here and anchored for the night."

"Did you see Ted Slater?"

Nora shook her head. "Only his lights. I've been thinking about it—what we might have seen. But I really wasn't paying attention. Everything on the boat had been thrown helter-skelter. By the time we put things to rights and ate supper, another storm rolled over us. It started with a few drops of rain pinging on the cockpit sole. No wind. I thought we might just swing a little on the anchor. But the next thing I knew, lightning was everywhere. I was thrown into the stove." Nora rubbed her upper arm absently. "Everything went black. We'd taken a hit on the mast. After, the harbor was totally dark. The ambient light from shore was no use at all."

Frank glanced at the sailboat anchored in the harbor. "I'm glad it wasn't too bad."

"How can you say that?" Her question dripped with outrage. "The only reason we didn't burn—or sink—was because the strike went to the grounding plate at the bottom of the keel. But it blew the electronics—the VHF radio—all the instruments. The distributor, starter, alternator—all burned black. Battery cables, hoses. No lights. No bilge pump. No engine. How can you say it wasn't too bad?"

"Calm down, Nonnie. How would I know?" The old endearment fell easily from his lips. "So is the boat yours?" Nora nodded. "I'm glad you finally got her."

"I bought her right after we . . . She was secondhand, of course. Nothing beats being on the water. But after last night . . ."

Frank wrenched his focus from the quiver in Nora's voice back to the business at hand. "So last night was the big storm. And you saw nothing out of the ordinary."

Nora considered. "Nothing. We saw lights from several of the houses. I heard music, but I'm not sure where it came from. I woke in the middle of the night and noticed that Ted's lights were still on." She glanced sideways at Frank. "I thought he might be entertaining. Which is why we didn't row ashore till mid-morning."

"What about other boats?"

Nora shook her head. "If there had been another boat, the skipper would have called a tow for us."

Frank tilted his head. "Surely you have a cell phone. Did that get fried too?"

"We left them ashore on purpose—to get away from it all." She took a deep breath. "I still need to call the marina and get *Duet* towed."

"Not till we're done with the crime scene."

"Frank, be reasonable! *Duet* had nothing to do with anything. Ted was dead long before we even got here."

"And you know this how?"

"The smell, of course." Nora shuddered. "And the way he looked."

Of course she would draw the right inference. "So where were you Friday night?" Frank held up a hand. "Just routine questions. I have to ask everybody."

"Home. Grading papers." Nora plucked at her pant leg. "How am I going to get them finished now? Damn!"

"Were you alone?"

"Grading papers is not a social activity."

When Frank interviewed Van, he confirmed Nora's version of all that had transpired. His stiff manner and formal speech gave the impression of someone older than his apparent age of forty or so. Frank said, "I'd think you'd want to sail longer than a day."

"Always. But this trip was a bonus. We had not expected to sail at all."

"What changed?"

"Nora had lent her boat to Lydia Howard—President Howard's wife—for a Wednesday-to-Sunday sail. It is my understanding that John's fund-raising trip was canceled, so Lydia cut her sail short. She returned *Duet* to the college mooring basin around noon yesterday."

Frank made a note to follow up with Nora. Why hadn't she mentioned that? Then again, why would she? Frank tried to be objective. He had nothing against van Pelt except that he was good-looking in a solemn sort of way and took overnight sails with Nora—something he had never done. None of which should matter to a happily married man. *Didn't* matter.

He had no reason to think that Nora or Van killed Ted Slater on Friday and then arranged to sail in on Saturday to find the body on Sunday. He closed his notebook and said that they were free to go as soon as Madeline Goldberg gave the all clear.

Frank rejoined Madeline and Joe. "Someone's wiped down the faucets and other surfaces in the bathroom and kitchen," she said. "I'll come back to the less likely places later. You can search here now—but touch only the surfaces already dusted. And I want prints from all of you."

"They're already on file!" Joe said.

Madeline didn't look up. "Yes, but I like to take my own. Humor me."

Frank watched her work. "We think there was a woman here. I'd appreciate anything you can give me from the bedroom." Madeline nodded.

Frank and Joe trailed after her to the bedroom, taking notes. "Let's see. We have several strands of long, brown hair here." Madeline mixed a yellow powder and liquid. "Imdamediome—great stuff." She applied the mixture to the condom wrapper. "Voila! Two prints on the condom wrapper. You want to bet on his and hers? And what's this? Could be thumbprints on the headboard—left and right—but they've been wiped over, nothing usable." She worked on the back of the headboard in silence, then chortled, "Pay dirt! We've got a couple of smudges and *six* good ones! Now, let's see. More prints on the lamp, different yet." She looked at Frank, her eyebrows reaching for her hairline. "This room got a lot of traffic."

Frank's relief that the long hair was brown faded. The possibility still existed that some of the fingerprints were Nora's. "I'll want comparisons with the ones on the phone."

"Sure thing." Madeline moved back to the outer room, started dusting the bar and the liquor bottles. "We've got at least two sets here that we haven't seen before." She started around the periphery of the room, concentrating the electrostatic duster on the sections of floor that had no rugs. She examined the bathroom and kitchen floors, using amido black solution to raise telltale signs of blood. She signaled Frank and Joe that they could walk around again and, in response to Frank's inquiry, said, "It's a mixed bag. Someone cleaned up, all right. The remains of bloody tracks are everywhere, crossing and recrossing the kitchen, the bathroom, and the rugs—but no useable treads. Everything's pretty smudged, except for a couple of half prints under the wet bar, where someone's toes were off the rug. It looks to me like men's shoes, maybe size eight D. All the bloody prints are indistinct, but at least some of them are longer and narrower than the ones under the cabinet."

Madeline made measurements, collected fibers and other trace evidence, working methodically from the periphery of the living room toward the body. As she measured the blood spatter patterns and lifted fingerprints, she continued. "It looks like your perp is right-handed, maybe five-seven to five feet nine inches tall. Someone sat there after getting bloody," she said, gesturing toward the two-seater. "Maybe there were two assailants." Finally, she examined the corpse, measuring the temperature of both the body and air before turning off the gas fire.

Frank joined the sheriff outside. "It's going to be a long day: someone's tidied up the crime scene. Why don't you come on in? Just give me a minute to talk to the *Record Observer* and clear out some of the unnecessary people."

"Great. Not much going on out here. About an hour or so ago, a West College kid stopped by. Said he worked for Professor Slater and needed to deliver some exams." Jake gestured toward the yellow tape. "He could see it's a crime scene and started asking questions. I saw him talking to the *Record Observer* guy—maybe half an hour. He seemed pretty shaken up when he left."

"Did you get his name?"

"Schuyler Buckner Brady—the Third. Goes by Sky."

Dark had fallen before Goldberg gave the all clear to remove the body. The forensic investigator—one of four emergency medical technicians who volunteered to do that work—arrived to handle the paperwork and pronounce the body dead. The Newman Funeral Home hearse was close behind, come to transport the body to the Baltimore City Morgue. Frank dispatched Sy Brown to follow the hearse, maintain the chain of custody, and get a receipt for the body.

By the time Goldberg finished, hundreds of evidence bags—tagged, labeled, and initialed—filled the foyer. Fingerprints of at least five people besides the victim dotted various surfaces: the Bombay Sapphire gin bottle, the Knob Creek bourbon bottle, the nightstand, several cabinets, the desk, the front door latch, and the glass found under the body. The dishwasher held a full dinner service for two, including wineglasses and one tumbler that matched the one under the body. There was no empty wine bottle in the trash, no open wine bottle anywhere in the house. The bathroom wastebasket was empty. There were no sheets or towels in the hamper, the washer, or the dryer.

Frank turned to Joe Jamieson, slumped wearily against the doorframe. "I don't know exactly what or how much, but stuff's definitely missing. The perp probably hauled it away. But get someone out here to drag the harbor tomorrow anyway. And bag everything from the trashcan outside too—just in case."

Joe's "Sure thing" came with a yawn.

They'd found nothing to identify Slater's female visitor unless it was the elegant black umbrella from the hall closet, the initials L.S. inlaid in brass on the wooden handle. That could belong to a man, of course—though it looked dainty to Frank. The black lace bra in the dresser was probably too common to be helpful. None of the near neighbors to the west on the harbor were home for questioning, but the neighbor at 210 Old Wharf Lane told Sy he had seen a red sports car leaving Slater's drive on Friday afternoon, throwing gravel and nearly taking out his mailbox on the way. He couldn't give a description. No one else had either seen or heard anything suspicious.

Frank exhaled wearily as he thought of the investigation ahead: getting in touch with the Human Resources Office at West College about next of kin; questioning Slater's family and colleagues about enemies; identifying L.S. and the driver of the red sports car; going through Slater's bank records, his address book, his calendar. The start of a murder investigation always felt like the beginning of an interminable uphill climb.

Decades-old images of Nora Perry plagued his drive home: pacing in front of the classroom, patting the figure-eight twist at the nape of her neck, striding across campus, dancing naked in the moonlight with her hair flowing free. The memories flickered in his head like scenes from an ancient home movie. He'd thought he got over her years ago.

CHAPTER THREE

Sky drove back to campus thinking about Professor Slater. Dead. He remembered the President's Farewell to Summer Party. Sky had been tending bar, part of his work-study job, when Slater had strolled up to the portable bar and said, "I say, Brady. You do remember that you're supposed to be my teaching assistant this term, don't you? Let's get one thing clear. I won't have my work put off while you dragoon unsuspecting high schoolers into applying for admission or lead the swim team to fame and glory—or pour drinks for the president." The remark smarted. Sky passed it off with a joke about his dedication but silently vowed Slater would have no cause for criticism. Grading the multiple-choice part of Friday's exam had been his most important assignment so far. Professor Slater had ordered them marked and delivered to his house by mid-afternoon on Sunday. And now he was dead. Sky glanced at the jumble of papers on the seat beside him. What the hell should he do with them now?

When Sky walked in, his roommate sat at the computer. Without looking up, Brad said, "Where the hell've you been?" He swiveled around. "Hey, what's up? You look like hell." Sky sank onto his bed and dropped his head onto his fists. "C'mon, man, speak to me. Did you wreck your car? What?"

Finally, Sky whispered, "It's Professor Slater. He's dead."

"Holy shit! *Dead?* How? What happened? Holy shit!"

Sky stared into space. "I went to his place to drop off the exams, and there were all these people and police cars. They said it was a crime scene, and no one was allowed in. But people were talking. The guy from the *Record Observer* said it was murder, that someone had

20

bludgeoned him to death." As he talked, Sky's voice rose in pitch. "The police are still there."

Someone pounded on the door. Louisa shouted, "Hey, guys, open up! Time to eat. You didn't go without me, did you?"

Sky blinked, shaking his head. "Geez. I forgot about Louisa."

Brad opened the door. Louisa strode into the room saying, "Okay, guys, move it, move it, move it. Haul your asses out of here." She had been pretty tightly wrapped recently. She stopped short when she saw Sky. "What is it?"

Brad rocked from foot to foot. Sky held out his hand. "Oh, Weezie—Jesus, you better come sit down." Louisa, pale and still, just looked at him. He thought she might faint. She walked stiffly to the bed and sat beside him. He took her hand in both of his. "I don't know how to tell you this. But . . . That is . . . I mean . . . Ted Slater's dead! I was just at his house. They're saying his head was bashed in."

The last tinge of pink gracing her cheeks drained away. "Dead? When? What happened?"

Sky leaned forward, elbows on knees, and stared at the floor between his feet. "I don't know. Someone said a couple of sailors found him. People're saying it must be murder. The guy from the *Record Observer* had been there since late this morning—seemed to know everything. He said there was a lot of blood and stench and insects. He must've been dead for days." Sky cut a sideways look at Louisa. "Sorry, Weezie. I shouldn't've said . . . But it's probably gonna be all over the papers by tomorrow."

Louisa frowned. "Days? It can't be more than two days." Sky and Brad stared at her. "I mean, didn't you talk to him on Friday about the exam?"

Sky tried to read her expressionless face, white as a peeled potato. "No. That was Wednesday. I just monitored the exam Friday afternoon."

Brad broke in. "Hey, if this is gonna be in the paper and everything, we oughta tell College Relations. And what about the president? Did anybody call President Howard?" Sky shrugged. "People are gonna be calling him, for sure." Brad rubbed his hands together as he talked. "We gotta tell a couple of the VIPs what's up."

Sky considered it. "Yeah, well, you got a point."

Louisa stood up. "I don't feel like eating after all." She left without looking back.

Brad said, "You work the president's parties all the time. You think we ought to call or go over to his house?"

Sky didn't answer. He stared at the closed door. Two days ago. Friday. Louisa had borrowed his car. That night she came back with a banged-up face and said she had taken a header on the curb outside Baxter Hall. And now, the way she was acting. *Christ*, he thought. *No way. No way.*

CHAPTER FOUR

Nora pulled the dinghy parallel with Slater's dock and scrambled in. "Don't go all macho on me. There's no reason for you to row with a strained back and an injured shoulder." They had sailed together often over the past two months, but Nora suspected that her colleague still felt awkward being rowed about by a woman. Van glanced back toward Ted's patio. Maybe he was concerned about being observed. But he stepped into the middle of the dink without demur and settled onto the stern seat. Nora braced her feet against his seat for maximum thrust and pulled toward *Duet*.

Boarding *Duet* from the stern, Nora clambered up the ladder and secured the dink. She started to offer Van a hand up but realized in time that that would add insult to his injury. Instead, she set about coiling lines and stuffing debris into garbage bags. Now that Frank had finally released them and a towboat was on the way, she was impatient to get going. Caustic air billowed up from the cabin, a remnant of the electrical fire and meltdown. She wondered how long the stench would permeate the cabin, how much repairs would cost, when the towboat would arrive. She came topside to stretch her back and scanned the harbor. The old town water tank soared above the tree line, a century-old sentinel that still dominated the center of the village. Closer to hand, sawgrass sharp and rough enough to cut flesh shared the shoreline with tall flowering tufts of light brown sedge, short stretches of sand, and private seawalls of wood or riprap. Gulls perched on the pilings of Slater's dock, facing into the breeze. From markings on the pilings and the brown stalks of the grasses, Nora estimated that the tidal change in the harbor wasn't much more than a foot. She caught a whiff of rotted sea grasses and decaying fish, the musty odor of sun-baked, salt-covered rocks—pleasantly natural contrasts to the chemical smell of last night's electrical fires. Or the cloying stench of dead bodies. In one place the generally low-lying land formed an elevated plateau on which stood the Bollingly Estate, captured by the British in the war of 1812. How could a setting so serene hold the gore and blood that had once been Ted Slater?

Her gaze moved uneasily to Van on the foredeck. His summer employment as a sailing instructor at the Gibson Island Yacht Club kept him fit and bleached his straight brown hair almost blond. Well-worn jeans, boat shoes without socks, and an old white cotton sweater with the outline of a Navy anchor stitched on the front. His clothes suited him. He winced retrieving her brass anchor light from the bowstay, and Nora wondered just how serious his injuries were.

Nora perched on a cockpit cushion near the helm. Settling onto the cushion beside her, Van turned the light over in his hands, unscrewing the cap to get a better look at the ground glass lens. "Good news: neither the lens nor the brass canister was damaged. Replace the battery and it will be fine." He handed the light to Nora.

"Thank goodness. It was a gift from a friend in Maine." Nora stared across the harbor. "He finally grew too old and ill to sail. He mailed the light to me just two days before he died." She cleared her throat. "This week was her maiden voyage on *Duet*."

"She's a beauty. I much prefer an anchor light hung at the bow in the old fashioned way, compared to the modern ones at the tops of masts." Van looked from Ted Slater's house to his little landing dock on the point, where the old ferry dock used to be. "Had you been in Ted's house before?"

"Not often. And not recently. The views are wonderful." Nora swept her arm in a broad arc. "If I weren't so happy where I am, Queenstown harbor would be the place for me. Would have been, before today." She looked at her watch. "Where the hell is the towboat?"

"This murder will certainly shock the campus. How do you think his students will take it?"

Nora cocked one eyebrow. "Hard. Most students loved him. He was reputed to be knowledgeable, witty, suave, and to go the extra mile with any student who needed or wanted help."

"I heard he came from wealth."

"W-e-ll . . ." Nora zipped her windbreaker. "I don't know about coming from wealth, but when his parents died—both of them, in a car crash—what with their retirement accounts and the house and insurance and everything, I think he inherited a bundle. Rumor has it that consulting work doubled his faculty salary and then some. His house looks like it, anyway! He has a lot of art, including at least a few important pieces." Nora stood as the towboat chugged toward the mouth of the harbor. "Ahhhh. At last."

The towboat slid to a stop near the bow and Van moved forward. The operator cupped his hands around his mouth and shouted to Van, "Skipper, do you know how to rig the scufflehead?"

"Yes!" He caught the scuffle in midair, fed the double lines through the port and starboard fairleads and secured them to the bow cleat.

The operator smiled. "Good job, skipper. I'll keep you on a short tow line, maybe thirty feet, so stay directly astern. We'll make better time if you don't wander all over the goddamn bay."

Van chuckled as he returned to the cockpit. "Did you hear the towboat operator's comment about steering?"

Nora glowered, her body rigid, right hand gripping the oak tiller. She struggled to stifle her anger before answering. "As if we didn't know how to take a tow." The words sounded petulant and peevish, even to her own ear. She thrust the tiller into Van's hand and turned aft.

He brought *Duet* in line with the towboat as it churned toward the Chester River. "What is wrong?"

"Why didn't you tell the towboat operator that you aren't the skipper?"

"What?"

"Why didn't you tell him? Did you *want* him to think you are the skipper?"

Van fell back, looking stunned. "I did not intentionally mislead him."

"But you didn't correct him, either!"

"I was securing the towline. Why does that offend you?"

"He called you skipper *twice*. It's just so typical, always assuming the man is in charge of a boat. And you played into it!"

"I was just attending to business. Tell me. Do all feminists have hair triggers?"

"If they're worth their salt—yes."

Van made a half bow. "I apologize for the offense. It will not happen again." A smile twitched at the corner of his mouth.

Realizing that her reaction was over the top, she tried to match his tone when she said, "Thank you." When she touched his cheek, he placed a kiss in her palm, folded her fingers around it, then dropped his free arm across her shoulder.

Nora inhaled deeply. "I'm sorry I couldn't control my boat. Sorry I injured you."

"For God's sake, Nora, it was not your fault. Anyone would lose control of a boat if the key came out of the rudder post in a storm. Get over it. Please."

"Done. I'll not mention it again." She stared at their churning wake. "Pretty ironic, huh? We seldom get above five knots under sail. But here we are in a disabled boat going twice that fast." Nora felt like she would cry any minute. "The damage to my boat—it just hurts so much. I was wakeful all night. And then finding Ted. Everything's getting to me."

By late afternoon they were a few miles from the entrance to the Kent Island narrows. Van went forward to check the tow line and gave a thumbs-up to the operator. On his way back to the cockpit, he examined a deck fitting and the twisted strands of the stainless steel port shroud. He said, "The deck fitting loosened, and the port shroud is partially severed"

Nora sighed. "At least we won't lose the mast."

"We will know more once *Duet* is hauled. But given the voltage that came down the mast and shrouds, my guess is that there will be hull damage on the keel around the grounding plate."

Words and tone right out of a physics professor's mouth. Nora grinned crookedly. "On the bright side, it could have happened in early summer and ruined the whole season."

"Atta girl."

The first slang expression she'd ever heard from Van! Once when he said, "Let us depart," Nora had laughed. At his questioning look, she explained: "Anybody else would have said, 'Let's go.'" He had flushed and said, "My father disdained contractions. He said that at best they are examples of uncultured language and at worst, they are evidence of lazy habits of thought. I learned well." Nora had apologized for laughing and assured him that his speech fell pleasantly on her ear. A strange bird. A physics professor, but he seemed to be a romantic, quiet and intense. One time he said that he was a born poet who stumbled into technology. She suspected that his sex life was as conservative as his life in general. What would he think if he knew of her '60s sexual standards? What would he do if she ever tried to get physical with him? Did he know that she and Frank had been lovers? Probably. It hadn't been a secret—had been the talk of Centreville at the time. So many years later, she hadn't expected such a gut-felt response to seeing him again. She shifted uncomfortably against the abrasive thoughts. "Have you thought about who might have killed Ted?"

Van shook his head. "I just keep thinking that when we anchored in the harbor, Ted was lying dead in his house."

"Me, too. A little. But mostly I think about the body. Finding his body was the most horrifying experience of my life. I'll never forget the stench. Unfortunately. Olfactory memories have an uncanny ability to summon the past. No doubt I'll live with this for the rest of my life."

"I did not see him clearly, only out of the corner of my eye. But one could not avoid the smell."

"The blood. The bugs. And his skin—it didn't even look human. Who could have done such a thing? And why?"

Van ran a thumb along his jaw. "Do you suppose Captain Pierce suspects us? I read somewhere that the person who finds the body is often the perpetrator."

The suggestion surprised Nora. "Frank? Suspect us? No way."

"You must admit he did not seem especially friendly."

"No. Well. We hadn't talked in years. Look," she said, pointing skyward. More than a hundred geese in chevron formation were flying south.

Van said, "That is the prettiest thing I have seen on this trip—with the exception of you, through the forward hatch, fast asleep—and certainly an improvement over the murder scene."

Nora's heartbeat skipped a couple of times. She motioned toward the mainsail, partially burned and melted on the boom. "I suppose I should try to get that off."

Van said, "Take the helm. I will attend to the main."

"Get real. Don't aggravate your injuries." Nora struggled to get the melted nylon lines loose from the clips, then started peeling the mainsail off the boom, stuffing the remnants into the sail bag.

After several minutes, Van said, "By the way, have you heard anything about John Howard being a candidate for the presidency of another college? Clyde Barnes was talking about it in the locker room last week."

"If Clyde's talking about it, it's hardly a secret anymore. Nevertheless, please don't repeat what I'm about to say." Van nodded his assent. "He's a candidate at Waldorf College. I'm one of his references. I was on the search committee when he was hired at West, you know. Anyway, a faculty member on the Waldorf search committee phoned me. They are screening possibles for off-campus interviews. The names of candidates always get out then, so I guess everyone will know soon."

"Why would anybody wish to be a president twice? The hassles, the travel, always asking for money . . ." Van shifted to the other side and steered with his right hand.

Nora said, "Would you like a break?" Van shook his head. "John feels he's done most of what he set out to do here—curriculum, endowment, physical plant. He said it's time for new challenges. Lydia's very ambitious, too, and *her* success is being the wife of a successful president. Maybe Centreville and West College no longer offer a broad enough venue for them." Nora looked impatiently at the towboat. "This is going to take a while. I need to do something useful." She retrieved her *Ship's Log*.

Detail. Precision. As a physicist, and son of an architectural engineer, these qualities touched Van's core. Nora logged every sail, however brief, and anyone else who sailed *Duet* had to commit to doing the same: the vessel's location, the compass courses sailed, distances, comments on weather conditions and events of the sail. She said the sheer completeness of it pleased her, but she used the entries for a practical purpose as well: to refine her *Book of Words*, a notebook that contained detailed information about the workings of *Duet* and important information about channels and anchorages. He would emulate Nora's practices if ever he could afford a boat of his own—if he finished paying college bills for his four children before he was too old and feeble to hoist a sail.

As Nora leaned over the fold-down table, Van knew what she would be writing: "Sunday, October 26; mostly sunny. Marsh Pt.

towboat arrived at 16:35." The long auburn braid falling over her left shoulder made her seem warmer and less imperious, less of an elder statesperson, than the figure-eight twist at the nape of her neck which was her hairstyle on campus.

During Van's first semester at West College six years ago, Professor Nora Butcher Perry had been one of the employees honored for twenty years of service. Their paths had seldom crossed. They were separated not only by rank and department, but by their personal lives as well: she was single but integrated into the campus social life; he was married, with four teenage children, a loner by inclination, set apart from other new faculty by age and from others his age by inexperience. She owned a big brick house near campus and a sailboat. He rented a college house on Faculty Row and had no easy access to sailing outside his summer employment at the yacht club. She was an excellent teacher and a respected scholar whereas he was yet to be judged. She chaired her department and powerful committees that Van scarcely even thought about. Of formidable size and demeanor, she was a staunch feminist. Those first years, he could not imagine talking easily with her.

Van steered almost without thinking, the product of the summer's experience with *Duet*. Last fall, his youngest had matriculated at Rutgers, freeing up Van's evenings and weekends. The bruising left behind by Sheila's desertion was less tender. And he and Nora had discovered a shared interest in choral music. At the president's graduation party in May, when Nora invited him to sail, he had accepted.

Van had been pleasantly surprised by her skill as a sailor and even more surprised by the ease he felt in her company. She seemed to feel the same. She was closer to him in every way than he had imagined— even age. She had been one of the youngest faculty members ever hired at West, whereas he came late to the academic life. Despite the twenty-year difference in their tenure, she was only nine years his senior.

"Why did you name her *Duet*? If that is not too personal a question."

Nora looked up. "Not at all. I'll tell anyone who wants to know. Her name when I bought her—*Trade Winds*—didn't appeal to me. An old friend from graduate school suggested *Duet*. She knows how I love music." Nora grinned. "Also, she said something about me and my boat, two independent broads who could make beautiful music together. It seemed right."

Van grinned in return, his impressions of Nora confirmed by her old friend.

"Why do you ask?"

"I just wondered," he said, relieved that Nora did not question him further. He paused. "Where did Lydia anchor Friday night, anyway?"

"Friday? Let me see." Nora paged back through the log, and read the entry: "16:15 hrs, dropped the anchor 1 mi. up Swan Creek past Gratitude Marina; 5 ft. of water; wind NW at 8 K. Watched 2 blue herons around half-sunken skiff near duck blind on western shore of creek." She looked up. "That's where we gunkholed during our sail a couple of weeks ago. I took pictures of that rotting skiff at ebb tide. Remember? Pretty dramatic—the way light from the setting sun slanted low over the water."

"That was the best fall break I have had since coming to West!" They had sailed most of the week of the break and it was the first—and till now, the only—sail that had kept them out overnight. The intimacy of the close quarters produced a frizzle of excitement that Van had not expected, and did not mention now. That week cemented their growing friendship.

Stowing the log, Nora said, "I know I'm just torturing myself, but I really want to see the damage one more time."

While she poked her head into the engine compartment and uttered a litany of expletives, Van thought about her modes of self-presentation. The first—the only one he'd known until recently—was the Campus Nora: tweed jackets in earth tones, pants or mid-calf A-line skirts, flat shoes or boots, hair pulled back in a tight figure-eight twist at the nape of her neck. She favored massive, attention-grabbing earrings and multiple rings that emphasized her sweeping gestures. She moved confidently, spoke decisively, was friendly but businesslike, supportive but demanding.

While Nora examined the ship-to-shore radio and confirmed that it was, indeed, as communicative as a stump, he thought about the Sailing Nora: twill pants and long-sleeved shirts, busy-patterned wool sweaters and plain microfleece, an old yachting cap, her hair in a single loose French braid down her back. Her movements were quick but unhurried, her manner teasing but considerate.

When Nora came topside after finishing her inspection, she had tears in her eyes. She said only, "My poor, beautiful boat." And Van recognized the third Nora, discovered on this trip, whom he couldn't quite label: softer, volatile, hair a veritable riot. He thought about Nora being comfortable enough to remove completely the mask of professionalism. He pondered his own propensity toward privacy.

As the towboat approached the channel's half-way point, it slowed to a crawl, engine coughing black smoke. When the operator signaled, Nora went forward. He shouted, "My engine's overheated, damn it. Drop the tow line and drift off the channel. I'll be back as soon as I can—or I'll send somebody from the marina to get you."

She prepared the anchor as *Duet* swung slowly sideways to the wind and drifted off the channel. The anchor set, she rejoined Van. "Good grief. What more can happen to us?" While she spoke, she took a couple of bearings on nearby channel markers. "Here's hoping the anchor holds—tricky to set it without power." She watched the towboat disappear around the next bend and choked back a sob. Her voice quavered when she said, "He'll probably make it to the marina. And we're only about twenty minutes out. Help should be here soon."

As the sun sank, fatigue and the chill in the air began to get to her. When Van rose and stretched his back, one arm draped over the boom now denuded of the partially burned mainsail, Nora's feet picked up a familiar thump on the cockpit sole. Van seemed to feel it, too. "Damn. Our keel just kissed the bottom." They exchange knowing looks. Last spring they'd talked about the value of having knowledgeable feet that keep one from falling overboard, that brace the body in a stiff breeze when the gunwale's awash, that sense trouble from vibrations or unusual thumps—as when a keel hits the bottom. She sighed. "I should never have asked what more could go wrong."

Van chuckled. "Remember the lines about Kent Narrows from Stone and Blanchard? 'Keel boats should proceed with caution. The bottom is hard sand and you can't slither through a few inches of soft mud, as you can in so many parts of the Chesapeake . . . The channel is very narrow, and if you have an absent-minded professor in your crew, take the helm yourself.'"

"But we aren't even underway," Nora wailed.

Van tilted his head and closed his eyes. "Do you hear what I hear?"

Nora listened. "I don't hear anything."

"Well, your ears *are* nine years older than mine."

She was taken aback until she saw a smile twitch the corner of his mouth. Deciding that his teasing about their ages was a good sign, she responded in kind. "That's not funny, young man! What do you hear?"

Van opened the starboard cockpit locker and Nora, too, heard the trickle of water. "How bad is it?"

"I cannot tell. The bilge is a black hole."

Reflexively, Nora pulled the switch for the electric bilge pump. Nothing. She smacked her forehead with the heel of her hand. Nothing electric. "Stupid, stupid, stupid."

Van aimed the beam of the searchlight into the bilge. "If it does not get worse, we can keep up with it with the hand pump." He reached into the locker and began to pump. Again nothing. "Damn it, Nora, how long has it been since you used this pump?"

Nora realized that she wasn't the only one feeling the strain, and kept her voice neutral. "Over a year. Maybe the summer before this one. Maybe longer."

"Well, it is dry as toast." He unscrewed the cap and poured water into the cylinder, soaking the leather plunger. Five minutes later, when he pumped, oily bilge water flowed into the cockpit and drained out through the scuppers.

Nora traced the horizon, thinking that if they sank this close to the marina, she might just lose it completely. Seeing Van struggle to keep up the pace, she said, "Let me take a turn." Van hesitated. "After all, it is my boat." Without a word, Van relinquished the pump and turned aside. Nora recognized the signs of his withdrawal—and thought she knew the reason: his sensitivity about their relative economic circumstances. Working the pump, she said, "I'm sorry. I didn't mean that—you know—the way it came out." Van stuffed his fists into his pockets and did not respond. Nora wondered what he was thinking but was too stubborn to say anything more. Pumping was strenuous. She was determined not to wimp out.

Van said, "I see a workboat. I think it is from Marsh Point Marina."

Nora looked toward the bend in the channel. A searchlight beam swept back and forth as the boat came closer. Soon the beam was fixed steadily on *Duet.*

"I think help is about to arrive."

She continued pumping.

A distant voice called, "Professor Perry, is that you?"

Nora straightened her back and shouted, "Yes. Sid?"

"Yep, it's me. I'll pull along side." Sid threw a single line to Van and turned to Nora. "Here's what you need." He handed up a twelve volt power pack and a small pump mounted on 2 x 4s.

Nora gaped. "How did you know we are taking on water?"

"The towboat operator said you might be, but he wasn't sure. I decided to play it safe." He flipped a cigarette butt into the bay.

"He noticed? Why didn't he say anything to us? We didn't discover it until about an hour ago." Nora pushed aside her chagrin. "By the way, this is Professor van Pelt."

"Two professors on the same boat? Lots of brain power. Too bad that's all the power you got." Sid grinned and nodded toward *Duet.* "What happened?" His face was shadowy, almost grotesque against the darkening sky, illuminated only by stray light from the lamp hooked near his belly.

"God got mad and fried my boat."

Sid chuckled as he prepared to tow *Duet.* "The slings are already in the water. We should have her hauled by seven o'clock."

He was as good as his word, the best wharfinger in the business. At the marina, two helpers guided *Duet* over the slings.

Nora and Van watched the lift pull *Duet* out of the water and settle her on a cradle. Van said, "Just what we expected."

Nora's throat felt tight. The grounding plate had come loose from the keel. "Poor baby," was all she could manage. She dashed a tear from her cheek and tried to be stoic. She feared that Van held a poor opinion of her outbursts. Finding Ted's body had shaken her. And over all lay the weight of disappointment that her sailing season had ended so disastrously.

Sid came along the dock, his yellow foul-weather gear open to the night air, exposing portions of a well worn navy blue turtleneck. He took a drag on his cigarette. "I guess you see where the discharge plate at the bottom of the keel is partly separated from the hull. Happens a lot with lightning strikes—or maybe it was when she kissed the bottom and the hull torqued. Anyway, it's fixable." Sid talked about damage Nora already knew. "I'll put a crew on *Duet* first thing in the morning, and call you with an estimate. Have you thought about how you're gonna get back to Centreville?"

Nora shrugged. "I guess we'll get a taxi."

"No need. I'll give you a lift. I gotta leave soon anyway. Got a meeting in Church Hill."

They piled into Sid's pickup at a quarter before eight. Sid lit another cigarette and cracked the driver's window. By the time they passed Queenstown water tower, going north on Route 18, Nora's head was resting against Van's shoulder. Sid's truck swayed along the gently winding two-lane road. The rolling farmland, dotted with big old houses set back from the road, slid across her field of vision. The moonlight made everything look serene.

Nora woke when the engine stopped. They were at the West College dock.

Sid said, "Don't worry about *Duet,* now. We'll clear out your gear and stow it in a locker till you're ready to pick it up. Just give me a heads-up." Nora nodded, and handed over the keys.

Standing under the parking lot light, Van said, "Would you care to have supper at my place? I feel that I owe you a lot for the sails we have had." Nora's spurt of pleasure at the invitation dampened at his reference to feelings of obligation. He said, "I know you need to prepare for classes tomorrow, but if we do not linger, there will still be time. I could get my laboratory demonstration ready afterward."

Nora studied his face, trying to read his feelings. He looked both eager and anxious. Finally she said, "Damn! That would be great. But I really have to get back. Those Intro papers on Freud and the research proposals from Social Psych are screaming to be read."

CHAPTER FIVE

Nora drove away from the dock feeling hollow, thinking she might call Van when she got home, just to talk over the day some more. "Whoa, girl," she said into the dark. "What makes you think he'd welcome more talk tonight? After all the blowups over the last couple of days? Besides, we both have work to do."

The soft glow of yard lights greeted her as she pulled into her driveway. She parked in the garage and carried things she'd brought from *Duet* into the kitchen. The message light on her answering machine flashed "8." She hit the play button and put the reefing knife into the miscellany drawer beside the sink. A marginal student wanted to know whether she'd graded Friday's papers. Nora pushed "delete" and set the CD case on the counter next to the radio. While her mother's disembodied voice asked whether Nora would be home for Christmas, she shelved the *Ship's Log* in her study and dropped the GPS into a drawer.

The third message came from Nora's favorite student: "Dr. Perry, this is Louisa Smallwood. I know it's Sunday but something's happened and I really need to talk to you. Please call." She sounded strained.

The next five messages all came from Louisa, each at a higher pitch of anxiety, ending with one on the brink of hysteria at 8:05 p.m.: "Dr. Perry, *where are you? Please, please* call! I *must* talk to you. It doesn't matter what time! I can't sleep anyway till you call, so please, please call! Even if it's 3:00 in the morning, it doesn't matter. I've got to talk to you. There's no one else!" She ended on a strangled sob. Nora stared at the answering machine. She had never heard Louisa so out-of-control. Even last spring, talking to Nora about having been raped, she'd wept quietly. Nora steeled herself for disaster and dialed Louisa's number.

"Hello!"

"Louisa, this is Nora Perry. What's happened?"

"Oh, Dr. Perry, thank God! I—I . . ." Louisa sobbed.

"Take your time, Louisa. Calm down. Try to tell me what's happened."

"I need to talk to you."

"Of course. First thing in the morn—"

"No! I mean now! I've got to talk to you tonight."

Nora frowned at the clock: nearly 8:30. She thought of her lecture and student papers. She massaged her forehead. "Okay. Where are you? Where shall I meet you?"

"I'll come there. Now." The line went dead.

Nora replaced the receiver slowly, wondering. Louisa was the daughter she would never have, and wishing for Louisa's happiness came near to wishing for her own. This could be a hellish night—on top of two truly hellish days. Nora washed her face and scrambled into a sweatsuit, anxiety surging. She turned on the porch light just as Louisa arrived.

The red, swollen eyes, the split lip, and the yellow remains of a bad bruise on Louisa's left cheek took Nora aback. Louisa catapulted into her arms, clutching her as though she were a lifeline, sobbing into her neck. Nora patted her back, murmuring wordless sounds of comfort. When the wild sobbing subsided, Nora managed to disentangle herself. "Come sit down. Here's a box of tissues. How about some hot chocolate?" Nora guided Louisa to the oak table, then set about making the hot chocolate as though she hadn't noticed that the young woman practically collapsed into the chair. The matter-of-fact approach only partially succeeded: by the time the milk was hot, Louisa seemed coherent but still highly agitated.

"Now, tell me what's upset you." Nora dropped into the chair opposite Louisa and lifted her mug.

"Ted Slater's dead and I'm going to be charged with murder!" Louisa keened.

"What?" Nora set her mug down so abruptly that the hot chocolate slopped out. How had the word spread so fast? She sucked her burned fingers, resisting a temptation to swear, and spoke quietly. "How do you know? What happened?"

"Sky went to his house. This afternoon. To deliver his multiple choice exams. The police wouldn't let him in. They said he was *murdered.*"

Nora pushed aside her shock at Louisa's knowledge and tried to deal with her near-hysteria. "Louisa, get a grip. You can do it. Just start at the beginning. Why would the police suspect you?"

Louisa took a long, shuddering breath. "I went to his house—to Ted's house—on Friday—to get my umbrella. He was supposed to be in class but he was *there*. Naked. And he laughed and said I wanted sex, but I *didn't*, I swear I didn't, and he—he hit me. And now he's been dead for days and the police are going to find out I was there and they'll think I'm a murderer but I just defended myself, and it isn't fair! He shouldn't be able to hurt me anymore. And I don't know what to *do!*" The note of hysteria was back.

"Louisa. Slow down. Look at me. Are you saying Ted Slater *attacked* you?"

Louisa looked away, laid aside a balled-up tissue. "I know it was stupid—stupid—but I had that umbrella custom made, during my semester in London. I scrimped and saved to buy it." She dabbed her cheeks with a fresh tissue. "Afterwards—after that night in December—I told myself, 'It's just an umbrella.' But—but it felt like he had a sliver of me. And as long as he had it, I couldn't be free of him."

Nora's thoughts tumbled one over another. "Are you saying Ted Slater is the man who raped you last December?" She asked question after question, quietly, patiently, until she finally knew the whole of what Louisa labored to tell. She tried to get her head around it, to reconcile what Louisa said with the Ted Slater she thought she knew. "Louisa, you must tell the police."

"I can't! I won't! I want to go home! They don't have any record of my fingerprints. If I go home, they won't find me!"

"Louisa, be reasonable. You asked me what to do and I'm telling you: you must talk to the police." She did not add, "Or I will have to."

"But then they'll know . . . I never told anyone that it was Ted who . . . Or about the abortion. They'll have to *know* all of that! What will people think of me? I just can't!"

While Nora talked, she tried to digest the fact that Louisa had kept from her anything as important—as traumatic—as an abortion.

"If what you tell them isn't important to his death, not many people would have to know. You can ask them to keep it confidential." Tears continued to flow from Louisa's reddened eyes, but she seemed calmer—or maybe just worn out. "I know the County Sheriff's chief deputy, Frank Pierce. He's in charge of the case. He would be a good person to talk to." Panic flashed in Louisa's eyes. "Really. I mean it. I've known him more than twenty-five years, since *he* was a student at West, and he's good—a good policeman and a good person." Louisa gnawed her lower lip, doubt clear in her eyes. "I'll go with you if you want."

Louisa's head drooped. "If you think . . . If I really have to do it . . ." She whimpered. "It doesn't have to be now, does it?"

"No. Of course not. I'm sure tomorrow would be fine."

"Will you call him? I don't want to talk about it over the phone. And I do want you to be there. Please." Louisa's voice quavered. "Will he question me at the police station?"

"I don't know. I'll ask. I'll call you as soon as something is arranged." Nora squeezed Louisa's hand. "It's going to be all right. You haven't done anything criminal and nothing bad is going to happen to you. I promise."

The chocolate had lost its heat but they drank it anyway and talked quietly for another hour, Nora biting back an urge to tell Louisa what she had seen, Louisa spilling the aftermath of her date rape. "For weeks after it happened, I dreamed in screaming colors—dreamed I wore a chrome yellow dress splashed with blood and everyone I passed knew what had happened. And Ted laughed at my tears—just like that night." She wiped tears from her cheeks now and dropped the tissue onto the mound of soggy tissues growing at her elbow. "Maybe you'll think I'm an awful person. But, you know, if nobody had to know about Ted and me—if the police didn't find out I'd been there—I would be glad he's dead."

"Of course you're not an awful person. If all you said is true—I mean, he must have hurt you terribly. Try not to worry about gossip. Or anything." Nora patted Louisa's arm. "Your friends and your mother will stand by you. You've told me how exasperating your mother is—but she'll stand by you now. And you know you can count on me."

By the time she left, Louisa seemed completely drained. Nora walked out with her. "Are you all right to drive? Would you like me to take you back?"

"No. No. I'll be okay. Besides, I have to get Sky's car back." She dropped into the driver's seat, shoulders drooping.

Turning back into the house, Nora weighed the pros and cons of calling Frank. In times past she wouldn't have hesitated, but now 11:00 seemed too late. She'd probably wake him, and maybe his wife and children, too. And it wasn't as though Louisa knew anything about the actual murder. Early tomorrow morning would do.

She wandered around the house, picking things up and setting them down again. What she really wanted was to talk with Van. And now there was actually something new to talk about. On the third ring, she felt the presumptuousness of a call. The receiver was halfway to the cradle when Van's "Hello?" came across the line.

"Van, it's Nora. I hope I didn't wake you."

"No, of course not," he said, his voice thick with sleep. "Is something wrong?"

"It's Louisa Smallwood."

"Oh. What about her?"

"Van, she knows Ted Slater is dead."

"Really? How?"

"Sky Brady told her. He heard about it when—." Nora was well aware that she almost never told a short story, and Van seemed to be listening patiently, but this time she caught herself up short. "The thing is, she came over here tonight, crying hysterically. She knows Ted has been dead for several days." She paused. "And she may have been the last person to see him alive."

"Except the murderer, of course. Or are you saying Louisa *is* the murderer?"

"Of course not!" Nora wondered at her own vehemence, and the tiny trickle of doubt she stifled. "But she went to his house on Friday afternoon and—spoke to him there."

Van sounded more awake when he said, "Why would she go there? And why come to you about it?"

What could she say without breaking Louisa's confidences? "I can't tell you everything, but Louisa came to me because I counseled her last spring. So tonight I told her she's got to tell the police she was there.

Probably she can help set the time of death. I said I'd arrange for her to talk with Frank Pierce, and go with her, just to be supportive."

"What would you like me to do?"

"Do? Oh. Well . . . nothing." Nora twirled a wispy curl around her finger. "I mean, there's nothing *to* do. I just called because I needed to talk to a friend. It's been a wearing night."

"Oh."

"Look, I'm sorry. I shouldn't have called so late. I'll let you get to bed." Nora felt awkward. "Good night."

"No! Wait. I mean . . . I will come over tomorrow and we can talk about it then. If you want."

"Oh." Nora's spirits lifted. "Thanks. How about lunch here? There's always soup."

"That would be fine."

"Fine."

"Well. Good night then."

"Good night."

Nora got into bed comforted. Inclined against the walnut headboard, she picked up the student papers she'd planned to finish before turning in. She couldn't stay focused. Visions of Ted's body intruded. Would she ever be able to put those images aside? And nothing in her own youth had generated the kind of hysteria Louisa exhibited. But if it had, to whom would she have turned for solace? No one. That realization strengthened her resolve to help Louisa if she could. No one should be so alone. Did Louisa's upset mean she was holding something back? Could she possibly have done murder? Nora couldn't believe it. But believing Ted Slater was a rapist was difficult, too.

Work was impossible. Laying the papers aside for the night, she vowed to return them within the week and clicked off the light, hoping the topic of tomorrow's lecture was fresh enough to get her through class without further preparation.

She rolled onto her left side, thoughts still roiling. Had she and Van seen *anything* of importance Saturday night?

CHAPTER SIX

Frank was about to go into the briefing when the duty officer buzzed. "Nora Perry's on the phone. I told her you have a meeting, but when she said it's about Ted Slater, I thought you might want to take it."

"Right." Frank punched the lighted button. "What's up? Did you remember something?"

"Good morning to you, too, Frank."

The amusement in her tone stopped him short. He pinched the bridge of his nose and stifled the impatience in his own voice. "Sorry. How did you sleep?"

"Not well. How are Claire and the boys?"

"Everyone's fine. Except for Claire's morning sickness." For no rational reason, telling Nora—even indirectly—that Claire was pregnant felt awkward.

"You're expecting another child? Should I offer congratulations or condolences?"

Frank forced a chuckle. "Everyone's been on my case. I shouldn't have been so adamant that we were done after the twins. We didn't plan a third, but we're happy about it now. We're hoping for a girl this time. But that isn't why you called. Why are you beating around the bush?"

"When I got home last night—about 8:15—I had phone messages and . . . The bottom line is, I talked to a person who saw Ted Slater late Friday afternoon."

"Who?"

"In a minute, Frank. Just hold your horses." Nora's take-charge tone carried Frank back to his days as a student in her class. Badgering would do no good. Frank tapped a pencil on his yellow pad and waited for her to choose her words. "It's a young woman, a student, and she's scared. She's afraid you'll think she's involved."

"She is."

"You know what I mean. She's afraid you'll suspect her. When you talk with her, she'd like to have me there for moral support."

"No problem."

"Well, um—could you talk to her at my house?"

Frank considered. "Yeah, I could do that. She'll have to come in to make a formal statement, but that could be later."

"How about 1:30 today? Would that work for you?"

"Sure. I'll see you then."

"Great. 'Bye."

"Nora."

"Yes?"

"Aren't you forgetting something?" Frank waited. "What's her name?"

"Oh. Louisa Smallwood."

The chitchat stopped as Frank entered the briefing room, and all eyes turned in his direction. He took the chair at the end of the table opposite the sheriff and picked up his coffee mug before speaking. "I just talked to Nora Perry, calling to give us a little help in our investigation." His gaze swept the table, gathering everyone's full attention. "The name of a woman who was at his house late Friday afternoon." Raised eyebrows, open mouths, and mild oaths greeted his statement. Frank summarized his conversation with Nora. "So, if we want to stay ahead of the bystanders, we better step on out." He ticked off an item on the list in front of him. "Sy, what do we have on next of kin?"

"Nothing. No letters or cards in his desk." Sy leafed through his notebook. "Speed dial on his phones had the weather hot line, the state lottery info line, and the carryout numbers for Bread and Soup and Coliseum Pizza. His address book doesn't have Mom or Dad or anything, and if anyone's named Slater, there's no way to know. He only put in first names and phone numbers, plus a few businesses—like, 'E' has Ellen, Elaine, and Edwards Pharmacy. Like that." Sy smirked. "Women's names outnumber men's by about three to one."

"Okay. Use the reverse directory to put full names on the phone numbers. Joe and I will start with the personnel office at the college, see what they can tell us about next of kin. And somebody's gotta talk to the president." Frank tilted his head at the sheriff. "You want to take that, Jake?"

"You're in charge. Go for it." Jake's blue eyes stabbed each officer in turn. "We've all got to remember that they're not going to be happy with us nosing around campus." His gaze landed on Frank. "Maybe they won't get their shorts in as much of a twist talking to an alum."

The personnel department at West College consisted of the Director of Human Resources and one secretary, shoehorned into a former supply room in the basement of Old Main. Frank sat by the door with the secretary's desk hard by his right elbow. Joe took a straight-backed padded chair wedged between filing cabinets and the front wall. The clutter gave a whole new meaning to paper pushers. A lone spider plant hung from the ceiling beside the single window high on the outside wall. The phone rang incessantly and the secretary fielded the calls with pleasant efficiency. She buzzed her boss when his phone light went out.

The director opened the connecting door almost immediately and stepped into the reception area with his hand already extended. "Hello, I'm Jim Thomas." His voice sounded like Johnny Cash but his appearance was closer to Woody Allen.

Joe and Frank followed Thomas into a small inner office, just as cluttered as the waiting area and even more cramped. Everyone settled into chairs and the officers produced IDs. Joe said, "I can see you're pretty busy this morning. Thanks for seeing us."

"Yes, it's always something. Right now we're finalizing the annual employee recognition ceremony. But what can I do for you? Is one of our employees in trouble?"

"You might say that. One of your employees is dead."

The dark eyes behind the thick lenses grew round as full moons. "Who? What happened?"

"Theodore Slater. He was found in his home yesterday morning, murdered."

Thomas looked from one to the other, blinking rapidly, and murmured, "Oh, my." He coughed dryly. "The poor man. Have you told the dean? His department chair? I wonder how we're going to cover his classes. There will be a memorial service, of course. Oh, dear." The gentle musing seemed incongruent with the deep gravelly voice.

Joe said, "We want to notify his next of kin. Can you help us with that?"

"Oh. Oh. Yes, of course." Thomas swiveled his chair and plucked a folder labeled "Slater, T." from a lateral file. He talked as he paged through the contents. "Unless I'm misremembering, his next of kin is his wife—his second wife—Suzanne." Joe and Frank exchanged looks. "Ah, yes, here it is. Suzanne Slater, 104 Water Street, Chestertown, Maryland. Do you want the phone number too?" Thomas wrote as he spoke.

Joe said, "Were they separated or what?"

"Yes. It's been a couple of years now, but as far as I know, they aren't divorced. He left her on as next of kin *and* as beneficiary of his college life insurance." Thomas propped his elbows on his chair arms and made a tent of his fingers. "I brought it up a couple of times. Earlier this fall he got quite huffy, said he was more than capable of handling his own affairs, and that when and if he needed to make changes, *he* would get in touch with *me*."

Frank raised an eyebrow. "Was it a big policy?"

"The college pays for coverage in the amount of one year's salary. Ted paid to increase that to twice his salary—the maximum our policy allows." Thomas tapped the file. "But that's not where the big money is. He's always made the maximum contribution to TIAA/CREF—our retirement plan. I'd guess that's worth ten times the life insurance, more in the long run. And qualified retirement accounts are marital property. If they're still married, he couldn't have cut her out unless she consented in writing."

"Would she have any way of knowing that?" Joe asked.

"I might have just mentioned something once. But it's pretty much common knowledge these days anyway." Thomas shifted in his chair. "A while back, Mrs. Slater's attorney was asking about it. I told her she would have to get in touch with TIAA/CREF."

"I see. What about family? Parents? Siblings?"

"I've never heard anything about siblings—but then I might not. I believe both his parents are deceased. Mrs. Slater would know, of course."

Frank spoke up. "When someone is murdered like this—not incidental to another crime—the key is usually in who the victim was. What kind of person was Ted Slater?"

Thomas shuffled papers back into the folder, not meeting Frank's eye. "I suppose that depends on who you ask, doesn't it?"

"I'm asking *you*." Frank paused. "Don't want to speak ill of the dead?"

Spots of color bloomed on Thomas' cheeks.

Joe leaned forward. "I'm sure you want to help, Mr. Thomas, and the best way to do that is to speak up. It could be hearsay or impressions, not necessarily facts. We won't go telling other people what you say."

Thomas drew a deep breath and exhaled slowly. "Personally, I didn't like him much. And there were rumors that his marriage—both marriages, actually—were pretty volatile. I don't really know." Thomas paused. "But to be fair, I've got to say the buildings and grounds crew, the custodial staff, the food services people—they all liked him. He went out of his way to know who does what, to ask about family, especially kids. The secretarial staff was practically a fan club."

"Who would know about his marriages?" Joe asked.

"Other than the two wives, I couldn't say."

"What about friends? Who did he see socially?"

"My impression is that he was pretty much a loner. I did hear that he played poker with Ray Martin—our bookstore manager."

Joe noted the name. "What else can you tell us?"

"Nothing right off hand. I'll read through his personnel file, though, see if there's anything that might help."

"No offense, Mr. Thomas, but I'd rather do the reading myself." Frank leaned forward, reaching across the desk.

Jim Thomas snatched up the folder and clutched it to his chest. "I can't let you do that—not till I've talked to the college attorney." Jim Thomas thrust out his chin. "I'll call the attorney today. Your best bet is to talk with his departmental colleagues. And his wife."

Joe glanced at Frank. "Well, then, I guess that's it for now. Can we use your phone to call the president?"

"Sure. I'll dial for you." Thomas sounded wary, and he replaced the personnel folder in the file cabinet before turning to the phone.

Leaving Old Main, Joe said, "Jeezooey. I've seen jail cells bigger than that office."

Frank laughed. "West College changes about as slowly as hell freezes. You can't expect a lot of investment in something as newfangled as Human Resources. I did a paper on the history of the college when I was a student. West started as a Methodist seminary in 1784, with seven students. One Methodist minister was the entire faculty. It took from then till 1846 to get up to forty-six students and four faculty. That's when it was chartered as West College, and Old Main was the first building constructed after that. I'd bet Jim Thomas is delighted to have any space at all in a building that set in history."

Joe's grunt did not encourage more.

The walk from Old Main to Ozmon House took less than ten minutes. Frank set a brisk pace. Approaching the president's house, Joe said, "I suppose this is the second oldest building on campus." He sounded breathless.

Frank slowed the pace. "Could be. I always thought Old Main was the oldest, but now that I think about it, this house is pre-Civil War. Maybe it's the oldest. Anyway, the college didn't buy the Ozmon farm till 1900." He glanced at the renovated and expanded farmhouse, wood, Federal style. "I haven't been much involved with the college as an alum. Most of what I know about the current president comes from town gossip or mailings to alumni. He had a traditional academic career: bachelor's degree from Randolph Macon, M.S. and Ph.D. in mathematics from Duke. His specialty was something to do with code breaking. He was under fifty when he came to West College seven years ago, which makes him mid-fifties or so now."

"Is he likely to give us any trouble?" Joe's breathing still sounded labored.

Frank slowed his pace more. "I wouldn't think so. He's built the best relationship between the college and the town in living memory—and that doesn't happen if you ride roughshod over people. Of course, that might change when it comes to a murder investigation." Stepping onto the porch Frank added, "I doubt we'll get anything useful here.

But Jake thinks there'd be hell to pay if we tried to question people on campus without paying our respects."

★   ★   ★

John Howard had taken the call from Frank on the phone in the upstairs hall. Lydia called up, "Who was that?"

"Frank Pierce." He spoke as he descended the stairs. "He and a colleague are coming over. It's about Ted Slater, of course. I thought here would be better than my office."

"Yes, of course. I probably should offer coffee." Lydia turned toward the kitchen. "People expect hospitality here."

John entered the parlor putting on his presidential persona—tucking in the tails of his lightly starched white shirt, tightening his belt a notch, putting on his suit jacket—holding his apprehension in check. Last night, after Sky and Brad left, Lydia had urged caution, suggesting he do nothing until he talked with the police. But John had felt compelled to call the chairman of the board, and college staff who would have to manage the situation once it became public.

Everyone he called expressed shock and wondered aloud about the circumstances. Some assumed a random act of violence. Others said that if it was murder, there must have been some strong motive, although no one voiced any. The chairman of the board said, "I know you'll handle the fall-out, John. Let me know if there's anything I can do." The dean of students' concerns focused on student upset and the possible need for counseling. The academic vice president said she would arrange to cover his classes. The chaplain wanted to talk about the memorial service. The director of PR said he'd draft a press release and a campus notice. "I just hope no scandals peek out of the closet."

Lydia's opinion was that the college certainly wouldn't be held responsible for the murder of a faculty member in his own home, in a different town. Nevertheless, she acknowledged that the publicity might—just might—have a deleterious effect on John's candidacy at Waldorf. He shifted uneasily. Any threat to his career was a threat to both of them. Last night, awakened by troubled dreams, John had looked at his sleeping wife, grateful for her presence. Their marriage wasn't as passionate as it once had been, but Lydia was unfailingly helpful and supportive. She was always gracious, and cultivated people important to his work so well that only the most sensitive and persistent observer would have detected ulterior motives in her friendly overtures. He could count on her now as always.

The doorbell rang, ending John's musings.

The three men shook hands. Frank scrutinized John Howard, noticing his close shave, and intense blue eyes behind dark framed glasses. The president tilted his head toward the parlor. "We can talk in here." He moved easily, a man of average height, beginning to lose hair and gain weight.

Frank's gaze swept the hall and the parlor as he passed through. An antique gold-framed mirror hung over a small table. Framed portraits, paintings, and historical documents reminded him of a museum. Matching stuffed chairs and sofa formed a comfortable circle around the coffee table. Overall, an impressive blend of college showplace and personal home. Once seated, Frank said, "You were expecting my call?"

"Yes. I assumed you would want to talk with me about Ted Slater's murder. It's shocking. Nothing like this ever happened at the college before." John radiated confidence, energy, and a keen intelligence.

"How do you know about Ted Slater death? *What* do you know?" Frank tried to keep testiness out of his voice.

John said, "Not much, actually," and Frank heard an echo of Nora saying the same thing. He wondered how many people "didn't know much" about Slater's murder—and just how much tougher it was going to make his job.

John continued. "Two West College students came to the house—Sky Brady and Brad Longstreet. They're roommates." He must have noticed Frank's scowl, for he added, "Don't be angry with them. They just thought that, as president, I should know that a member of my faculty had been murdered."

Frank was not mollified. "Exactly what did they say?"

"Sky said that he went to Ted's house to deliver exams and heard that he was dead—probably murdered. With all the police and bystanders around, Sky thought we should know, before the press started calling."

"We? Who else did they tell?" Frank's voice was tight and he saw the president stiffen.

"My wife was here when they came. They were going to tell our PR director, but I said I'd take care of it."

At the chill in John's voice, Frank decided to ease off. He relaxed his posture, crossed one leg over the other, and adopted a casual tone. "Yes, of course. Tell me what you have done in the way of damage control."

As Frank had hoped, the president also seemed to relax. He matched Frank's posture, and a friendlier note returned to his voice. "We've done very little so far. It hasn't been necessary. We've prepared a brief statement—factual information about Ted's employment, a sentence that he will be sorely missed in the classroom—that sort of thing. We will give it to any media people who call. We'd like to put out a more personal notice to employees and trustees as soon as possible."

While he spoke, Lydia set a tray on the coffee table. All three men followed her actions appreciatively—attention she seemed to take for granted. Lydia Cutler Howard, five feet seven, trim and fit, was in her early fifties and aging well. Frank doubted she had ever been beautiful, but had often heard her described that way, so something—liveliness, wit, charm?—created that illusion.

John turned to his wife. "Lydia, this is Sgt. Joe Jamieson, of the Queen Anne's County Sheriff's Office. You've met Frank Pierce. They're here about Ted."

"Of course. How do you do?" she shook hands with Joe and turned to Frank. "Captain Pierce. Unfortunately, this is a less pleasant occasion than alumni functions. How are you?" Frank noticed both her firm grasp and the slight pallor beneath her tan. Her small bones and graceful movements implied softness and fragility, but her gaze was level, her manner cool and contained.

She took a seat beside her husband. "Would you like coffee? Or tea?"

They both took coffee. While Lydia served, John continued. "As I was saying, we'd like to get on with the campus formalities. When will we get the green light?"

Frank said, "Probably tomorrow, or maybe the day after. We just want to notify the next of kin. We learned this morning that his wife, Suzanne, lives in Chestertown. We'll see her as soon as possible."

"Suzanne Slater isn't his wife!"

The intensity of Lydia's voice, its note of scorn, caused Frank to murmur an especially quiet, "Oh?"

"They've been divorced well over a year—as everyone knows."

"I believe Ted told us so himself," John added.

"Mmmm, well, we were told by Jim Thomas that Suzanne Slater is still listed as his next of kin."

"Really?" John seemed surprised.

Lydia's lip curled humorlessly. "Ted was just full of surprises."

Frank looked from one to the other. "It helps if we get to know the victim. What kind of person was he?"

They both paused. John Howard spoke first. "He was very personable, of course—a good conversationalist, well read, well traveled. We invited him here often. We enjoyed his company." He paused. "Ted held strong opinions and presented them forcefully, but he wasn't active in campus governance." He paused again. "Some colleagues didn't approve of his consulting work."

Lydia Howard said, "He was Machiavellian."

Frank leaned forward. "What do you mean?"

Lydia bit her lower lip and looked aside. "Nothing, really. It was just an impression I had."

Frank spoke quietly. "I really need your help in understanding Ted Slater. We're not talking facts here. What gave you the impression he was Machiavellian?"

Lydia bit her lip again. "He always seemed to be on the make. You know. Using people, making every social event a networking opportunity. He flattered me outrageously, but only because I'm John's wife." She seemed to catch John's look of surprise because she added, "It's true, John. I don't mean he was obnoxious. Quite the contrary. He was charming, but he didn't care for people as people."

"What about friends? Social activities?"

John said, "He was very present on campus—attending concerts, lectures, plays, athletic events. But I don't know who his particular friends are—were. His departmental colleagues would know. Have you spoken with Clyde Barnes? He chairs the Economics and Management Department."

"Not yet," Joe said. "We heard something about a poker group. Would you know anything about that? Who was in it?" Both Howards denied any knowledge of a poker group.

"What about women friends?" Neither responded immediately. Joe added, "I mean, a good looking man, seemingly unattached, you'd think there would be."

John nodded. "I'm sure there were. But I don't know who."

Lydia said, "After Suzanne, I don't remember that he ever brought a guest to college functions."

They chatted a few more minutes, mostly about the college and whether the murder was likely to cause problems for admissions or fund raising. Both Howards expressed fervent hopes that the case would be solved quickly. John asked, "Do you have any leads at all?"

Joe said, "Well, sir, that sort of thing is kept confidential. You understand."

Frank thought giving a little might be more fruitful. "We don't have anything approaching a lead yet. But Nora Perry—Were you aware that she and Hendrick van Pelt found the body? They may know more than they've told us, and a female student was at Slater's house Friday afternoon."

John made a startled noise. Lydia rattled her cup onto the coffee table, spilling tea into the saucer. "That's impossible."

Simultaneously John said, "That's absurd. I can't imagine that one of our students—let alone any of our faculty—would be involved." He paused. "Well, I suppose I can *imagine* it. But I hate to think . . ."

Their denials were only what Frank had expected of the presidential couple. "We aren't jumping to conclusions, but we have to cover all the bases."

Walking back across campus, Joe said, "Well, I guess that takes care of any niceties we owe the college bigwigs."

"Mmmm," Frank murmured. And then, "Have Sy check Slater's address book. See if there is a 'Lydia' listed."

CHAPTER SEVEN

Nora and Van had just finished lunch when Frank arrived, a few minutes early. As she and Frank entered the sitting room, Nora said, "We're just having coffee. You two didn't meet under the best of circumstances. Let's start over." Smiling to cover her anxiety, she made a broad flourish, as though presenting a game show prize for audience appreciation. "Franklin Jefferson Pierce, Captain and Chief Deputy of the Queen Anne's County Sheriff's Office. He has a West College degree and a fine baritone voice, but uses only the former." She made a sweeping gesture toward Van and a slight bow in his direction. "Hendrick van Pelt, a.k.a. Van, faculty member extraordinaire in the Physics Department, sailor, and mainstay of the tenor section of the Corsica Chorale."

Van shifted from one foot to the other and Frank looked sharply at Nora. The two men shook hands, unsmiling.

Nora turned to Frank. "Coffee?" Frank nodded, sat down at the table, and took a cookie without waiting to be invited. Nora added milk and two spoons of sugar to Frank's coffee before bringing the mug to the table. Van eyed the mug—speculatively, she thought—and she realized what she had done. He sat straighter and folded his napkin. "Let me give you a refill," she said.

"No, thank you. It is time for me to go. For me to be present when Louisa arrives would be improper." Van nodded to Frank and turned to Nora. "Thank you for lunch. The food was superb, the river views spectacular, and your company delightful, as always."

Nora refrained from commenting on his sudden return to the formal politeness that had marked their early acquaintance. She walked him to the door. "I'll see you at chorus rehearsal?"

"Yes. Of course. And thank you again for lunch."

Frank was scanning the room when Nora returned. She expected a comment about changes over the ten years since he'd last been there. What he said was, "So, is he the current boyfriend?"

"No! Of course not. He's a colleague and a sailing companion."

"You acted more than companionable in Queenstown. Why 'Of course not'?"

Nora tilted her head. "For one thing, he's still getting over a fairly brutal divorce. Two years ago he returned from a professional meeting to find his wife had run off with a bartender from the Gibson Island Yacht Club, taking everything but his toothbrush and the kitchen sink."

"Mmmmm."

"Besides, he's much too young."

Frank peered at her, his eyes partially hooded. "How much too young?"

"Nine years." Nora colored, recalling that at twenty-six, she'd told Frank the three year difference in their ages made her feel like she was dating her kid brother. But the issue that caused their final separation ten years ago had been marriage—Frank's desire to share a home and family versus Nora's stated intention never to be a wife or mother.

Frank's only comment was another, "Mmmmm." He finished his cookie and reached for another. "Now, before the Smallwood girl gets here, I want to make sure we understand each other. It's your house, and she wants you here, but it's my interview. You've got to let me conduct it."

"Of course."

"I mean, I need to ask questions. Don't get all motherly if she gets upset or cries or something."

"I wouldn't." Nora felt offended that he would even suggest such a thing.

"Good. I guess we have an understanding." Louisa's arrival ended the awkward exchange.

Louisa was pale, her "How do you do?" barely audible. She perched nervously on the chair opposite Frank and glanced at him furtively. Probably she had not expected her interrogator to be a black man. He sized up the young woman: slender, good bones, wide-set eyes, generous mouth, and long brown hair—beautiful in an unconventional way—and extremely edgy. First names and a relaxed approach would get more information than hard questioning. He leaned back and put his hands in his pockets. "Nora tells me you saw Ted Slater on Friday afternoon." Louisa nodded. "Tell me about it."

Louisa studied her hands, knotted in her lap. She unclenched them, spread her fingers on the blue denim, and kneaded her thighs. Blue smudges under her eyes showed nearly as dark as the bruise on her left cheek. Frank waited patiently. At last she spoke. "I wasn't there long. I went to get my umbrella. I thought he was in class. It was Friday afternoon and he was supposed to be in class. I went into the bedroom to look for it—for my umbrella—and he came out of the bathroom and caught me. We . . . had a fight." Louisa touched her left cheek absently. "I ran out and drove back to the dorm." Her eyes darted to Frank's face and away again. "He was alive when I left!" Another fleeting look at Frank. "That's all I know."

"Let me just make sure I have this straight. You went to his house when you thought he wouldn't be there." Louisa nodded. "What time was that?"

"I don't know exactly. I left campus about 3:30, I guess."

"You have a key?"

Louisa started, then stared at her hands as if they held the answer. "No. I thought the door would be unlocked."

Frank studied her through narrowed eyes. "Was his door always unlocked?" Frank kept his questions flat, hoping to mask the implied knowledge of "always."

Louisa's voice sunk almost to a whisper. "I don't know. It's just . . . Lots of people leave their doors unlocked around here. Lots of the time."

"And was his door unlocked on Friday afternoon?"

"Yes."

"Did you knock?"

"No."

"So, you just walked in, and went into the bedroom searching for your umbrella. Slater came out of the bathroom and found you there." Louisa nodded. "Tell me about the fight."

Louisa's eyes skittered to Nora's face, then came to rest on the river view. She spoke slowly. "He pushed me down on the bed. He wanted to—have sex—and when I wouldn't, he hit me." She touched the left side of her face. "I got away from him and ran."

"How far toward having sex did you go?" Louisa wrinkled her brow and Frank said, "Did you take off your clothes? Did he put on a condom?"

"No!" She flicked a look at Nora. "I was just sitting on the side of the bed. I had all my clothes on. And he pushed me down."

"He hit you. Did you hit him?"

"Hit him? No." By now, Louisa's face was scarlet.

"Come on, Louisa. It would be natural if you hit him back. A slap maybe? In self defense?"

"No. I told you, I didn't *hit* him. I . . . twisted away from him. And ran."

What college coed would be embarrassed by such prim sex talk in this day and age? There must be more. "What time did you leave?"

"I'm not sure. I guess I was there about fifteen minutes. Maybe twenty."

Frank asked several more questions, pinning down times. Then, "You left before 5:00?"

"Yes. I was back in my room by then."

"What was he wearing when you left?"

Color ebbed and flowed in her face. "A robe. A short kimono sort of thing, silk, with a belt."

"Anything else?" Louisa looked away and shook her head. "Did you eat or drink anything while you were there?"

Louisa's "No" sounded surprised.

"And did you find your umbrella?"

"No."

"Where did you look? Besides the bedroom."

"I didn't look anyplace else."

Frank leaned forward, putting bite in the words. "You went there specifically—for the sole purpose—of getting your umbrella and only looked in the bedroom?"

Louisa pulled back but her voice was steady. "The last time I saw it, it was in the bedroom closet. I went there first. Then, like I said . . . I ran out. I didn't look anywhere else. I just ran."

"Mmmmm. Why was your umbrella in Ted Slater's house?"

Louisa looked at Nora, who patted her hand and murmured, "It's okay. Just tell Frank about it."

Louisa squared her shoulders, took a deep breath, and for the first time met Frank's eye. "How much of this do you really want to hear?"

"Everything. Tell me everything."

"Last fall, I had a class with him. I . . . I had a crush on him. Lots of the women students did!" Her tone was a mix of defiance and defensiveness. "He was sophisticated and funny and charming. He said I was beautiful. The smartest woman he'd ever taught." Her voice trailed off. Her eyes returned to the river. When she resumed, the words tumbled out in a heap. "We saw each other—outside of class, I mean. He said things, like I was his biggest challenge ever and what fun it would be to seduce me. Saying it in a teasing way, you know? I was flattered." Louisa gnawed her lower lip. Frank waited through her silence. "I usually stayed on campus after exams, to work the holiday parties. I work for Food Services. And last year, on December 19th I went to his house for dinner." She glanced at Frank. "Do you really want all the details?"

"Sometimes the details are the most important."

Louisa sighed. "He gave me martinis before dinner—I'd never had a martini before—and a glass of wine with dinner. I got drunk out of my skull and I threw up—barely made it to the bathroom in time— and then collapsed across the bed. He was solicitous and gentle. He took my clothes off and tucked me in." Louisa fiddled with her water glass. "Then he got in beside me. When I said I didn't want to have sex, he just laughed. I told him I was a virgin and he said that was just great—that he was very good with virgins—that I'd enjoy it." Louisa's eyes took on a haunted look. "I cried and struggled, but I didn't seem to have any *strength*. He made love to me anyway. He *raped* me. And then he told me to stop crying so he could sleep. I guess I just passed out after that." She paused. "He—he forced me to do it again the next morning and then he drove me back to campus. I didn't see him after that. I mean, just by accident, on campus."

"You said he forced you to do it again. Did he beat you?" Louisa stared at him blankly. "Answer me. Did he hit you? Threaten physical harm? Restrain you in any way?"

Louisa seemed to grow smaller in her chair, her voice barely a whisper. "No. He just grabbed my shoulders and shook me. But . . .

but I was in *his* house and he said he wouldn't take me home till after we did it again. He said things like, 'When you're no longer a virgin, you're no longer a virgin. What does it matter?' And it's *true*. I'd . . . He . . ." Tears coursed down her cheeks and she dried her face with her sleeve. "I was afraid that if I didn't let him do what he wanted he would talk about it—about me—on campus. I just wanted it to be over."

"So you cooperated."

"No! I didn't *cooperate*. I just . . . let him do it." Sobs mangled the words.

Nora leaned forward. "He didn't have to beat her or tie her up to make it rape. He got her drunk. She said 'no'. That's enough!"

"I'm just trying to understand the relationship here." Frank looked stonily at Nora, holding her gaze long enough to remind her of their understanding before turning back to Louisa. "You said he made love to you and you said he raped you. Which was it?"

Louisa dried her face again and then clenched her hands in her lap. "I mean . . . he did the sorts of things . . . It was like he wanted me to like it. He kissed my breasts and licked me . . . down there." A single tear trickled down her cheek and she dashed it away.

Frank started to ask whether she *had* liked it, but Nora's expression made him change the question. "How did you feel about all this?"

"Stupid. Embarrassed. Humiliated. I *told* him to stop. But he held me down, said I didn't have a choice anymore. He wouldn't let me go and I felt so *helpless*. I just wanted it to be over."

"Why didn't you report it?"

Louisa shook her head. "I was too ashamed. I sort of told Dr. Perry last spring, but not his name." Louisa again stared at her hands.

"Sounds like you're still upset."

"Wouldn't you be?"

"This isn't about me. Were you angry enough to kill him?"

Nora gasped. Louisa blinked. After a moment she said, very quietly, "Yes. Gladly." She didn't meet his eyes. "But I didn't. I swear I didn't."

Frank looked steadily at Louisa. "So tell me what you did when you ran out of the bedroom. Where did you go? What did you do Friday night and Saturday?"

Louisa drew a deep breath. "I got out of there as fast as I could. I guess I drove back to campus pretty fast. I don't really remember. I was so upset—I was crying. I went to my room and just stayed there."

"All weekend? You didn't see anyone or talk to anyone?"

"Well, sure. I mean, on Friday I went straight to my room and stayed there."

"So no one can vouch for when you got back."

"Sky Brady can."

Frank let impatience seep into his tone. "You just said . . ." Louisa made a small whimpering noise but Frank talked over it. "Was Sky Brady in your room with you?"

Louisa twisted her fingers together. "No! I saw him in the hall, on the way to my room. I was crying, and my lip was bleeding. He asked what happened. I said I'd tripped on the curb outside the dorm and fell on my face. He said I should go to the Health Center. But I just wanted to lie down. He brought me ice in a towel. Later he brought me some soup. I told him I wanted to sleep and not to come over any more, and he didn't."

"What time did he bring you the soup?"

"Five-thirty, six o'clock."

"And you didn't see or talk to anyone after that?" Louisa shook her head. "What about Saturday?"

"I stayed in my room. I looked like hell and I felt worse. Sky knocked in the middle of the morning. I told him to bug off, that I wanted to be alone. I didn't go out till Sunday brunch."

"You just stayed in your room. For thirty-six hours. Because of a split lip and a black eye?"

"If *you'd* ever been raped, you'd damn well know you don't feel very social afterwards!" Her fury seemed to be spent as quickly as it had come. "That's what it was like last Friday, like it had happened all over again. I couldn't keep my mind on anything else." She slumped back in her chair. "Believe what you want. I stayed in my room. And I cried a lot."

"Have you talked to anyone else about this?"

Louisa's eyes sought Nora, who nodded encouragement. "Dr. Perry. After Sky told me Ted had been murdered."

"Sky Brady? Did he know about the rape?"

"No, not really."

Frank's gut told him there was more she wasn't telling and exasperation sharpened his tone. "What do you mean, 'not really'?"

Louisa braided her fingers together. "I mean, the only person I talked to about what happened—either time—was Professor Perry. But last spring . . . Sky knew that I'd been raped but—you know, just the fact of it. I didn't tell him what happened—details or anything. And I didn't tell him it was Ted Slater."

"So you didn't tell Brady about being at Slater's on Friday?"

"No."

"But he did tell you about the murder?"

"Yes. But not much. It was just, you know, really traumatic for him. He'd heard there was lots of blood, and insects."

Frank rubbed his chin. He'd have to try to pin down what Brady had said to whom. "So far, you're the last person to see him alive. You're going to have to come down to the station and make a formal statement. And we'll need your fingerprints, to help identify ones we found in the house."

"I'm supposed to work later this afternoon." She sounded tentative. "But . . ." She turned to Nora. "Could you come with me now?"

Nora looked at Frank and he nodded almost imperceptibly. "Sure, I'll come."

Frank deposited them in the waiting room. "Make yourselves comfortable. I'll only be a minute." He signaled the duty officer to buzz him through.

Louisa lowered herself stiffly onto a chair, staring at her hands again, apparently oblivious to her surroundings. Nora surveyed the room. Everything from the buff colored walls to the green speckled vinyl tile floor to the hanging philodendron screamed "Institutional Décor!" There wasn't a magazine or newspaper anywhere, and Nora hadn't brought a book. She read the walls—plaques, citations, notices—the titles of informational brochures, and business cards. A nearby door held a sign printed in tall red capital letters: RUNAWAYS AND STATUS OFFENDERS CANNOT BE PLACED IN A CELL—JUVENILES CHARGED WITH A CRIME CAN BE PLACED IN A CELL FOR A MAXIMUM OF SIX (6) HOURS WITH SEPARATION FROM ADULTS. NO EXCEPTIONS. She'd just read TIPS LINE, 758-6666, when Frank opened the door. "Follow me." His loose, swinging gait was as graceful as ever.

Louisa and Nora followed, through a maze of corridors carpeted in institutional tweed, through a room much like a West College classroom, into an interrogation room. One wall included a two-way mirror. Frank motioned Louisa and Nora to seats facing the mirror. He sat opposite. Sgt. Jamieson had already claimed one end of the plain rectangular table. Everyone was polite, but Nora did not find the blank gray walls, hard chairs, and bare table conducive to relaxation.

"This is an official statement. Both Sgt. Jamieson and I will be present throughout. The session will be recorded. Your statement will be typed and you will be asked to read and sign it." Frank turned on the recorder. "This is Capt. Franklin J. Pierce, interviewing Louisa Smallwood concerning the murder of Theodore Slater. Also in the room are Sgt. Joseph Jamieson and Prof. Nora Perry. Prof. Perry is here at Ms. Smallwood's request." He added the date and time and turned to Louisa. "Now, you are not required to tell us anything, but I urge you to give a complete and accurate statement. If you have nothing to hide, you should do everything you can to help us clear up this murder. Do you understand?" Louisa nodded. "You need to speak your answers."

Louisa exhaled slowly. "Yes. I understand."

When it was over, Louisa drooped like a half-dead daisy. Nora drove her to her dorm.

While Nora drove home, Frank reported to Jake Bentley. "She had motive and opportunity and the means were at hand. She admits she was there. She has brown hair and the tech found brown hair on the rug by the bed. She *claims* she went there to get her umbrella. Pretty lame if you ask me. She also says he date raped her last December, but maybe that's just what she's calling it now. She admits she hated the guy enough to kill him. She has a banged-up face she says he gave her, but swears she didn't hit back."

"Do you believe any of it?"

Frank considered. "Slater might have been a man who'd let her just run away in the middle of a fight. But guys in general—well, I doubt it. But if she's telling the truth, she's holding something back—like maybe what she did when Slater caught her."

"Good work. It would be a real coup if we could wrap this thing up fast."

"I'll call Pikesville, see if we can't get the fingerprint info out of them sooner rather than later. Could you lean on the Baltimore City Morgue for me? I need the time of death pinned down. I think he died Friday night, but heat from the fireplace makes it a tough call."

"Sure, no problem. Just let me know whose arm I need to twist. And see what else you can get on the girl." Jake tucked in his chin and looked at Frank from under bushy eyebrows. Frank knew that look—and braced himself. "You know, Frank, you might want to step down from this one." Jake cleared his throat. "It's common knowledge you and Nora Perry were an item. Now she finds a body and you're the chief investigator. People are gonna wonder."

Frank held his temper. "I'm the most experienced investigator you've got. Are you more interested in solving this case or in keeping up appearances?"

"What if she becomes a suspect?"

"That ain't gonna happen, Jake."

"See what I mean? It's that attitude. It just doesn't look kosher."

"Are you ordering me off this case?"

"Well, no. Not ordering."

"Then here's the deal. I'll keep you informed every step of the way. If any evidence turns up linking Nora to the crime—or if you find some conflict of interest is affecting my investigation—I'll step aside. Otherwise, I'm on it."

Eventually, Jake nodded. "You got it. I'll let you run with it as long as I can."

CHAPTER EIGHT

In the early dark, Joe and Sy rang Suzanne Slater's doorbell. The porch light came on and the door opened, only as wide as the security chain, revealing a narrow slice of a tall woman. "Yes?"

"I'm Sgt. Joe Jamieson of the Queen Anne's County Sheriff's Office. This is Detective Seymour Brown." Both men flipped open their IDs. "We'd like to talk to you."

"I didn't get a good look at your IDs. Let me see them again." They held the IDs steady for a lengthy scrutiny before she unchained the door. She could have passed for a gypsy fortuneteller: brown wavy hair past her shoulders, a black leotard, an Indian print skirt, long silver earrings, silver bangle bracelets, and bare feet. She said, "A woman can't be too careful these days."

Joe said, "Not a problem. It's always good to be cautious."

"Well, then, how can I help you?"

She sounded like a sales clerk in a posh store. Joe said, "We want to talk to you about Ted Slater."

Her face clouded. "What if *I* don't want to talk about *him?*"

Sy scowled. Joe said mildly, "Is there some reason you don't want to talk about him?"

"Yeah. He's an asshole." For several seconds nobody moved, then she stepped aside. "I guess you'd better come in."

She led them into a small room smelling faintly of incense. Joe wasn't sure whether the furnishings were Indian or Turkish or what: woven rugs, embroidered leather cushions, hammered brass and silver. She waved them to the sofa and took the chair opposite. "So why are you here?"

"Are you—or were you—married to Ted Slater?"

She looked wary. "Yes."

"Well—which is it? Are you or were you?"

"Technically, we're still married. But we haven't lived together for over two years. What's this about?" She sounded irritated.

Joe cleared his throat. "The West College personnel office has you down as his next of kin. I'm just confirming the relationship."

"Next of kin? Is he in the hospital or what?"

Joe and Sy exchanged a look. "He's dead."

"Really? Seriously? Was it a car accident? I mean . . . I didn't really think . . . He's really dead?"

Joe nodded. She was younger than he'd first thought—probably not more than twenty-five or twenty-six. Her surprise seemed genuine—or maybe just a little overdone.

Suzanne beamed. "Hallelujah! Free at last!" She looked from one detective to the other. "Thank you. That's the best news I've had in a long time."

Joe shifted uneasily in his chair and Sy's face registered rigid disapproval.

"Don't look so shocked. It's not like I'm the grieving widow. His being dead is about the best thing that could happen to me. That bastard made my life a living hell!"

"How was that?"

Suzanne rose from her chair and paced. "He acted more like a jailer than a husband. He questioned everything I did, ordered me around. He'd promise to change, but . . ." She stopped. "Two years of that before I finally saw the writing on the wall. On my face, actually: he broke my nose and loosened two teeth. It was the second time he'd hit me."

Joe cleared his throat again. "Uh. Why aren't you divorced?"

Suzanne lifted her chin. "Money. I dropped out of college to marry him and never even had a job. He gave me a weekly allowance but the credit cards, all the bank accounts and everything, were in his name. He said, 'I don't want you to worry your pretty little head about money.' I actually thought that was romantic. How could anybody have been so dumb? When I left the hospital, I had nothing but the clothes on my back." Suzanne whirled to face Joe. "This calls for a celebration. What will you have? Beer? Wine?"

Sy said, "We're on duty, ma'am."

"Suit yourselves. I don't mind drinking alone." She returned from the kitchen with the smell of curry clinging to her clothes, carrying a glass of red wine. She drank about a third of it before setting the glass on the table at her elbow.

Joe said, "So how did not getting a divorce help you? With money, I mean."

Suzanne gazed at him steadily. "He claimed he wanted to get back together—said he wanted another chance. He said that as long as I was his wife, he'd take care of me—and if I got an apartment nearby, he'd pay for it. I needed him to tide me over. I had to find a job, establish credit, buy furniture . . ." Her mouth twisted into an ugly line. "Later I realized how much power he still had, holding the purse strings."

Joe surveyed the room. "You seem to be doing all right."

"I get along okay now. No thanks to him." Her bracelets jingled as she brushed an invisible something from her skirt. "He wouldn't let go. He refused to sign a separation agreement. Refused to get a lawyer. Missed meetings with my lawyer. He'd take papers for review and then never return them. He stonewalled every step of the way—smiling soulfully and saying he wanted to get back together."

"You sound pretty angry."

"Why wouldn't I? He seduced me when I was practically a child. Before we married—and for a few months after—he treated me like a princess. And the sex was great. But the more I tried to grow up, the more I wanted any kind of independence, the more he ground me under his heel." Anger flashed in her eyes as she finished. "All I got from that bastard was a taste for fine wine and art and a shit load of practice following orders." Her voice softened. "Two years of therapy and support groups and I still have trouble standing up for my rights."

Whether she was a vulnerable child acting brassy or a bitch acting vulnerable, Joe still had to get the same information. He said, "I see. Do you know whether your husband had a will?"

Suzanne narrowed her eyes and sipped her wine. "No."

Joe continued. "Either way, now he's dead, you'll get at least some of his property."

"It isn't all *his* property. Most of it's *marital* property! I'm entitled. My lawyer said so." Suzanne lifted her chin. "The hell that bastard put me through, I'm entitled to everything I can get and then some."

"Do you know of anyone else who might benefit from your husband's death? A relative perhaps?"

"No." Her voice turned guarded. "You never told me how he died. *Was* it a car accident?"

"It looks like he was murdered, ma'am."

"Murdered! When? Where? How?"

Was her surprise real? "In his house. A blow to the head." Joe tried to sound casual. "Just for the record, ma'am, where were you this past weekend?"

"Why? Do you think *I* killed him?"

"It's the sort of question we ask a lot of people in a case like this. So, tell me about your weekend."

"I worked and shopped and hung out here."

"We need more detail than that, ma'am."

Exaggerated patience dropped over Suzanne's face. She rolled her eyes ceilingward as she intoned, "We close the shop at 5:00 in the off season, and after work on Friday I came home. I spent the evening watching TV. Saturday I worked nine to five, Sunday one to four. Saturday I did grocery shopping after work and then came home. Sunday morning I went to church. Sunday evening I did laundry and paid bills." She looked at Joe. "Satisfied?"

"Did you see anyone or talk to anyone when you weren't at work? Could anyone vouch for your whereabouts?"

"No."

"What kind of car do you drive?"

"A three-year-old white Toyota Corolla."

"Do you still have a key to your husband's house?"

Suzanne shook her head. "He changed the locks. Not that that means anything. Ted never locked the house—except right after I left, when he was trying to keep me from getting my things. Otherwise anyone could waltz in there, practically any time."

Joe ran his thumbnail along his jaw. "Do you know anyone with a red sports car?"

"Why?"

Sy said, "We're asking the questions here. You just answer them." Joe frowned and shook his head. Sy clamped his mouth shut.

Suzanne stood up, rigid as a porch pillar. "I don't believe I care to do that. Please leave."

Sy rose but Joe remained seated. "Just a couple more questions, ma'am. Other than yourself, who would be his next of kin?"

She seemed to weigh the pros and cons of answering before saying, "There's no one close. His parents died years ago. No brothers or sisters, just a couple of aunts and uncles, and some cousins somewhere, I think. Ted never talked about family. I don't even know their names."

"What about his friends? Who would they be?"

Suzanne laughed bitterly. "Ted wouldn't have *friends*—only girlfriends. And I wouldn't know them."

"When was the last time you saw your husband?"

Suzanne glared from one to the other. "I want you to leave. Now."

"We heard—"

"I'm not answering any more questions! Will you leave, or do I have to call the Chestertown police?"

Sy stiffened, about to protest, but Joe waved him into silence and rose slowly to his feet. As they reached the door, Joe said, "Thank you for your time and your help. If you think of anything more we should know, give me a call." He held out his card. Suzanne didn't take it. He laid it on a little table by the door as they left.

The door snicked shut behind the officers, the small sound hanging in the silent hall. Suzanne leaned against the wall, then sank to the floor cross-legged, fighting to marshal her thoughts while the curry in the kitchen scorched. Eventually they would question her again. They'd ask again about the last time she had seen Ted, the last time she had been to the house.

CHAPTER NINE

Hurrying toward the Baldwin Fine Arts Building, Van saw Raoul swing his car off North Hibernia, into the lot by Physical Plant. The choral director jumped out, briefcase in hand, and half-trotted toward the rehearsal hall. Van picked up his pace. Raoul was hell on latecomers.

The president's announcement about Ted Slater had come out that afternoon—a discreet statement that he had been found in his home on Sunday, followed by the usual laudatory things said about the dead. Rumors that he had been murdered already buzzed. Pushing open the door to the rehearsal hall, Van speculated about the mood of the singers—probably unruly. Raoul would bring them to order if anyone could. During his year singing with the chorus, Van had found refuge in the weekly rehearsals. Tonight, more than anything else, he wanted a respite from thinking about Slater. Not likely. But maybe no one knew he'd seen the body.

Van slipped into place three minutes before rehearsal began. Glancing over the chorus, he recognized the back of Nora's head. How was she bearing up? As Raoul arranged music at the podium, snatches of conversation confirmed Van's expectations: virtually everyone was talking about Slater's death. Clyde Barnes declared with loud authority that it was murder, adding, "And furthermore, I have a damned good idea who did it!"

Gerry Foster demurred. "Oh, come now, Clyde! You couldn't possibly—"

Clyde puffed out his chest. "I assure you, Gerald, I know whereof I speak!" His glance gathered in those in closest proximity. "I didn't have the office next to Ted's all those years without learning a thing or two. Why, I could tell you—"

"Warm up!" Raoul boomed, striking a C major chord, unceremoniously cutting off Clyde's comments and causing the just-in-time arrivals to scurry to their places.

As Van left the hall, Nora fell into step beside him. While he wondered whether to mention Frank Pierce, or ask about the interview with Louisa, Nora said, "I think I need a friend tonight. How about a beer? Or coffee? I could follow you down to The Pub." Van's mood spiked up a notch.

Cars and pick-ups jammed the parking lot at Corsica's Lighthouse Pub, a place favored by the college crowd because it was on the edge of town toward campus. Van and Nora stopped just inside the door. Nora said, "Wow. And it's a weeknight."

Noting the noise level in the bar, they turned right into the dining room and scanned the crowded tables. Van said, "It seems the whole chorus had the same idea."

As they claimed a table, Clyde approached, beer in hand. Van leaned close to Nora and whispered, "Damn. Here comes Motor Mouth."

"Hello, Nora, Van." Clyde pulled out a chair and straddled it. "Pretty hot news about Ted. Not that it's surprising, when you think about it. What *do* you think about it?"

Nora said, "I don't want to talk about Ted Slater. You can either like that or lump it." She set her jaw in a way that said persisting would be counterproductive.

Clyde held up his hands as if warding off a blow. "Fine, fine." He raised his chin and narrowed his eyes to slits. "But I hear you two were anchored off Slater's property when he was killed."

Nora looked as stunned as Van felt. She said, "Good grief, where do you hear such things?"

"Oh, a little birdie told me. Doesn't that make you suspects or something?" Clyde grinned at Nora. "Some people might think your presence there was suspicious—that boat trouble was just an excuse to be there. But not me. Besides, I happen to know at least two people with lots stronger motives." He stopped talking and smirked, looking from one to the other, obviously waiting to be asked.

Nora toyed with her coffee cup, saying nothing. Van was not inclined to give Clyde the satisfaction of a question, either. But there was no better source of campus gossip than Clyde Barnes—if he didn't turn coy and hoard his secrets. So Van adopted a skeptical tone and asked, "And who might they be?"

"Two unhappy women from his past."

Van said, "There must be at least two unhappy women in any man's past."

Clyde cast a withering look at Van but addressed Nora. "Far be it from me to speak ill of the dead, but Ted was not a gentleman where women were concerned." Nora's only response was a frown and silence. "Two weeks ago, maybe three, that Smallwood girl was in his office, arguing with him. They kept their voices down, but I could hear enough to know this was *not* a friendly exchange." Clyde pursed his lips in righteous disapproval. "A year ago she was hanging around all the time, giggling and blushing, spending hours in his office getting *extra help* on her coursework. As if a candidate for Phi Beta Kappa needed it. Who did they think they were fooling?" He sniffed. "Then spring semester, nothing. My guess is, he seduced her and then dumped her, she wanted to have another go at it this fall, and he told her to get lost. And you know what they say about a woman scorned."

Nora stiffened, her face like thunder. "For God's sake, knock it off. You're spreading malicious gossip about an excellent student who never did a thing to you! Why don't you mind your own damned business for a change?"

Clyde fell momentarily speechless. He habitually curried Nora's favor, so Van expected him to drop the subject. Instead, Clyde said, "Of course, there were other women students—usually one a year. Idol worship in the fall, true love in the spring and a fade-out over the summer. Always the same—except with Smallwood it ended sooner."

"Are you telling me you knew he abused his position as a faculty member—repeatedly—and you did nothing to stop it?" Van had never seen Nora so angry.

Clyde tried a sheepish grin and a shrug. Nora scowled at him. When Clyde spoke again, his tone was a defensive half whine. "What was I supposed to do? There's no law against sex between consenting adults, you know, even when one happens to be a faculty member and the other is a student. None of them ever made a sexual harassment complaint." Nora opened her mouth to respond but Clyde hurried on. "Besides, I don't really think it was a student—Smallwood or anyone else. My money is on Suzanne Slater."

Nora gasped and Van tried to mask his astonishment when he asked, "Why would his ex-wife want to kill him? *She* left *him,* didn't she?"

Clyde looked triumphant. "But she wasn't his *ex*-wife. They never divorced."

"Of course they were divorced." Nora snorted. "Ted talked about it!"

Clyde peered down his nose at her. "There's talk and then there's truth. She was in his office last month, a real shouting match. At least, *she* was shouting. I couldn't hear him very well. She called him a sonofabitch and demanded to know why he was stonewalling on the separation agreement, why the hell didn't he get a lawyer, why wouldn't he sign the papers, and on and on. At one point she said, 'You've got to let me go! ' and Ted said, 'Oh, really?' and laughed. Then *she* yelled, 'Goddamn you Ted, I could kill you with my bare hands!' and some other stuff I didn't catch. I think she threw a bunch of papers at him before she stormed out. Trust me. She did it," Clyde said, pushing back his chair. He hustled toward a man who had just come in. "Hey, Eric!"

Clyde's strident voice and incessant talk, even from across the room, drove Nora and Van from their table in the dining area to one as far removed as possible, in the octagonal annex near the emergency exit. As they sat down, Nora said, "The good news is, Clyde didn't say anything about us finding the body. If Clyde doesn't know, nobody knows." Her voice was tight.

"Do you think he really believes Suzanne or Louisa killed Ted?"

Nora lifted a shoulder. "With Clyde you never know whether he's speaking from conviction or saying whatever will hold the crowd."

Van squinted at the brownish-gray floor tiles in the annex, trying to recall a distant conversation. "Don't you know Ted's ex-wife? Or wife, as the case may be."

"I know both of his wives—slightly. I've lost track of Barbara, but Suzanne lives in Chestertown. She took one of my classes before she dropped out—smart and witty but incredibly naïve. Didn't I tell you that already? I saw her at campus functions sometimes when she and Ted were married, but I discouraged any friendship. It was always 'Ted says this' and 'Ted likes that,' and what Ted had 'let' her do—not a thought in her head that he didn't put there. She's the kind of submissive, wishy-washy woman that drives me nuts!" Nora fell silent for a moment. "I haven't seen her in ages. Are you wondering whether Suzanne could be a murderer?"

"More precisely, I am trying to assess the accuracy of Clyde's statements." Van leaned closer, striving to be heard over the pub noises without speaking too loudly. "Did you know about—or even suspect—that Ted habitually had relationships with women students?"

"Not till tonight! I knew Suzanne had been his student before they married, but more than that—if I'd had any idea, I would have put a stop to it. He didn't have tenure. It wouldn't have been all that complicated. There is no place on this faculty for people who exploit and abuse students. That Clyde knew and did nothing about it . . . He makes me mad enough to spit!"

As Nora spoke, her voice rose in both pitch and volume. Such naked emotion made Van squirm, and he sought a shift in direction. "It is not likely that he fabricated the incident with Suzanne—not completely. Some of his comments had the ring of truth."

"Even if there was an argument, I bet he exaggerated it for effect. Although there were rumors of some pretty violent scenes around the time of their divorce—around the time everyone thinks they got divorced!"

"Physical violence?"

Nora tilted her head. "Not that anyone ever witnessed, as far as I know. Just violent language. But at this point, there isn't much I'd put past Ted Slater! Clyde might be wrong about them still being married. But in any case, I'm absolutely certain he's wrong about Louisa."

"Wrong about what?"

"Everything. Well, maybe not *everything*. But wrong about Ted dumping her."

"Perhaps so, but until a better suspect comes along, she is it. Why do you suppose they were arguing in his office a few weeks ago?"

A shadow seemed to pass over Nora's countenance. "I don't know. Louisa didn't mention any arguments this fall. But I can't believe she killed him. So, we'd better find someone better!"

"What do you mean, *we*? This is a police matter." Van signaled for another beer.

"But the police don't care about Louisa. They just want to find the killer. And mistakes *are* made . . . all the time!"

"Not *all* of the time," Van murmured. Nora pursed her lips and Van inferred that she did not appreciate his scientific precision.

She said, "The point is that we care—I do, anyway—and someone who cares is going to try a lot harder to find the real killer."

Van paused while the waitress set his beer on the table and departed. "But you cannot know that Louisa did not do it. What if she did?" He couldn't suppress a hint of irritation.

Nora jutted out her chin. "She didn't." Was she really sure of Louisa's innocence, or was she just being stubborn? She leaned forward. "Don't you want to know who did do it? Who subjected us to—*that*? I don't know that I'll ever get the sight of Ted's body out of my mind. Or the smell." She shuddered. "You seem fixated on details and hair-splitting precision. Where are your feelings in all of this? Don't you care about the people involved?"

Van thought of Winston Churchill's definition of a fanatic: someone who cannot change his mind or the subject. He assessed his options: leave the investigation to the police and thereby distance himself from Nora, or acquiesce against his inclinations. He did not wish to dwell on Nora's growing importance to him. But it would not hurt to tidy up a loose end or two. "Living in the county seat, we could easily check divorce records. I would be willing to go to the county clerk's office after my classes tomorrow and do that."

Nora smiled and Van noticed the beginnings of crow's feet at the corners of her eyes. Her hand covered his. "Thank you. I know this isn't your thing, and I do appreciate your willingness to help."

They fell silent once more. For Van, it was not one of their comfortable silences. He nursed his beer, noticing Nora's cheekbones, the half moons of her eyelashes when she looked down, the fine red mesh created by the light behind a curly wisp of her hair. He wondered whether the uneasiness he felt would continue, would diminish the quality of their friendship.

Nora finished her coffee. "What are you thinking?"

"Oh, nothing really." He paused. "Is it not strange that one's life can be touched by such violence and one's daily activities continue in their ordinary paths? We found a murder victim, but we still write exams, advise students, attend committee meetings, and draft scholarly papers as if our lives were unchanged." Nora nodded. After another moment, Van said, "Is it time to go? I will see you to your car."

As Van turned off Corsica Neck Road onto North Hibernia, he thought about things he and Nora had not said. She had not mentioned the police interview with Louisa and he had not thought it appropriate to inquire. She had not mentioned Frank Pierce, either. He wondered at the significance of her silence. His inclinations regarding this investigation and Nora's were almost diametrical opposites, their levels of emotional involvement vastly different. And that was a combustible combination. Van went to sleep contemplating the bleary line between reasonable accommodation and being a pushover.

CHAPTER TEN

Jake Bentley wore his suit like a uniform. Standing beside Frank's desk, he said, "You've got to keep me up to speed on this. I need to know everything." A little thick around the middle, Jake stood ramrod straight, feet slightly apart, reminiscent of a military man at parade rest—a staff sergeant, perhaps, proud of his record and the sharp crease in his pants. He twirled his pen and added, "I want to know whatever you know, as soon as you know it."

Sometimes Jake's repetitions irritated Frank, sometimes they amused him. Today he chose to be amused, and adopted a sardonic tone. "Sure thing, Jake. You're The Man."

Jake stopped contemplating his pen and looked up from under bushy red eyebrows. "I'm not saying you can't handle it. Nobody else around here even comes close to your—hold on." Jake reached for Frank's ringing phone, the stretch landing his belly on the edge of the desk. "This is Jake . . . Well tell him Frank will call back. And hold all calls till we're finished here." He slammed the phone back into its cradle and scowled at Frank. "As I was saying, I'm up for re-election next year. I don't want voters thinking I've been out to lunch on this one."

Jake answering his phone felt arrogant to Frank. His focus on re-election felt like the big city politics Frank had deplored in Philadelphia. He chose not to say so, the pencil tapping on his yellow pad the only sign of his emotions. "Sure, Jake," he repeated. "I'm on your team, remember?"

When Jake first ran for sheriff eight years ago, Frank had openly supported him against the incumbent of decades. By then, Frank had tolerated his boss's bigotry, old boy network, and lackluster performance for four years. One of them had to go. People recognized campaigning for his boss's opponent as a hell of a strong endorsement. Too much of a politician to forget his friends from that tough campaign, Jake had been ready to give Frank any breaks he reasonably could. None were needed.

"But it isn't just next year's election. You know that, don't you, Frank? As long as we don't have the killer, we can't be sure this was personal to Ted Slater. What if this turns out to be a serial killer's first victim? Someone's always the first."

"Don't worry, Jake. Only dead fish float with the current. We'll swim wherever we have to."

When Jake left, Frank sat for a few minutes, reminding himself of all the ways Centreville was better than Philadelphia—or any other big city. Eventually he grabbed his notebook and prepared to interview more of Slater's neighbors. He dusted the toe of his right shoe against the back of his left pant leg, then shifted his weight to accommodate the other shoe, a habit that drove his mother crazy. Claire didn't like it much, either. He straightened his tie and ran a finger along his pencil-thin-mustache, aware that his colleagues sometimes called him Dapper Dan.

Driving to Queenstown along the gently winding, two-lane road, he thought about his return to Centreville. He could have gone to the top in Philadelphia, but after thirteen years, he'd had it. Urban crime and departmental politics drained his spirit. When a job opened up in the Queen Anne's County Sheriff's Office, he'd applied—shocking family, colleagues, and Nora. He'd returned to Centreville hoping things would work out with her. They hadn't. She was too damned adamantly single. But he'd never regretted his decision to return. Now he had Claire, and two wonderful children. He'd never regretted that, either. Still, finding Nora at the crime scene—upset, stressed—dragged old feelings to the fore. As the road slipped away behind him, he sorted through those feelings. He still wanted to comfort and protect her, still wanted to absorb her calm and her passion. Her regard and approval still meant a lot to him. And right now, he'd give a lot to talk over the case, and pick her brain. As that last thought surfaced he passed the "Welcome to Queenstown" sign and turned on Salthouse Cove Lane.

The Grube residence faced the harbor. Frank took advantage of his early arrival to walk the property. The lawn sloped to the water's edge. An eighteen-foot runabout rested on her hoist and a small skiff tugged gently on her mooring line. Gazing at the skiff, Frank remembered seeing a boat like it during a walk along a dock with Nora. He'd said something about the biggest, most elaborate rowboat he'd ever seen. Nora had laughed at his landlubber vocabulary and explained that it was a skiff: longer and wider at the beam than a rowboat, with a small foredeck. Frank had laughed, too, and said, "If you row it with oars, it ought to be called a rowboat." Nora had said, "What about the Viking longboats?" They had been young then, and laughed together often. Why think of that now? Frank threw off the memory and trudged to the end of the dock. Looking back, to his right a stand of evergreens and oaks marked the boundary, the adjoining property visible only from the second floor of the Grubes' house. Spectacular views across the water, but no good view of Slater's house. Frank checked his watch and retraced his steps to the front door.

"Mr. Grube? I'm Captain Pierce," he said, displaying his credentials.

"Come in, come in. We've been expecting you." Owen Grube turned back into the house, calling, "Ruthie? Captain Pierce is here."

The Grubes denied knowing Slater personally, but reported seeing him sometimes at Potter's Pantry, the little general store on Main Street, often in the company of good-looking women.

"Anyone in particular?"

"Not recently." Owen's voice sounded wistful. "The last steady one was about a year ago, a young woman we saw several times last fall."

"Can you describe her?"

"Gosh, I don't . . ." He blinked rapidly and turned to his wife as if checking whether he should have noticed the young woman's looks.

Mrs. Grube's voice rang with authority. "She was above average height—maybe five feet, eight inches—and slim—with straight, shoulder-length hair. I'd have to say she was moderately attractive—or would have been if she'd ever tried to fix herself up." Mrs. Grube was on the heavy side of plump, stiff and primly groomed. "Her mouth was too wide—she couldn't do much about that, of course—but she needn't have been so frumpy. I never saw her in anything except jeans or shorts or something of that sort. She sounded smart, too." Mrs. Grube's tone conveyed that being smart was as unforgivable as being frumpy. "Probably she was a college student. He was a professor, you know."

Frank thought she was describing Louisa. "Do you know her name?"

"I don't remember."

"Were you aware of other visitors to Mr. Slater's house? Women *or* men?"

Owen blinked. "We couldn't see his place—only the Sasser's, and that's from the guest room."

His wife cut in indignantly, "We don't make a habit of spying on our neighbors, Captain."

"I notice that you have a boat. Do you go out often?"

Owen beamed. "I love to fish. Weather permitting. When the water's rougher than a stucco bathtub, I hit the showers." Owen chuckled. "But I go out most days."

Frank started to ask what could be seen from the water, but Mrs. Grube leaned forward, chest heaving, and said, "Owen, tell Captain Pierce about the sailboat." She turned to Frank. "That was probably someone visiting Mr. Slater."

"Good God, Ruthie, that was months ago."

"I know that! But I think you should tell him what we thought."

Owen looked at his wife and blinked several times, then glanced at Frank and rolled his eyes heavenward. Frank nodded and said, "Yes, Mr. Grube, tell me."

"It was in April, maybe May—last spring, anyway. We noticed this white sailboat anchored for three or four days off the old steamer wharf near Slater's dock. Gunkholers seldom stay here for more than a night—certainly not more than two. We thought the woman from that boat must be visiting Ted Slater." He leaned forward. "The boat was anchored close to his dock, you see. Besides, there weren't any cabin lights at night. It was always dark except for the anchor light. Ruthie and I decided that meant that no one was on board—unless, of course, they didn't need light for what they were doing." Owen chuckled.

Mrs. Grube frowned. "So obviously it was someone visiting Mr. Slater."

"Was it the young woman you mentioned earlier?"

Owen stroked his chin. "No, no. The woman I saw on the boat was middle-aged—well, older than twenty, anyway—but a real looker."

"Oh? You got a good look at her?"

Owen darted a look at his wife's pursed lips and narrowed eyes. "Well, no, not really. My wife and I are birdwatchers, see. We watch birds feeding on the sand spit at low tide, great blue herons in the marsh grasses, that sort of thing."

"I see," Frank said. "You happened to see the woman on one of those bird watching occasions."

"Yes. Yes, that's right." Owen winked at Frank.

Mrs. Grube could reveal her displeasures in utter silence, but this time she added words to her body language. "Yes, Owen's hands are sometimes *glued* to the binoculars. He's especially attracted to female birds."

Shit, Frank thought, *that'll stop Owen talking.* He said, "I suppose you had only a glimpse, but any description you could give me would be very helpful."

Owen looked at his wife, then back at Frank, and coughed into a meaty fist. "I only saw her that one time, mostly from the back, when she tied up the dinghy. She had short hair—either that, or it was up under her hat—a big hat. And she wore really big sunglasses, too. But she had a great figure." Another quick look at Ruthie. "I mean, she had long legs and . . . seemed very fit."

"You said she was middle-aged."

Owen fidgeted and said faintly, "Oh, well, it was just an impression I had, you know?"

"Was there anything unusual about the sailboat besides not having cabin lights at night?"

"I can't think of anything. I'm a stinkpotter myself, so if you wanted to know about *powerboats* . . . But a rag bag is a rag bag, pretty much."

"What about the name of the boat?"

Owen massaged his chin. "Well, now, I noticed it at the time, but I can't say as I remember it now. There've been a lot of boats in here since."

It was a long shot, but Frank asked, "By any chance, was that sailboat anchored in the harbor on Friday night?"

"Not that I saw. There was a boat, but not that one."

"Are you sure it wasn't the same boat?"

"I'm positive," Owen said. "In the first place, the Friday one wasn't white. I don't know what color it was, but it wasn't white. Even in the light of a half moon, you can tell a white hull." After a pause he added, "And in the second place, it had a different anchor light."

"Different how?"

"Well, it wasn't a fixed one at the top of the mast. It was a transportable one—like a lantern—hung near the bow of the boat, maybe seven or eight feet above the deck. And it was bright. I've never noticed one quite like it before." Owen folded his hands on his belly, resting his case. That was the last Frank could get out of him.

Walking to the next interview, Frank shook his head. Not a hell of a lot to report to Jake. Louisa was old news. But the woman with the boat might mean something.

CHAPTER ELEVEN

Frank thought the place had potential: Twelve Loverlee Lane, between the Grubes and Slater. He knocked. A busty blond wearing a tight black skirt that ended a foot above her knees flung open the door. "*You* must be Captain Pierce! I've been *expecting* you. I'm Mrs. Sasser, of course—Mrs. Mark Sasser—*Mary* Sasser, that is." Her words came light and breathy.

"Good afternoon, Mrs. Sasser. May I come in?"

"Please do," she said, turning toward the living room. "I'm *so* sorry Mark isn't here. He called around noon to say he couldn't make it. I told him you'd want to talk with *both* of us. But you know how he can be sometimes." She looked over her shoulder at Frank and giggled. "Well, no, you don't know, do you? How could you?" She smiled brightly. "But I surely will try to be helpful in any way I can."

Frank waited for her to sit, and when she perched on the edge of an enormous beige overstuffed chair, he took the one opposite. He realized his mistake as soon as he sank into its depths—not a posture conducive to conducting a business-like interview. "Mrs. Sasser, how well did you know Ted Slater?"

"Oh, my God! We were *shocked* when we heard what had happened. I never thought that something like that could happen in *Queenstown*. And right next door, too." Her prattle flowed on, her delicate, long-fingered hands fluttering like butterfly wings.

Frank cut in mildly: "Mrs. Sasser, I know murder is upsetting. But you need to focus. Did you know Ted Slater well?"

"Oh, dear, I was babbling wasn't I? I'm *so* sorry, Captain. I know I talk a lot. Mark says I talk such drivel sometimes that it drives him absolutely *crazy*—but of course he doesn't mean that *literally*."

Was she stonewalling? Frank struggled to sit straighter. "Mrs. Sasser! Tell me about Ted Slater. Did you ever see his visitors?" The effort to be forceful while sunk in a chair that curved his spine and brought his knees almost as high as his armpits put an edge on his tone.

Mary Sasser giggled. "Sorry. I knew him pretty well, actually. As a *neighbor,* you know. Not that we were exactly good friends or anything."

Taking advantage of her momentary responsiveness, he repeated, "Please tell me about him, anything you can."

"I can tell you that he really liked it when I called him doctor. He wasn't a *real* doctor, of course. He was the thinking kind of doctor. He taught business courses at West College. But then you know that, don't you? How silly of me!" Her giggle rippled forth.

"When did Ted Slater tell you he had a doctorate?"

Mary Sasser's blue eyes opened wide. "Oh, he never *told* me! That would have been ever so conceited, don't you think? And besides, everyone knows college professors are doctors. I wouldn't have to be told *that.* But like I said, when I called him 'doctor' I could tell he was pleased, even though he never actually said . . ."

Frank jotted "ego" on his notepad and cut in again. "Yes, thank you. What else can you tell me about him?"

Mrs. Sasser rolled her eyes. "He was ever so handsome—like a soap opera star, if you ask me—and of course you *did* ask me, didn't you?" She giggled. Frank decided that a little giggling went a long way. "And he was a sharp dresser, right out of *GQ.* From what *I* saw, I'd say he was *very* taken with the ladies."

"What did you see, ma'am?"

"A *lot* of female visitors."

"Anyone in particular?"

Mrs. Sasser tugged at the hem of her skirt, to no noticeable effect. "Mark told me I should watch my tongue. He thinks I'm not very *discreet,*" she confided. "But telling the *police* isn't the same as telling just *anyone,* now is it?" Mrs. Sasser bounced a little on the edge of her chair and leaned forward. "There was a mystery woman in his life." She paused. "Well, I suppose she wasn't a mystery to *him.* Maybe I should say there was a mystery woman in *my* life, because I certainly did find it mysterious." Frank took a deep breath and waited for her to say something concrete. "The last several months I've seen this one woman a lot, maybe four or five times a month. Sometimes I would see him drive away and then he'd be back again, with her, and then she'd be there for *days*. Well, sometimes it was only a few hours. But if you ask *me*—and of course you did ask me, didn't you? Well, it must have been his current *amour*." Her tone changed from conspiratorial to peevish. "But he never introduced her. That was the mystery. He *always* introduced us before. We never bumped into her in the yard or in town or anything."

"But you can describe her?"

Mrs. Sasser's brow clouded. "Well, no, not really." Her voice rising to a wail of disappointment, she added, "She always wore a hat and sunglasses!"

"Anything at all would be helpful, ma'am—height, weight. Was she white?"

"Of *course* she was white." Mary Sasser's eyes widened. "Oh." She looked away and again tugged at the hem of her skirt. "I mean, yes, she was." She hurried on, "And she had great legs and a good figure."

"Age? Hair color?"

"I really couldn't say, but I had the *impression* that she was older than his usual girlfriends. But there were the glasses, you know, and the hats."

Frank cut in. "Let's talk about boats."

"Boats?" Mary Sasser seemed nonplused, but only momentarily. "There are hundreds of boats, Captain." Her tone was teasing. "This *is* a harbor, after all!"

Frank spoke through clenched teeth. "But did any boats near Slater's dock attract your attention?"

"Well, to tell you the truth, Captain, *boats* don't really attract my attention." She giggled and leaned forward, the low V of her silk shirt offering a view of considerable cleavage. "Mark's always saying, 'Mary, how can you possibly live right on the harbor and not know a ketch from a sloop?' and I say, 'It's easy!' and—"

"So you didn't notice a boat anchored here for several days last spring?"

"Well of *course* I noticed *that*. Why didn't you say so? It was there for most of a week."

Frank swallowed his exasperation. "Okay, so what can you tell me about that boat? Or the person sailing it?"

"Not a thing! It was just a plain white sailboat. I didn't see it coming or going, never saw anyone on board. But we probably have a *picture* of it!" she said triumphantly.

"What?"

"Yes, indeed! My husband is a photographer—quite a good one, he could be a professional—and as you can imagine, the sunsets from the porch are *beautiful*. Mark takes pictures of them all the time. He really is an *artist*, you know."

Frank's excitement battled his frustration. "I'm sure. Tell me about the boat picture."

"Well. Mark was taking a sunset series last spring. You know, the same time every night for a month? About a week into it, *just* before the timer went off, this white sailboat came into the viewfinder. He yelled, 'God damn it!' He was *so* angry. And then the boat just stayed there for *days* and he could never get a clear shot that didn't have the boat in it, so after it left, he had to start over."

"And he kept the picture?"

"I would *think* so. He keeps everything. After he developed it, he said the boat made a nice foreground focus or something."

"I'd like to see it."

"Mark has thousands of pictures. I'd have *no idea* where to look! But I could ask—"

Frank cut in, "If your husband can find the picture, I want it. And what about last Friday? Were any boats anchored here?"

"Well, you know, very few boats gunkhole this time of year." She said it casually but looked intently at Frank before she laughed and said, "When Mark says I know *nothing* about boats, he's exaggerating. I know that 'gunkhole' means anchoring in a harbor—or a creek or a cove—rather than tying up to a dock. This late in the season, boats don't anchor out much. And besides, we weren't home on Friday night, so I *couldn't* have seen a boat, could I?" She looked at Frank earnestly. "But I saw a boat on *Saturday* night. Does that help?"

Frank stifled his irritation. "Go back a bit. Are you aware of any other women who visited? Besides the mystery woman?"

"Not recently. He seems to be—I mean, *seemed* to be—involved with one woman at a time. He was married when he moved in, you know. Suzanne Slater was *absolutely gorgeous*. But what would you expect? He was so handsome and all. She was the *second* Mrs. Slater, but I never knew the first. She'd been one of his students, I think—Suzanne, that is—but maybe the first Mrs. Slater, too. He seemed to have a *thing* for good looking students." She wriggled a little and folded her hands in her lap. "Before the mystery woman, there was this brown haired girl, Louise somebody. About a year ago."

"And what did 'Louise' look like?"

"Young, of course. They all were. She was a student, I'm sure. Mark says I jump to conclusions, but I can't help *thinking*. I'm not a *stump* or something." Frank tapped his pen on his notepad and Mary Sasser said, "Oh, right. Well, let's say she was in her early twenties. Medium tall. She had long, sort of medium brown hair."

"Have you seen her recently? Over last weekend, maybe?"

"Nooooo. I don't remember seeing her since last winter. But speaking of boats! *Louise* anchored here a couple of times last fall! But not overnight, I think."

Frank started upright but then sank back into his chair. "Are you sure?"

"Of course I'm sure!" Mary Sasser sounded offended. "I *met* her, didn't I? And she waved to me the second time she anchored there, because we'd met by then, hadn't we?"

"If your husband has pictures of Louise's boat, too, that would be very helpful. What about men? Would you have noticed any men visiting?"

"Of course I would have noticed—if there had been any worth noticing!"

"Meaning?"

"Well, I can only think of two men. That handsome young hunk in the red sports car—now, *he* was worth noticing—he came a couple of times, I think. I never spoke to him, but he *exuded* masculinity." She glanced wistfully toward the window. "If you could bottle that, you'd make a fortune." She turned her gaze back to Frank. "And then there was that man he played poker with, I can't remember his name, something starting with an *M*, I think. I spoke to him a few times. He dressed well enough, but he was *not* very attractive, if you ask me—too thin, and going bald. He was *polite* enough, but not *forthcoming*."

"You seem to know quite a lot about Mr. Slater's social life."

"Well, we *are* neighbors. Were. One can't help but notice things. And one always tries to be *friendly* with one's neighbors, after all."

"How friendly?"

"How friendly?" She turned scarlet and spoke quickly. "Just—friendly—you know. Like, a couple of months ago Ted invited us for cocktails. Ted was a *very* charming host and absolutely *nothing* unusual happened."

"So what made that cocktail party worth mentioning?"

She plucked at the hem of her skirt. "Oh, *God!* Mark would just *kill* me if he knew I said anything. Well, not *really*, of course, but I do hope you won't mention that I told you."

"You haven't told me anything yet."

Mary's tongue darted across her upper lip. "Well, when we got ready to leave, Ted got our jackets. He handed Mark's to him, but he held mine for me—which was, of course, the *gentlemanly* thing to do. But after I'd slid my arms into the sleeves, he kept his hands on my shoulders for what seemed like a long time, and of course I felt uncomfortable with that." She flicked a look at Frank. "And then, as he showed us to the door, he slid his hand down my back and he . . . Well, he patted my behind. Mark saw, and he was *furious.* Well, indignant, anyway. He didn't say anything then, of course, because we were *guests.* And anyway, we were leaving. But later he said that he wasn't surprised, a man with all those women, that he'd never trusted Ted, and that I should be *very careful* in the future and that I should not be alone with Ted, ever." She paused, then added wistfully, "We've been fairly distant since then."

Frank heaved himself out of the armchair, straightened his shoulders, and tried to ease his muscles a bit. "I appreciate the time you've given me. As long as I'm here, I'd like to look around outside. You needn't accompany me."

She leaned forward, again offering Frank a view of her cleavage, and smiled up at him. "Look all you want!" She rose gracefully and held out her hand. "I'll have Mark call you about the picture. I'm *sure* he will be able to find it."

Frank surveyed the property line. Trees and heavy underbrush gave Slater's house privacy but there was one line of sight where the bay window in Slater's dining room was clearly visible. And sighting boats anchored off Slater's dock would be easy. He wondered how he could identify Mary Sasser's mystery woman. And he wondered just how friendly Mary Sasser and Ted Slater had been.

CHAPTER TWELVE

Frank drove past the Bollingly estate and turned into the gravel driveway Slater had shared with Joseph Douden. Douden's front entry offered a view of Slater's house, partially occluded by hemlocks. He had a clear view of the circular driveway, and part of the porch.

As Frank reached for the handsome brass knocker, the door swung wide. A frail old man, somewhat stooped, extended his hand. "Captain Pierce, I presume. Come in." He pointed to the front room with his cane. He shuffled his feet, trying to take the first step without losing his balance. "Parkinson's," he said.

Sitting down across from Douden, Frank said, "As I told you on the phone, I'm investigating your neighbor's death."

"Murder, Officer Pierce. His murder."

"Well, that's not official." At the look of scorn on Douden's face, he added, "Yet. Although it almost certainly was murder. So, how well did you know Ted Slater?"

"Pretty well, as neighbors go. I liked him. After my wife died a couple of years ago, he checked on me pretty regularly. Sometimes he took me shopping in Chestertown. I don't drive any more. I still have a car but God only knows why. I guess it keeps me from feeling trapped." Douden chuckled.

Frank assessed his witness: old-fashioned in manner and dress, probably a big man on campus, back when football players wore leather helmets. "So he was a friend?"

"Sort of. Want some sherry?"

"Thank you, no."

"Against the rules, I suppose. Well, I'm going to have some." He leaned his cane against the frayed and darkened chair arm and reached for the decanter and glass on the table beside him. "When you get to be my age, you make your own rules." With that he launched into a monologue on aging, coping with Parkinson's, and living life to the fullest, clearly more interested in having an audience than in assisting Frank.

Frank listened patiently for a few minutes—he always treated the elderly with respect—before returning to his questions. "What can you tell me about Ted Slater?"

Douden flapped one hand over and back. "He was kind enough to me, but more than a little full of himself. He put on airs about everything from his art collection to his cooking—liked to wear silk smoking jackets and brag about his travels. And he had one eager prick for the women." Frank made a small noise and Douden said, "When you get to be my age, you might as well say what you mean. If you knew anything at all about Ted Slater, you knew that women were drawn to him like bees to honey—or moths to a light bulb. Young ones. Old ones. Good looking ones. They came by car. They came by boat." His eyes twinkled at Frank. "They came on foot through a break in the hedge."

"Meaning?"

"Well, Mary Sasser didn't have need of mechanized transportation, did she?" He sounded less judgmental than amused.

"Slater had an affair with Mary Sasser?"

"Oh, I don't know that they ever actually got down to it, but I'd be willing to bet she wanted to. He probably enjoyed keeping her dangling. Or maybe they did it and just didn't tell me!" Douden chuckled again. "But I doubt it. He always had all the women he could service—younger and even better looking. He introduced me to a lot of them."

"What can you tell me about the current woman in his life?"

"Not a hell of a lot. I never met her." Douden confirmed what the other neighbors had said about the woman's visits, hats and sunglasses. "Now why would a man who shows off his trophies not show off this one? My guess is she was married. And probably from around here, or who would give a damn?" Douden hadn't noticed any boats at Slater's place, either last spring or last Friday.

Frank asked about other visitors during the weekend. Douden took a handkerchief from his pants pocket, wiped drool from his mouth and chin, his face animated. "Last Thursday or Friday, mid-afternoon or so, a young woman in a red sports car drove out of here like greased ape shit, throwing gravel all over the place. I was watching a cardinal at the birdbath till she scared him off. When she hit the black top, you could have heard the screech of the tires all the way to the post office. She nearly took out my mailbox."

Frank was sure he was describing Louisa's leaving, but he asked anyway. "Can you describe the woman? The car?"

"Well, like I said, it was a real streak-of-lightening sports car. A convertible, I think, but with the top up."

Frank leaned forward. "And the woman?"

"Just a blur, really. My vision isn't what it used to be."

"But you think she was young?"

The old man reached for his sherry. "I can't imagine a mature woman driving like that."

"What about other visitors?"

"No one interesting. Just that poker buddy in the old Subaru. He was there again. Friday—or maybe Thursday. I can't be sure."

"And who was this?"

Douden shrugged. "Just some guy Ted played poker with. I can't remember his name. I only met him once—a long time ago—but once was enough. Sleek on the outside, but he can't hold his liquor—or wasn't that night, anyway. When you get to be my age, you don't want to waste time on the likes of him." Douden said the man was skinny and losing his hair, and that he drove a four-door, tan Subaru that was frequently but not regularly parked in Slater's driveway.

Frank made a note to check on the cars driven by all Slater's poker buddies. He had only one name so far, Ray Martin. Douden's physical description fit Mary Sasser's man whose name started with M. "And you said his car was there last week?"

Douden nodded. "About 7:00—during *The News Hour with Jim Lehrer*, anyway." He drained his sherry glass and refilled it. "Now you tell me, why would a classy stud like Ted Slater have a friend like that? Not that they seemed all that friendly. But he's the only man I ever saw there except Mark Sasser. I asked Ted once, asked him outright. He just grinned and said, 'He amuses me.' Now what do you think he meant by that?" Mr. Douden's voice trailed away.

On the way back to his office, Frank mulled over the scraps of information about the mystery woman, the red sports car, and the poker pal. Not much to go on. He inhaled gloomily, feeling as though he was breathing in a black cloud.

CHAPTER THIRTEEN

Nora's plan was sketchy. She would leave right after class, arrive in the late morning at the shop where Suzanne Slater worked, strike up a conversation, and invite her to lunch. Then what could be more natural than to talk about the murder?

The night's rain and wind had littered the back roads with leaves and small branches, but the fall foliage remained impressive. A line of mature cedars, dark green sentinels along the shoulder of the road, accented the gold and red. Nora drove, too keyed up to savor the view. She parked on High Street within a block of the shop, dreading that Suzanne already had lunch plans, or had taken the day off, or was suffering the flu and not eating anything. She should have phoned ahead.

Nora paused—peering in the window, ostensibly examining the display—trying to quiet her breathing. "Well, here goes nothing," she muttered, pushing through the door. A dumpy woman in too-tight jeans and a cranberry colored sweatshirt was talking to Suzanne about a watercolor featuring the weathered remains of a barn. "Well, really, I don't believe I should have to pay full price if the frame is all damaged." Chunky diamonds flashed on age-spotted hands.

Suzanne's voice held no trace of exasperation. "As I said, Mrs. Johnson, the frame isn't damaged. It's distressed wood. The artist deemed it appropriate for this subject. The piece is with us on consignment, so we can't change the frame unless the artist agrees. I happen to know he's out of town. But I could call him when he returns." After the briefest of pauses, she continued pleasantly, "Of course, in the meantime, the painting might be sold, and it *is* one of a kind. But you seem doubtful about it anyway." Suzanne reached for the painting. Mrs. Johnson gripped the frame reflexively. "Well, if the artist really meant it to be like this . . ."

She's good, thought Nora, *really good.* While Mrs. Johnson struggled to extricate her platinum credit card from her pants pocket, Nora studied Suzanne. She hadn't changed noticeably since Nora last saw her—still looked like a New York fashion maven. Her hair was braided and coiled on top of her head, and she was dressed in black from earrings to shoes, the monotone relieved only by a five-inch silver and enamel peacock on her left shoulder and a heavy silver bangle on her right wrist. Nora saw her own reflection in the mirrored wall. The faun wool pants, forest green silk shirt, and tweed jacket suited her. But she felt every one of her fifty-one years, and dowdy. As the door closed behind Mrs. Johnson, Nora gathered her chutzpah and put on a happy face. "Hello, Suzanne. You look marvelous! It seems like forever since I last saw you."

"Nora Perry! It *has* been forever. How are you?"

"About as you would expect at this point in the semester—more frazzled by the hour. I'm interested in earrings. Do you have any particular recommendations?"

"For you or for a gift?"

"For me."

Suzanne scrutinized Nora, briefly but thoroughly. Nora waited, intensely aware of the few glints of silver in her copper colored hair, of her broad face and heavy bones. She resisted an impulse to smooth her eyebrows or adjust the lapels of her jacket. "You can carry a lot of weight," Suzanne said. The remark startled Nora, but Suzanne didn't seem to notice as she turned to a display case by the wall. "These, for example. They make a bold statement. And although they have the visual weight I mentioned, they're actually quite comfortable to wear."

Nora had no intention of buying earrings, but perused the display at length. The choices were seductively unusual. She bought two-inch discs made of overlapping shapes in paper-thin gold, silver, and copper. Taking the proffered package, Nora looked at her watch and feigned spontaneity. "How about a bite of lunch?" She waved the small box and added, "My treat, to celebrate this fabulous find!"

"Sure, why not? Let me tell Marge." Suzanne returned from the small office in the back corner wearing a serape woven in shades of teal, coral, beige, and black. Nora wondered what the people of Chestertown thought of her. But if Suzanne felt at all uncomfortable—or even self-aware—she gave no sign.

They settled themselves at the Fish Whistle Inn and ordered. While Nora sought the right opener, Suzanne said, "How are people at the college taking Ted's murder?"

Nora tried to sound casual. "As you might expect—with all manner of speculation."

"I heard you found the body."

"It was ugly. Traumatic." Nora shuddered. "I don't like to think about it, let alone talk about it." And besides, if Suzanne did it, Nora didn't want to give anything away. "But how are you doing?"

"Me? It's so good to finally have that sonofabitch out of my life, I'm practically dancing in the streets." She spoke quietly, without emphasis. "And according to the police, Jim Thomas told them I'm Ted's heir. What could be better than that?" She paused with her soupspoon in mid air. "The world's a better place without Ted in it. Everyone who really knew him must feel the same."

That comment surprised Nora a lot less than it would have a week earlier. While they attended to their sandwiches, Nora searched furiously for a way to keep their focus on the murder, to determine Suzanne's whereabouts on Friday night. But Suzanne stayed with the topic on her own. "We could have a celebration. But I suppose no gathering of Slater haters would be complete without Ray Martin, and *that* would certainly throw a wet blanket on things. He is one of the most disagreeable people I've ever met."

Nora tried not to show her surprise. The Ray Martin she knew seemed a little slow to warm up, but nice—friendly with students and faculty. On the other hand, she'd been pretty off-target on Ted, so . . . "Disagreeable? In what way?"

Suzanne fiddled with her bracelet, apparently considering her response. "He's an ugly drunk." Nora suppressed a gasp. Suzanne continued, "He would be okay when he picked Ted up, quiet and polite. But when he brought Ted home after a night of cards, he was always sloshed. And then he was loud, vulgar, made suggestive comments . . . He creeped me out. One time I told Ted I didn't think he should hang out with an alcoholic. Ted just laughed and said something about

Ray's twin vices, alcohol and gambling." She glanced at Nora. "*I* never saw Ray violent, but Ted had a split lip about a month ago, said Ray attacked him. He laughed about it."

Nora doubted that two such different people lived in Ray Martin's skin, but she'd come for information, not argument. "Why do you think Ray was a Slater hater?"

"Ted was blackmailing him."

Nora jerked upright. "Blackmailing him? For what? Are you sure?"

"It started about three years ago. I still lived with Ted then. Ray gave him cash, regular as clockwork, the first day of each month." Suzanne added creamer to her coffee. "He brought the money to the house sometimes. I asked Ted about it. He just laughed and said, 'Knowledge is power—and power pays. Although in this case, it doesn't pay very well.' Sometimes, for no reason at all, he'd call Ray up at the last minute and say, 'You drive to the game tonight,' and Ray always did." She seemed to realize Nora was puzzled because she added, "They were in a poker group, every other Friday. In public, Ted was all hail-fellow-well-met, like they were the best of buddies. But Ray was afraid of Ted. I could tell—the one thing he and I had in common." Suzanne fell silent, gazing in the direction of the menu board. "Blackmail was the only reason I could think of for the money, for being a doormat."

"What do you think Ted had on Ray?"

"I don't know. Though of course I wondered. You know, Ray used to work for Fairfax County, and Ted drove over to Virginia a couple of times a month to consult. Maybe he learned something about Ray, some kind of trouble when Ray was building inspector."

"Hmmm. Could be." Nora remembered a scene at the president's Farewell to Summer party. Ray stood in the middle of the lawn, diet cola in hand, talking to two faculty members. Slater had strolled over, clapped him on the shoulder, and smiled broadly. "Hello, Ray, what's up? Are we expecting great profits from the bookstore again this year?" At the time, it seemed like cocktail party chitchat and Nora had been surprised that Ray seemed so hostile though he'd said only, "Profit enough."

Suzanne's voice recalled Nora to the present. "I could never figure out why Ted treated people the way he did. Some he walked all over, and others, he couldn't do enough to be nice. I used to think he was nice to the powerless, but then he should have been nice to me." She sounded distant and tearful. "With me, there was no such thing as submissive enough. He barked arbitrary orders, just to watch me scramble. 'Give me a gin and tonic,' he'd say. 'No, not that glass, one of the blue ones.'"

"It must have been awful," Nora said, and added gently, "There were rumors that he beat you."

Suzanne grimaced. "Only at the end. Before, it was just control and domination. He was older—more experienced—and at first, it seemed natural for him to make all the decisions. His taking care of me felt romantic. But I grew up, you know? When I wanted a more equal relationship, he turned petty, telling me how to do every little thing."

"But—but did you ever refuse?"

Suzanne grimaced. "Not often. He said I was a slovenly housekeeper, disgustingly disorganized. He'd badger me for days, talk about my stubbornness for hours, not even letting me sleep. It was easier just to give in right away. When I finally refused absolutely, he beat me." She sounded mournful. "He apologized and brought me presents, said it wouldn't happen again. But it did, a few months later. That's when I left. I should have left the first time—before the first time—but I was so weak."

Nora put her hand on Suzanne's forearm. "You're not weak, Suzanne! It takes great strength to get out of an abusive relationship. You're a survivor. You got out, and you're alive to tell the tale."

Suzanne blew her nose and lifted her chin. "Yes, and I have you to thank for it."

"Me? I never did anything. I only wish I had. I had no idea . . ."

"I only took your Intro class so you probably don't even remember. But I've admired you ever since my student days. You were my role model—living, breathing proof that a woman could make it on her own. And be happy!" Nora marveled—not for the first time—at the long-term impact teachers can have without even being aware. "So when my old roommate picked me up at the hospital—that last time Ted beat me—I thought of you and never went back."

Nora squeezed Suzanne's hand. "I only wish I'd known . . ."

"How could you? I didn't *want* anyone to know. It was too humiliating."

"So what are you going to do now?"

Suzanne looked out the restaurant window. "I like it here. And I don't have any close family. My mother died last year, and her estate is settled now. I used the money to make a down payment on one of the row houses on Water Street. It really eased my money situation, so I could push Ted harder on the divorce. Now I guess I'll be able to buy into the business as well. Things are really turning around."

"You said you've talked with someone from the sheriff's office?"

Suzanne summarized the interview, ending with, "I don't have anyone to vouch for my whereabouts the weekend Ted was killed. They'll question me again. The estranged wife is just too good a target." Nora murmured sympathetically.

The topics of Ted's murder and Suzanne's ordeal exhausted, the remainder of lunch passed pleasantly in talk of local events, the books they'd been reading, and fashion until Suzanne looked at her watch. "Oh, my gosh. I've got to get back to work." They parted with promises to get together again before long.

Nora meandered up High Street, window shopping and enjoying the crisp autumn air, the Halloween decorations everywhere. Bales of hay, pumpkins, corn shocks, and pots of mums decorated the sidewalk in front of the Kent County News offices. An elaborate garland of evergreens and gourds bedecked the Chesapeake Bank and Trust above its wide front door and down the sides. The entire town sported a festive air, and Nora reveled in the glory of the fall day. She browsed at The Compleat Bookseller and stopped at the White Swan Tavern for tea and scones. She pondered what Suzanne had said about Ted and Ray. Could it be true? She didn't notice the time till nearly five o'clock.

Nora lit the fire in her sitting room and relaxed in the near dark, nursing the first of her two nightly scotches. Thoughts of Suzanne swirled. She'd hated Ted enough to have killed him. She was strong enough to have done it. His death set her up financially. And it sounded like she had—or could have had—opportunity. Surely Suzanne was a good possibility. But Nora would much rather it be someone else.

Her hand was halfway to the phone when she checked the motion. Calling Van at this hour on a Friday night presumed a lot. She'd probably interrupt his dinner—if he was home. And anyway, she'd see him tomorrow.

She sank back into her chair, savoring the black of night, no lights visible through the patio doors. Living at the edge of moving waters made her feel in touch with the world. During daylight, the river changed hour to hour. But at night, the blackness expanded her space and fed her imagination. She felt more alone, and somehow freer in the night. A line from a friend's letter came to mind: "Light the fire, swing the chair around, and let peaceful evening in."

CHAPTER FOURTEEN

Nora propped her elbows on the oak table, surveying a watery world in shades of gray. Rain on the sliding glass doors curtained the scene with silver ribbons. The river ran slate, the fog was pussy willows and smoke. A perfect day to slugabed, reading trashy novels and eating bonbons. Or to don something soft and comfy and spend the day in the kitchen making soup, baking bread and custard, maybe roasting a Cornish game hen and a potato for dinner. She could retrieve *Duet's* gear from Marsh Point Marina on a better day. But her work schedule would just get tighter as the semester progressed. She carried her dishes to the kitchen, resignation settling in. Yes, she'd pick up the gear as planned—unless Van wanted to cancel. She poured a second cup of tea just as the phone rang.

"Good morning, Nora. What time would you like me to arrive at the marina?"

"Good morning to you, too." Amusement warmed her voice when she added, "We lie, of course. The morning is perfectly foul. Do you really want to drive to the Narrows today? I could haul it in two trips some other time—save you the trouble."

"There are other things I could do, but nothing I would rather do."

Nora laughed. "Damn. I half hoped you would be my excuse to wait for nicer weather and fritter away today."

She could hear the smile in his voice when he said, "Not a chance."

"Okay, then. Let's meet about noon, at the Harris Crab House. We can load up after lunch"

The rain sliced sideways, driven by a thirty-mile-an-hour wind, as Nora climbed the wooden stairs to the restaurant. She went straight to the women's room and shucked her dripping slicker. Although the hood had protected her braid, the hair around her face clung to cheeks and forehead in soggy ringlets. She used paper towels to blot as much of the dampness from her face and hair as she conveniently could and called it good enough.

Van sat by the window, watching workboats go through the Narrows. He rose as Nora approached the table and held her chair.

Nora grinned. "We look like a couple of drowned rats! You're a real trooper for coming out in this."

Van slicked back his damp hair. "A little exposure to the elements is good for the soul. Besides, if I had not, you would have had to make at least two trips—and would have been at least twice as wet for twice as long."

"Thanks for sharing the pain."

A waitress laid placemats in front of them. "Hi. My name is Lisa, and I'll be your server today." As she spoke, she flourished a black felt-tipped pen and wrote "Lisa" on the heavy brown paper that covered the table, and under that the date before which a customer had to be born in order to be served alcohol. "Anything to drink?"

Van glanced at Nora. "Would mulled cider suit you?"

"Sounds great."

"Okay, then, two mugs of cider, please." They quickly agreed on Chesapeake Crab Chowder and an order of French fries to share—the latter a particular vice of Nora's.

Over their soup, Van said, "Let me tell you about my trip to the county courthouse yesterday. Have you been in there?"

"Only the Clerk of the Courts office."

"It's pretty interesting, actually. A lot of people call it the Old Courthouse, but it dates from the 1790s. The *real* old courthouse—the original Queen Anne's County Courthouse—was built in 1708, in Queenstown. Did you know it's still there? The wooden building at the corner of Main and Del Rhodes." He spoke with such enthusiasm that Nora couldn't help smiling. Although Van and Frank hadn't warmed up to each other, they had a lot in common—including a passion for architecture and history. Maybe someday her two favorite men would be friends. When she tuned back in, Van was saying, "Still, the *new* Old Courthouse here in Centreville is an interesting building. I expected a stately interior. What I did not expect was a shabby stairwell to the lower level—concrete steps with iron treads and a wainscot painted vibrant orange."

He sounded so mournful that Nora could not help teasing. "So rampant poor taste offended the son of an architect?"

He chuckled. "I confess that I was disappointed."

Nora leaned forward. "But you found . . . ?"

"That anyone can walk in and check on anybody. Civil and criminal actions are matters of public record—everything, except adoptions and cases involving minors." He shook his head. "That such personal information is so public does not feel right. But I did not cavil." He placed his hand over his heart and adopted a tone of exaggerated sincerity that amused Nora. "True to my word, I searched the Civil Action Dockets covering the entire period from Slater's marriage to the present. I even checked under Baker, just in case Suzanne had resumed her maiden name."

"Being your usual thorough self, in other words."

"Yes. Well. But I found no record of divorce." He fished a French fry from the edge of the plate.

Nora leaned forward. "That's what Suzanne said! She's been trying to get a divorce for two years and Ted was stonewalling—wouldn't even sign a separation agreement."

A frown flashed across Van's face but when he continued his tone was light. "But the saga is not over. I decided to check on a will as well as marriage and divorce records. I left the courthouse, braved the chilly northwest wind and went to the Liberty Building." As he spoke he turned up his collar and rubbed his hands together. "Risking everything from frostbite to hypothermia, I never faltered in my pursuit of the whole truth."

Nora laughed. "You're such a ham. No wonder students enjoy your courses."

"Is that last French fry yours or mine?"

"Yours."

Van plucked it from the paper plate and popped it into his mouth. "In the office of the Register of Wills, I learned that Slater had no will on file in Centreville. So we do not know for sure, but if he died intestate—his parents dead and leaving no children—Suzanne will get everything."

"*She* thinks she's his heir, anyway. The police told her that Jim Thomas had told them so." Nora felt ebullient.

A note of exasperation surfaced in Van's voice. "It would seem that the errand you talked me into was not only unpleasant, it was a waste of time."

Nora wanted to remind him that he had volunteered, but instead tried to reason him out of his anger. "It wasn't a waste of time!" She punched him lightly on the shoulder and added, "What sort of scientist are you, if you don't believe in the confirmation of evidence from multiple sources?" Van still glared, so she hurried on: "But I have more." Nora filled in details of her lunch with Suzanne, reliving during various parts of the retelling the outrage, disgust, and sympathy she'd felt for Suzanne. "So if Suzanne is right about the blackmail, Ray had a motive, too!" Van said nothing. "So, what do you think?"

"I think we should consider whether anything supports Suzanne's assertion. What might he have been blackmailing Ray about?"

Nora turned her gaze to the wind-driven rain pelting the window. "Well, Suzanne believes that Ray has a drinking problem. And apparently he gambles. But I think it's more likely to be related to his work." She told Van Suzanne's speculation that Ted might have discovered something from Ray's past. Van drummed his fingers on the table. "What is it?" she asked.

"The only out-of-the-ordinary association I have for Ray Martin is that September when everyone was wondering whether he was going to be fired—after the bookstore robbery. But that was three years ago."

"Van, that's it!" Nora smacked the table, then rubbed her stinging fingers. "It fits! Suzanne said the payments started after she and Ted were married awhile but before they separated! Three years is just right!"

Van said, "Hmmmm. Right before classes started—sixty thousand dollars in cash—more than any other time of the year—and none of it ever recovered. Perhaps he would pay blackmail to keep his theft unconfirmed."

"For God's sake, Van, don't be such a skeptic. That's got to be it! Now Frank will have to see that lots of people could have wanted Ted dead, not just Louisa."

"Calm down, Nora. We do not really know anything."

"Of course we do. It makes such perfect sense."

"Logic and conjecture are not facts. We are simply spinning hypotheses." He sounded like someone exasperated but trying to sound patient.

"Well, then, we'll have to get evidence."

"What do you mean, *we* will have to get evidence? That is not our business."

"But—but—oh, all right." Irritation seeped into her tone. "We'll hand it over to Frank and let *him* get the evidence."

Resistance settled on Van's face. "What if we are wrong? An innocent person would be harassed by the police and it would be our fault. We cannot go to the police with a conglomeration of rumors, hearsay, and wishes." Van shifted in his chair, his determination clear.

Exasperation welled in Nora's breast. "Really, Van, you can't have it both ways. Either we investigate or the police investigate."

"What about the alternative that we just leave it alone? The police may come across it on their own."

"Or not! I suppose you'd be perfectly okay with that." Her words sounded more sarcastic than she intended.

Van locked his fingers together. "I do not wish to discuss it further." His withdrawal brought on a lengthy silence.

Eventually, Nora said, "You're right, of course. About going to the police." She spoke softly, hoping to soothe his riled feelings. "We should not do so without more information." She laid her hand on his forearm and tried to be persuasive. "Ray is more likely to talk freely with a man. And you have such a quiet, non-judgmental manner. You'd be much more successful than I could be."

Van drew back from her touch. "That is not something I wish to do."

Seeing the stubborn set of his jaw, Nora capitulated. "Oh, well, it was worth a shot. I'll talk to Ray."

"You will do no such thing! It could be dangerous."

Nora felt color bloom high on her cheeks. She scowled at Van. "Since when do you tell me what I can and cannot do?"

"I did not mean to presume . . . I apologize, both for the tone and for the phrasing." Van drew an unsteady breath. "But—please reconsider.

If you seriously believe that Ray Martin might have murdered Ted, what would keep him from attacking you as well?"

"Ray Martin? He wouldn't." She paused. "Besides, I would be careful. I'd meet him in daylight, in a public place. And I'd let him know that you know I'm meeting him."

Van shook his head. "The prospect makes me very uncomfortable."

"But *someone* needs to do it."

By the end of the conversation, Van had conceded that one of them would confront Ray Martin, and Nora had conceded that Van would be the one to do so. Nora wanted to put the tension behind them, but she couldn't help adding, "As long as we're both clear that I'm agreeing in the spirit of compromise, not because you forbade me."

"Some compromise! I should have agreed to your request immediately and saved both of us the aggravation." But Van seemed to share her desire to smooth things over, for he chuckled—albeit not convincingly—and added, "Nora, you could coax the spots off a leopard. It is just fortunate for the world that you are with Superman on the side of truth, justice, and the American way!"

Having agreed that Van would speak with Ray Martin as soon as he could arrange it, their talk turned to other matters. They touched on campus events, the chorale, and John Howard's candidacy at Waldorf. Interspersed were recollections of sailing. Van told how he rode out a bad storm tied up at the pier just below the window where they sat. But one way and another, the murder kept intruding. During one lengthy pause, Nora followed Van's gaze to the droplets of water running down the windowpane in random, crooked paths. When his eyes flicked from her face to her hair to her hands, she asked, "What are you thinking?"

He shifted in his chair. "Oh, nothing much. I was wondering whether a mathematician familiar with random theory could write a formula to account for the way raindrops run down windowpanes." He paused. "I don't believe the wind and rain will lessen any time soon."

Nora thought how attractive, thoughtful, kind and gentle he was, and speculated that he probably would remarry before long. Men mostly did. What she said was, "I guess physics is never far from your thoughts."

Van pulled his sleeve back from his watch. "It is 1:30. Shall we go?" At Nora's nod, he signaled Lisa for the check. He took several folded bills from his pocket.

Nora put her hand on his and said, "No, please. This is my treat. A small thank-you for driving down in the rain to help me."

He seemed inclined to resist, but after a pause said, "Thank you."

Rain pelted them mercilessly as they trooped back and forth between the storage locker and their cars, loading *Duet's* anchor, anchor chain and shackles, sails, and other gear. By the time they finished, both cars were stuffed. Nora felt soggy as a dunked donut. Closing the car door, she was assaulted by the stench wafting up from melted Dacron sails, the singed canvas toolbox, the damp cabin curtains, and every other cloth thing.

During the drive to Centreville, her mood sunk lower and lower. She couldn't put aside her need to have closure on Ted's murder, bolstered by her concern for Louisa. Louisa had told her that Ted was naked when she left him, but she'd told Frank that he was wearing a satin robe. Was she confused? And what about the abortion? And the argument Clyde said he heard? Nora had to get to the bottom of things. But she mustn't lose Van's friendship over it.

At her house, Van quickly unloaded the cars. He did most of the heavy lifting while Nora separated things that could be stowed in the garage from those that needed to be discarded, dried, cleaned, or repaired.

When they finished, Nora said, "How about coffee? Or a drink?"

"I could use something to take the chill out of my bones."

"Well, then, turn on the gas logs in the sitting room and I'll bring scotch for both of us."

They talked long of music and sailing, of the work that *Duet* needed. Nora steered her talk carefully away from murder, and Van seemed to follow her lead willingly. When he rose to go, Nora took his face in her hands and said, "Thank you for being such a dear friend."

Van kissed her gently, an exploratory kiss that triggered a lurch deep in her middle. Her breath came faster. "Oh, Van." She kissed him in return, feeling the solid muscles in his back, the soft warmth of his lips, and the arousal of his manhood.

Van leaned back, searching her face. "You cannot help but know . . . I feel incredibly drawn to you." One finger traced the curve of her cheek. "I very much want to be with you. Intimately."

The passion lacking in his stilted words was clear in his tone. The strength of his feelings rang a warning bell in a corner of Nora's consciousness. What was she doing? They needed to talk first—to be clear with each other. "I'm drawn to you, too—more powerfully than I can ever remember. I'd like nothing better than to make love with you." As Van leaned in to kiss her again, she turned her face aside. "But you need to understand . . ." She felt suddenly defensive, but continued, "I care for you deeply, and I want you. And maybe I am being presumptuous, given that you've never so much as mentioned . . . But I am not a marrying sort of woman." Van stepped back but she caught his hands and drew him toward the sofa. "Please. Just listen." She fought to control the tremor in her voice. "I've had lovers over the years. And sometimes love. I've had proposals I actually thought about accepting." She looked hard at Van. "But too often among my family and friends, I've seen women turn into wives. And why? It isn't as though they could count on husbands to take care of them, not even financially. I've seen too much grinding down poverty, too many women working to support husbands and children, too much heartbreak and depression in my mother, sister, aunts, and cousins whose marriages ended in divorce after ten, twenty, or thirty years. That is not for me." She squeezed his hands in both of hers and searched his face. "You needed to know that—before rather than after."

Van remained silent for so long that she dreaded hearing his words. He said, "My marriage failed. But it did not undermine my belief in marriage—did not destroy my hope for a better marriage in the future. I want nothing more than to be happily married."

Nora breathed deeply. "Are you saying that if marriage is off the table, so is an affair?"

"I guess that *is* what I am saying. A sexual affair that is predetermined not to lead anywhere—I do not think that would suit me."

She shrugged one shoulder and released his hands. "Well, then. I guess we'll forego sex." The thought of all she was losing nearly choked her. She cleared her throat and tried for a light tone. "So how do you feel about remaining friends?"

"Yes. Absolutely. I would hate to lose that." He stood. "But now, I really must be going."

Nora showed him to the door. When he said goodnight, he brushed her cheek with a fraternal kiss. Climbing into bed, she tried to stifle her feelings of loss. Already she cared for Van more than she had realized. Did she really want to risk losing his friendship after an affair was over? And an affair was *always* over eventually. So probably it was just as well that he had scruples about the sort of relationship she had suggested. Nora mused over relationships she had buried—in anger or in sorrow, by dint of will or by sheer neglect. She was not a woman for a lifetime of dependency and vulnerability. She did not need a man in her life—did not *want* a man in her life—not in that way. Not now. Not ever! Her night thoughts were as gray as the day had been.

CHAPTER FIFTEEN

Van slept poorly. Thoughts that usually carried him to peaceful sleep—thoughts of Nora and sailing, plans to divide lilies in his garden—had been pushed aside by the emotions of the day. Searching court records had brought his own divorce to the fore. Sheila was the first woman he ever had sex with, and he'd dropped out of the Maritime Academy to marry her because he believed himself to be the father of her unborn child. Maybe he was. What was definite was that his commitment to his marriage vows had thrust him into middle age incredibly inexperienced with women—sexually or emotionally. How was he to respond to a woman like Nora? Was it really his commitment to marriage that held him back, or was he just afraid she'd find him inept? That the prospect of interviewing Ray Martin was a welcome distraction testified to the depth of his anguish. He punched his pillow and turned his mind to it.

He was not fearful. Ray would never be mistaken for a mob muscle man. Van could take him if it came to a fight. But the interview was bound to be awkward, maybe hostile. He thought about the questions he needed to ask, and the words that might elicit answers.

When he awoke from a murky half sleep, he arose tired but resolved: he would get through it as quickly as possible, and in the future he would spend less time mucking about in other people's business.

A minority of faculty—Van among them—still "dressed" to teach. He selected a tie, remembering his father's instruction: "Van, no matter how tall you grow, always start with the wide end hanging to the bottom of your crotch. Once tied, it will be just the right length to cover your belt buckle." He had just finished dressing when the phone rang. "Van Pelt here . . . Oh, good morning, Nora. Is everything all right?"

"Everything's fine. Are you still planning to talk with Ray today?"

"Yes. But I am not happy about it. Fact-finding is one thing. But trying to get a man to incriminate himself sits uneasily on my conscience. I did not sleep well."

"Ummm. I was a little restless myself. I know I—sort of wrangled you into this. I just called to lend moral support and to wish you luck."

Emotions he had tried to suppress flooded back: anger at Nora for pressuring him into this meeting, disappointment in himself for caving in, distaste for prying into another's life, an intense wish to protect the woman he cared for—and intense discomfort that he has exposed his caring. When he said, "I appreciate your concern," the words fell cool and distant.

"Look, Van, if you really feel that this is wrong—unethical or something—just call it off."

He paused. "Once I make a commitment, I fulfill it. Ray expects to have lunch with me at the student center."

His assertion seemed to wash away Nora's doubts, even their shadows. Relief rang clear in her voice when she said, "Great. So, what reason did you give him?"

"I said that there is a matter I wish to discuss with him. Look, Nora, I have to get to class. If you are going to be home tonight, I will call and share the details."

"I'll be home. Would you like to come over instead?"

Van considered. "I will call or come over about 8:00. Is that all right? We will talk in any event."

"Sure, that's fine. Till 8:00. And good luck."

Van unlocked his office in the Pinder Science Complex. Books on acoustics and optics, plus a few on astronomy, filled a wall of shelves. Over his desk, a bulletin board displayed pictures of his children, a calendar featuring photographs of wooden boats, and his class schedule. Beside the window hung a framed cross-stitch sampler his older daughter had made when he was in graduate school: Van Pelt's Law—Things Take Longer Than They Do.

Van leafed through the assigned chapter, reviewing the substance of the day's lecture. He never used lecture notes. If he referred to the same old dog-eared notes semester after semester, he would become bored and so, too, would his students. If student evaluations were any indication, his method worked. Satisfied that he had the material in his head, he entered the adjacent lab, concerns about the lunch meeting pushed aside.

Ray Martin groaned, set his feet on the bedroom floor, and resigned himself to facing the day. He held his head, resolving to lay off the bourbon—as he did every morning. But since his mama got too bad to live with him, every long evening alone dissolved that resolution. He showered, and shaved meticulously. Mostly bald at the crown, he kept his sparse graying hair trimmed short. Unruly eyebrows exaggerated his sunken cheeks, and he realized that he should trim them. But not now. He swallowed a couple of aspirin, and swooshed mouthwash.

Ray pulled a favorite suit from his closet—brown, with pencil stripes of pale blue and melon—old, but of good quality, and tailored to his thin frame. His model of sartorial splendor was Fred Astaire in those old high society movies. The blue shirt would do nicely. He added a brown leather belt and highly polished brown shoes. He searched his tie rack for the striped tie he always wore with this suit. A small gravy spot dotted one edge. Probably no one would notice, but he put that tie aside and chose another. If his mama were here, she'd have used spot remover on it. His eyes grew moist thinking about his mother's Alzheimer's. He picked up his Cross pen and matching pencil. Image was everything.

The microwave beeped. Ray retrieved the mug of yesterday's coffee and stared out the window at railroad tracks long out of use. He had no stomach for breakfast. There wasn't much food in the place anyway. He gulped coffee. Someday he would hit the jackpot, retire, and take care of his mama the way she deserved. But today wasn't that day. He stubbed out his cigarette in a saucer already overflowing with butts. In four years he would be sixty. That was his target—retiring at sixty. But right now, trying to make ends meet had him stretched thinner than a rubber band.

Ray arrived at the bookstore still a little hung over from last night's libations. As he moved through the aisles, making his presence felt, he smiled and greeted each employee by name. "Michelle, that Halloween display's been very effective. We've sold twice as many cards and candles as this time last year. Keep up the good work."

"Thanks, Ray. I think we can use the same approach for Thanksgiving and Christmas."

Ray closed his office door, relieved to let the mask drop, and turned on the computer. He'd hired an assistant manager to handle the details, a compulsive little twit who checked and double-checked everything. He spent his days tidying shelf stock and poring over accounts and inventories. It freed Ray to focus on the bigger issues of transforming the bookstore. He surfed the web daily for new marketing ideas, for successful ploys like the Halloween merchandizing, that he could adopt or adapt—plus, it allowed him to keep track of the odds on the ponies, and major sports teams.

His job security depended on change, on upping profits, on developing his next great idea. His eye fell on the handsome, gold plated desk set President Howard gave him, a thank-you for taking the bookstore from major liability to significant asset. But maybe profits wouldn't be enough. His boss had cooled off after the robbery. Ray had asked Syd what he was supposed to have done, what he was accused of. Syd had said, "No one's accusing you of anything, Ray. It's just—well, a robbery raises concerns. And it happened on your watch. That's all." Three years later, and Syd had never let up. One lousy time he came in a little tipsy, and Syd put him on probation. He could be out of a job in three months.

Ray opened his calendar. Right, van Pelt for lunch. What's that really about? When faculty called, he got complaints about the cost of text books, or about how publisher delays in shipping messed up their course schedules. The books for van Pelt's Intro class last spring arrived three weeks into the term. Ray dabbed his forehead with a handkerchief. Professor van Pelt, rising faculty star—a complaint from him would carry major weight with Syd. The more he pondered, the more his hands shook. Ray wiped his forehead again. At 11:00, he unlocked the bottom drawer of his desk, pulled out a blue and tan thermos, and took a long pull of bourbon. As his appointment with Van approached, the bourbon in the thermos diminished, along with

Ray's headache. The hair of the dog. But he was still in control. He chewed a couple of cough drops.

Van paused in the doorway of Ray's office. "Hello, Ray. Ready for lunch?"

Ray looked up from a pile of paperwork, glancing over his half glasses. "Yeah, sure. In just a minute."

Van leaned against the doorjamb, looking around Ray's office—neat and tidy as his own, and twice the size. Ray had an oak desk rather than a metal one, and an upholstered chair for visitors. Framed awards and certificates hung on the wall. The most recent, silver framed, from the National Association of College and University Business Officers, recognized Ray for outstanding achievement the previous year.

Ray coughed into his fist and popped a cough drop. "Fall cold. I get one every year." He shuffled papers into piles, collected his coat and gestured his intention to depart. Van trailed after him out of the store, across the broad entrance hall, and into the snack bar.

They filed through the cafeteria line at Chum's in silence, then took an empty table in a corner of the food court. Van had expected small talk because Ray always conversed freely at college functions. It didn't happen. Van tried, but carrying the conversational ball alone was wearing. After several minutes, he turned to the ostensible reason for the meeting, how the purchase and resale of used textbooks could benefit students and the bookstore.

During Van's monologue, Ray rolled his cough drop from one cheek to the other and said nothing. Van finished by asking, "So what do you think?"

Ray pursed his lips. "Well, professor, I appreciate the suggestion. I really do. You're the first faculty member in my six years here to try to make a helpful suggestion. Mostly, I just hear complaints." His smile held an apologetic tinge. "To tell the truth, handling used textbooks isn't a new idea. I've considered it. But there isn't much profit margin. It requires enormous amounts of storage space, a lot of staff time, maybe even additional seasonal employees." He rolled his cough drop to the other cheek and looked doleful.

"But," Van began, then reconsidered. Arguing would only make his real goal tougher to achieve. "I see. Thanks for listening. How about a walk?" He stood as he spoke, eager to escape the cloud of cough drop fumes.

Once outside, Van assumed the air of a man enjoying a fine fall day while he wondered how to broach the questioning. Ray trudged beside him. Eventually, Van said, "So, what do you think about Ted Slater's murder?"

"Why should I think anything about it?" Ray looked startled.

"Well . . . because you knew the man!"

"Not well, I didn't. Not really." Ray picked up the pace and Van lengthened his stride to keep up. "I don't have all that much to do with faculty, socially."

Van tried to sound casual. "I heard you played poker together."

Ray slowed and threw a sideways look at Van. "Where did you hear that?"

"Around."

"Yeah, well, it was no big deal. We played with three townies sometimes."

"Every other week," Van insisted.

"So what if we did? There's nothing wrong with a little game of poker among friends."

"So you and Slater *were* friends?"

"Yeah, sure. I mean, just poker buddies." Ray licked his lips. "But I'm all cut up about it. Naturally." Ray licked his lips again. "Because we were pals. You know."

"Is that why you were paying him off? Because you were pals?"

The afternoon sun beamed down on Ray's partially bald head and half glasses. Sweat glistened on his forehead. Ray fished out his last cigarette and lit it with a steady hand, slowly crumpled the empty pack, and stuffed it into his pocket. He turned a piercing glare on Van. "I'm thinking that used book crap at lunch was a smoke screen for this. Why is my relationship with Ted Slater—or anybody else—any business of yours? What the hell do you really want?"

Ray's tone made Van doubly regretful that he had agreed to question him, but his query was probably as good a launching pad as any that might come along. Suspended between his promise to Nora and his aversion to prying into another's affairs, Van drew a deep breath and said, "What do I want? I want to know why you paid Ted Slater

111

every month for three years. Was he blackmailing you for the bookstore robbery?" He studied Ray's face and waited for the explosion.

Ray reached slowly for the cigarette in his mouth, took one long draw, then dropped it on the pavement and flattened it with the toe of his shoe. His eyes met Van's and he pointed to the squashed butt. "That's you," he said, the words almost a whisper. He turned and walked away.

For a moment, Van felt rooted to the spot. He'd imagined dozens of possible reactions, but certainly not this one. Half an hour ago, he'd felt confident in his mission, even if a little uncomfortable being a predator. He'd felt sympathy for Ray. But now he felt defeated. And just a little threatened. He looked at the cigarette ground into the pavement. What did Ray really mean by that?

After supper, Van drove to Nora's. Together they assembled a picture of Ted Slater's emotional and physical abuse of others, of his need to torment and dominate. Van concluded, "So we know of two victims for sure: Louisa and Suzanne. Ray didn't admit a thing. I'm sorry about that." Van looked at Nora and tried to quell his feelings of failure. "But there must be something to Suzanne's story, else why would Ray react the way he did? And if there are three victims, there are bound to be others."

"Why he paid Ted doesn't really matter. The important thing is that he had some motive, as did Suzanne. We don't really know about alibis for Friday night, but Louisa can no longer be the sole suspect. When we tell Frank, he's bound to see that."

The prospect of going to the police still made Van feel like a war time collaborator or something. And he didn't relish the idea of telling Frank Pierce about his abortive interview attempt. He shifted uneasily in his chair. "On the other hand—unless you posit a conspiracy—only one of them could be the killer. That means we are intentionally getting at least one more innocent person into trouble. I don't like it."

"But what if Ray or Suzanne *did* kill him? Do you honestly feel that it's better to let a guilty person off than to get an innocent one into temporary trouble? And what if we remain silent and an innocent person—Louisa—is *convicted?*"

"That is catastrophic thinking. You are letting your imagination run away with you."

"I'm doing no such thing! Innocent people are convicted all the time. Like all the men serving prison sentences who were freed when new DNA techniques were applied to old evidence."

Van could not argue with her logic. And he doubted he could stop her knee-jerk defense of Louisa. "You are right. Captain Pierce needs to know these things." He tried to take comfort from the thought that once everything was handed over to the authorities, he could wash his hands of it.

CHAPTER SIXTEEN

"Really, Van. If you're not comfortable talking with Frank, you can always leave." Nora's words stung.

"It is my house, remember?"

"So? Do you think Frank and I would make off with the furniture?" Van stifled an urge to say that he'd never mistake her for Sheila. Nora, looking abashed, added, "I'm sorry. I didn't mean . . . But you're the one who said it would be more convenient to meet here."

"And so it is."

His attempt at a reasonable tone seemed to fuel Nora's anger. She chopped the air with both hands as she paced. "My point is that you don't *have* to stay! If this discussion is offensive to you, maybe you should go back to your office—or to another part of the house, even— and I'll deal with it."

"I will stay, goddamn it!"

Nora stopped and turned, arms akimbo. "Well, stay then! But do quit going on about it!" Before either could say more, the doorbell rang.

Van stalked to the door, still rigid with anger. "Good afternoon, Captain. We are in the living room." Was he imagining it, or did Frank look from him to the high color in Nora's cheeks in a way that suggested he had overheard them from the porch? "Would you like a cup of coffee?"

"Sure. That would be great."

"Nora?"

"Yes, please." She didn't meet his eye.

Assembling the coffee tray, Van took several deep breaths and wrestled some semblance of control back into place.

★   ★   ★

While Van worked in the kitchen, Frank and Nora exchanged perfunctory comments on the weather and local events. Frank wandered around the living room, sizing up his host. A large picture reminiscent of Picasso hung over the fireplace. The cherry furniture, Shaker style, was sparse but graceful. Frank ran a finger over the edge of an end table.

Nora said, "He built most of it. When Sheila left, she took everything."

Frank examined the beautifully finished crates opposite the fireplace, the plethora of books and small objects that counterbalanced the conventional good taste of the rest of the room. Non-fiction, music, and art books. A model sailboat, an intricately twisted piece of driftwood, and three perfect shells. A picture of four attractive young people who must be his children. So, van Pelt was probably traditional, serious, quiet. And if Nora was interested in him, he must be smart as well.

When Van returned with coffee, he glanced at Nora sitting at one end of the sofa, hesitated an instant, then took the chair opposite. Frank reached for a coffee mug, the conflict he'd suspected at the door confirmed. "So, Nora, you said you wanted to talk about Ted Slater's murder."

"Yes. We—I—Well, you know, everyone is talking about it, and we've heard things." She glanced at Van. "People have told us things— things that maybe you haven't heard."

Frank watched her, head tilted, wondering what he was in for.

Nora's words came fast. "At the rehearsal of the Chorale on Tuesday, and in The Pub afterward, Clyde Barnes said he knows a thing or two about the murder. Of course, one can't believe every word Clyde says. Sometimes he just talks for effect. He even suggested that Van and I might be suspects, just because we were anchored off Slater's dock on Saturday night! God only knows how he came to know *that*. But he often has surprisingly accurate information—"

Frank cut in. "Before we get into the gossip, tell me about Queenstown harbor. What's it like to sail in there?"

Nora sounded relieved when she said, "It's small and shallow, so easy to run aground. I've done it myself. The bottom is forgiving, so it's mostly an embarrassment—unless one's sailing alone: winching off can be a *major* pain in the ass."

"Would you need to be a good sailor to go in there alone?"

Van said, "Moderately so." Nora nodded agreement.

"What about after dark?"

"Sailing in the dark is always more difficult. This anchorage—the size, the depth, the sunken pilings from the old wharf—would be something of a challenge, but certainly doable if you were familiar with the place."

Nora chimed in, "And night doesn't necessarily mean dark. Depending on the moon, it can be quite bright. Why all this interest in the harbor? Do you think the murderer *sailed* in?"

"It's one possibility." Frank pinched the bridge of his nose. "It seems that Slater's women friends sometimes came by boat." He cocked his head at Nora. "I heard that Louisa sailed in there a couple of times last fall. Do you know how well she sails?"

"Louisa did not sail into Queenstown harbor in the dark of night and kill Ted Slater! It's a preposterous suggestion. Louisa doesn't even have a boat!"

"She doesn't have a car, either, but she drove over there." Frank kept the comment mild. "Is she a good enough sailor or not?"

"She's co-captain of the college racing team. So, yes, she's good enough." The reply sounded grudging. "But Louisa didn't do it!"

Frank leaned back in his chair. "Well, if *you're* convinced, I might as well ignore real evidence."

Nora sat up straighter. "Or try looking at all of it for a change! There are plenty of other suspects—with just as much motive and opportunity as Louisa! That's what I was trying to tell you. Clyde said that Ted and Suzanne weren't really divorced and that they had a major row in Ted's office recently. He said she shouted something like, 'I could kill you with my bare hands.' So . . ." Nora shifted in her chair. "So, we talked it over and decided that Van would go to the courthouse and check the public records." Frank wondered what she wasn't telling him.

Van took up the narrative. "I found no record of divorce and there is no will on file. If she knew there was no will, plus the divorce issues, those things could constitute a motive."

Did they think he was too stupid to have thought of that? Frank held in his annoyance and merely said, "Mmmm."

Nora picked up the recital. "Of course you must know all of this because Suzanne said that the police questioned her already."

"You talked with Suzanne Slater?" Frank let a touch of exasperation show. "When?"

"On Halloween Friday. I went to the shop where she works and I bought earrings and then . . . invited her to lunch."

"You pumped her."

Nora clenched her teeth and her voice had a colder edge when she replied. "It wasn't necessary to *pump* Suzanne! She brought the subject up herself. And much of what she said was quite revealing." She paused. "But really, Frank, if you don't want to know what we found out, you might as well leave!" Nora glanced at Van and color suffused her high cheekbones. She grinned ruefully and added, "It isn't as though we're in your house or something."

Frank noticed the byplay, filed it for future consideration, wondering yet again about the exact nature of Nora's relationship with Van. "Of course I'm interested."

"Suzanne said that Ted was blackmailing Ray Martin for the last three years!"

Frank tried never to show surprise at what suspects or witnesses said. He looked hard at Nora. "Tell me *exactly* what she said."

Nora repeated their exchange and reminded Frank about the bookstore robbery. "So we decided—well, actually, I persuaded Van to talk with Ray, to see whether he could confirm the things Suzanne said." His anger must have shown because Nora lifted her chin and said, "It really didn't seem responsible to come to you with completely unsubstantiated rumor."

Frank snorted and Van said, "Actually, it was I who resisted. I am not comfortable with rumor mongering. But having decided to talk with you, let me tell you of my talk with Ray Martin." He did so, concisely but in detail, sparing himself not at all, before concluding, "So we have nothing in his own words about any blackmail. But from his reaction, I really do believe there was something to it. Ray seems to have had motive, and no doubt you could determine opportunity. Although, personally, I still doubt he had the gumption to have done it."

Nora cut in. "Well, I don't think Suzanne did it, either. But the point is that people other than Louisa had reason to kill Ted Slater. And who knows how many more are out there?"

Frank said, "Give it a rest, Nora. You're the psychologist. I shouldn't have to tell you that anyone is capable of anything, given the right circumstances. The question isn't whether Ray Martin could do murder, but whether he did *this* murder. The same goes for Suzanne Slater and Louisa Smallwood." Seeing the stubborn set of Nora's jaw, he added, "There's no one whose intellect—whose opinions—I respect more than yours. But you don't have all the facts, Nonnie. I have reasons to doubt Louisa Smallwood's story."

Van had a sinking feeling that the nickname signaled ongoing intimacy—more than the old flame he'd heard about—but reminded himself that that shouldn't matter to him anymore. Frank's voice brought him back to the conversation at hand. "I can't tell you the details, but she's been lying up one side and down the other. I have proof."

"There must be some explanation."

"There always is." A twisted grin accompanied Frank's comment. "But I'm keeping an open mind anyway."

"Frank, be fair!"

Knowing how Nora felt about Louisa made Van want to say something supportive but neither Nora nor Frank gave him a chance.

"Nora, give me *some* credit. Do you think I don't know how to do my job? Or that I can't be trusted?"

"Neither. And you know it! It's just—"

"It's just that you don't know anything about the investigation. I'll talk with Ray Martin. And I already told you I'm trying to track down a woman who sailed in there last spring. I'm also trying to find the most recent girlfriend—who may be yet another suspect. Even if she had nothing to do with his death, a lover probably knows something about his relationships, maybe about feuds or grudges. Can you help me with any of that? What women do you know who sail?"

Nora flared. "Why only women? It could have been some man Ted pissed off. It could have been a jealous husband. It could have been a thief!"

Van had seldom seen Nora so combative. He said, "Now, Nora," in a tone he immediately regretted and hurriedly turned to Frank. "We are practically on the Bay. Nearly everyone here sails."

"Okay, okay. But can you tell me about other women in Ted Slater's life? Or anyone in his life, for that matter?"

Both Nora and Van said, "No." Nora added, "We never knew that he *had* women in his life till recently. He must have been incredibly discreet."

"Look, I appreciate the information. I really do. And if anything else comes your way—*happens* to come your way—I want to know it." He drew a long, slow breath, and looked at Nora as he spoke. "But this is a police investigation of murder. It's my job, not yours, and I can't have you going off interrogating people, maybe contaminating witness testimony. It's one thing to cooperate with the investigation; it's another thing altogether to interfere. Keep your nose out of it."

Nora's cheeks flamed. Van was too gentlemanly to say, "That's what I told her." Instead, he cleared his throat and spoke politely. "Of course we understand your position, Captain. We wish only to be of assistance."

"Good. As long as we understand each other."

After seeing Frank out, Van carried the coffee tray to the kitchen. When he returned, he saw tears on Nora's cheeks. He dropped onto the sofa beside her. "Are you all right?" She turned away and Van put his hands on her rigid shoulders. She shrugged him off. His voice was gentle. "Nora, what is it?"

She whirled to face him. "I'm so mad I could spit!" Van jerked back from her fury. "I'm mad at Frank for going all high and mighty and condescending. I'm mad at the way the two of you are just—*male bonding* all over this case. I'm mad at—What the hell's so funny?"

Van spoke through his laughter. "I actually thought you needed comfort!"

Nora scowled at him uncertainly, then smiled. Her giggle turned to laughter. The tension release made the whole scene seem funnier than it was, and Van laughed till his belly hurt. Nora said, "Tears are my inevitable response to impotent rage." She giggled again. "So now you know."

Van said, "I do not shed tears but I surely do know the feeling." He brushed the last tear from her cheek. "Nora, I . . ." The heat of her thigh seared his, and the scent of her came gentle as a breath. He kissed her softly, then long and deep, and she kissed him.

The doorbell rang and they jumped apart, breathing hard. Nora said, "Frank?"

Van went to the door and returned carrying a small parcel. "It was UPS. A book I ordered." Nora stood near the sofa. Van put his hands on her shoulders and drew her to him.

She leaned slightly away. "Have you changed your mind?"

Van stepped back immediately. "Sorry. I—wasn't thinking." He thought she was going to say something but she turned to the sofa, gathering her jacket and briefcase.

She said, "Well. I guess I'd better get going." She did not meet his eyes.

Van said, "Of course. I need to get back to my office, too." But he knew the afternoon was shot. He felt embarrassed, caught up in thoughts of having stepped over a boundary, pondering how he could restore his equilibrium—or even his dignity.

Nora walked rapidly away, her thoughts in turmoil. Of course Van hadn't changed his mind. He was not capricious. She felt stupid, stupid, stupid.

CHAPTER SEVENTEEN

Frank sat at his desk, reading arrest summaries, when Jake arrived. "Morning, Frank. Fill me in."

Frank grimaced. "Professors Perry and Van Pelt seem determined to play detective. It really pisses me off. I told them to mind their own business and leave the investigation to us. Van seemed okay with that, but Nora may be a problem. She's convinced the Smallwood girl didn't do it."

"So, convince her otherwise. Now, where are we?"

Frank summarized his interviews. "Everything Nora and Van said has been corroborated. I still have to talk to Ray Martin. Slater's cleaning woman, Natasha Brown, just got back from West Virginia. She was visiting family. But I interviewed her this morning. She worked for Slater over two years, Mondays and Thursdays, doing laundry and cleaning. She was there the day before he was killed, so the clean sheets and towels *she* put out had to have been replaced on Friday. Also, she grocery shopped for him that Thursday. Because he wanted lamb chops and salad greens for two—which she thought was fancier than what a man would cook for another man—she concluded that he was entertaining a woman. And that fits with what we think went down that night."

"What did she have to say about female visitors?"

"She mentioned Louisa and the Sasser woman. Says their behavior in her presence was always quite proper—and that what they did when they were alone was their own business." Frank cocked one eyebrow at Jake. "She thinks that a vigorous man in his prime has needs, whether he's married or not."

Jake grinned. "Pretty damned tolerant."

"Especially for the daughter of a Southern Baptist preacher." Frank referred to his notebook. "She says she hasn't seen the Smallwood girl since the first of the year, but that Mary Sasser stopped by whenever she thought Slater was home. She hasn't seen our mystery woman." Frank flipped the page in his notebook. "She said, 'But the sheets tell their own tale. He's been seeing someone for six months or more.' And a few weeks ago, she noticed a black lace bra in his underwear drawer. So that gives us something of a timeline for the one we found at the scene."

"Slater was a real piece of work."

Frank nodded. "So far, he seems like a love or hate kind of guy. On the one hand you have Smallwood and Suzanne Slater. On the other, you have the secretarial staff and grounds crew at the college, Douden and now Natasha Brown. His cleaning woman thinks he practically walked on water—gave her paid time off when her daughter was in the hospital, sent a basket of flowers when her dog died. She actually got teary talking about him."

"You think there was something more between them than employer-employee?"

"No way. My gut couldn't be that wrong. Besides, Slater liked them young. She's just a really nice lady. Didn't seem to hold anything back. And she gave me the names of a couple of the poker pals: Ray Martin again, and Christopher Halter."

"Have you talked to any of the poker guys?"

"I'm working on it." In casual deference to his boss, Frank outlined the next steps, knowing Jake would not object. "I'll start with Christopher Halter. He can give me any names I don't have. I'll hit all of them today, including Martin."

Jake's parting tone was grim. "We have a long way to go, but I know I can count on you to get us there." Frank couldn't tell whether he was being praised for what he'd done or pressured for what remained. He grabbed his coat and headed for the door.

CHAPTER EIGHTEEN

Christopher Halter answered the door in his sock feet, wearing jeans and a T-shirt. Fit, his four decades or so showed mainly in his thinning hair. "Come on in," he said, his voice deep and melodious. He ushered Frank to a small back room sparsely furnished as an office. "Not exactly a palace, but it's got everything I need." He lifted one foot, wiggled his toes. "And I can kick my shoes off any time I want."

Frank looked around. "You work from home?"

"Telemarketing."

From that one word Frank pegged him as a smooth talker who could say whatever he thought his listener wanted to hear. Something to watch for. "I'll try not to take a lot of your time. Just tell me about Ted Slater."

"I don't know much about his personal life, but I liked him fine. He was a slick bastard, played a real competitive game—but that describes us all!" Halter grinned broadly as he said it.

"What about women? Did you know any of the women in his life?"

"I only wish! Every time I saw him with a woman, she was a real knockout. But I never met any of them. And Ted wasn't a man to talk. I mean, just in generalities. No details, not even first names."

"What about male friends?"

Halter cracked his knuckles. "I don't know any except for our poker group. Like I said, I liked him. All of us did. He was just a regular guy, not putting on airs about teaching at the college or anything—although sometimes he'd sort of pull rank on Ray Martin. Ray works at the college, too, you know."

"So what about Ray Martin? What's he like?"

Halter made the transition to talking about Ray Martin with no apparent curiosity. "Ray's a pretty shrewd card player. Has one hell of a memory. He wins his share of the time, maybe a little more than his share." Halter winked at Frank, adding, "Which is probably just as well. He can be a pretty sore loser. A few drinks and he gets pretty funny. But as the night wears on and the booze flows, sometimes he gets pretty explosive, you know? Don't get me wrong. Ray's an okay guy. When he wins, he's real open-handed—buying drinks and stuff. And who'd ever expect that? I mean, he's got a good job at the college, but he lives in a dump. We always try to set the game someplace else."

"How serious is he about gambling? Would you say he's a compulsive gambler?"

Halter leaned back, rocking his swivel chair a little, and laced his fingers across his belt buckle. "Well, gambling is surely in Ray's soul. The casinos in Atlantic City pull him like the moon pulls the tides."

"What does he say about work?"

"He doesn't talk about work. Except sometimes he brags about how much money the bookstore makes, and his big salary when he was building inspector over in Fairfax County. Of course, maybe some of that's hype. He can tell good stories. And like I said, damned funny, too."

"Have you noticed any changes recently?"

"No, I can't say that I have, except his bets may be smaller these days—smaller than two or three years ago. And lately he'd been pretty depressed about putting his mother in a nursing home."

Halter said the other members of the poker group were Gary Cloonan and Tony Schiavoni.

"What about Cloonan and Schiavoni? How did they get along with Slater?"

"Why, just like everybody else. You know. Buddies."

"No fights? No grudges? No money owed?"

"Naw, none of that—none that I ever knew about, anyway. The worst I ever saw was when Slater would ride Tony about goldbricking—you know? After Tony went on worker's comp. Tony worked as a mason until a cinderblock wall collapsed on him—during the construction of Queenstown Discount Plaza. Tony'd get pretty ticked. Sometimes Ted didn't know when enough was enough, you know? But that wasn't really serious." Frank asked several more questions, but it seemed Halter really couldn't tell him anything more.

Frank drove to Anthony Schiavoni's apartment across town. Tony confirmed Chris Halter's comments. He added, "Gary and Chris got along well with Slater—but then Chris gets along with everybody."

Frank asked about Ray Martin and Slater. "Mostly they got along. But there was this one night a month or so ago. Slater was busting on me about being on the dole, living off charity, and like that. He really had a bug up his ass. After awhile, he saw I was getting pretty hot under the collar, like, and then he turned on Ray. Well, really, it was Ray's mom. She has Alzheimer's, and Ted was saying how when somebody loses their marbles, they might as well just be put out of their misery, they're no good to anybody, God never meant there to be two-legged vegetables, stuff like that. Ray told him a couple of times to lay off, but he just kept on. Ray yelled something about Slater being a sonofabitch not even a mother could love, so how could he know anything about it. Slater had had a few. He laughed, and said in this real smarmy voice, 'And just what kind of love did Mama give you, Ray? The kind that made you want to change her diapers?' Ray jumped on Ted, grabbed him by the shirt and laid one on him. He was trying to beat the shit out of Ted's face till we pulled him off." Tony shook his head. "I'd never seen Ray like that before."

"You were surprised?"

"Well, yeah. Sure. Least ways, I never seen it coming. But looking back, I can see it, you know? He's always taking her candy or something special to eat, or flowers from the Acme, or something. And after he's had a few too many, sometimes he gets all weepy about how she used to be and how it breaks his heart the way she is now. When Ray cries, that's a sure sign it's time to fold our cards." Tony raised his chin with the air of someone offering a deep insight. "You really shouldn't mess with a man's love for his mother."

Frank nodded. "And what about Slater? What did he do?"

"Nothing. I guess he was too surprised at first, and we pulled Ray off him pretty quick. When Ted got up, he sort of mopped at his face and his shirt with his handkerchief and said something about how did

Ray think he was gonna pay for that. Blood'll ruin a white shirt every time."

Frank asked a few more questions but he learned nothing more.

Just before lunch Frank walked into Cloonan's Convenience Store on Liberty Street, owned and operated by Gary Cloonan. Not much of a talker, what Cloonan did say indicated that his views of his fellow poker players were much the same as those Frank had heard already. He confirmed Halter's report of the way Slater treated Tony Schiavoni. He confirmed Schiavoni's version of Ray Martin's fight with Slater but with less detail. According to Cloonan, they all were good buddies and nobody held any grudges. Nobody had mentioned the fight again.

Leaving Cloonan's, Frank realized that if he was going to get back to his office in time for the interview with Mark Sasser, he'd better step on it. He put aside thoughts of the poker group and concentrated on questions he wanted to ask Sasser.

CHAPTER NINETEEN

Mark Sasser arrived at Frank's office at 4:30, walking fast, a little out of breath. He looked like an aging football player: beefy shoulders, thighs that strained the seams of gabardine slacks with every step, the line of his jaw made indistinct by time and added weight.

Sasser extended his hand. "Here's the picture. You can keep it. I have the negative."

The picture showed a white-hulled sailboat against a sunset sky. Frank turned it over. On the back, in a small, precise hand was printed "Sailboat at sunset, May 22." "Thanks. I appreciate your help. Sorry to have taken you out of your way."

"No problem." He turned to go.

"Wait." Frank laid aside the picture. "We need to talk. Sit down."

Sasser looked surprised and wary but said, "Sure. Fine. I'm not in a big hurry to get home." He dropped into the chair across from Frank. "Mary's out with the girls tonight. What's up?"

"Start with the picture. You're sure it's the boat your wife mentioned to me?"

"Yeah—the one that sailed into my sunset series last spring."

"Right." Frank tilted his head and spoke softly. "So your wife told you about our interview?"

Mark Sasser shifted his position, muscles tensing, his elaborately casual words strung on a taut wire. "Sure. I know you talked to her. So?"

"We discussed your relationship with Ted Slater." Sasser scowled. Frank kept his tone neutral. "I need to know as much about Slater as possible."

Mark folded his arms across his chest. "I never liked him much. I didn't trust him any farther than I could throw this desk."

"Why not?"

"With Ted Slater around, men had better lock up their wives and daughters." His grin looked forced. "That bastard would screw any woman from sixteen to sixty–if she was good looking enough."

Frank waited long enough for emphasis, then said, "Was your wife one of them?"

Sasser shifted in his chair. "Leave my wife out of this! I don't like it when strangers pry into things that are none of their damn business."

"But murder is my business."

Mark leaned forward, trembling hands clasped tightly between his knees. Frank waited through a long pause. When Sasser spoke, face and voice conveyed resignation. "I don't know. I hope not. But Mary's a good looking woman, lively—and she's a tease. She can't help it."

"You told her to stay away from Slater."

"That's right."

"Because of Slater's reputation with women, or because of Mary?"

"I saw them—twice. I went to the kitchen for ice one time and caught them kissing. Ted made a joke about Mary being irresistible, and they both laughed. But . . ." Sasser was a man in pain. "Then there was the time I saw him feeling her ass. He was supposed to be helping her with her coat. It made me crazy. That's when I—I put my foot down—told Mary to stay away from him. That's all there was to it."

"You didn't say anything to him? Do anything?"

"No. Maybe I should have." Mark looked away. "But I thought . . . I didn't want to force the issue." Frank thought he was probably lying, but decided to let it slide for now. Mark leaned back in his chair and crossed his legs, his upper body limp. "I love Mary, you know? I can't believe she'd cheat on me. But she—gets high doing something a little naughty. And she can be really gullible. I always worried that she'd get tangled up with Ted and then not know how to get loose."

Something in his recital made Frank wonder about Mark Sasser's performance in bed. "Just for the record, where were you that Friday and Saturday?"

"What? I need an alibi?"

"I'm asking everybody."

Mark pinched his lower lip. "Friday? I worked, of course. I closed on a big account that afternoon. Then Mary met me for dinner at the Hotel Imperial in Chestertown. I guess we got home about 9:30 or so. On Saturday we ran errands in the morning. In the afternoon, Mary did grocery shopping and I watched football."

"Did you see anyone—talk to anyone? Besides your wife, I mean."

"Nobody who's likely to remember. Maybe the waitress Friday night, but she was really busy. And buying an extension cord at the hardware store doesn't attract a lot of attention! If you want an alibi, I'm probably shit out of luck," he said ruefully, adding a boyish smile.

Frank thought that smile had probably served Mark Sasser well most of his life. "Did you see anything that weekend?" Frank tapped the photograph. "This boat, maybe?"

"As far as I know, I never saw that boat again." Frank pressed for anything out of the ordinary. Mark insisted there was nothing. He hadn't looked at the harbor Friday night, saw one boat anchored in the storm on Saturday, saw light from Slater's house both nights. In short, he hadn't noticed a thing.

"I'll need fingerprints from you and your wife. My sergeant will take yours now and she can come in as soon as it's convenient." Frank extended his hand. "Thanks again for the photograph."

Frank studied the photograph—clearly a white sailboat. He opened the small magnifying glass attached to his key ring and tried to find something—anything—to identify the boat. But the angle was such that neither the registration number on the bow nor the name was visible. Nothing but three black numbers—232—on the sail. If sail numbers meant anything, he might have something. Too bad he hadn't shared Nora's passion for sailing. He might have learned something that would help him now. He phoned the Maryland Natural Resources Police and learned that numbers displayed on sails usually match the hull number.

"What kind of sailboat is it?"

"Hell, I don't know. I can hardly tell a yacht from a tug."

"You have a picture? Fax me a copy. I'll try to identify the manufacturer. With the manufacturer and the hull number, Natural

Resources can find out who the Registration Card was issued to. The vessel registration number, the hull number, the length of the boat, and the owner are in the computer. It might take awhile, though. The file isn't organized by hull numbers."

"I'll fax it now. Give me a call as soon as you find anything, okay?" Frank gave his number. "Ask for Captain Pierce."

Within an hour Frank knew that the boat was a thirty-two-foot sloop built by the Pearson Yacht Company in 1971. Frank called the office of Natural Resources in Baltimore. Yes, they would do a search, and yes, like car titles, certificates of vessels cannot be transferred. Owners are obliged to report when a vessel is sold, to whom, and at what price.

Frank felt a frizzle of excitement. "How long will it take to do the search?"

"Hard to say. Could be as long as a week. There are a hell of a lot of sailboats on the Maryland waters of the Chesapeake."

"Yeah, well, you know it's a murder investigation. Do the best you can. Call me as soon as you have anything."

Clearing his desk to leave, Frank wondered what Mark and Mary Sasser would talk about when she returned from her outing with the ladies. He felt sorry for Mark, for any bastard who was that uncertain about his wife. Was he jealous enough to kill?

CHAPTER TWENTY

At 5:40, Frank walked to Ray Martin's place on Railroad Avenue, across the street and only a few hundred yards from the Sheriff's Office. Light from the Acme fell on the old-fashioned railroad crossing sign marking the abandoned track, a reminder of the days when Centreville had two important canneries.

Ray lived in a brown shingled house adjacent to the grade crossing, formerly single family, now two apartments. A label beside the front door read, "R. Martin, Second Floor." No doorbell. Frank banged on the door. When he got no reply, he opened the door onto a narrow entry. Two old ceiling fixtures cast dim pools of light on a shabby stairwell. Frank would have been surprised if Ray's poker pals hadn't said he lived in a dump.

He knocked on the door at the top of the stairs, caught the sound of a toilet flushing. A voice called, "Just a minute." The man who opened the door looked like he'd had a long day—eyes hollow, shoulders sagging. Frank rated the quality of his suit pants, shirt, and loosened tie several cuts above the dim light and shabby stairwell. The man's "Yes?" was noncommittal.

"Ray Martin? I'm Captain Pierce of the Queen Anne's County Sheriff's Office."

"Yes?"

"I want to talk to you about Ted Slater. May I come in?"

Ray hesitated, then gestured him into the kitchen. He raised the remnants of a drink in his left hand as if to say, "Want one?" Frank shook his head, wondering whether it was Ray's first drink of the day. Ray leaned against the counter, nursing his whiskey in silence, while Frank looked around. The mess was more consistent with the stairwell than with the dapper clothes. Frank said, "So, tell me about Ted Slater."

Ray frowned. "What's to tell? He's dead."

"I understand that you were in the same poker group. Is that right?"

Ray took a swallow of bourbon, probably considering his answer before he said, "Right. You want to sit down?" He swept a pile of newspapers from a kitchen chair. Frank sat and pushed aside a dirty coffee cup to lean his elbows on the table.

Ray said, "I'm not much of a housekeeper, I guess. It was better when my mother lived with me." He stared vacantly at the wall.

Frank said, "I guess your mother meant a lot to you."

"Yeah. She still does." His voice quavered. He refreshed his drink and plopped into the chair across from Frank.

"I understand you had a fight with Ted Slater over your mother." Ray looked startled. "Your poker buddies told me."

Ray leaned back, relaxing a little. "Yeah. Right. The sonofabitch had it coming."

"So tell me about it."

"What's to tell? He had no call to insult my mother. When he wouldn't lay off, I pasted him one." Ray clamped his mouth shut.

"So which was worse, his comments about your mother or the blackmail?"

Ray slammed his fist on the table and swore under his breath. "Who the hell've you been talking to? van Pelt?"

"Who doesn't matter. Ted Slater blackmailed you—for three years—over the bookstore robbery."

Ray yelped. "That's bullshit. I told you then and I tell you now: I didn't rob the bookstore—had nothing to do with it." He peered at Frank through half-closed lids. "Sometimes Slater floated me a loan. That's all. The only money I gave Slater was for I.O.U.s."

"Every month?"

"Well, you know, interest. Sometimes it took more than a month to pay him back."

Frank looked hard at Ray. "So, what happens to your gambling debts now that he's dead?"

Ray's jaw muscles tightened. "Jesus Christ! You don't think *I* killed him, do you? If I were gonna kill the bastard, I'd've done it years ago!

Ted Slater had other enemies besides me." Ray lit a cigarette, a slight tremor in his hands.

"So who were some of those other enemies?"

"How the hell would I know? I'm just saying, there had to be some."

Frank hammered on him for half an hour but got nothing more. Ray smoked and drank steadily throughout. His enunciation grew careful but not slurred. Frank thought only a pretty heavy hitter could carry his liquor like that. For no reason Frank could fathom, Ray suddenly said, "I didn't do anything in Fairfax County, either, but they sacked me anyway. You can check it."

Frank grinned. "I have. You were up for assault and battery in Vienna, Virginia."

Ray looked sideways at Frank. "I mean, I was never in trouble over anything *important* there. That was just a fight in a bar." Ray moved to the sink with what Frank thought was careful steadiness and poured the last of the bourbon into his glass. "There goes another dead soldier." He held the bottle at arm's length over a grocery bag of trash and let it fall.

"Listen up, Ray. Where were you on the weekend Slater was murdered?"

Ray slowly tapped a cigarette from a soft pack, lit it, and dropped the match into the sink. "Atlantic City."

"Give me the details."

Ray squinted. "I left Centreville, from my apartment here, after work on Friday and drove to Atlantic City. I stopped for a bite right after I crossed the Delaware Memorial Bridge. I hit Atlantic City about 10:00."

"And?"

Ray shrugged. "I got a room, went to Trump's Casino, and played black jack—a couple hours."

"A room where?"

"Christ, I dunno! Some little dump off the strip."

"What about a receipt? A credit card slip?"

"I pay cash. I probably trashed the receipt."

"You aren't doing yourself any good here, Ray. I'd like to believe you but you just aren't giving me anything."

Ray shifted in his chair. "Look, I swear, all I remember is the room—brown and green. Near the ice machine. And cheap. I always go cheap on the room. But they had a good bar brand." He lifted his glass. "I like my bourbon."

"Did you win?"

"Probably not. I didn't have much when I got home. But usually I win. I like the wheel best. Brings me luck. Someday, the wheel's gonna roll me right outta this nothing burg."

"When did you get home?"

"Sunday. Noon maybe."

"When was the last time you saw Slater?"

Ray focused cunning eyes on Frank. "Thursday."

"Tell me." Frank grabbed Ray by the shirtfront and got in his face. "And don't lie, you sorry sonofabitch!"

"It's not my fault the bastard's dead!" Ray tried to pull away. "I went there Thursday. Slater was all fancied up in his smoking jacket. He told me to fuck off. I told him I got his note telling me to pay up, but it was no good. I didn't have any more money. He said, 'You'll find a way, Ray. Or you'll regret it.' I did everything but get down on my knees. The bastard wouldn't budge. Finally, the fucker threw me out." His eyes darted back and forth, a cornered mouse who just wanted to be left alone. "I thought maybe—you know—he was gonna hire some goons to rough me up or something."

"Listen to me, Ray. That Atlantic City story is one piss poor alibi. Are you hearing me, Ray? You could end up on the hook for this murder if I don't find someone better. You'd best figure out how you can help me out here." He let go of Ray's shirt front, pushing him back into his chair.

When Frank left, Ray sat slumped at the table, mumbling, "Not my fault. Not my fault."

Frank walked slowly back to his office. He dispatched Joe to Atlantic City to check the motels where Ray might have stayed, and to check the casinos' play cards, the closed-circuit TV surveillance of the gaming tables, the ever-present clock monitor. They'd pin down Ray's every hour.

If they turned up enough pieces, eventually the picture would come clear. But today's haul just added to the jumble: Ray Martin's gambling debts and capacity for violence, Mark Sasser's doubts about his wife, and an unidentified sailboat that might or might not be relevant. The flotsam of the case weighed heavily on Frank. He drove home on automatic pilot, too tired to think.

CHAPTER TWENTY-ONE

Frank stopped at Jake's open door. "Hey, boss. I just wanted to let you know I'm on my way out. Our interview with the dean was a bust: every comment cautious and guarded, no serious complaints against Slater. Ditto his departmental colleagues: they seemed more interested in pumping us than in providing information. They disapproved of his consulting work—and probably wished they had a little of that kind of action—but they didn't tell us anything we hadn't already heard elsewhere."

"What about that sex with women students business?"

Frank grunted. "Both the dean and his department chair assured us that if there had ever been a complaint of sexual harassment, they would have acted swiftly and decisively to deal with it. That's a quote."

"Yeah. Right. But they didn't deny that he was involved with students."

"Nope. And—according to Clyde Barnes—Slater and the Smallwood girl had a row in Slater's office a couple of weeks before the murder—an encounter she conveniently forgot to mention to me. So, I've got to go around that barn again." Frank shifted his weight and leaned against the doorjamb. "On the good news side: the Department of Natural Resources identified the boat that was anchored off Slater's dock for four days last spring as a thirty-two foot Pearson named *Confederate*, registered to West College." Jake whistled. "Corporate ownership isn't as close a tie as I would have liked. But Louisa's access to college boats gave her another means of getting to and from Slater's house. I think she anchored in Queenstown Harbor last spring—and never mentioned it. I think she lied about what happened with Slater and when." Frank straightened up. "I'm on my way over to the college now, see what I can find out about *Confederate*."

Paul Zimmerman managed the college-owned fleet of sailboats. He explained to Frank that the college kept seven sailboats on moorings near the college dock from mid-April to mid-October. Maintaining the fleet during the college's sailing camp was a big part of his job during the summers. "But they've been put up for the winter now. We hauled them on October 15th."

"All of them? Including *Confederate*?" Frank asked.

Paul cast a pitying eye on Frank and drawled, "Naw. I'm talkin' about the student boats, the Flying Scots. *Confederate* ain't no little Flying Scot. She's a thirty-two-foot Pearson, assigned to the president. I don't handle her. She's kept tied to the dock behind the president's house. Saves Mrs. President the trouble of rowing out to a mooring."

Frank fell silent, mulling over Paul's information, and let Joe pick up the questioning. "Is that where *Confederate* is now?"

Paul shook his head and rolled his eyes. "Not this late in the season. Mrs. President took her down to Marsh Point Marina and had 'er hauled. She's too big for us to handle here. She took her down 'bout the same time we hauled the racing boats. I don't know exactly, but you could ask Mrs. President."

Frank roused himself. "So Mrs. Howard does most of the sailing? Where does she sail?"

Paul leaned back in his chair, thrust his hands in his pockets. "She's a mighty fine sailor. Lots of little day sails or half-day sails here on the river. Sometimes she's gone for three or four days—like to Annapolis and back. For long trips, she goes out with President Howard—but I guess he didn't have much time for that this summer."

"I see. Well, thanks for your time, Mr. Zimmerman." Joe turned to Frank, who shook his head almost imperceptibly. "If I have any more questions, I'll get back to you."

As they left the office, Zimmerman said, "Say, Sheriff, what's this all about?"

"I wish I knew!" Frank grinned. "I'm trying to get leads on a couple of boats, but if you're sure about when all the college boats were hauled, I guess it couldn't have been any of them."

"Is one of our kids in trouble? They wouldn't use our boats for anything really bad. A little night racing or something like that, maybe, but nothing *bad*. The kids who sail are good kids!"

Frank said, "Yeah, I'm sure you're right. Besides the Pearson and the Flying Scots, are there any other boats?"

"Not college boats. Three employees moor boats here, but the only one still in the water after the fifteenth was *Duet*." Paul chuckled. "That Professor Perry is always the first one in the water and the last one out. Now she is one fine sailing woman!" He rubbed his chin. "That's about it. Sometimes a transient ties up—but not often. We're pretty far up the river. I haven't seen a transient in a couple of months."

Frank digested the new information as he and Joe hiked back across campus. He didn't think Nora lied to him about when she took her boat out. But could Louisa have taken it without asking? Or van Pelt? But what could Van have had against Slater? There was no "Lydia" in Slater's address book, but if she anchored *Confederate* there last spring . . . Then he remembered: Nora had loaned her boat to Lydia Howard. He decided not to speak to Lydia just yet. He needed to be a lot surer before he raised such an explosive possibility about the wife of the president of West College.

Back in the office, Frank arranged with Joe to interview Martin MacPhee that evening, then turned to the phone. First he called the wharfinger at Marsh Point Marina. "Yeah, *Confederate*'s here. Hauled her the sixteenth of last month." Then Frank called Owen Grube. Grube was alone and freely admitted watching the woman on the sailboat longer than he'd let on, but he could not add substantially to his earlier description. He guffawed heartily. "I'm not much of a face man, myself. I focus on tits and ass and that doesn't leave much time for anything from the neck up!" Frank buzzed Jake and brought him up to speed. Jake said, "I hope to God this doesn't turn into a blow-up between my office and West College!" On his way to the parking lot, Frank detoured to check the fingerprint file. All the ones he'd asked for were there.

Driving home, he struggled to throw off his frustration. There were too goddamned many people who hated the man's guts! As soon as he seemed to be getting a solid case against Louisa, along came Suzanne Slater and Ray Martin, now the possibility of Lydia Howard, or Mary Sasser—or more likely, Mark—had to be thrown into the pot. And who knew how many others? And what about that black lace bra? Loose ends frayed his nerves.

Frank sighed. In his mind, black lace against white flesh would always mean Nora. She was the only white woman he'd ever dated. Not that others hadn't turned him on. But Nora was the only one who ever roused a passion strong enough to overcome his upbringing, his mother's warnings against all the evils that befell black men in mixed marriages. Maybe it *would* have been a disaster. It was a moot point now. Frank shook his head to rid himself of the thought and parked the car. Time to focus on home. He bent his mind to it as he opened the back door.

After dinner, Frank picked Joe up at the station on his way to Queenstown. They traveled mostly in silence while Frank mulled over Claire's disappointment that he was spending yet another evening working. He'd assured her that he would keep it as short as possible, but she was not mollified.

Frank and Joe arrived at the MacPhee residence two minutes early. Frank wiped nonexistent dust from the toes of his shoes and pushed the doorbell. A middle-aged man, of average height, with a barrel chest and no evidence of a waist, swung open the door. "You must be Sheriff Pierce."

"Captain Pierce, actually. The sheriff is my boss. This is Sergeant Jamieson." They stepped into the hall as Mrs. MacPhee came from the kitchen, drying her hands on her apron.

Martin MacPhee said, "This is my wife Elsie," and led them into the dining room where a framed diploma was prominently hung: Clarkson College, Potsdam, New York, Bachelor of Science in Mechanical Engineering. Martin MacPhee lowered his bulk into a chair, leaned on his right arm, and crossed his legs. Elsie gathered napkins left behind after dinner. The officers remained standing until Mrs. MacPhee was seated—erect, both feet on the floor, hands folded on the table in front of her.

"We want to talk with you about Ted Slater."

Elsie said, "We heard you've been talking to all the neighbors."

Martin said, "Sure thing. Shoot."

The MacPhees knew nothing of Slater's private life, had little in common with him, and lived too far away to have seen anything at his house. When Frank raised the question of sailboats anchored near Slater's dock, MacPhee slapped his beefy hands onto the arms of his chair and pushed up. "Come out on the deck. There's something I want to show you." He switched on the outside light and removed the plastic cover from a Schmidt telescope set on a tripod, a permanent installation. "See this? It's the primary reason I stay in Queenstown and commute to Baltimore every day. In the city, there's too much ground light to see a good night sky."

Frank nodded polite assent. "Very interesting.

Joe muttered, "I don't see how the night sky is going to help us catch a murderer on the ground."

"You just might be wrong about that. Hear me out. My field is optics. I study light. And not all light is in the sky!"

Frank decided he would get farthest letting MacPhee follow his own path. "And?"

MacPhee shifted his weight, pointing to the red flasher at the harbor's entrance. "I can see from the flasher there to well beyond Salthouse Cove."

"Can you see Slater's dock?"

"Sure. On a clear day I can count the feathers on the gulls sitting on his pilings."

"So, you certainly could see boats there," Frank said.

"I could if I wanted to. But as I said, optics is my real passion. I care less about the boats than I do about their lights. I work for a company that develops specialized lights for boats—and other vehicles, even NASA spacecraft."

Frank perked up. "Have you seen some special boat light here?"

"I sure have. First, you've got to understand that sailboats manufactured in the last thirty years have fixed anchor lights built into the masthead. I developed the design and my company holds the patent." MacPhee's voice radiated pride. As he talked, he reached through the v-neck of his sweater to retrieve a crumpled box of cigarettes. He continued as he puffed. "Before the masthead light, boats flew the anchor light at the bow, hung just high enough to be seen at night by approaching watercraft. Those older anchor lights—

essentially lanterns—were powered by a six volt battery—and didn't give off much light."

Frank sneaked a peek at his watch. "So, did you see one of these masthead lights or an old one? What are you driving at?"

MacPhee raised a fat, nicotine-stained finger. "Hear me out, Captain. I'm getting to that. What I saw was a bright anchor light not at the masthead. Now, I did my senior thesis at Clarkson on an optical analysis of Fresnel light patterns, but I lived here twenty years without ever seeing a single Fresnel. There are only a handful of anchor lights like that around any more. They were expensive, and the company that made them went belly-up." MacPhee flipped his cigarette butt into the night air. "But I finally saw one! It was Friday, four weeks ago today. I came out on the deck for a smoke after dinner and I saw this bright anchor light hanging on the bow of a sailboat near Slater's dock. The Fresnel is brighter than the old battery style anchor lights by a factor of ten, and I said to myself—"

"Friday? You're sure it was Friday?"

"Yep. I left for California Saturday morning." MacPhee ushered Frank and Joe into his study, where he pulled a photograph out of a file drawer, checked the date, and said, "I was pretty certain that the light was a Fresnel just eye-balling it, but I put my camera on the scope and took an infrared exposure. I mean, when would I get another chance? My technician at work did a spectral analysis, and I reconstructed the lens from the patterns. I was right," he said, apparently happy to have an appreciative audience.

Frank reached eagerly for the photograph but saw nothing there except bands of colored light. "Do you have anything that would show the actual boat?"

"Sorry. Like I said, the boat itself didn't really interest me."

When Frank got home, Claire closed her book, unsmiling. He'd been gone three hours. He apologized. She listened silently to his summary of the evening, then gave his cheek a brush with her lips and said, "I'm going to bed." When he climbed into bed beside her, she seemed already asleep. Maybe being pregnant was making her more demanding. But it wouldn't hurt to pick up some flowers tomorrow.

He felt tired and deflated. This lens business should be unusual enough to track—if not the murderer, a witness who could lead him to the murderer. There had to be a connection, and he'd find it. But where to start? That was his last thought as sleep washed over him.

CHAPTER TWENTY-TWO

"Are you and Mary about to head back to Queenstown?" Mark's brother asked.

"If Mary can tear herself away." Mark looked at her as he spoke. He saw the swell of her breast and the curve of her thigh under her short straight skirt, and suddenly he had a vision of his wife naked, of watching his wife being screwed by his brother. It would be better than the mirrors! Maybe the three of them . . . He choked off an impulse to urge Jason to come home with them. His desires left him shaken, and he said scarcely another word as he and Mary made their farewells.

Mark knew he had drunk too much when he had to try three times to get the key into the ignition. He backed carefully onto the street, thankful that Mary was already dozing off. An alcohol-induced lethargy weighed on him, but he resolved to make it back to Queenstown. He hoped Mary would stay asleep, knew he had to concentrate on driving. He hunched over the steering wheel of the Cadillac, determination in his beefy shoulders and knotted brow.

But he couldn't stay focused on driving. The nightmare visit intruded. Mary hated going to Salem, but why couldn't she at least try to understand that it wasn't his fault? His mother was just like that. Why couldn't Mary shrug it off instead of making his life a misery? After all, it was only for holidays. Who wanted to spend Thanksgiving—or any of the other big holidays—alone anyway? Okay, so she and Mom didn't get all warm and fuzzy together. But what about him? Dad always favored Jason, praised the successful executive, the go-getter at the Kellogg Plastics Corporation. Mark never let that get in the way of spending time with his family. But not Mary. Oh, no. Her mood began to sour days ago, and today it had absolutely curdled—grown worse

and worse from the minute they got out of bed. And then going on—
again—about kids of their own, about adopting kids of their own—as
if that weren't an oxymoron. Why didn't Mary just get over it?

Mark's vision blurred, but cleared a little when he squinted. He'd
squinted through nearly closed eyelids when he saw Jason and Mary.
They thought he was sleeping. He saw Mary batting her eyelashes
at Jason, pressing her leg against his. Jason, motionless, murmured
something Mark couldn't hear. Mary leaned into Jason's arm and said
something indecipherable in return. Watching turned Mark on but
Mary refused to indulge his taste for sex videos. Watching her and
Jason was better. It was real. Mark's own organ had grown big and stiff.
God, he hadn't had such a hard-on in a long, long time. He nearly side-
swiped a parked car and adrenaline coursed through his body.

He shook his head vigorously to clear his senses. He'd done this
before, and he could do it again. Besides, Thanksgiving wasn't a night
for a big police presence. "It's not New Year's Eve, for Christ sake." He
turned off the heater and cracked the window on the driver's side.

He pulled into the driveway about 11:00. "We're home." Mary
didn't stir. He shook her shoulder. "C'mon, babe. It's time to wake up
and go to bed." He snickered and got out of the car. Mary came awake
slowly. When he tried to help her out of the car, she lashed out, batting
his hand away.

Suddenly Mark felt more aggrieved than tired. "Why the hell did
you do that? I got us home in one piece. The least you can do is get
your sorry ass into the house!"

"Oh, just shut up." Mary got out of the car and slammed the door.
"You *know* riding in the car makes me sleepy."

"*Booze* makes you sleepy." In his affront, Mark forgot that he had
wanted her to sleep. "You sure as hell weren't keeping me company on
the drive back. I could've gone to sleep at the wheel. We could've been
killed. I suppose it's just too much to expect you to care about your
husband."

"I said, 'Shut up.'"

He couldn't tell whether Mary was tired or just bored. He sank
into his easy chair, the reality of his marriage closing in on him. The
arousal he'd felt in Salem had disappeared, beaten down by grief that
his wife needed to flaunt herself in front of other men. The loathing he
felt for his own voyeurism, for his prurient arousal, fell on Mary. She

threw her purse on the hall chair without saying a word and proceeded to the liquor cabinet in the dining room. "Don't you know when to stop?"

Mary focused on the bottle as she poured. "A night cap," she said, turning to offer Mark a wordless toast, spilling part of her drink as she did so.

"Don't you want ice? Only dedicated drunks take their whiskey neat."

"I don't need *ice*. I've got *you*," she replied, steadying herself on the back of a nearby chair.

He was sober enough to realize that he should let the remark go, but not sober enough to do so. "And you're a sex-starved bitch! Jesus, you wiggle your ass at anything in pants." He dropped his head into his hands.

Mary glared, one fist on her jutting hip. "Well, it isn't as if wiggling my ass at *you* would do any good. These days you're either too *drunk* to notice or too *limp* to do anything about it."

Mark's face burned, but the truth of it silenced an immediate retort. He again saw his wife sitting so close to Jason that their thighs touched. Mark's voice was a strangled whisper when he said, "I notice all right. I saw you and Jason, how you rubbed his leg and pressed your tit against his arm. Christ, anyone could have seen you! Mom . . . He's family, for God's sake. Have you no decency?"

"Not much." Mary laughed. "Exactly what do you imagine I did with your precious brother?" She cupped her breasts in her hands, thrusting her pelvis at her husband in three quick bumps. Mark averted his gaze.

When she laughed again, he leaped up, grabbed her shoulders, and shook her till her head bobbed. "I've seen you, bitch. I've seen you with Jason and I've seen you with Slater. You're nothing but a whoring slut!" He dropped his hands and turned from her. "I'm glad that son-of-a-bitch is dead. Maybe I'll get a few weeks peace—days, anyway—before you pick up the next guy."

Mark had turned toward the living room when he felt the blow. He touched the side of his head and felt blood as Mary's glass spun to a stop at his feet. He whirled back and slapped her. "You want rough, I'll give you rough!" he said, slapping her again. "I've heard how Slater treated women. Is this how you like it? Is it?"

Mary brought her heel down hard on his foot and writhed out of his grasp. She seemed suddenly sober. Her look was poison, her voice dead level. "You better never raise a hand to me again unless you want some of what *else* Ted Slater got!" The expression on her face made the threat real. Mark forced a laugh. She licked a drop of blood from her lip. "I *mean* it, Mark. If you ever hit me again, you better just *kill* me, because if you don't, I'll sure as hell kill *you*. Maybe not right away. But given the opportunity, sugar, *anyone* can bash somebody's head in, and don't we both just know it?"

The words hung between them, heavy and black. Mark's heart pounded. Mary swayed toward the sofa and fell onto it. She turned her face into the cushions and began to cry. His rage drowned in her tears. He pulled the ottoman close and rubbed his hand across her back until she was quiet. He thought about Ted Slater, about seeing Ted's hands on Mary and lunging at him in rage. His first blow had landed with a gratifying crunch, but after that the fucker dodged and sidestepped and landed punches of his own. Ted had laughed when Mark's nose spurted blood. Mark closed his eyes, conjuring a picture of Ted's blood and brains on the slate hearth. His gratitude to Mary for not telling Pierce about that fight smothered the last of his rage.

CHAPTER TWENTY-THREE

Frank pulled the Slater file to prep for his meeting with Jake. He scanned the Death Certificate: *Immediate Cause of Death – Respiratory Failure; Underlying Cause of Death – Brain Stem Injury*. Frank skimmed the autopsy report—*open skull fracture, carotid artery ruptured, subdural hematoma, epidural bleeding, fractured right mandible, right pupil dilated. Estimated time of death: 7-10 pm, Friday, October 24. Legal time of death: 5:35 pm, Sunday, October 26. Manner of death: homicide.*

Photographs taken during the autopsy made his stomach lurch. He turned them face down and stared out the window. Frank's revulsion wasn't just for Slater, but for a world in which anyone could die that way. He felt grateful that years on the force had not hardened him beyond feeling—and grateful that he had left Philadelphia.

He finished the report from the OCME. The loose ends weighed him down and wore him out. Could Thanksgiving have been only yesterday?

Jake pulled his chair up beside Frank's desk. "Whatcha got, Frank?"

"Nothing startling in the autopsy." Frank pushed it toward him. "You'll be surprised to know that somebody bashed in the poor bugger's head."

Jake grimaced. "Yeah. Big surprise."

"Most of the important stuff is in the Crime Lab Report."

Jake held the file, unopened. "Tell me,"

"His stomach was full–everything from nuts to salad greens. Blood alcohol of .05, maybe from gin and wine. He'd had sexual intercourse recently. And here's one for you, Jake–somebody bit his dick."

The Sheriff winced. "Can we make anything of that?"

"In locker room jokes, lots. Otherwise, no. The bruise was a few hours old when he died, but without knowing how much of a hard-on he had when he was bitten—the 'degree of tumescence' as the report so politely puts it—there's no way to identify the mouth from these marks."

Jake shook his head, grinning. "How about DNA?"

"Yeah, some. No usable secretions on him—too old and adulterated—but there were two profiles on the glass under the body, one his, one unidentified. We've also got a profile on brown hair that Goldberg found by the bed, maybe Smallwood's, but that profile *doesn't* match the one on the glass. That's it for DNA."

"What about the missing poker?"

"Still missing. But the poker's got to be the murder weapon. According to forensics, the wounds were all made by the same weapon, consistent with the size and weight of the other fireplace tools in the set. My guess is, the poker was dumped along with the sheets and towels. When somebody cleans up a crime scene the way they did this one, they sure as hell aren't going to leave the murder weapon. We dragged Queenstown harbor but got nothing." Frank swiveled in his chair.

"So, what else do we know?"

"The prints on the gin bottle and the condom wrapper—besides Slater's—belong to Louisa Smallwood. She said she was in and out in a few minutes, no refreshments, no sex. So she lied about that, and who knows what else?" Frank paged through the report for Jake's benefit. "Fingerprints—besides Smallwood's: Nora Perry, Natasha Brown, Ray Martin, Suzanne Slater, Mark and Mary Sasser, unidentified ones on some liquor bottles, and a different unidentified set on the headboard of the bed."

"Jesus. Can we eliminate anybody?"

Frank stared at the Union Pacific calendar over the filing cabinet. "The cleaning woman's out. She liked Slater, she had no motive, and her daughter confirms that she arrived in West Virginia in time for dinner on Friday. No apparent motive for Perry or van Pelt, either. But technically, Brown is the only one in the clear."

Jake crossed his legs and clasped his hands around one knee. "Jesus H. Christ."

"Some of the unidentified prints may belong to the mystery woman. But frankly, Jake, I feel like a kid playing blind man's bluff, racing around catching air." Frank snapped the file shut. "My guess is she's married. The black lace bra might be hers. Suzanne Slater might have left it behind. Or Mary Sasser or some one-night-stand. It's too big for the Smallwood girl. Other than its size, the only thing we have on the bra is that Brown saw it in his dresser four or five weeks before the murder. So it just may belong to the mystery woman." Frank girded himself for what he was about to say, for Jake's displeasure after. "I'm pretty sure the mystery woman is Lydia Howard."

Jake was silent so long that sweat popped out on Frank's upper lip. Finally Jake said, "How sure are you? You go around saying things like that, you better be pretty damned sure."

"Look at the evidence. Her boat was in Queenstown harbor several days last spring. None of the neighbors got a good look at his current lay. And she reacted pretty strongly when I mentioned that Slater was still married." He paused. "She was out in Nora Perry's boat when Slater bought the farm. I don't have anything tying her to the scene, but she might know something."

"So you want to confront her. Jesus H. Christ." Jake tapped his toe. "I expected you to solve this thing weeks ago."

Frank refused to be baited. He patiently went over it all again. "I was hoping the stuff about sailboats would turn into a clear lead, but so far, no. Smallwood is captain of the college sailing team. She sailed to Queenstown a couple of times about a year ago. But she doesn't have access to the boat that was there last spring. The Howards use that boat. And all of the college boats—including the Howards'—were already out for the winter when Slater bought it. A boat with a distinctive anchor light anchored there Friday night, but I haven't found a way to trace it to Smallwood or Lydia." Frank retrieved the report. "Anyway, from the blood spatters and the wounds, the murderer was right handed, five foot eight or taller. The footprints are puzzling, though. The ones that tracked blood aren't as distinct as Goldberg thought they should have been."

Jake scowled at Frank. "Both our asses are on the line on this one, Frank. You do know that, don't you? And I'm still worried that you heading up a case that involves your old flame could come back to bite us."

Frank held onto his temper with both hands. "I already told you, Jake: there's nothing throwing suspicion on Nora. Zip. Nada. Zero. Besides, that's been over for ten years!"

Jake looked at him for several seconds. "I'm just saying, that kind of gossip dies hard in a town like this. There could be some who would say it wouldn't be zip, nada, and zero if someone else was doing the looking. If we don't solve this thing, come election time next year, we could both be unemployed." He looked at his watch. "I've got to get to Chestertown. Keep me posted."

Frank slumped in his chair and wallowed in indignation at the length of small town memories and the human capacity to distrust law enforcement. He put it aside to think about Lydia as the mystery woman, and whether she was even there that Friday. He had to do something to get the case moving. Now. Catching people on Friday of a holiday weekend would be tough, but he'd see as many as he could. Louisa Smallwood would have to wait until after the Thanksgiving recess, but some of the others might be around. He'd try to shake something loose.

Frank and Joe mounted the narrow stairs and pounded on Ray Martin's apartment door. No answer, but they could hear voices. Joe knocked again, then tried the knob. "Unlocked."

Ray faced the TV, his back to the door. "Hello, Ray. Frank Pierce."

"Christ, man, I know who you are." He scowled at Joe in the doorway. "And I sure as hell don't remember *him*."

"This is Sergeant Joe Jamieson." Frank took a seat uninvited. "It's about this Slater murder." He considered Ray's lethargic disregard. Depression, maybe? If he could get a better feel for what made the man tick, he might be able to eliminate him as a suspect—or jump him to the top of the list. Frank tilted his head toward the wall behind Martin's chair and Joe moved to lean quietly against the wall. A glass rested on the table at Ray's elbow, adding another white ring to the array already there. "Isn't it a little early in the day to be hitting the bottle?"

"It's always happy hour somewhere." Ray fished a cigarette from a half-empty pack. "And what better way to spend my time off? I sure as hell can't afford to go anywhere this time of the month." He punched the TV remote and highlights from Macy's Thanksgiving Day Parade flashed across the screen. "Funny how the casinos won't let you play without money."

"So you've got lots of time to talk to me," Frank said. Maybe the bourbon would lubricate the interrogation.

Ray jutted his chin toward the TV but turned his eyes toward Frank. "What's that got to do with the price of tea in China? You gonna try to get me to incriminate myself?"

"Could you incriminate yourself, Ray? You got something to hide?"

"Hell, no." Ray shrugged. "Just nothing to say." He lit the cigarette he'd been holding and flipped the used wooden match into a wastebasket beside the TV table.

"Talk to me anyway, Ray."

He jutted out his chin. "I've got nothing to say about Slater's murder, so get the fuck outta here." He slouched back in his chair, mumbling about an attorney.

Joe threw a warning look at Frank, a caution Frank ignored. "So don't talk about Slater. Talk about your family. No harm in that."

Ray coughed, rolled his eyes, and reached for the bottle of bourbon on the floor beside his chair. "Fat lot of good it'll do you." He stared at the TV screen. "My old man was a drunk. A mean drunk. He walked out on my eighth birthday." Ray shifted his stare to a spot over the TV. "It was a while before we realized he'd gone for good that time." He spoke with the quiet heat of long-held hatred. "That turned out to be the best birthday of my life."

Frank let the ensuing silence ride. Ray still sounded sober, more testimony to his tolerance for alcohol. "Mama did the best she could for me and my sister. The woman was next thing to a saint. She could have married again, a fine looking woman like her, but she never did. Said her children would never have a stepfather as long as she could keep body and soul together. She lived with me till about a year ago." Tears roughened Ray's voice. "Christ, I miss her. It breaks my heart when I go see her and she doesn't even know who I am."

Frank searched Ray's face. "You came to West College six years ago?"

"Yeah, that's right."

"And before that you were a building inspector for Fairfax County. What about the trouble you got into there?" Frank asked.

"That was nothing." Ray stretched his legs out and crossed his ankles. "I wasn't an engineer or anything, but I was good enough, sort of mechanically inclined. I missed a code violation when I signed off on an electrical refitting job. Another inspector had it in for me, told our boss I'd taken a bribe. I didn't! No evidence that I did. But there were rumors, and the county let me go. Like I said, there wasn't any proof. I think my boss felt bad about losing me. He recommended me for the bookstore job here."

"I know how gossip can grind somebody up. I've been there myself. I feel for you." Frank made his voice sympathetic. The grain of truth in his comment was the furor in Centreville when he started dating Nora after college. But mostly he was just playing Ray. "You know what's odd, though? Going from building inspector to bookstore manager. How did you swing that?"

"What? You want my whole damn history? I worked for a bookstore chain for ten years. But the pay wasn't as good as a county job, and the benefits couldn't hold a candle. But I never had any trouble there!"

Frank raised his eyebrows. "So, what about the rumors here? The robbery?"

"I keep telling you—telling everybody. I didn't rob the damned bookstore!"

"Sure, Ray, sure," he said soothingly. Feinting toward the window, he whirled back to Ray, his voice menacing. "Suppose I told you I have proof."

Ray took a drag on his cigarette, squinting against the smoke. "Go fuck yourself. If you had proof, you'd have arrested me by now."

"Too bad. Robbery's better than murder. How did your fingerprints get on the bottle of bourbon at Slater's place?"

Ray tongued his upper lip and turned his head away. "I told you. I was there the night before he was killed—when I went to tell him I couldn't pay any more. He said we should sit down, talk like civilized men. He invited me to help myself to a drink, so I did."

"Last time you said he threw you out. Now you say you were drinking buddies. Which is it?"

Ray stubbed out his cigarette. "Both. First we had a drink, then he threw me out."

"How about the prints on his desk?"

"Maybe I sort of leaned on it."

"Inside the drawer?"

Ray squirmed in his chair and cast a sideways look at Frank. "Okay, okay. It was when he went to take a leak. I was looking for my markers. Without them, he'd have no proof I owed him anything. But the bastard must've hid them." His voice slid into a whine. "I didn't find a one."

Three times Frank went over Ray's account of his movements the night of the murder but got nothing new. Even so, he said, "Ray, I think your sorry ass is in a sling on this one."

"Check the casinos. They know I was there, goddamnit!"

Ray struggled to his feet, his thoughts circling. "Fuck those bastards. Nobody's gonna get Ray Martin," he promised the empty room. He yanked open the kitchen drawer where he kept important papers and fumbled through them. He found it: a chit from the Golden Rainbow Motel for two nights, Friday and Saturday, October 24 and 25. He'd produce it if he had to, if they didn't find the place he'd really stayed. He waved the slip of paper. "You gotta get up pretty early in the morning to put one over on Ray Martin, *Captain* Pierce. When you told me Atlantic City was no alibi at all without proof, what'd ya think? I was gonna roll over and play dead?" Ray laughed. "All I had t'do was call my old buddy at the Rainbow and say, 'It's payback time.'" He put the receipt back in the drawer, sliding it under a pile of bills with exaggerated care. Returning to his chair, he patted himself on the back for keeping his cool—first with van Pelt and later with Pierce. How the hell did the professor tumble to the blackmail? But he didn't let van Pelt rattle him. Well, maybe for a minute. But he had a story ready by the time Pierce asked the same questions. "Pretty damned funny, Pierce thinking he could trip me up just hammerin' on the same questions. Well, that sure as hell didn't work. Nosiree. Fuck those bastards. Nobody's gonna pin anything on Ray Martin."

Suzanne Slater agreed to see Frank mid-afternoon. He pressed hard on her whereabouts the Friday of the murder. The owner had verified her story: except for lunch, she wasn't out of the shop all day. But even if she worked until five, she could have made it to Queenstown in time to kill him.

"We found your prints on the desk at your husband's house. How did they get there? And when?"

"They must be ancient! I haven't been in the house for a couple of months."

Madeline Goldberg thought the prints were fresh, but there's no solid way to date prints. Frank scowled. "Exactly when were you there last?"

"Mid-September." Suzanne looked him in the eye, speaking quietly. "I went to deliver his copy of the separation agreement. He'd said he would sign."

"What did he say when you gave him the papers?"

"He wasn't there. And I didn't expect him to be. I knew he had a class. I just left the papers on his desk."

"If you didn't want to see him, why didn't you just mail them? Or send them by courier?"

"I . . . Those couriers charge an arm and a leg. And the mail's slow. I was in a hurry to get the agreement signed—so I could get on with the divorce." Suzanne studied her fingernails. "Besides, I wanted to check his desk—for the document on asset distribution we'd agreed to. I needed to give it to the judge. God, what a nightmare. I'd already signed. He hadn't."

"That must have pissed you off."

Suzanne shifted her gaze to her other hand. "I realized that leaving papers there wouldn't do any good. So I took everything to his office. But nothing worked with Ted. We had a big row. Clyde Barnes, the bastard, loved every minute of it."

"Professor Barnes says you told your husband that you had to have money, says you yelled that you could kill him. Is that right?"

"Clyde Barnes is a damned gossip! Anyone can say something like that in the heat of an argument. It didn't mean a thing."

"And what about needing money?"

Suzanne shifted in her chair. "I'm not in financial difficulty. Not any more. I just wanted to get what rightfully belonged to me."

"Exactly when did you break into your husband's house?"

"I didn't break in. The door wasn't locked. I think he went back to leaving it unlocked after I got my belongings."

"So when was it that you didn't break in?"

"I told you: at least a month before he died!" Suzanne's face turned an ugly, mottled red. "I don't remember the exact date. It was around the middle of September."

"And that row in his office was the last time you saw your husband?" Suzanne nodded. "Did you talk with him after that?"

"Oh, yeah. Too much. He called at least once a week about one thing or another—but really just to remind me he was in the driver's seat."

Frank flipped back through his notebook, underlining phrases and making checkmarks, while Suzanne watched, her body tense. Frank looked up, his face bland. "There's just one more little thing. We found a black lace bra in the bedroom dresser. How would your husband come to have that, all this time after you left?"

"How the hell should I know? It probably isn't even mine."

"I believe it is. I believe you two had sex for old times' sake—probably more than once—and that you were there a lot more recently than a month before he was killed."

"I don't give a damn what you believe!" Suzanne stood, fists clenched. "Am I under arrest?"

"Not yet."

"Then get out. I'm through answering questions."

Frank persisted until Suzanne picked up her purse and flung open the front door, calling over her shoulder, "Lock the door when you leave."

En route to Queenstown, Frank mulled over the interview with Susanne Slater, strong and controlled beyond her years. He was torn between irritation and admiration.

Mary Sasser met him at the door. "Oh, my. Aren't *you* the busy bee—and on a holiday weekend, too." She giggled. "Did you have a nice Thanksgiving?" Face powder and blusher didn't quite hide a blue bruise on her left cheek.

"Yes, thanks."

Mark joined them in the living room just as Mary said, "So, what brings you here today, Frank? Did you miss me?" Mark winced and glared at his wife. "I was just *kidding*," she said, glaring back.

"I'm afraid this is serious," Frank interjected.

"What could be that serious?"

Mark snarled, "For God's sake, Mary, give it a rest. He's here on business." He motioned Frank to sit.

Their tension filled the room like fog. Frank sat on the couch. Mark dropped down next to him. "I want to know when you two were last in Slater's house."

"Oh, for goodness *sake*," Mary said. Mark looked like he tasted bile.

"Mark, your prints were found on a bottle of Benedictine."

Mark shrugged. "So? We were there for cocktails and dinner. After dinner, Ted set out cordials and asked me to serve."

"When was that?"

"Probably a couple of months before the murder."

"And you haven't been in the house since then?"

"No. I told you, I didn't like him and I didn't trust him. There was no reason to visit."

Mary added, "I'm sure Mark's right. That must be when it was." Her smile reminded Frank of a toothpaste ad.

Frank said, "We found *your* prints on an empty tuna fish can in the garbage bin. Are you telling me those are from the dinner party a couple of months ago?"

The question hung in the air until even Mary seemed to realize there was no way out. She cast a beseeching look at Mark. "I had lunch with Ted the day before the murder."

Mark jumped up. "Goddamn it, Mary, I told you . . . !" He drew a deep breath. "Where else did you find Mary's prints?"

Mary whispered, "Nothing ever really *happened*."

Frank said, "We found a black lace bra in his bureau."

Both stared at him. Mary said, "It probably belonged to Suzanne."

The muscle along Mark's jaw rippled, he breathed fast and shallow. "That bastard deserved to die!"

"And maybe you saw to it that he did," Frank said quietly. The remainder of the interview added nothing. Frank left feeling that his only major accomplishment was sowing marital discord.

Monday morning Frank told the Dean of Students that he wanted to speak with Louisa Smallwood in private, on campus rather than at the Sheriff's Office if possible. Technically, he didn't have to go through the dean, but Jake wanted him to do whatever he could to keep town-gown relations civil. The dean checked Louisa's class schedule and suggested one o'clock. "I'll call back to confirm that after I check with Louisa. You can use the little conference room beside my office."

Frank spent the morning reviewing the case. Many questions plagued him, especially who left the fingerprints Goldberg found on the headboard of the bed, and whose DNA was on the glass beneath Slater's body. The dean's call interrupted his study. The meeting was set, the conference room reserved for an hour.

The dean greeted Frank, hand extended. "Hi, I'm Doug Jay. I don't think we've met. Come in. Have a seat." Frank followed him into the office. "Is Louisa Smallwood a suspect in Ted Slater's murder?"

"She's a person of interest. What can you tell me about her?"

"I can't release confidential information, but I'll tell you what I can." He said that Louisa was extremely bright, majoring in economics with a minor in psychology. She was a Trustee Scholar, which paid most of her tuition. She was on the work-study plan, employed in the college's food service since her freshman year. She was active on campus, captain of the sailing team. There was no record of any disciplinary action against her.

Frank thanked him just as Louisa arrived. The dean showed them into the conference room, closing the door as he left. Frank said, "Sit down, Louisa. Try to relax."

"Relax? You've got to be kidding. What do you want?"

"Let's start with what you haven't told me."

Louisa looked startled. "What do you mean?"

"I mean, tell me why you went to Slater's office a couple of weeks before he was murdered. What were the two of you fighting about?"

"We weren't fighting." Louisa massaged her forehead as if she had a headache, and Frank wondered what story she would come up with next. "I was tending bar at the Trustees reception that first Friday in October when he—he baited me, about my umbrella. He knew how important it was to me. He came up to my station, with half a dozen people standing around, and said, 'That item you left with me, Louisa. Feel free to come by for it any time that's convenient.' I said—you know, because of the bystanders—I said, 'Thanks. Or maybe you could bring it to campus.' He said, 'I'll try to remember to do that.' He smirked and left. After that, nothing. So I went to his office."

Frank layered his voice with impatience. "Yeah, yeah. But what happened in his office?"

"Nothing! I mean, I asked for my umbrella, told him it was really important to me. He laughed and said he had grown quite fond of it, that he might just like to keep it as a souvenir of all we'd shared. I was so frustrated—I felt so helpless—I just burst into tears. And then I left."

Frank shook his head. "You expect me to believe that? You lied to me before. I think you're doing it again."

"I haven't lied." Her voice quavered, but she met his eyes steadily.

"You told me you had nothing to drink at Slater's house."

"I didn't."

"We found your fingerprints on a Bombay Gin bottle. You lied." She started to speak but Frank held up a hand. "And we found your fingerprints on a condom wrapper on the night stand by his bed, too." Frank leaned forward, grim faced, disbelief reverberating in his tone. "You lied about sex. And I don't like that."

Louisa's hands began to shake. She wiped away a tear with the sleeve of her sweatshirt, a painfully childlike gesture, but her voice was firm when she said, "I didn't lie. I swear." She took a deep breath. "I went for my umbrella. But when I got there, I just really wanted to punish him. So I dumped his gin down the sink. I know it sounds pretty lame, but that's what I did." She looked at Frank. "The condom was part of the punishment, too. I was going to put pinpricks in some of them but then I realized that that would hurt his partners, not him."

"So, you had nothing to drink and no sex?"

"Like I told you before, Ted wanted to have sex but I refused." Color spread across her cheeks.

"So why was the condom wrapper empty?"

"Empty? *I* don't know."

Frank tilted his head, his eyes boring into her till she shifted in her chair. "And now you've told me absolutely everything?"

"Yes. Except . . ." She spoke barely above a whisper, looking only at her clenched hands. "I told him I was having my period, thinking that that would turn him off. It didn't. He grabbed me by the hair and pushed my head into his lap, saying it was one way or the other. The whole thing made me sick. I . . . bit him. He yelled—cursed at me—and hit me. That's when I ran out."

"You bit his penis." He took her through the story three times, asking again and again about this detail or that, but Louisa swore that there was nothing more to tell. Finally Frank said, "We found some hair on the floor beside the bed. Maybe it's yours. I'd like a strand or two to test." She yanked out a couple of strands of hair. Frank put them in an evidence envelope. "Professor Perry told me that you're a sailor—co-captain of the sailing team."

The shift in direction seemed to surprise Louisa, but for the first time during the interrogation, she offered a faint smile as she replied, "Yes, I am."

"Did you learn to sail at West?"

"Oh, no. My cousin Jack taught me when I was nine. He had a little eight-foot catboat. I learned on that."

"Where do you sail now?"

"When school's in session, just on the Corsica. That's where our racecourse is. We used to have longer races, but a student drowned in the Chester River. He was practicing on his own, nothing official, but after that, the college restricted us. It's too bad but I can see the point. A lot of the kids are pretty inexperienced and the Chester can boil something fierce in a fifteen knot breeze."

"Have you ever sailed into Queenstown harbor?"

Louisa nodded. "Before the racing boats were restricted to the Corsica, I took one of the Flying Scots in there."

"Tell me about a Flying Scot."

She seemed to choose her words. "Well, they're built for racing, sloop rigged, fitted with dagger centerboards, about nineteen feet long overall. They're really stripped down for speed."

"Have you ever anchored overnight in Queenstown?"

"You don't anchor overnight in a Scot." She sounded amused. "There's no place to sleep."

"I see," said Frank. "Have you ever anchored there in another boat?"

"I don't have access to another boat. Besides, I never stayed at Ted's overnight." Her brow clouded. "I mean, except that one night last December."

"How did you get to Slater's house during the months the two of you were involved?"

"He'd pick me up and drop me off by Carnegie Library. The same day." Louisa seemed calm, relieved to have the interview winding down.

Frank leaned on his desk, mulling over the day's interviews. For the first time, he thought Nora might be right about Louisa. In his gut, he felt she was telling the truth now. He hoped so, for the girl's sake and for Nora's. Still, he wasn't ready to count her out completely. If Louisa was no longer the prime suspect, who should be? Jake would ask that first thing, and Frank had no idea what he would say.

CHAPTER TWENTY-FOUR

John Howard tied his red, white and green striped necktie. "I told Frank Pierce I'll speak to Nora about staying out of the Slater investigation."

Lydia paused with an earring halfway to her left ear, studying John's reflection in the bedroom mirror beside her own. "Why?"

"Apparently she's championing the Smallwood girl. And has taken it upon herself to help." He frowned at the knot of his tie. "She and van Pelt actually questioned people." John turned to her, smiling. "My guess is she's just being an academic, sure her brain has more horsepower than anyone else's. But you can see how that might ruffle official feathers. So I said I'd speak to her."

Lydia addressed his reflected profile. "But not tonight. This is a party, after all." Twice a year the Howards invited employees and their spouses, trustees, and important townspeople to a gala at Ozmon House. "Besides, if Frank hasn't mentioned it recently, chances are it's no longer a problem. You might not have to deal with it at all." Lydia paused. "You don't want to risk antagonizing one of your references for the Waldorf presidency unless it's absolutely necessary."

"Mmmm. Maybe you're right."

Virtually everyone treated the president's annual winter party as a Christmas party, and dressed accordingly. Lydia, however, would wear a simple blue wool dress and diamonds. She refused to don the cliché red, white, green, or any combination thereof during this season.

She returned to the task of selecting jewelry. For the Cutlers, gift-giving occasions always meant jewelry. She fingered a ruby and pearl brooch, a gift from her parents when John was inaugurated as president of West College. Daddy knew it as much her achievement as John's and had marked the occasion accordingly.

Yes, Daddy was proud of her. And of John. She paused, watching John's reflection as he left. At first Daddy had resisted John Howard as a suitor, urging his only child to "marry a nice Jewish boy." But apart from religion, John's Virginia pedigree and professional prospects were all Sam Cutler could have wanted. Nothing pleased him more these days than to go to a meeting of the Institute of Scrap Recycling Industries and drop a comment or two about "my son-in-law, the president of West College."

When Daddy was pleased, he was also generous. Not that John would ever take money from the Cutlers—not directly. When he was in graduate school, his scruples in that regard had made her life more difficult than it needed to be. But he couldn't really object to personal presents, and the tradition of jewelry for Lydia was strong. Lydia returned the laden jewelry box to her dresser drawer. John had never objected to his in-laws' philanthropy, either: Sam and Rachel Cutler donated handsomely to every academic and charitable institution with which Lydia affiliated. It had not been difficult for her to have a friend of a friend make the search committee at Waldorf College aware of this. It might not help, but it couldn't hurt.

Turning from the mirror, she moaned softly. Ted Slater had been a big mistake. He could have ruined their chances at Waldorf—their marriage—their lives. She shuddered. She'd planned to end the relationship when they moved to Waldorf—and even if they didn't. She wished he'd known that. Now, with luck, even John need never know. And maybe the Waldorf presidency would put her and John back on their old footing.

The student workers' chatter and laughter drifted up the stairwell, recalling her to her role as hostess. Catching sight of her brooding countenance in the mirror, Lydia replaced her frown with a mask of contentment and ease. When she descended the ornately carved staircase, anyone watching would have thought her regal. No one *was* watching—but a great actress performs as much for the role as for the audience.

A flurry of activity filled the downstairs. Sky dashed through the kitchen door, nearly colliding with Louisa. "Hello, Weezie Small. Help me with my cummerbund?" Sky grinned.

Louisa took the strip of bright blue, grinning in return and saying brightly, "I've heard that most men your age are actually able to dress themselves."

"What's the fun in that?" Their eyes met and both looked quickly away. Sky joined a group discussing the Flyers game. Louisa returned to the preparation of hors d'oeuvre trays. It was typical of their interactions since Thanksgiving—since Sky asked her to marry him and she refused. Sky said what had happened with Slater didn't matter, but Louisa feared that it would always stand between them, would eventually destroy them.

"Okay, folks, move it, move it, move it. It's time to be out there." The director of food services was always hyper, especially at the president's big parties.

No guests had arrived when Louisa moved to the corner of the large gathering room where a chest of drawers on casters stood away from the wall. The drawers were fake, but from the back she had access to shelves lined with liquor bottles. Sky waited behind another portable bar in the dining room, but she resolved to avoid him. Why make misery? She busied herself getting the bar ready and taking in the grandeur of the gathering room—the tall windows fitted with interior shutters, the double fireplace, the restfulness of the gray-green woodwork against the off-white walls. She hoped someday to have a house like this.

Clyde Barnes and Josh Allison arrived early and stood before the fireplace in the dining room, drinks in hand. Over the mantel hung an etching of the campus with an insert of Old Main in the lower left corner. Clyde gestured toward the etching with his drink. "I like that etching, Josh. It's one of your best. You gave it to the Howards, didn't you?" Josh nodded. "When?"

"A couple of years ago—when they celebrated their fifth year at West."

"Wasn't that about the time you were promoted to full professor?"

That sort of sly innuendo made Clyde one of the least liked members of the faculty. Josh refused to be baited, stared stonily at Clyde, and said, "Yes."

He turned to leave but stopped when Clyde whistled, then said, "How about our illustrious bookstore manager?" Josh followed Clyde's gaze to Ray Martin, near the refreshment table in the gathering room, talking with a small group of people. Josh noticed that Ray was even better groomed than usual. His dark suit and white shirt looked tailored, his hair recently cut. Clyde continued, "He really needs to get more involved on campus—stop being such a loner."

"Come on, Clyde, it's the season for a little Christian charity. Everyone knows he's had a rough time—his mother's illness and all."

"Word is, he has a drinking problem."

"I've never seen him drink," Josh protested.

"Oh, not around campus, not at a party like this. But I heard he's a different man with his card-playing buddies—really knocks 'em back, life of the party. You wouldn't suspect it, would you? A straight-laced sod like that leading a double life?" Clyde laughed. "And speaking of card-playing buddies, have you heard anything about the murder case?"

"Give it a rest, Clyde. This is neither the time nor the place." Josh escaped before Clyde could launch an attack on anyone else.

John Howard circulated among his guests, smiling and chatting. The winter party served as his bellwether for the second half of the academic year, and this year, all signs looked good. If this turned out to be his last year at West College, he wanted it to be very good indeed. "Hello, Louisa. My usual, please. You're looking a little tired."

"Oh, well, it's the end of the term." She pulled a glass from the tray at her side.

"How was your fall semester?"

"Good. I finished the research for my honors thesis and I've started the writing." As she talked, Louisa picked up the marked scotch bottle and poured a hefty slug of apple juice over ice. Every student who tended bar knew of his deception, but everyone else said he was a man who could drink hard and keep his head.

John nodded. "Glad to hear it. Thanks." He lifted his glass to her before joining Van and Nora.

Lydia talked with two of the vice presidents, smiling and nodding, making appropriately happy noises as they discussed enrollment projections. The West College budget was tuition driven, so enrollment—whether up or down—was always a hot topic. The conversation demanded only part of her attention. The other part monitored the progress of the party: the student workers, the buffet service, the tenor of guests' moods.

When John approached Van and Nora, Lydia joined them, too, arriving just as Van said, "Actually, discussion of the murder is way down the list. Our primary topic is sailing. I am trying to convince Nora to publish her ship's logs." He bowed ever so slightly in her direction. "Good evening, Lydia. It is a very successful party, as always." Nora made a gesture of protest but Van talked on. "No, no, I am serious. You would need only to expand the prose a bit, emphasizing things the weekender might find interesting. For example, the story behind the sunken pilings from the old ferry wharf in Queenstown Harbor." Lydia caught her breath, but Van's voice remained mild when he continued, "Or the lighthouse off Bloody Point, knocked cockeyed by ice flows; that old sunken skiff on Swan Creek; how Ordinary Point got its name. You could write about the challenges of night sailing. You could make it more personal with anecdotes from various sails, recipes, the challenges of cooking a three-course meal on a two-burner stove." Van was on a roll and Lydia breathed more easily. "I envision something like *Blue Highways*. Only on water, of course. Who wrote that? William Least Heat Moon?"

Nora laughed. "Forget it. I'm so not in his league. The sailing logs are for my personal perusal, for chilly nights in the off-season when I want nothing more than to curl up with a book I can put down without regret any time sleep overtakes me." She turned to Lydia. "On a more seasonal subject: I'm going Christmas shopping in Philadelphia next week. Would you care to join me?"

"Maybe. I'll let you know tomorrow."

John glanced across the room. "Will you excuse me? Liz Johnson needs to leave early and I want to speak with her before she goes." Lydia watched as he strode away, the muscle along her jaw tightening.

"How's the fund-raising going?" Nora asked.

Lydia answered automatically, her eyes on John and Liz. "Oh, the money is coming in, but it's been very demanding. Rounding out the funding for upgrading residence halls has kept John on the road quite a bit." She turned an appreciative gaze on the copper and gold embroidery of Nora's jacket. "That jacket is spectacular."

Nora's laugh sounded self-conscious. "Thank you. I wanted something as festive as the occasion."

"Well, it's always refreshing to see someone at this party who isn't done up in Christmas colors!" She smiled. "I suppose I should mingle. I'll talk with you tomorrow."

Elizabeth Johnson and John were laughing when Lydia turned in their direction. Her gaze swept from Liz's sensuous, laughing mouth to her strappy sandals, trying to remain objective. Liz's laugh served her well as a fund-raiser. Her strengths dovetailed perfectly with John's. Whereas John was always the president, Liz could be many things to many people. Not that she was acting, just calling forth different aspects of her personality. John dropped his hand onto Liz' shoulder. When he said, "Liz, we need to get closure with the Bennets and the Cabots," Lydia released her pent up breath.

Lydia said farewell to Liz just as Frank and Claire arrived. "I'm so glad you both could come."

John shook Frank's hand and clapped him on the shoulder. "It's good to see you socially. We're a bit ahead of you, but that way to the bar." He waved toward the gathering room. Lydia wondered whether she needed to warn Frank off talk of the murder but said nothing. He probably knew better.

When Frank saw that both bars were staffed by people involved in the Slater murder investigation, he couldn't resist a little police humor, though he didn't expect Claire to appreciate it. He leaned close to her ear and whispered, "Fortunately, Slater was bludgeoned, not poisoned. Even the investigating officer should be safe with a drink." He steered Claire to Louisa's station. "Hello, Louisa."

Louisa nodded. "Captain Pierce."

"Let me introduce you to my wife, Claire." He put his hand on Claire's shoulder. "This is Louisa Smallwood, a student at West. And a bartender as well, apparently."

"How do you do? What would you like to drink?"

Frank ordered bourbon and water. Claire asked, "What are your choices for the designated driver?"

"Seltzer with lemon or lime, Coke, 7-Up, orange, tomato, or apple juice." Louisa talked fast. Claire ordered a 7-Up. Louisa poured their drinks without looking at Frank. Not a sadistic man, as soon as they had their drinks, he steered Claire's toward Sheriff Bentley.

"Why, Frank, I haven't seen you at one of these shindigs before. Evening, Claire."

"Hello, Jake." Frank smiled wryly. "Nothing like a little murder to up my importance to the college."

Jake scowled. "Zip it, Frank. Not here, not now."

Frank stifled an urge to tell his boss to stuff it. Did Jake really think he would say something inappropriate to a civilian? He wasn't about to talk murder with any of the partiers. Keeping his tone neutral he said, "How bad is it?" His gesture included the party at large.

"Not bad at all. The food's excellent, the talk's generally interesting. It'll do you good to mix in these circles."

Typical. Jake was always the politician.

Lydia joined them "This is a party now. You two are *not* to talk shop."

Jake gave a mock salute and said, "Yes, Ma'am," and Frank allowed himself to be led away for introductions. Apparently he wasn't the only one with murder on his mind.

As Claire moved heavily toward the buffet, one hand on her distended belly, a brassy blond approached, glass in hand, her eyes and smile too bright for this to be her first drink. "Why *hello* there!" She extended her hand in a theatrical sweep. "You must be Captain Pierce's *wife*. You are absolutely gorgeous—but then such a handsome man *would* have a beautiful wife, wouldn't he?" Claire was speechless. "My name is Mary Sasser. I was a neighbor of poor Ted Slater's! Maybe your husband has mentioned me?" She sounded hopeful.

"He isn't supposed to talk about the people involved in an investigation."

"Well, no, I suppose that wouldn't be very *professional*. And I'm sure Captain Pierce is *terribly* professional."

Before Claire could think of an appropriate response, a big burly man took Mary Sasser's elbow. "Honey, I think it's time we get a little something to eat." He nodded to Claire. "Excuse us, please."

Mary spoke a little more loudly. "But, Mark, honey, I was just getting acquainted with Mrs. Pierce. Don't you even want to *meet* her?"

Mark looked pained. "How do you do, Mrs. Pierce? Come along, Mary." He tightened his grip on Mary's elbow and turned her toward the buffet table. His voice was low but intense. "What are you thinking, Mary?"

Mary hissed, "You're hurting my *arm!*"

The man loosened his grip with a perfunctory, "Sorry."

Claire saw Frank across the gathering room, looking in the direction of the grand piano. Turning to follow his gaze, she saw a tall red-head whose hair was intricately wound and plaited, with wispy curls around her face and at her neckline. The woman talked animatedly and laughed joyfully. Claire joined her husband. "Do you know that woman?"

"Yes. Nora Perry."

"The woman who directed your honors' thesis?" Claire looked again. "She seems awfully young to have been one of your professors."

"West College was her first job after graduate school. In my junior year, I was a student rep on the search committee. She was twenty-five then." Frank faced Claire and added, "If I remember correctly. The man with her is Josh Allison, a member of the Art Department. He's new since my time, but you've probably seen some of his work—in shows here, in Chestertown galleries. One of his etchings hangs over the fireplace in the dining room. Would you like to see it?"

As Frank tried to change the subject, the pieces fell into place for Claire. Nora Perry must be the faculty member Frank had had a crush on when he was an undergraduate. Was she also the white woman Frank had dated—had wanted to marry—after he returned to Centreville? Even though Frank's family—or Centreville gossips—would have told her a hundred times over, Claire's pride had always kept her from trying to find out something Frank was so unwilling to discuss. But now she said, "Aren't you going to say hello to Dr. Perry?"

Frank studied her face before he said, "Would you like to meet her?"

"Yes. Of course I want to meet someone who's been so important to you."

Was it her imagination, or did Frank fortify himself with an especially deep breath before saying, "Okay. You got it." He took her elbow and moved toward Nora and Josh.

Nora turned in their direction and smiled. "Frank. Happy holidays." She turned to Claire. "You must be Claire. It's hard to believe we haven't met."

"Claire, let me introduce Nora Perry and Josh Allison."

"Hello. Frank tells me you both are on the faculty at West." The ensuing exchange might have been heard among any four people at the party. Claire took the opportunity to surreptitiously inspect every square inch of Nora Perry. She thought she knew why Frank had never mentioned that she was so young. Or so attractive. Claire suddenly felt intensely aware of her own pregnant profile.

Lydia had announced early in John's presidency that they both turned into pumpkins at midnight. From eleven o'clock on, either John or Lydia lingered near the front door, bidding farewell to their guests. They had the ease and understanding—the synchronicity of intention and action—that come from thirty years of shared success. People departed in twos and threes and small groups, making their way down the icy path, telling each other what a wonderful party it had been.

John lay on his side, watching his wife. Her jewel cases were back in the top drawer of the dresser, the blue gown back in the closet. When she slipped into bed beside him, he turned off the light and rolled onto his back. Lydia moved closer and turned onto her side so that her hips and feet touched him. The contact was familiar, the intimacy comforting. John said, "The evening went well, don't you think?"

"Yes, it did. But if we invite this many people again, we need to use the glassed-in porch, too. Tonight was a bit crowded."

"Mmmm. Good idea."

"You didn't say anything to Nora, did you?"

"About the murder investigation? No. You were right. This wasn't the right time."

"She and Van came together tonight. They're together a lot these days. Do you think something is going on there?" Lydia yawned.

"I have no idea."

John plumped up his pillow. "Frank and Claire seemed to fit in well. Maybe we should put his name forward for alumni trustee. We need more minority participation, and he seems to have a good head on his shoulders. His age is about right. We couldn't expect him to give much money, but then alumni trustees sometimes can't. Indirectly, though, his presence would help with charitable and educational foundations, and with some individual solicitations—anywhere minority representation is noticed. And he's interested in West." Lydia said nothing. He patted her haunch and said, "Good night, my dear."

Lydia's answering, "Good night," was muffled by the bedclothes.

John rolled onto his side and tried to remember when they stopped kissing goodnight. It had been years ago.

John had known Lydia was the right woman for him within a week of meeting her. They married a month after Lydia was graduated from Randolph Macon Women's College. Her parents gave them a honeymoon trip to Europe as a wedding present, but as soon as they returned from Rome, John was back in graduate school. Living on his graduate student stipend was a big adjustment for Lydia—a *big* adjustment. But she'd soldiered on, taking a secretarial position in the English Department at Duke, not complaining more than other grad students' wives.

John's parents had tried to argue him out of marrying the daughter of a Harrisburg, Pennsylvania scrap recycler right up until the last possible minute when a gentleman might honorably have withdrawn. But when John and Lydia named their first son James Leonard Howard after John's father, it made all the difference. So something good came from the trials of that unplanned pregnancy.

The memory of that time still made his adrenaline spike. He shifted positions and slowed his breathing. The need to get a job that could support a wife and child had put almost unbearable pressure on him to write his dissertation and put graduate school behind him. He'd never been as desperate again, thank God. From his first job as an assistant professor of mathematics at Lawrence College, their lives had gotten better and better. Lydia was his partner, his confidante, his best friend. There was nothing he didn't share with her, nothing except that one desperate act.

Now John needed a change in his life. They both needed it. If not this year, then next. At first, the West College presidency had felt like the pinnacle of his career. But after accomplishing so much—improving the physical plant, the endowment, enrollment—he needed new challenges. More importantly, his marriage needed them. It was still solid. There was no doubt in his mind about that. But things hadn't been right between them for a year or more. For awhile, he was concerned about her drinking, but that seemed to be under control now.

John shifted restlessly, seeking to still his night thoughts. He could see the curve of his wife's hip in the moonlight, smell her fragrance. He thought about touching her hair but did not. He didn't know why she had become involved with Ted Slater. If she never talked about it—if he never knew her reasons—he could live with that. He just wanted his life back the way it had been. She thought he didn't know. He didn't, in any explicit, factual way. But he was too attuned to his wife's tone, her moods, her body language not to know when her relationship with Slater became intimate, too attuned not to attach his own explanation when she stopped accompanying him on fundraising trips. Still, he'd avoided real, concrete evidence, right up to that Friday night. The low, insinuating voice on the telephone saying that his wife was with Ted Slater, that he'd seen her, that she could be in "a shit load of trouble" if she wasn't careful. There had not been another call.

John pulled his knees into the fetal position. Slater's death had only partly cleared the way for them. Whatever had led to the affair in the first place still had to be dealt with. And it would be.

He turned on his side and fitted his body to his wife's like a spoon. He put his arm around her waist and breathed her scent. He slept.

CHAPTER TWENTY-FIVE

John put aside the Sunday paper as Lydia entered the den. She looked pale. "Are you all right, my dear?"

"Of course," she said, her voice listless.

John patted the sofa beside him and she sat. He took her hand. "What is it?" Lydia stared at the carpet, saying nothing. "Tell me what's bothering you."

"I'm worried about the Waldorf presidency."

"Is that all?" He shook his head. "We have a good chance—a very good chance. But the on-campus interviews aren't for another two and a half weeks. It isn't like you to get all worked up so far ahead."

"Suppose it doesn't work out."

He kept his tone bland. "We could do worse than stay at West. If I don't get the Waldorf offer, it isn't the end of the world. We'll find some other presidency."

"But not this year." Lydia drew a deep breath, exhaled slowly, and picked up the front section of the paper.

As the afternoon wore on, Lydia grew inattentive. His efforts to draw her out rebuffed, John eventually turned on the TV. By early evening, Lydia had made several trips to the portable bar in the gathering room, excused herself after eating little supper, and retired to bed. He wondered if his earlier conclusion that she had her drinking under control had been premature. He suspected that Ted Slater was heavy on her mind, and perhaps heavy on her heart. Should he broach the subject? He weighed the pros and cons. The sound of the TV faded as he nodded off. By the time he went to bed, Lydia was asleep.

★　　　★　　　★

John had set out breakfast in the kitchen nook when Lydia came downstairs. Her "Good morning. You're up early," was subdued—as one might expect of someone slightly hung over. They lingered over coffee, reading Monday's newspaper, discussing the latest Middle East crisis, bemoaning the Baltimore Ravens' failure to make the play-offs. Everything seemed to be back to normal as they discussed their plans for the day and week.

John left for his office in Old Main, stepping into a mild winter day. Most of the ice that covered the flagstone walk on Saturday had melted. Small banks of plowed snow lined the campus roadways, the fluffy whiteness turned to slush and streams of melt-water. The place felt deserted. In his second year at West, John had convinced the Board of Trustees to give employees an extended winter holiday with pay. The Board had been reluctant, but John argued that increased productivity both before and after the holiday recess would be worth it. The change made him popular on campus and the results were all he had hoped they would be. John came to the office most days during the recess and accomplished twice as much as when college was in session. His vice presidents often came in as well, for the same reason. As he swung open the heavy door and stepped into the foyer of Old Main, he put aside thoughts of Lydia and Waldorf and focused on the morning's agenda.

John reviewed the fund-raising report Liz had left on his desk. Flipping through the pages, he reflected on year-to-date achievements, progress on the Alumni Fund, and Corporate and Foundation Gifts. Bottom lines far ahead of last year. His spirits lifted. Work seldom failed to provide an escape.

John dialed Liz's number. "I just read your report. Great work . . . Are you ready to discuss our January visits? . . . No, no. I'll come to your office."

Liz's door was open. "Good morning, John. Your party was lovely—the best yet."

"Thanks. We thought it went well—in spite of the snow." John took a seat across from Liz at the little conference table.

She cleared her throat. "Before we get down to business, there's something else we need to talk about." Faint pink tinted her cheeks, her usual smile and ebullience missing. "Lydia called me last night. Did you know?"

"No. What was that about?" Liz looked away. "What's wrong?"

She bit her lower lip. "Lydia thinks you and I are having an affair." She stood abruptly and fled to the window.

John was too stunned to speak. An affair with one of his vice presidents—with any employee—was unthinkable. That Lydia thought him capable of such a thing—and that having thought it, she did not talk to him—wounded John. He felt acutely embarrassed that his wife had made a spectacle of herself. Angry that she had involved him in such an awkward situation. Liz turned back, tears shining in her eyes. Under other circumstances, he would have patted her shoulder. But Lydia's accusation left him motionless. His relationship with Liz could never be the same.

Liz said, "I just . . . don't know where this is coming from."

John pulled himself together. "I don't know either. Exactly what did she say?"

"She said, 'I've had my suspicions for quite awhile now.' She said she knows what we get up to when we travel together." Liz ran a hand through her short blonde hair. "She . . . she sounded like she'd been drinking." Liz looked away. "She said that you seem happy when you're around me—relaxed, laughing—that you're not like that with other women. That's as specific as she got."

John and Liz had an exceptionally good working relationship. They shared each other's hopes for the institution they served. But his feelings for her were nothing like his love for Lydia. He said, "I'll talk with her." If Lydia suspected an affair, why did she stop going on fundraising trips with him? He'd attributed her coolness to decades of marriage. And, more recently, to Ted Slater. His loyalty to Lydia would not allow him to share these thoughts with Liz—with anyone. He leaned forward. "Liz, you're the best VP for Development I could have. Don't worry. Everything will work out."

Liz dried her tears as she walked briskly back to the table. "Okay, then. Let's get to work." John heard the forced lightness.

They set a schedule for visits to donors in New England, speaking more brightly and smiling more often than the task warranted. John recalled the old adage: act the way you want to feel. It didn't seem to work. He left the office mentally rehearsing the forthcoming confrontation with Lydia.

On the walk home, he considered several possible openings and thought about the right time to broach the subject. He steeled himself to behave normally in the interim.

Lydia was working at the kitchen counter. John joined her, kissing her cheek as usual in greeting. She said, "Hello, my dear. Did you have a good meeting with Liz?"

"Very productive." Did she think Liz wouldn't have told him about the phone call? Did she not remember making the call?

Before he could decide what to say next, Lydia continued. "Good. Listen, Frank called. He wants to talk to us, before Christmas if possible." Lydia carried their lunch plates to the table. "I told him that if he didn't hear from us, we'd see him about two o'clock this afternoon."

John wanted to clear the air with his wife, but it was not a discussion to have boxed in by an appointment. He shifted mental gears and said, "That's fine. Perhaps I'll have a chance to feel him out about serving on the Board of Trustees. I called Victor before I left the office, and he seemed pretty certain that he could get the Committee on Board Membership to bring Frank's name up at the January meeting."

Lunch passed pleasantly enough on the surface, although talk was sporadic and John had little appetite. Lydia seemed distracted. Perhaps he'd attributed too much of Lydia's behavior this past year to Ted Slater. Perhaps the problem—or a big part of it—had been her belief that he was having an affair with Liz. A suspicion that he didn't know his wife as well as he had thought left John shaken. He searched for an innocuous topic. "Why didn't you accept Nora's invitation to go shopping in Philadelphia?"

"Oh, it's a long drive. I just don't feel like it." Lydia shifted in her chair. "I do have a little more shopping to do, though. Would you mind if I went to Chestertown tomorrow?"

"No, of course not. It would be good for you to get out for a few hours."

"It might take the better part of the day. The stores will be crowded and the clerks tired." Lydia talked as she cleared the table. "Honestly, shopping for presents, sometimes I regret our decision to celebrate both Christian and Jewish holidays."

The ringing of the doorbell ended the stop-gap conversation.

CHAPTER TWENTY-SIX

Lydia escorted Frank into the front room. John said, "Good afternoon, Frank."

"Good afternoon, sir." Frank put a briefcase on the floor and took a notepad from his pocket.

Lydia smiled but mentally braced herself. From Frank's formality, she inferred that the interview was official business, and likely to be unpleasant. Both men declined her offer of coffee.

John said, "So, what can we do for you?"

"I have a few more questions about Ted Slater's murder." Lydia felt blood rise in her cheeks. Frank leaned forward in his chair. "This is awkward, given your positions and my ties to the college. But I'm sure you want to cooperate."

Lydia said, "Of course," striving to sound natural. She poured coffee for herself.

"Paul Zimmerman told me that *Confederate* is assigned to you, for your use only. Is that right?"

"Yes," she and John said in unison, exchanging surprised looks. John continued, "The boat belongs to the college, but many people think it's ours."

"So, have you sailed her into Queenstown harbor often?"

John said, "No. I seldom have time to sail more than an hour or two. I don't go out of the Corsica unless it's a real vacation, a sail well beyond Queenstown."

Lydia shifted her gaze from John to Frank. "I sail often, especially when John's away. But I've never sailed into Queenstown."

Frank cocked one eyebrow. "According to Slater's neighbors, *Confederate* was anchored there last spring."

Who could know that? Lydia decided to brazen it out and lifted her chin. "There must be some mistake. The boat they saw couldn't have been ours."

"I have a photograph of the boat in Queenstown harbor. The Department of Natural Resources identified it as *Confederate*."

Frank's tone said as clearly as his words that more denials would be fruitless. Nevertheless, Lydia answered vehemently. "I tell you, there must be some mistake. And what does a boat anchored there months ago have to do with anything anyway?" she demanded. "You said you wanted to talk to us about Ted's death."

"Tell me about your affair with him."

"We weren't having an affair!"

Frank leaned forward. "We can do this the easy way, here, in the privacy of your home. Or I can take you down to the Sheriff's Office. One way or the other. But I will get the truth. So, tell me about the affair."

Lydia drew herself up. "Do what you have to do. I have nothing to say."

"Okay." Frank rose from his chair. "Let's go."

John turned to her. "Lydia . . . I already know. Here is better. Tell him."

She read certainty in his eyes. "Oh, God, John." She had planned what she would do if John ever found out about Ted—what she would say, how she would say it. But those mental rehearsals involved only the two of them. She stared past the white knuckles of her clenched hands. What did John know? How did he find out? How much did she absolutely have to tell? Both men waited silently for her to speak.

Lydia straightened her shoulders, took a deep breath, and unclasped her hands. She spoke directly to Frank, her voice low and calm, her gaze steady. "You've heard that Ted Slater could be very charming. He chose to be very charming to me." Her lips twisted. "One might say he danced attendance at every opportunity—attentive, complimentary, witty. He was a pleasant addition to parties and we invited him often. That's all there was to it until last January."

She paused, struggling to clear her thoughts. "Are you sure you don't want coffee, Captain? John?" She was gratified to see that the carafe she held was steady as she refilled her cup. She drew another deep breath. "I'd rather not go into painful details. They couldn't be important to your case."

"That's not for you to decide," Frank snapped, then added more gently, "When did you last sail into Queenstown harbor?"

Lydia shifted slightly. "I sailed to Queenstown only that once, the first time I took *Confederate* out last spring. John was on a fundraising trip with Liz Johnson. I anchored just off his dock and we stayed at his house. Queenstown harbor is small, and I realized that if I anchored there repeatedly, it would be noticed." Her smile was humorless. "Apparently repetition wasn't necessary. So that's it. A common story— pitiful, perhaps, but it has nothing to do with Ted's death."

Frank said, "I'll take that coffee now." Lydia poured and Frank added milk and sugar. "When was the last time you saw Slater?"

Frank's tone was friendlier and Lydia willed herself to relax. "I last saw him privately—I assume that's what you mean—Thursday of the week before he died." She ventured a look at John. He sat motionless, his face an expressionless mask.

"Tell me about it."

Lydia again glanced at John. He seemed to be bracing himself to hear what he'd said he already knew. "Ted has—had—a Tuesday-Thursday class that ended at noon. I parked at the shopping center in Chestertown. He picked me up there and we drove to his house. We had a bite of lunch and then . . ." Lydia clasped her hands. "Surely you don't need details."

"You made love."

Lydia spoke quietly. "Not love. Sex. We had sex. He drove me back to the parking lot afterwards and I was home before five."

"How was your relationship? Any problems?"

Lydia tried to read Frank's expression. "You mean, did I want him dead? No, of course not!"

"So everything was just as hot and heavy as ever between the two of you?"

Lydia stifled an angry retort. Her voice was shaky and low when she said, "Not exactly." She hoped John would believe her. "The fact is, I realized months ago that the affair was a mistake. I wanted to get my marriage back on the old footing and having an affair with Ted wasn't the way to do it."

"What did Slater say when you told him?"

Lydia fixed her eyes on Frank. She couldn't look at John. "I hadn't told him. He wasn't a man to take rejection well. He could have made it very—awkward—being faculty and all. I thought he would tire of the affair soon—couldn't imagine that he wouldn't. Otherwise, I counted on our move to Waldorf to put an end to it."

"So you hadn't seen him for the eight days before he was murdered." Frank tapped his pen against his notebook.

"That's right. Except in public. There was a lecture in our visiting artist series that we both attended in the middle of the week, but we barely exchanged greetings. We always kept our distance at such events. I don't remember seeing him any other time."

"What about the weekend he was killed? Did you sail to Queenstown?"

She chose her words carefully. "I was supposed to have Nora Perry's boat from Wednesday to Sunday. But then John's trip was canceled, so I came home early, around noon on Saturday."

"And Friday?"

"I was anchored in Swan Creek, a mile or so past Gratitude Marina."

"Were other boats anchored in Swan Creek that night?"

"Not when I arrived. After supper I stayed below, reading Waldorf College materials. I heard an engine and looked out. I couldn't see much of the boat coming up the creek, just its running lights. It must have been about nine o'clock. But they couldn't see me either."

"Did you speak to anyone? Could anyone confirm that you were anchored in Swan Creek on Friday night?"

Lydia straightened her back. "I said I was anchored there. That should be enough." The strength of her voice surprised her.

"Not by a long shot. Your lover was murdered." Lydia couldn't help wincing. "So is there any way to substantiate your story?"

"I spoke to no one. I have no corroboration at all unless you count the log, and I suppose you wouldn't since I wrote it myself."

"What log?"

"Nora's ship's log. Everyone who sails on *Duet* keeps a record of courses taken, places visited, notes on the weather—things like that. I recorded my sail in her log."

"Well, it's better than nothing," Frank said. "Where's the log now?"

"I assume Nora has it."

"I'll ask her." He turned to John. "Now, then. You said you knew about your wife's affair. When did you find out? And how?"

John seemed to shrink into himself. "I just knew. We've been married thirty years. I know my wife." John looked at her. "A year, year and a half ago, Lydia was acting—I don't know. I guess I'd call it acting with reckless disregard. Drinking. Moody. Then last fall I began to notice a change when Ted was around. She was more vivacious, more engaged. At parties she talked to him more than to others. She followed him with her eyes." John looked at Lydia again, twisting her heart. She blinked back tears. It was the tone John used when his emotions ran high but he wanted to appear cool and detached. She ached at being the cause of that tone. "Last January—in conjunction with the winter meeting of the Board of Trustees—we had a party. Ted was one of the faculty members present. That's when I knew they had become— intimate. The way they smiled at each other. A change in tone when they talked. Things like that. I know it isn't proof. I didn't need proof. I knew."

"What did you do about it?"

"Do? I bided my time. And I applied for the presidency at Waldorf."

Frank snorted. "You expect me to believe you weren't angry—you weren't jealous."

John shrugged. "I was hurt. I was bewildered. But there was no reason to be jealous." It sounded remarkably like the truth to Lydia. "What Ted Slater had with my wife was nothing compared to our marriage." She relaxed a fraction, marginally reassured.

"He had sex with your wife. You call that nothing?"

"I'm just saying that sex . . . sex isn't who we are. What we have is stronger than a physical union. Believe me or not, that's the truth." John tilted his head. He actually smiled a little. "We all live under the same sky, Frank, but we don't all have the same horizon."

"And you never said anything to your wife or to Slater?"

"No."

Frank shook his head, in disbelief or disgust, it wasn't clear which. "So when did you last see Ted Slater?"

"I saw Ted on campus the day before the murder. I expected to be out of town until Sunday, a fundraising tour of New England, but

Ms. Johnson called the night before we were to leave. Two of our three appointments had been canceled so we decided to reschedule the whole thing."

"When was that?"

"Wednesday night."

"Then you were in Centreville during the next four days?"

"Yes."

"So when you saw Ted Slater, what happened?"

John recrossed his legs and shifted his weight onto his other elbow. "Nothing unusual. He was coming out of the student center as I was going in. He was surprised to see me, said 'I thought you were off raising big bucks for dear old West.' He said he'd just made an appointment for the next week, that there was something he'd been meaning to take up with me."

Lydia gasped and both men looked at her. "Oh, God. He really was going to . . ." She fought to control the tremor in her voice. "To tell you about us."

Frank turned back to John. "Did Slater say what he wanted to see you about?"

"No. I said I could see him that afternoon or just about any time the next day. But Ted said, 'No, no. Next week will be fine. I hope you enjoy your weekend as much as I'm going to enjoy mine.'" John grimaced. "Then we went our separate ways. As nearly as I can remember, that was it."

"Where were you that Friday night?"

"I was home."

"And is there anyone who can vouch for you?"

"I wouldn't think so. Unless someone walked by and saw me through the window. I was around and about earlier, but I stayed home that night, reading and listening to WBJC. I didn't talk to anyone."

Frank said he would need fingerprints. "I can take them now if you want." They nodded wordlessly. Frank took their prints and thanked them for their cooperation.

Lydia closed the door behind Frank and sagged wearily against it. "Oh, John, what have I done? I should never have . . . I'm so sorry." She burst into tears.

"For God's sake, Lydia, get control of yourself."

"I . . ." Lydia covered her face with her hands.

John paced back and forth. "You've been drinking like there's no tomorrow."

"I . . . Everything is just so . . . I should never have taken up with Ted." For a moment she couldn't speak through her anguish. "Maybe, if you hadn't fallen in love with Liz . . ."

John stopped, wide eyed. "I've never loved Liz! How could you think such a thing?" She could only stare at him, hope and joy struggling against disbelief. "And if you did think it, why didn't you come to me? Why the hell did you call Liz?"

"Call Liz?" Lydia bowed her head and closed her eyes, as the hazy memory drifted back. "I'm so sorry. It was a stupid thing to do, but I couldn't stop myself. I can't remember much of that call. I hope I didn't say anything too awful to Liz. "

"Lydia, listen to me." John gripped her shoulders. "The only way we can survive this is to stick together. If you aren't careful, your drinking will ruin us. Now it's all I can do to look Liz in the eye. Things will never be the same with her."

"I'm sorry, John. I am." Her voice was thick when she added, "I never wanted to hurt you. You must know that." She rested her hands on his chest. "I've always tried to do what's best for you, for the children. For us. Even with Ted." She started to pull back but John put his arms around her. "We were careful. Most of the time we met in Delaware or Baltimore, so no one would know. I realized months ago that I had to get him out of my life. Out of our lives. I'd give anything to just—undo—Ted. Oh, God. If it weren't for me, you would never have . . . I've screwed everything up so royally."

"Shhhh. I meant what I said to Frank. I've come to terms with Ted Slater. With *everything*. Don't worry. It will be all right. I promise." Lydia sobbed and John folded her into his arms, murmuring indistinguishable words of comfort against her hair—words she wasn't sure he could really mean.

CHAPTER TWENTY-SEVEN

Just before noon, Nora parked off Arch Street, a couple of blocks from the Philadelphia Convention Center. A raw wind blew. The flurries predicted for later weren't supposed to amount to much. Lydia had declined her invitation, but Christmas shopping alone would be more efficient anyway. She crossed Broad Street, hurrying toward the river. "If it weren't for the last minute, a lot of things would never get done," she muttered.

She went first to Reading Market. She wandered the aisles, taking in the sights, sounds, and smells. Fresh fish eyed her warily from beds of ice, whole fowl hung beside sausages and hams, every kind of baked goods from seven grain bread to cream puffs filled one case after another, fresh vegetables and fruits reflected the tastes as well as the bounty of South America and Australia. She inspected a supply of esoteric kitchen utensils from France, Italy, and China. And then there were cookbooks.

The revolving bookcase beside Nora's favorite chair stood half empty, the books piled on the ottoman and scattered on the floor. In her study, desk drawers and filing cabinets hung open, books and papers helter-skelter, two shelves of personal journals and ship's logs spilled across the floor.

Nora left the cookbook stalls feeling sheepish that the first purchase of her Christmas shopping trip had been for herself. She set off in pursuit of lunch, abandoning all thought of healthful eating to splurge on a German knockwurst with kraut at a busy counter. She devoured her treat perched on a backless stool, elbows braced on the counter, coat unbuttoned, the meal washed down with Dortmunder Aktien. Something about the Market made everyone hurry. Three men elbowed for her stool when she slid off. A lead-gray sky and a strong westerly wind greeted her when she turned right on Market and headed toward Lord and Taylor's.

A clear glass bowl filled with red, green, gold and silver ornaments fell from the top of Nora's drop-front secretary. A black boot crushed two of them and gloved fingers rifled the pigeonholes and drawers.

Nora left Lord and Taylor's at 2:30 lugging two shopping bags of presents. Driven by a capricious wind, snowflakes danced in the air and disappeared as soon as they landed. Nora's fourth grade teacher had talked about Wilson "Snowflake" Bentley who lived in Jericho, Vermont, and discovered the six-sided crystalline structure of snowflakes. She marveled at the mystery of human memory, how something from her childhood came suddenly to mind.

She meandered toward Liberty Plaza, a few blocks west of City Hall, swallowing the recurring aftertaste of knockwurst. During one of their sails, when *Duet* pounded against the weather all morning, Van had said, "Take chocolate and warm Coke for lunch. It is the only diet that tastes the same coming up as going down." He claimed he'd learned that secret at the Maritime Academy, but she half suspected he'd been pulling her leg.

Black boots stepped boldly across Nora's bedroom. The book that was Nora's current bedtime reading thumped to the floor. Gloved hands jerked open the drawer of her bedside table.

En route to Broad Street, Nora stopped at the Calderwood Gallery. "Just looking," she said. She spent enough time silently wandering around the shop to discourage the constant attendance of the manager. Eventually she returned to stand before a smallish painting—perhaps twelve by sixteen inches—which up close seemed completely abstract but which with distance resolved into a landscape. The ambiguity of the painting intrigued her and she bought it.

The gloved hand swept two pale green wineglasses to the floor. The booted foot kicked an unbroken candlestick under the table.

At 5:10 Nora paid the parking lot attendant and drove toward the Schuylkill. Traffic was heavy. The combination of rush hour and snow wore on her. By the time she got to Wilmington, she needed renewal. She bought coffee at the rest stop on the Delaware Turnpike. Thank goodness Route 213 through Galena and Chestertown had little traffic. She stopped at Cloonan's in Centreville for gas and a quart of milk, greeting Gary Cloonan and both of the other customers by name—definitely a rural comfort. In ten more minutes she was home.

Nora gathered an armload of packages and struggled through the utility room to the kitchen. She dumped everything, including her coat, on the kitchen counter and turned to the refrigerator. It was 8:30 and she felt famished.

With unthinking economy of movement, she set a pot of minestrone on the stove. She would watch a little TV and retire before the eleven o'clock news. She put placemat, tableware, napkin, and a tin of Melba toast on the oak table, hunger narrowing her focus. A few minutes later, she carried a bowl of soup and a glass of wine to the table.

Glancing toward the far end of the room, she saw the empty revolving bookcase. "What the hell?" She took a step forward before she froze in place, thoughts churning. *Oh, my God!*

Her tongue felt cottony. She looked from the books on the ottoman to the ones on the floor beside her chair—books that had been in the bookcase when she left that morning. She glanced toward the other end of the room. The drop-front secretary was in disarray. She stood motionless, listening, asking the silence whether she was alone. She took one slow step back and then another, her heart pounding like a long distance runner's.

Nora inched backwards toward the kitchen, her breath coming hard. She threw one look in the direction of the hall and another toward the door to the dining room, afraid to turn her back on any part of the house she had not yet entered. She bumped into the counter and gasped convulsively. She snatched up her purse and—just in case—a fine long butcher knife. She ran to the garage, wrenched open the car door and lunged into the driver's seat, pushing the button to lock the doors. Her hand trembled as she fumbled with the ignition key. "Shit, shit, shit!" she shouted, searching the floor for her key ring. She forced herself to take slow, deep breaths, got the key into the ignition and backed the car out.

Nora stopped under a street light. She dialed 911 on her cell phone and tried to calm her breathing.

The dispatcher at the QAC Sheriff's Office beeped Joe Jamieson and Sy Brown. "Nora Perry, reporting a B&E at her house. She lives at the end of Corsica Point Lane but she called from her car. She'll wait for you where Corsica Point joins 304. She doesn't know whether the intruder is still in the house."

By the time Jamieson and Brown got to Nora's car, she was calm enough to wonder whether she had overreacted. They drove in tandem to her house and pulled into the driveway. Jamieson said, "You wait here till we check things out." Nora felt a spurt of adrenaline as they drew their guns. The men went through the garage and into the house through the utility room door. They found no one.

Nora joined them in the kitchen, feeling a little foolish.

Sy Brown frowned at Nora, then dismissively resumed his straight ahead gaze, managing wordlessly to convey "featherheaded broad." Nora's cheeks flamed. Joe spoke easily, "Well, now, I'd say someone was after something here. We'll have to dust for prints and all. But first you need to walk us through, tell us what's missing. Let's start here," he said, waving toward the door to the dining room.

Entering the dining room, tears burned Nora's eyes. The doors to the china cabinet and the corner cupboard hung open. Depression Glass, candle sticks, and crystal vases lay at their feet, a riot of pink, green, yellow, blue and crystal. Someone had swept everything within arm's reach onto the Oriental carpet—thankfully, breaking only two wine glasses. The highest and lowest shelves were unscathed. Her maternal grandmother's carnival glass vase rested safely on the fireplace mantel, the arrangement of white carnations and nandina berries nodding undisturbed over the litter. Two chairs were overturned. But all her silver was in the wooden chests and silver-cloth bags. As far as she could tell, nothing had been taken.

The intruder had rifled the drop front secretary by the sitting room door. Some papers had been stuffed back in the drawer, others strewn on the floor among bits of broken glass Christmas balls. "This is where I do household accounts—pay bills—keep the information on appliances—things like that. I'll look carefully when it's okay to handle things, but I can't think of anything that would interest a thief."

In her bedroom, only the bedside table seemed to have been searched. The $250 she kept in the drawer was gone, but her jewelry armoire was undisturbed. "This is just the costume stuff," Nora said. "Silver, wood, bone, stone beads . . . nothing of much value." She went to the closet shelf where she kept her good jewelry—pearls, semiprecious stones set in gold, and a few pieces with diamonds. Everything was there. She just didn't understand. "Why wouldn't a thief take these things?"

Sy cut in impatiently. "It wasn't that kind of robbery. It's obvious that someone was in search of paper—and cash, maybe. But probably a legal document, photos, incriminating correspondence. Do you have anything like that around?"

Nora shook her head. "I have legal documents—a living will, the deed to the house, things like that—but nothing worth anything to anyone else."

Her upstairs study showed signs of a thorough search, desk drawers and file cabinets open, papers and books disarranged. Whole shelves of personal journals and ship's logs littered the floor. As far as Nora could tell, nothing was missing.

Returning downstairs, the three of them sat at the oak table. Joe said, "So, Professor, let's take this from the top. When did you leave today? When did you get home? What did you do when you got here?"

Nora pushed aside the bowl of soup, now cold. She recounted all she could remember of her actions. Her earlier discomfort returned, adding a note of defensiveness when she said, "I had no way of knowing whether someone was still here. And from what I've read and heard, the absolute worst situation is being *alone* with someone who intends bodily harm."

Sy rolled his eyes but Joe assured her that she had done exactly the right thing. "Now, tell me, who knew you were going to be gone?"

"No one who would do this! I told Van—Hendrick van Pelt—and Lydia and John Howard at a party Saturday night. One of them might have mentioned it to someone. Or we might have been overheard by any one of dozens of people. I might have mentioned it to others. I don't remember. It wasn't a secret."

"Was the house locked?"

Nora raised her left eyebrow and smiled ruefully. "Sort of. Everything was locked except the front door."

"You don't lock the front door." Sy's comment held an edge of disbelief.

Joe gave him a withering look and said, "Well, lots of people around here don't. So, the sliding glass doors along the back of the house were locked? The garage door? And all the windows?"

"Yes, that's right."

"So, as far as we know, the burglar most likely came through the unlocked front door. Who knows you don't lock the door?"

"Pretty much everyone who's ever been here," she blurted.

"Do you have any idea who might have burglarized your house, or what the burglar might have been looking for? Have you pissed anyone off lately?"

Nora considered the question, toying with the unused soupspoon. After a moment she said, "I'm completely flummoxed. Nothing seems to have been stolen except the cash. Nothing of value was destroyed— not even the Depression Glass, except for one pitcher—and the two wine glasses." Tears misted her eyes as she thought of the Greek Key pitcher she had hunted for so long, now smashed. "As far as I know, no one has anything against me personally unless it might be a disgruntled student." She paused to think. "One student was especially put out this semester—Dave Langdon. His family is rich, he's a super athlete, and I guess he thought a passing grade was a given. Well, it wasn't, and now he won't graduate this year. He ranted and raved at my office last week, said I'd be sorry and all that." Nora paused again. "But I can't believe he really did anything. I've been teaching for more than twenty-five years. Lots of students get upset but no one has ever actually done anything. And besides, Dave wouldn't need to steal money."

Joe pursed his lips. "You never know. Taking the money could be a cover. Does this kid live around here?"

"In Baltimore, I think."

"That's within striking distance. We'll check it out." He closed his notebook. "That about wraps it up for tonight. Leave everything just as it is. I'll have a couple of people here first thing in the morning to dust for prints. They'll print you then, too. And tomorrow we'll check outside for whatever might be there. I don't want to screw things up prancing around in the dark. But before we go, we'll check for signs of forced entry."

On his way out, Joe said, "Now you just relax and get a good night's sleep. B&Es like this, the perps don't come back the same night." That possibility had not occurred to Nora. She was not reassured when he continued, "But take all reasonable precautions anyway." He pushed the lock button on the front door with his pen as he and Brown left.

On the way to their patrol car, Sy lit a cigarette. Joe said, "Hey, you know Jake doesn't want us smoking on duty."

"Yeah, well, that's not reasonable. I don't smoke in the car, and who's to be the wiser? Unless you rat me out."

Joe shook his head. "When you get done, put the butt in your pocket. We don't want to find evidence tomorrow morning that an officer of the Queen Anne's County Sheriff's Office burglarized Professor Perry's house."

CHAPTER TWENTY-EIGHT

Frank picked up Joe's report on the burglary the next morning. "What the hell?" He flipped through the pages and then called Nora. "Are you all right?"

She said, "Oh, sure," but in an uncharacteristically wan voice. "I wasn't even here when it happened."

Frank reigned in his adrenaline and tried to sound casual. "I'm busy this morning, but how about I come by this afternoon?"

"That would be fine. But I'm okay. Really." Frank listened for the message under her words and thought she sounded stressed. "I just feel a little—I don't know—violated? Some stranger going through my things gives me the creeps."

"If it makes you feel better, you can believe it was a friend who trashed your house."

"That's not funny, Frank."

"Yeah, well. Police humor. Sorry. I'll see you after lunch. You hang tough now."

Despite his attempt to lighten Nora's mood, the burglary made Frank uneasy. In his experience, the perps in random vandalism ripped up furniture, smashed TVs, dumped kitchen cupboards, slashed paintings, urinated and defecated on the victims' clothes. None of that here. He drummed his fingers on the folder. Someone in it for profit would take electronics, jewelry, and anything else that could be fenced. A break-in this selective smacked of personal malice. In spite of the ten-year hiatus in their relationship, some things never changed. He felt protective.

Seated at her oak table, coffee mugs steaming, Nora realized that Frank's concern comforted her. "Even after all these years, I feel that you're one of the best friends I've ever had. I need a friend right now." She reached across the table to squeeze his forearm. "Thanks for coming."

Frank laid his hand over hers. "Nora, I'll always be here for you. Always." She tried not to show her surprise. He cleared his throat and let go of her hand. When he continued, his tone was again impersonal. "Now, tell me about this burglary," he said.

She repeated what she had told his detectives, then slumped back in her chair. "And that's all I have to say about the blankety-blank burglary," she added, forcing a chuckle.

"Have my detectives finished up here?"

"As of this morning, thank goodness. But I can't say cleaning up fingerprint powder and broken glass is my idea of a fun Christmas Eve day! Let's talk about something more pleasant. What's up with you?"

"Claire's feeling bulkier every day. Having a baby is something better to have done than to be doing. Other than that, it's the Slater case. It just hangs on."

Nora noticed that she found a discussion of the murder more appealing than a conversation about Claire's pregnancy. "Do you have any hot new suspects? Or newly hot suspects? Tell all."

"Now, Nora, you know I can't talk about suspects."

She grinned. "I'll talk about them then. I've been thinking a lot about how the murderer got to Ted's and how he—or she—left." She ticked off the possibilities. "And I think the Sassers were acting suspicious the other night."

Frank glared. "How many times do I have to tell you not to play detective?"

Nora made a face at him. "I didn't do a thing! But I'm not deaf and blind. Didn't Claire tell you about the Sassers? At the Howards' party?"

"What about them? That Mary was tipsy?"

"Don't you think it's odd that Mark got so bent out of shape because she talked with Claire?"

"Maybe not." He looked at her, head tilted. "Lots of people don't want the police to notice them."

"But maybe so." Nora tilted her head, mimicking his gesture and tone. Years ago, she'd often teased him that way. Excusing herself, she went to the kitchen for more coffee. Frank remained at the table aligning, as best he could, the straight edge of the placemat with the outer edge of the oval table. "What do you know about Lydia's relationship with Slater?"

She stopped, coffeepot in hand. "Why? Do you think Lydia is involved in Ted's murder?"

"There you go, jumping to conclusions. I didn't say anything about Lydia Howard being involved. But to solve this thing, I need to know the man—his life, his loves, his hates. So, were they good friends? Spend time together?"

Nora refilled their mugs before answering. She considered telling him about seeing them together at a party, but what she interpreted as intimacy seemed too ephemeral to mention. She knew nothing concrete. "I don't really know."

"Speaking of Lydia, she said you have a ship's log that includes info on every sail *Duet* makes." Nora nodded. "I'd like to read it."

In spite of Frank's off-hand tone, his request sent Nora's antennae up. "Sure. Van has it now, but I'll get it back. Why do you want it?"

Frank ran the fingers of both hands through his hair. "I've been pushing this investigation for two months, getting nowhere. Too many people wanted the guy dead."

Nora made her own connections between his questions about Lydia and his request for the log, and decided to give his change of subject a pass. She said, "Suspects in this case seem to come up like flotsam on a rising tide."

Frank ran one finger idly around the rim of his mug. "Yeah, a rising tide of suspects. And those damned sailboats. I need to find the one Martin MacPhee saw anchored off Slater's dock the night of the murder. Maybe there's a witness, at least. God knows, I need one."

Nora pushed the milk jug and sugar bowl toward him. "So what do you know about this boat?"

"Not much about the boat itself. Grube said it wasn't white. MacPhee's a specialist in optics and he said that the anchor light had a Fresnel lens."

"So?"

"Apparently they're rare these days. It's the only one he'd ever seen on the Chesapeake. But how the hell am I going to find it?"

"Maybe Natural Resources could help."

"Nope. Their records don't include auxiliary equipment." He sounded exasperated.

"Buck up," she said, punching his shoulder. "You'll get a break soon."

Frank's cell phone rang. He checked the caller ID and answered "Claire? What's up?" Frank listened intently. "When?" He pushed his coffee mug away, his hand shaking. "How bad is it? . . . But if it's too early to tell . . . Of course I'll come . . . I'll be right home. You start packing." Frank closed the phone, looking dazed.

"What is it?" Nora put a hand on his shoulder. "Are the boys okay?"

"They're fine. It's Pop. He's had a heart attack." Frank didn't elaborate. Typical. "I'm on my way to Philadelphia. I don't know how long I'll be away—several days, at least, depending . . . I'll be in touch when I get back. Take care." On his way out the door he added, "Listen, don't broadcast anything I said about the case. And remember that I don't want you messing around in it." He paused on the threshold. "And lock your doors."

Van called to say that he wanted to deliver her Christmas present. "Sure. Come on over. I'm just wrapping the things I bought yesterday. You can take yours with you. Oh, and bring back *Duet's* log, too—if you're finished with it."

"Sure thing. I finished last night. You're still wrapping presents?"

Nora caught the note of incredulity in his question. "I have been sending after-Christmas presents for the last twenty-five years! Early on, I threw in the towel and gave myself over to the academic calendar. With exams sometimes running as late as the twenty-second, grades due by New Year's Eve, and all those student papers . . . anyway, everyone I care about enough to give a present knows to expect something by Twelfth Night." Hearing herself, Nora realized that she had not quite succeeded in stifling her defensiveness.

Van chuckled. "I wonder whether it is too late to shift my children to that schedule."

When Van arrived half-an-hour later, he carried *Duet's* log and Nora's gift. Their fingers touched as he handed over the parcels and both drew quickly apart. "Merry Christmas," he said.

"Thanks. Merry Christmas to you, too. Your present's over there, the one with the silver and blue paper. I know you can't stay long, but do you have time for hot chocolate? It's only 3:30."

"Hot chocolate sounds good." While she puttered in the kitchen, Van looked at ornaments on her Christmas tree. "So, besides shopping and decorating, what have you been doing the last couple of days?"

"Talking to sheriff's deputies and cleaning up the place." Nora told Van about the burglary.

"My God! You should have called. I would have come at once."

He sounded gratifyingly distressed on her behalf. "Thanks for the thought. I considered that, actually. But it was late by the time the police left and everything was a mess and they didn't want anything touched till after they'd been here this morning." Nora handed him a steaming ceramic mug. "Besides, I didn't want to give in to heebie-jeebies at being alone in my own house just because some stranger had been here." She tried for a note of comic outrage in her voice when she added, "I can't say Frank's suggestion that I might feel better if I thought a friend did it was much of a comfort!"

"Frank Pierce? I would have thought a burglary too low level for him to investigate personally." His voice was chilly.

"I suppose it is. He came by more as a friend than anything else." Van stiffened. Or did she imagine that? She hurried on. "I asked about the murder investigation, but—predictably—he wouldn't answer any questions." Van had been involved all along. Talking to him was hardly broadcasting anything. Applying the nit-picking precision so typical of academics, she felt free to tell Van of Frank's inquiries about Lydia and his request for the log. "Frank said he asked about Lydia in order to better understand Ted, but I'm sure he's interested in more than general background."

"You mean he no longer thinks Louisa committed the murder?"

"Oh, I'm sure she's still a suspect. Unfortunately."

"We should read the log—figure out why Frank wants it. But right now I have to get going." He carried his mug to the sink as he spoke. "I must buy groceries and meet my kids. I will call you after dinner, if I may."

After Van left, Nora felt a great need to *do* something. Frank probably would be in Philadelphia several days at least, and he wouldn't have asked for the log if he didn't think it important. She decided to mail it to him there. But she wanted to have it available when she talked with Van, too. In the end she photocopied the entries for October, appended a note, and addressed the copy to Frank at his parents' old address, hoping they still lived there, but figuring it wasn't a major loss if they didn't. She got to the post office twenty minutes before closing.

Van returned about nine o'clock. "I have set the children to decorating our tree. I am yours for the evening." They had coffee and chocolate cake at the oak table, the log unopened between them. Van downed a slug of coffee. "Some day I shall come here and you will offer me neither food nor drink and the shock will send me into cardiac arrest." Nora laughed. He pushed aside his cake plate. "So, what else is new in the investigation?"

Nora watched the dancing flames as she told him about Frank's search for a sailboat anchored near Slater's dock that Friday night. "But no luck so far and he's pretty discouraged. One of Slater's neighbors is an optics specialist. He saw an anchor light with a Fresnel lens flown from the bow of the boat—the only Fresnel lens he's ever seen on the Chesapeake. Frank thinks anything so rare should lead to the boat and thus to a witness, but so far—" She turned to see Van staring at her, mouth open in a very un-Van-like gape.

"Nora! *Your* anchor light has a Fresnel lens."

"It does? You're sure?"

"Absolutely. I took the lens out of the cap while we waited for the towboat to appear. You said it was a gift from a friend."

"Oh! You're talking about the antique light Tom gave me." Nora shook her head. "I'd just gotten it—had never used it before. How do you know it's a Fresnel lens?"

"From the cut. It is nothing like the molded plastic ones so common these days. The lens is glass, specially ground. It is the sort of thing a physicist knows. This physicist, anyway. Was he sure it was Friday night? We were there Saturday."

"Frank definitely said Friday, but who knows how sure the neighbor was. Damn. Where's Frank when we need him?" Nora controlled an impulse to call him immediately. "Are you thinking about probabilities?"

"Someone must. And that is what physicists do."

"That's what experimental psychologists do, too!" The retort left her lips before she realized he was baiting her.

Van held up his hands in mock surrender, but his tone was serious when he continued. "If this neighbor really did see the Fresnel lens on Friday night, the most likely explanation is that Lydia anchored *Duet* off Slater's dock the night he was murdered."

"But according to the log, Lydia was in Swan Creek," Nora protested weakly. She opened the log to Lydia's entries. The more she read them, the phonier they seemed. However, she saw nothing concretely amiss and dismissed her perceptions as the result of concentrating too narrowly—sort of like repeating a word fifty times in rapid succession and finding that part way through the exercise, the word started sounding very strange. "I think—perhaps Ted's neighbor was confused about which night he saw the Fresnel lens."

Van frowned and read through the entries again before saying, "We should consider whether she could actually have sailed the courses she recorded. Are your charts here?"

"They're in my sailing locker in the garage. I'll get them."

Nora spread Chart 4 on the table. Van said, "It's about twelve nautical miles from Swan Creek to G-9 off the Narrows, nine more to the college mooring basin."

"She called me at twelve-thirty, so she was back by then. At four knots, we're talking about five and a half hours, maybe six. She could have made it back if she got an early start, say around 07:00 hours."

Van fingered his chin, still frowning. "Look at the writing. The entries for Wednesday and Thursday probably were written while she was underway. But notice the penmanship for Friday. It is too neat. There are no corrections. And it is more complete than the others."

"So? Sometimes I just jot notes on a scrap of paper, then write the log entry after I've anchored for the night—especially when I'm sailing alone."

Van pressed open the log. "Yes, but look. Pages have been removed—with a razorblade or something of that sort. It is almost hidden in the binding." He rubbed the stubble on his cheek. "I think she fabricated this log."

"Maybe she just spilled something on it and took out a couple of pages."

"Nora, do not let your tender heart make you willfully blind to the evidence. She falsified the log."

Probably he was right, but she hated to admit the truth of it. "What with the anchor light and all, maybe she was in Queenstown harbor Friday night. But we need something more solid before we tell Frank. I mean, we could be involving an innocent woman in a murder case." She paused. "Well, maybe not *innocent*, if she and Slater were lovers, but . . . Lydia's entry about Swan Creek seems very familiar. Let me see the log." Van passed it across the table and Nora flipped through the pages to the entries for their trip into Swan Creek. "Listen to this." Nora read descriptions of the gray farmhouse, the barking dog, the great blue heron hock-high in water near the sea grasses, the sunset colors painting the western sky, the breeze, and the sunken skiff alongside a rotting log, looking both sinister and romantic.

Van smiled. "Do you hear why I think you should publish your logs?"

Nora basked in his praise, but said, "The point is not the writing. It's the timing. We anchored just after 16:00 hours. It was very nearly ebb tide. Do you remember that we could see the sunken skiff only at low tide?"

"Yes, now that you mention it. Why?"

"Well, listen to Lydia's entry two weeks later: 16:15 hours, dropped the anchor 1 mi. up Swan Creek past Gratitude Marina; 5 ft. of water; wind NW at 8 K. Watched 2 blue heron around sunken skiff near duck blind on western shore of creek, great sunset in background. Chicken and salad for dinner." Nora looked up.

Van's eyes widened. "All of the particulars are within a fraction of what we recorded—the time she anchored, the depth of the water. But she sailed two weeks later. She could not have seen the skiff at the same time we did. Where is your *Eldridge*?" Nora fetched it. Van turned to page 147 and noted the times of high tide and ebb tide on Friday, October 24, and Saturday, October 25, jotting them in the left margin of the chart. "Lydia would have arrived and departed within two hours of maximum flood. The skiff would have been under water. The only time she could have seen the sunken skiff would have been between midnight and 03:00 hours." Van pushed everything aside and leaned on his arms. "She used parts of your entry to fake hers—to camouflage where she really was on Friday night."

"I can't imagine Lydia killing anybody." Nora felt queasy. She wished for some other explanation, something that would absolve Lydia. "What are we going to do?"

"Hold on. Even if Lydia anchored in Queenstown on the night of the murder, it does not necessarily follow that she is the murderer." Van stood, arched his back, and suggested that they move to more comfortable chairs. "I am not sure what we should do with our findings, but we are not going to do anything with them at this hour on Christmas Eve." He dropped wearily into one of the club chairs, put his head back, and closed his eyes. "Did you tell Frank about seeing Lydia and Ted at the party?"

"I thought about it, but he asked what I *knew* and—as you've said so often—one's beliefs aren't knowledge. I decided not to. Do you think I made a mistake?" For reasons unexamined, she felt vulnerable and less self-confident than usual. Van did not immediately reply. "Van, suppose Lydia sailed into Queenstown harbor for an assignation with Ted and she saw the killer. Suppose she faked the log so no one would know she has this dangerous knowledge. She lied because she's afraid. Do you think that could be?" Van shrugged, quietly drumming his fingers on the arm of the chair. "Or maybe he was already dead, and she tried to hide that she was there so their affair would not be revealed." Van still said nothing. Nora sighed. "I just can't believe Lydia could kill anyone. If she *did*, there's got to be more going on."

Van opened one eye and cast an amused look in her direction. "Tell me, Nora, who among your friends and acquaintances *do* you believe capable of killing someone?"

Nora lifted one shoulder. "Point taken," she said, shifting her gaze to the flames in the fireplace.

Van yawned. "It is getting late. I apologize for fading but I am completely bushed. If you do not mind, I shall excuse myself—go home and see how the kids are doing with the tree."

"Of course I don't mind. You've earned an early night of it."

"As for the log and the lens—why not sleep on it for a few days? I expect that we shall tell Captain Pierce, but we should not do anything precipitously. Lydia was not in Swan Creek, but it is just barely possible that she was not in Queenstown harbor, either. And if she was there—as you pointed out—there are many possible reasons for not coming forward. One does not accuse the president's wife willy-nilly. I suggest that we discuss it early next week and make a decision then."

"As if we had a choice. We couldn't do anything tonight—or tomorrow either—and most likely not even the day after, because Frank probably will still be in Philadelphia with his father." She saw that he wasn't paying attention. "Don't forget your Christmas present this time."

Nora helped Van's arm find the sleeve of his coat, and as he turned to say goodbye, she kissed him on the cheek—the sort of kiss she would have given her mother, her cousin, a friend—and said, "Merry Christmas, Van." He tensed and drew back. Nora blushed and looked at her feet. How could he misinterpret her intentions? The next moment he was gone and she turned back into her sitting room, feeling hurt, and irritated that Van made everything so difficult.

Nora went early to bed but did not go quickly to sleep. She could not stop thinking about the murder and Lydia's probable—no, almost inevitable—involvement in it. She peered into the darkness and tried to sort through her thoughts and feelings, tried to decide what she should do. She gave thanks that she didn't have to do anything just yet. Maybe it was one of the Sassers after all.

CHAPTER TWENTY-NINE

"Why the hell am I doing this?" Suzanne stalked across the bedroom and yanked open the dresser drawer. "Everyone will be from Centreville. I've scarcely even seen these people since Ted. Why didn't I tell them that organizing the shelter volunteers was enough? But I'll be damned if I'll look as miserable as I feel." She pulled on a red turtleneck, and a black sweat suit with appliqués of holly and red and green plaid ribbon.

Driving into town along Liberty Street, distracted by dread, Suzanne missed the turn to the Senior Center. She realized her mistake when she got to Lawyer's Row, where her attorney's office used to be. "Damn." She turned onto Lawyer's Row to circle the block, reminding herself to pay attention to her driving, ignoring the historic buildings clustered along the way. If her memories of Centreville hadn't been polluted by Ted, she would have liked the small, friendly town with its roots in Colonial times.

The Senior Center was bustling when Suzanne arrived. Everyone she would be working with had been part of her life with Ted, would remind her of how much she once had loved him, of how degrading her marriage had become. Her heart pounded. She labored to breathe. She concentrated on walking steadily in spite of feeling lightheaded, and hid her anxiety behind a smile that felt plastic.

Two elderly women huddled outside the door, coats pulled tight around frail bodies, cigarette smoke dancing with falling snow. One woman puffed daintily, the other sucked greedily, and between draws they gossiped. A bent man with a whisker stubble shook snow off his watch cap as he joined them and lit a cigar. Suzanne drew one deep, smoke-filled breath and pushed through the door.

Several tables of card players filled the front room. In the big room beyond, white paper tablecloths printed with holly leaves covered rows of old folding tables, each surrounded by ten folding chairs. The president of the Farmers' Bank and her husband were setting red candles on each table. Half the chairs were occupied already, and it was only 11:00. A Christmas tree, lights blinking garishly, decorated the corner by the upright piano.

Suzanne paused beside the punch table. She put on a cheery voice and greeted the volunteer. "Happy holidays. How are things going?"

The woman tilted her head toward a group of boisterous children. "Guess," she said, ladling red liquid into small plastic cups. Most of the seniors seemed happy to have women and children from the domestic violence shelter sharing the holiday meal, but for a few, the Christmas spirit was in visible decline as they glared at the rowdy children. "Do you work at the college?" the volunteer asked.

"No. I'm the volunteer coordinator at the Shelter. And I ought to get to work." She turned toward the kitchen, struggling to control her emotions. So many children spending Christmas at the shelter tore at her heart. All had witnessed abuse. Some had been abused themselves. If she and Ted had had children, would he have hit them—or made them watch while he beat her? She shuddered and wondered whether he'd had time to be surprised by the first blow, to know how it felt to be on the receiving end. The thought welled up from her gut and knotted her stomach.

Even before Suzanne got to the kitchen, smells assaulted her. Pushing through the swinging door, she heard Clyde Barnes proclaiming that turkey should not be the traditional Christmas dinner. "Even Ben Franklin would agree. He wanted the turkey to be the national bird. No one would think of eating the national bird!"

Suzanne turned to Gerry Foster. "Who hung the mistletoe?" Her voice—so casual, so steady—surprised her.

"Clyde."

"I should have known," she said. She'd always disliked Clyde.

"As long as it's here . . ." Gerry brushed her cheek with a fraternal kiss. "Merry Christmas, Suzanne."

His friendly gesture poured balm on her bruised emotions. "Thanks. And the same to you." Maybe this wouldn't be so bad after all.

"I think it's wonderful that you and Nora recruited so many workers." Gerry nodded toward the room at large. "Most of these folks had no other place to go."

The praise brought color to Suzanne's cheeks. "Oh, I didn't do that much. Nora got the ones from the college. The Council President got townspeople to volunteer, too."

Clyde peered into the dining hall through the peephole in the kitchen door. "The troops are getting restless." Dinner had been announced for noon, but by eleven forty-five nearly every chair was taken, the noise level rising in proportion. Turning back he said, "Why, Suzanne. I haven't seen you since Ted was murdered. Merry Christmas."

Suzanne glared at him. Was his comment an intentional jibe or merely colossal insensitivity? Before she could think of a suitable reply, Clyde turned to work the crowd, behaving as though the whole event was his creation. She caught Nora's sympathetic smile across the work table.

Marvin "Marvel" Singleton wiped his brow. "We're about ready to serve. Are your crews ready?" The servers nodded. Marvel earned his nickname all over again running the high volume kitchen. "Okay, then. Let's roll." The crews swung into action, forming an assembly line to put food on plates.

Suzanne fingered the square in her pocket, her decision nearly final. It wasn't the best place or the best time. But if she put it off, she might not do it at all. Jake Bentley's presence was an unpleasant surprise. He'd done nothing to stop his officers from harassing her. She tried to avoid him but they kept crossing each other's paths in the kitchen.

As dessert ended, Raoul Martinez arrived, flying through the room like a woomera aimed at the piano. Nora had persuaded him to lead a carol sing. He swung the upright around so that he faced the room, put his foot on the loud pedal and, still standing, banged out the last four bars of "Joy to the World." "Sing it!" he shouted.

After several old standards, Raoul took requests. His energy and enthusiasm filled the room. Most of the seniors sang with gusto, especially the rollicking songs like "Rudolph" and "Jingle Bells." With a well-honed sense of when a crowd has had enough, Raoul ended with "Silent Night."

As the hall emptied, the volunteers cleaned up. Suzanne carried a laden tray into the kitchen just in time to hear Marvel saying, "Not what I would call a banquet, but I'm sure it was appreciated. Thanks a million. I hope Santa was good to all you hard-working galley drudges."

Clyde strolled in, surveyed the work table now covered with dirty plates, the garbage cans overflowing, the stove piled with crusted pots. Suzanne expected some wise crack or other—or a lame excuse for ducking out. Instead, he rolled up his sleeves and drew water into the deep, stainless steel double sink. He worked without a word washing plates and putting them in the rack for the three-minute steam bath. Suzanne thought there might be such a thing as Christmas spirit after all.

She stuffed spent candles, plastic cups, and soiled paper tablecloths into large plastic garbage bags and carried them to the bin outside the kitchen door. Again she fingered the square in her pocket. She might be putting her neck in a noose, but if Nora believed her . . . Suzanne shivered, pulled her courage around her like a cloak, and turned back inside. Nora was drying dishes as they came out of the steamer. Suzanne asked if they could talk, adding, "It won't take long."

"Sure. Give me a minute. I'm almost finished."

A short time later, Nora joined her at a bare table in the deserted dining room. "What's up?"

Suzanne scanned the room, making sure they were alone. She took a computer disk in a paperboard sleeve from her pocket and slid it toward Nora.

Nora raised one eyebrow. "What's this?"

"I don't know. It belonged to Ted. Maybe something to do with his classes. I put it on the computer at work, but it's gibberish—like it's in code or something." Suzanne felt sheepish. "I don't really understand computers."

Nora's eyes bored into her. "And you have it because . . .?"

Suzanne shifted in her chair, tossed her head, and said, "When Frank Pierce questioned me, I lied. I told him I hadn't been in Ted's house since September. The fact is—I was there around noon the day he was murdered." She looked wide-eyed at Nora, trying to appear innocent, daring her to be judgmental. Nora remained silent and unmoving. "Actually, I told him *part* of the truth. I did go there to retrieve papers related to our separation and divorce. My attorney didn't want Ted having documents I'd already signed. All that was true, it just happened in October, not when we had that row in his office in September. The row was about other papers. I just sort of combined the two incidents." Seeing Nora's puzzlement, she added, "I had to tell him something. They found my fingerprints on Ted's desk."

Nora traced the outline of a Christmas tree in the grain of the wooden table-top. "Why didn't you just tell the truth?"

"Yeah, right. The estranged wife just happened to drop in on the husband she hated the day he was murdered? The police are going to believe she didn't do it?" Nora frowned. "Sorry. I guess I'm a little stressed."

"Why give this to me? And why now?"

Suzanne recited her story with great concentration, hoping it didn't sound rehearsed. "The disk was with the papers I took. I discovered it a few days ago. I had no reason to open that folder after he was dead, but then I was cleaning up my desk . . ." She gnawed her lip. "At first I threw it in the wastebasket, but then I thought there might be something important on it—lists of assets or something that should come to me—because it was in the divorce folder. But it's just numbers and symbols." She leaned forward, her shoulders tight, scowling at the table. "That makes me think maybe it really is important—if he was saving stuff in code. If not important to me, then maybe to the college—or even to the police. It might have gotten into that folder by accident. But I can't read it and I didn't know who to turn to. Don't computers date files automatically? If the sheriff finds out about the disk, he might be able to figure out that I was there after I said I was— the day of the murder." She added a wheedling note to her voice. "I need someone I can trust."

"You should take it to your lawyer."

Suzanne's misery welled up. "I don't have a lawyer now. Her father died at Thanksgiving. He was a lawyer, too, and she's gone back to Alabama to be with her mother and take over his practice."

"Well, I'm not the right person for this." Nora pushed the disk back toward Suzanne. "If you really think it's important, it should go to the police."

Suzanne put a hand on Nora's arm. "Look, if I have to, I'll take it to Captain Pierce and tell him everything. But I heard he's out of town. If I hold onto this, I'll be tempted to get rid of it. I almost did already." Her voice took on a pleading note. "Please, take it. You work with computers all the time. Find out what's on it and then do whatever you think best. Maybe the police never need to know about it at all. Please." When Nora did not answer, she repeated, "Please," and pushed the disk back across the table.

She remained silent so long that Suzanne nearly stopped breathing. Finally Nora picked up the disk. "I'll see what I can do. But no matter what's on it, if the murderer isn't found soon, I'll tell Frank you were there. The timing might be important."

They parted. Suzanne wondered whether she'd made the right decision.

Nora sat at her computer, fingering the disk. She shouldn't have taken it. She had tried mightily to resist, thinking what Frank would say—what Van would say. Suzanne coming to her seemed odd— regardless of the long-standing respect and admiration she had professed during their lunch. Maybe she really didn't have anyone closer. What a sad thought. The anguish in Suzanne's voice had been real. Nora should keep her mitts off—give the disk to Frank as soon as possible. She had it now, though, and who knew when Frank would be back? And she had told Suzanne she would look.

She put the disk into her computer and brought up two small files, named *m* and *h*. Nora opened each of them, finding the indecipherable numbers, letters and symbols Suzanne had mentioned. "Damn!" Nora spent nearly an hour trying everything she could think of to open the files. The longer she worked, the more convinced she became that whatever was on the disk was important to finding Ted's killer.

She picked up the phone and started to punch in Van's number. She had steadfastly resisted the symbolic act of putting him on speed dial. After the first three numbers, she stopped. What was she thinking? He might be gracious about a call that interrupted his Christmas afternoon with family, but no amount of holiday cheer would neutralize his disapproval of what she had done. She put the disk back in its paperboard sleeve and dropped it in her desk drawer. If she wanted Van to help decipher the disk, she would need to choose her time and place carefully. Maybe after the concert.

That decision made, she showered, changed clothes, and tried to relax into her own Christmas rituals: a cup of eggnog and presents by the fire. Each present told her she was loved. She'd saved Van's present until last. The box was marked Fawcett Marine Supply, Annapolis. It contained a white cotton sweater on the front of which was stitched a Navy anchor. The accompanying note read, "Now we are twins." She took off her silk blouse and pulled the sweater on over her bare breasts. The impulse took her by surprise, but she kept the sweater on as she began her Christmas calls to family and friends, teasing them with hints about their presents yet to come. Two hours later, she moved to the dining room where her supper of cheese, bread, fruit and wine awaited. Through it all, thoughts of the computer disk biding time in her desk drawer crept into the corners of her mind—speculations about what was on it and whether she dared call Van.

CHAPTER THIRTY

On the surface, the Howards' holidays passed the same as any other year: Lydia and John had joined the senior Cutlers in Harrisburg for Hanukkah, and John's parents came to Centreville for Christmas. Over the years, both sets of in-laws had revealed their relief that this marriage had not driven a wedge between them and their child. Lydia had long suspected that gratitude had spawned graciousness in both couples.

No one did gracious like old line Virginians. In deference to Lydia's aversion to red and green, John's mother brought her usual centerpiece of cedar and beautyberry for the holiday table. Christmas day passed with customary civility and expressions of affection, Lydia struggling to keep in check anxiety about the forthcoming exposure of her affair.

When at last John's mother said she was about to come undone and his father declared that he needed to be well-rested for tomorrow's drive home, Lydia saw rather than heard John's tiny sigh, the subtle changes in his body and expression that signaled the lifting of carefully controlled tension. He was as anxious as she. As the guestroom door closed behind the senior Howards, he said, "How about a nightcap?"

"That would be lovely." That he offered her a drink—after what had happened with Liz—spoke volumes of his mood.

John moved to the portable bar. "Courvoisier?" She signaled her agreement, kicked off her shoes, and rested her feet on the coffee table. He delivered the brandies, pushing aside the candy plate to make space. They lifted the snifters and clinked the rims gently. "Merry Christmas, my dear."

"And to you." She sniffed the brandy and took a tiny sip of the fiery amber liquid. When she continued, she could not help sounding as sad as she felt. "Oh, John, this may have been the last normal holiday our family will ever share!"

John's voice was gentle. "We've hardly had time to think since Frank's visit, let alone time to talk. But we do need to talk . . . about our future."

Lydia drew a deep breath and looked at her husband. "Do you want a divorce?"

"Never," he said quietly. That single word swelled her heart and she realized how much she had feared the possibility. "Frank probably thought I was just putting a good face on it, but in the overall scheme of things, the affair really doesn't matter. Not now." He seemed to search for words. "I would be nothing without you, Lydia."

She gripped his hand. "We've always been a winning team. If we stick together, this won't defeat us." Finally, she broached the worry that had plagued her night hours. "We need to consider all the possibilities—not only what is inevitable, but also the best and worst case scenarios."

John poured a little more brandy from the cut glass decanter. Reflections from the fire danced on their glasses, incongruously merry. "Taking the inevitable first: there's no hope that your involvement with Slater will remain secret. Once a couple of people in the Sheriff's Office know, the word will spread through Centreville like a virus."

Lydia exhaled slowly. "I know. Then it's only a matter of time before it gets to Waldorf. Even if they make you an offer before then, they'd withdraw it—or buy you out. In the long run, it would be better if you withdraw first, citing personal and family reasons. They'll know what that means soon enough."

John nodded. "I'll get in touch with the search firm Monday. I need to be ahead of the gossip with the West College Board, too—before New Year's—before Frank gets back to town. If the Slater murder is cleared up soon, we may have enough support on the Board to weather this."

"No doubt a lot depends on how many sexual skeletons are rattling around in their closets!" Lydia massaged her temples. "But we seem to have slipped into the best case scenario. It's also possible that the Board will ask for your resignation." John stared at the floor, shoulders drooping. Interpreting his silence as defeatist thinking, she continued. "But even that wouldn't be fatal. Some of the Board members will support you no matter what, help you get another presidency, perhaps at a school like Antioch or Bennington, where everything's a little unorthodox anyway—some school where my affair might not be taken so seriously." John swirled his brandy, seeming to concentrate on the amber liquid washing the sides of the glass. How could he be so passive? When she spoke again, both exasperation and encouragement crept into her words. "I mean it. You're a good administrator, a great fund-raiser. Your wife's peccadillo won't wipe out decades of professional accomplishment. It will rouse sympathy and amusement as well as disapproval. You can come back from this, John. Trust me."

At that, he looked at her and smiled faintly. "I always have."

Lydia detected no irony. "And I've always been right. Sometimes you're too modest for your own good. Professionally, this is only a temporary setback. But the family . . ."

John took her hand. "They'll get over it."

"Some of them. Eventually. Daddy will be disappointed. But he's always assumed that whatever I do is, if not right, at least excusable, so he will be okay. And Mommy will understand. She'll love me still, warts and all." She toyed with John's fingers. "But your mother will never forgive me."

"She wouldn't want us to divorce."

"No, never that. She won't tear my page out of the family Bible or cut me dead in public. On the surface, probably no one will notice anything. But you've always been her fair-haired boy, and in her heart, she'll never forgive me." Lydia's unresisting acceptance of the inevitable crept into her voice.

John flinched. "Probably you're right. But we won't let it matter." They each retreated into thought. Lydia hated to consider her father-in-law's disapprobation—not only of her affair but also of John's reaction to it. Her face colored as she remembered the first Christmas after she and John married, when they'd spent the holiday at Willow Oaks. The men were in the library after dinner. Brandy was thick in his father's voice as he lectured John on the perils of being "pussy whipped." John's younger brothers had snickered. The harangue was clearly audible to the ladies in the drawing room across the hall. From that day to this, no one had mentioned it. But Lydia had learned a lesson that guided much of her behavior in the succeeding decades: she delivered her opinions, advice, guidance and preferences about John, his behavior, and his career in the privacy of their marriage bed. No one else knew the extent to which Lydia's hand had shaped his life. In his father's presence, she was particularly deferential. Still, she knew his father's opinion had never changed. From John's boyhood, his father had derided him for being weak-willed and indecisive, and no doubt John's acceptance of Lydia's infidelity would elicit scorn for his lack of dominion with his wife. Lydia resolutely turned such thoughts aside and said nothing of John's father.

John did not mention him either. "As far as the extended family is concerned . . . well, maybe they'll read it in the papers or something. My parents would never say anything." John emptied his glass. "At least our sons aren't in sensitive careers."

Lydia always dreaded the seething emotion that hid beneath John's carefully neutral voice. She decided to respond only to his words. "Thank God for small favors. But Jimmy is going to be upset."

John nodded. "He's always been the one who reacts to family tensions. It will help a lot if I talk to him, make him understand that I'm okay with—everything."

Lydia said, "Young Sam will be okay, of course. He rolls with the punches, and he's had so many bumpy relationships himself. We just need to make sure they hear it from us first." She watched the fire. "Even if I don't have to testify—even if there's never any official confirmation of the affair—the rumor of it will be reported." Resignation weighed her down. But one of them had to manage their future. Lydia straightened her shoulders and pushed her weariness aside. "If we're lucky, Frank will give us notice before he tells anyone else, so you can talk with the PR staff. You'll need a strategy as well as an official statement. We should present you as loyal, steadfast, committed to your marriage vows, magnanimous in forgiving your errant wife, confident of your future." She tried hard not to sound bitter when she continued. "I will be the loving but misguided wife whose personal insecurities made her vulnerable to seduction by a suave and charming womanizer." The pain in John's eyes before he turned away softened her tone. "I suppose we should count our blessings. It's better for me to be exposed as the one who acts on passion and impulse and for you to be strong and reliable, rather than the opposite."

Her voice trailed away and they fell silent, holding hands, staring into the dim glow of the dying fire. The clock on the mantel struck midnight before either of them spoke again, and then it was Lydia who said, "Being your wife is who I am, John. Nothing that happened between Ted and me touched that. You know I never meant to hurt you. You know I will protect you from the consequences of my folly if I can."

"And I, you," he said quietly, "And I, you." He squeezed her hand.

Lydia retired for the night still brooding on all they had left unsaid.

CHAPTER THIRTY-ONE

"Hang it up, Ray. Just hang it up! There's no way in hell we're taking her out of here."

Ray Martin had seldom seen his sister so angry. "You're a hardhearted woman, Mart. A real hardhearted woman. Look at this place!" Ray swept his arm toward the TV across the room. The gesture included the first floor lounge and the entire nursing home beyond—its locked doors, asphalt tile floors, stained carpets, and K-Mart art. Martha glared stonily ahead, but her eyes grew moist. Ray pressed his advantage, leaned toward her and whispered, "Smell it, Mart! And listen to it! They don't call this the screamer floor for nothing." He thrust out his chin, his face less than two feet from his sister's and hissed, "Is this what you want for our mother, Mart? Is it?" He spat out the words on a gust of bourbon, the smell mingling with the odors of medications and meals past, of bad breath and incontinence that already assaulted them.

She turned on him. "You look, Ray! Really look at her, for Chris'sake! She has *Alzheimer's*. She's never going to be any better than she is right now!" Martha pointed to a small woman in a print dress, one of the row of people staring at the cartoon antics of Christmas elves on TV.

Ray glanced at their mother and his voice turned surly. "She doesn't really need to be in this place. You know she doesn't."

"Oh, she could be lots of places, Ray. Lord knows I know that well enough! If she wasn't doped up there's no telling where she might be right now. She could be playing in the toilets. She could be taking other patients' medications. She could be halfway to downtown Baltimore and not even wearing her hat and coat!"

Their chairs hugged the wall of the lounge, perhaps twenty feet from the line of mesmerized TV watchers. Their mother must have sensed their conflict, for she set up a wordless high-pitched keening. "Now you've done it!" Ray snarled. "You *know* how she gets when you're riled up. Aren't you proud of yourself?"

"Me? I'm not the one started this. I was planning to just feed her a couple of Christmas cookies and go home!"

Soon other voices joined their mother's, and the wailing of the residents competed with the blare of the TV. A nurse and several aides hurried in. They wheeled the chairs apart, stroking hands and patting heads and talking calmly close to the residents' ears. A plump middle-aged aide approached Ray and Martha. Her voice was kind when she said, "Perhaps it's best if you leave now."

They each kissed their mother's cheek and said, "Merry Christmas, Mama." Martha stroked her mother's hair, but the gray tufts standing up like an egret's crest wouldn't lie down. Ray squeezed his mother's hand and Martha straightened the carnations in the wrist corsage they had brought. Their mother grinned vacantly.

They trudged in silence past the sparsely furnished rooms. In some, relatives hunched in straight chairs beside the cranked-up bed. In others, the resident lay alone. The faint strains of "Joy to the World" came from the left. An aide ushered them through the locked door of the ward. Neither responded to his cheery, "Merry Christmas."

The raw December wind cut against them. They buttoned their coats, pulled on hats and gloves, and tramped toward the parking lot. They did not look at each other, hardly said a word.

The bells on the Christmas wreath jingled as they opened the door to Martha's small duplex. The warm air carried the lingering smell of turkey and sweet potatoes from their midday meal. Martha's husband and two grandchildren sat together on the living room sofa watching Bing Crosby in *Holiday Inn*. Martha and Ray continued in silence to the kitchen.

Martha pushed aside the remains of pumpkin pie and fruitcake littering the table. Ray picked up the argument they had begun in the car, his words slow, his voice one of exaggerated reasonableness. "It just seems to me, Marty, that as long as Mama isn't violent, it's a shame to have her locked up like that. Especially at Christmas and all. I just want her to be somewhere better than that place."

Martha's temper flared anew. "*That place* is all you can afford, Ray. You get more money, we'll put her in a nicer place!"

"I don't have more money, Mart—not right now anyway—and you damn well know it!" He slapped the table, rattling the dishes, making Martha jump. He leaned toward her. "I've been paying Mama's way ever since she had to quit work. When are *you* gonna ante up?"

Martha raised her chin. "Don't talk crazy. You know Fred's on disability, and what with taking in the grandkids, it's all we can do to put food on the table some weeks. Why don't you get a better job? You can't tell me that rinky-dink college pays as well as the Fairfax County job did. What did you do to mess that up?"

"Get off my case, Mart! It's not my fault the county screwed me over!" Ray pulled a flask of bourbon from his pocket and took two swallows before putting it back.

"How much money goes for booze, Ray? How much do you throw away on the ponies?"

"Now, Mart, be reasonable. A man's got to have some way to unwind at the end of the day." Ray looked sideways at his sister. "Besides, things are going to get better, Mart. Soon. I've got prospects."

"Oh, yeah? What kind of prospects?"

Ray looked at her through slitted lids. "That's for me to know and you to find out! But right now, I'm tapped out, and if you can't contribute any money, you ought to be making some contribution in kind. You ought to bring Mama back here."

"You're dreaming, Ray. Or drunk! I've been there and I've done that and it just won't work." Ray started to protest but Martha talked over him, her voice louder. "I'm telling you, Ray, it won't work!" She glanced at the door to the living room, and her tone shifted to the one she used with her preschool grandkids, the words careful and quiet. "When it got so you couldn't leave Mama alone, I was more than willing to take her in. We didn't have the grandkids then and I was happy to do it. I was determined to take good care of her, too. I went to the library and read all about Alzheimer's. I found this list—*25 Tips for Making Your Home Safe and Comfortable*—and I did all of 'em, Ray, all the ones I could do in a rental." She jumped up, knocking over her chair. She wrenched open a cabinet door. "You see these locks, Ray?

They cost a fortune. I had to lock up all the cleaners, all the drugs and medicines, all the beer." She leaned on the table and spoke directly into Ray's face. "Have you ever tried to work in a kitchen where the knives are all in locked drawers and you have to plug in the microwave every time you're gonna use it?"

Martha sagged against the counter, her voice almost a whisper. "I put her clothes on backwards so she wouldn't take them off all the time, and then she wouldn't let me take them off at all! I had to give her a bath in her slip! It got to where she could only eat finger foods and I had to start getting diapers for her. It was always something." Martha paced, ringing her hands. She drew a shuddering breath and sank into a chair across from him. "I did the best I could as long as I could. Nothing was ever enough. Trying just wore me out."

"Mart, you did a great job. You really did. I just thought, maybe for a little while, till I can get her in a better place . . . Being here with you, with family, it would just be so much nicer than that place."

Martha's face crumpled. She put her head down on her arms and wept—wracking, nearly silent sobs, copious tears making dark circles on the sleeves of her red dress.

"Oh, Jesus, Mart! Don't do that. Don't cry. You know I can't stand it when you cry." But Martha couldn't or wouldn't stop. "Oh, Jesus," he repeated. He pulled a handkerchief from his hip pocket, wiped his eyes and blew his nose. "Look, just forget it. Forget I said anything. I'll take care of it." As he spoke he wrapped a handful of cookies in a paper towel and stuffed them into his jacket pocket. "Look, I'll be in touch, okay?" She gave no sign of having heard him. He banged out the back door.

Back at his apartment, Ray dumped his hat and coat on a kitchen chair. He took one long pull straight from the bourbon bottle, then poured more into a water glass, not bothering to add ice. He flopped down heavily at the table and munched a cookie. It wasn't as good as his mother used to make.

Ray thought about when his mother first came to live with him, how good everything had been and the laughs they'd had. He'd stayed home and sober a lot more then. They'd eat popcorn and play gin rummy all evening. "Christ, she was good at gin rummy!" She used to beat him as often as not. Sometimes they'd just watch TV or go for a walk around town when the weather was nice. No matter what she was doing, when he got home from work she'd put it aside and talk to him. He could still see her, right at that table, double solitaire spread out in front of her, and as soon as he came in the door, she'd just gather up the cards and say, "So, what kind of day did you have today?" She cooked for him, too, a good homemade dinner every night, and he never had to wonder whether there'd be clean socks in his drawer. Ray lifted his glass in a silent toast to the good times they'd had.

And then the other memories crept in. The time she'd called him at the bookstore, that plaintive note in her voice when she said, "Son, I can't seem to find the Acme." He noticed, after that, how she sometimes couldn't find the deck of cards or her glasses or her watch. And she cried a lot. The doctor referred them to a neurologist. Ray's eyes smarted as he remembered: she told the doctor that it was Wednesday instead of Friday, that it was the previous month, that it was last year. She didn't even know the name of the town where they lived. When she left a pot on the stove and set the place on fire, he'd had to get Martha to take her in.

The ceiling light turned Ray's tears into shiny rivulets on his cheeks. He poured another slug of bourbon, lit another cigarette, and noticed that his tongue and lips were growing numb. He dropped into his easy chair. "I'm gonna get you outta that place, Mama—put you someplace nice, where someone'll walk with you, not try to keep you in a fucking chair or bed. I'll do it, Mama! Soon. You see if I don't. You won't have to put up with that place much longer."

Ray tried to focus on his Big Plan. He lifted his glass, sing-songing to the empty room. "I know something you don't know, *Captain* Pierce! I know a whole lot of things you don't know!" A grin twisted Ray's lips. "You never found out I went back to Slater's on Friday. You don't know her Royal Highness Mrs. President Howard was there, too!" He laughed. "That old patio door was good as a mirror." He fell silent for a moment, sneering into a gloomy corner of the room, remembering. "And now the tide's gonna turn for old Ray Martin. It surely will!" Ray remembered stopping by his office, seeing President Howard walking toward Ozmon House. "Just one little phone call, cool as a cucumber: 'I saw your wife with Ted Slater. I saw what she did.'" Ray finished the bourbon. "I know how to take advantage when opportunity knocks. If that scumbag Slater could manage a little extortion, so can Ray Martin!" Ray leaned his head against the back of the chair as he mumbled, "You just hang on, Mama. Ray's gonna get you outta there. Yessir, we're gonna be set for life."

CHAPTER THIRTY-TWO

Frank and his mother sat at the kitchen table, taking their ease after cleaning up the remains of Christmas dinner. Claire had gone to her parents' house with the boys. Frank's siblings, aunts, and cousins had gone home. The clock chimed eleven. Pearl Pierce reached across the table and squeezed Frank's hand. "Thanks for coming, son. It's a comfort to have you here."

"Where else would I be, Mama?" He finished his cookie and reached for another.

"I don't know what I'll do if Cleveland doesn't make it." The laughter usually just under her words was gone, replaced by a tremor. "We were just kids when we married, too young to know what we were doing even though we thought we knew everything. I guess it was about equal parts goodwill and good luck that kept us together these fifty years and more. But now . . . I just don't know what I'd do without that man."

"It won't come to that, Mama. The doctor said he'll be fine. But if it *did* come to it, you'd do what had to be done." Frank squeezed her hand. "You always have. And it's always turned out all right."

"Sometimes I wonder. I've done my best, but it seems like mostly two steps forward and one step back. Whatever did I do to make Selma the way she is?" Pearl shook her head and plucked at the frayed edge of a potholder lying on the table.

Frank chuckled. "Mama, what did you expect, naming a girl born during school desegregation Selma? How could she not take some of that rebelliousness into herself?"

A rueful smile passed across Pearl's face. "I guess I can't say 'What's in a name' when we chose Franklin Jefferson Pierce for you, just hoping the name would make the man. And you're every bit the man we wanted you to be. Except maybe head of the Philadelphia Police Department."

Frank felt the familiar sting of having disappointed his parents. His family just didn't get it. He'd rather be Number Two in rural Queen Anne's County than go through life shackled to urban crime and the underbelly of humanity. Those thoughts remained unspoken. He said, "When do you want to take down the tree? I spoke with Claire and we'll stay till New Year's if you want."

"What about your work? A man in your position can't just be gone like that."

"I have more vacation time backed up than I can use, and before I left Centreville the Sheriff said I'm off for the next week regardless." Frank fiddled with the big red, white and green plaid tin that had held Christmas cookies every year as far back as he could remember, making no mention of his guilt about being gone in the middle of an important investigation, of the restlessness that had already begun. He took another cookie.

"I'll be more than glad to have you. I won't deny I can use the help." Pearl got a glass of milk for each of them. "It's a wonder to me that your sweet tooth hasn't made you run to fat years ago." She set the milk glasses at their places and wiped crumbs from the white plastic tablecloth, the one with big red poinsettias she always used from Thanksgiving till New Years. Frank drew the glass closer, moving it like a piece on a chessboard. "Tell me about this murder you've been working on."

His mother had always seemed able to read his mind. "It's still hanging. If you don't find the murderer in the first few days, odds are you're never going to find him—or her." Frank shook his head. "I'm not giving up, but I'm not making much headway." He told his mother about the case, about his frustration. "I tell you, the man was a real piece of work. I can't help thinking a lot of people are better off with him dead."

Pearl clucked sympathetically. "You see more wickedness in the world every day. But if anyone can solve it, Franklin, you can."

Her blind maternal confidence comforted Frank without reassuring him. "I hope you're right, Mama. But I keep running up against things I don't know anything about. Like those boats. I thought maybe Nora would have an idea, but she just suggested that I check with Natural Resources, and I'd already tried that."

Alarm flashed across Pearl's face. "You aren't seeing that Perry woman again are you? Franklin, she can only bring you to grief."

"No, Mama, I'm not *seeing* Nora. I'm a happily married man, remember?" Frank heard the trace of exasperation in his voice and continued flatly. "I hadn't even spoken to Nora in years. But then she found the body and our first suspect—a woman the dead man raped awhile back—is a student of hers, and a friend. Nora thinks she's innocent." He looked Pearl in the eye. "Frankly, Mama, that carries a lot of weight with me, though I'm careful not to let it affect the investigation. Nora's got a good brain and good instincts and I respect her opinion as much as anyone's." He put his hand on his mother's and said gently, "She's always going to be my friend, Mama. You might as well resign yourself to that."

"I'm not saying you've done anything wrong, son, but *please* be careful. I just don't want anything to bring misery to another one of my babies."

"Not to worry, Mama. I told you, I'm not seeing Nora." The clock in the living room struck midnight. "I guess Christmas is over. And we'd better get to bed. You need your rest."

Pearl pushed her chair back and picked up the remains of their snack. "Yes, I guess it's about that time. I want to get to the hospital by eight. Cleveland's thinking about that angioplasty and we need to talk. Good night, son. I'll see you in the morning." She kissed his forehead and left.

Frank listened to his mother's footsteps on the stairs. She walked like a woman half her age, and he was thankful for her strength and health. He felt lucky that both his parents were still alive. Taking Pop's place, carving the ham, seeing everyone gathered around the table the way his father usually did, he felt older—but not old enough to be the oldest man in the family. Frank felt sure his father would weather this heart attack, be back rooting for the 76ers and working on his model trains. But someday his parents would die, and who knew what would happen between now and then? He rose wearily and turned off the light. "Frank, you don't want to go down that road tonight." He climbed the stairs thinking about Claire, their sons, and their unborn child.

★   ★   ★

Back from the hospital, Frank picked up the mail in the front hall. A manila envelope addressed to him was partially exposed, jolting Frank's composure. He'd recognize Nora's looping half written, half printed script anywhere. Why would she write to him here? While his mother and siblings gathered in the kitchen, he retreated to the parlor and read the enclosed note:

> *My dear Frank—*
>
> *I hope your father is improving rapidly and that you and your family are sharing joy this holiday season. Please give my greetings to all.*
>
> *You will find enclosed a photocopy of my ship's log for October. You sounded eager to have it and, given your father's health, it seems likely that you will be away for some time. I didn't want to send the whole journal but trust that a month's worth of entries will give you the flavor of it and will cover any particular dates in which you may be interested. If not, you certainly are welcome to read the rest when you return.*
>
> *My thoughts are with you and with your mother.*
>
> > *As always,*
> > *Nora*

Copies of log entries, in several handwritings, were stapled together. He skimmed the first eighteen pages, noting that Nora had had a couple of day sails. She and Van sailed over the fall break, beginning October eleventh. Frank turned those pages quickly. When he came to Lydia's entries, he read them several times. Nothing seemed out of line. "But words on a page don't substantiate her claims about where she was and when, either," he told the empty room.

Few pages remained. Frank read carefully all that Van and Nora had written about sailing into Queenstown harbor on Saturday—the storms, the damage to *Duet*, their plans to use Slater's phone Sunday morning. Absolutely nothing helpful. So what was so important that it couldn't wait till his return? Was this just Nora being Nora, trying to be helpful? Or was he missing something?

CHAPTER THIRTY-THREE

The concert ended in thunderous applause and shouts of "Bravo!" The second half of *Messiah* was even better than the first. Nora laid her hand lightly on Van's forearm. "That was stunning!" The rough texture of his tweed jacket sent a shiver through her. She willed herself to ignore the faintly herbal scent of his aftershave and focus on how she could tell him about Suzanne's disk without triggering an explosion. "So, are you up for dessert?"

"Absolutely." Van took her arm as they inched their way through Baldwin Auditorium toward the oak double doors. "There is nothing I would like better just now than to sample the legendary Perry sweets." On the drive to her house, Nora mulled over his words, his tone, and concluded that he intended no double meaning—no retraction of their agreement to stay platonic.

"Nora, that minced fruit pie was excellent."

He waved off the coffee pot but Nora refilled her cup, hoping to prolong the pleasant part of the evening. "Thanks. Would you like to take the rest of it home?"

"That would be great. My children have devoured everything but some brick-dry fruitcake and a few candy canes." Van shook his head and laughed.

"The young amaze me, too. Some of the kids at the Senior Center Christmas meal ate like truckers but were slim as whippets!"

"How did that go, by the way?"

"The day was a seesaw." Nora shifted her gaze to the world beyond her sliding glass doors. The onyx bowl of the sky showed uniform black, but the river reflected an occasional glint of stray light from distant houses along the shore. "On the one hand, such generous giving by so many people was a joy. Even Clyde Barnes tackled the worst clean-up job without being asked—and without making a big show of it." She pushed the crumbs on her plate into a tiny mound. "On the other hand, many of the seniors were infirm and needy, some querulous and defeated—depressing examples of what it can mean to be old and alone. The women and children from the domestic violence shelter were physically and emotionally battle scarred—equally depressing examples of how debilitating and dangerous families can be."

Nora angled her head. "And then I came home to sanctuary, and thought how very, very fortunate I am. Opening presents, talking with family and friends, I felt well and truly loved. But down, too. I just teetered back and forth all day and into the night." She lifted one shoulder. "Half the time I was not fit company for myself—let alone for anyone else." In her summing-up-for-the-jury state of mind, she added, "Which just goes to show that Katharine Hepburn was right: it may be inevitable that men and women should come together, but how well suited are they to live together in the same house?"

Van looked sharply at her, then away. Or maybe she imagined that. She told herself to quit stalling and adopted a light tone. "But let me tell you about something that happened *completely* out of the blue." She repeated what Suzanne had said about the computer disk. "So she lied to Frank about the last time she was in the house. But I still can't believe she actually killed him. For one thing, she says she went there around noon and he was killed after dinner. If she went back later to do it, why bring up the computer disk at all?"

"Probably so you would think exactly that." He sounded stern and Nora wanted to protest but he kept talking. "So you are going to give it to Frank on her behalf—as soon as he returns?" Nora bit her lip and did not answer. Van's scowl made her squirm. "Surely you are not thinking of withholding potential evidence."

Nora cleared her throat. Embarrassment made her defensive. "The operative word here is *potential*. We don't really know. Besides, you are the one who didn't want to tell Frank our suspicions about Suzanne and Ray Martin. And you suggested that we sleep on it before deciding what to do about the log and my Fresnel lens. This must be at least as important as those." She paced by the patio door. "Besides, we'd said we'd discuss it before we did anything and . . ." Nora heard the wheedling note in her voice and left the sentence unfinished.

"I suppose that makes me at least partially responsible," Van said. He sounded testy. "So what *is* on the disk?"

Nora lifted one shoulder. "Damned if I know! I couldn't immediately read it and I didn't want to mess around."

"Let me see." Van pushed his chair back from the table and followed Nora to her study. He said, "First we need a blank disk. We will make a working copy, so we can hand over the original and say truthfully that we did not change it in any way." His actions fit his words. He handed the original to Nora when he finished. "We should do what we can to insure its integrity, even at this late date."

Why hadn't she thought about that? She put the disk into its paperboard folder, sealed it, and both she and Van initialed it across the seal. She leaned over his shoulder. "Okay, what've we got?"

"The files were saved in machine language." He reversed the procedure and pulled up only two files, *m* and *h*, a spreadsheet file and a text document. He opened *m*. The file contained dates going back three years, and sums of money. Entries at the end of each month, and additional small amounts posted irregularly, continued until the week before Slater was killed. "This appears to be a record of money Ray Martin paid Slater."

Nora studied the screen. "Every pay period. And I bet the others are Ted's share of Ray's poker winnings. Suzanne got it right. Ray was being blackmailed."

"This must have been a lot of money for Ray—money Ted did not even need. But he did need the power." Van looked like he'd touched slime. He opened *h*. "It's a letter, dated October 23rd." He read aloud:

Dear John:

> *It has come to my attention that some thirty years ago, you plagiarized your dissertation. (Lest you think I merely suspect plagiarism, I am enclosing a copy of the original work of Smythe T. Smith.) Plagiarism may be a minor crime in some arenas, and your academic and professional life since may have been without blemish, but for you, this is a secret worth keeping.*

And exactly what is it worth to you? A presidency? Two? To compromise my integrity by keeping such a secret is worth a great deal to me. The value of intangibles is always a thorny issue. But in this instance, I have no doubt that we can come to agreement. As a start, I want tenure and a promotion. This isn't merely a suggestion. It's a requirement. By rights, I should have been tenured already if this backwater college had ever adopted AAUP guidelines. But it's never too late to rectify past injustices. Do whatever you must to make it happen.

I've made an appointment for next week to discuss procedures to implement this change in my status.

Yours most sincerely,

Theodore J. Slater, M.A., C.P.A
Associate Professor

Stunned, Nora leaned closer to the screen, her shoulder touching Van's. He scrolled through the letter twice. Her "Holy shit" came out on a pent-up breath. "I don't know which is more unbelievable, that Ted would actually blackmail the president of West College or that John Howard would have done something he could be blackmailed for."

They returned to the sitting room. Van said, "You are pale. May I bring you a drink?"

"Yes, thanks." Her voice quavered. She sank into one of the leather club chairs by the fireplace. Van poured scotch on the rocks for each of them. Nora drank, hardly noticing the bite of the single malt. Van looked as distressed as she felt. She said, "This changes everything."

"Let us consider the possibilities." He sounded subdued. "Perhaps John killed Slater to end the blackmail and avoid exposure. Perhaps Slater's affair with Lydia had nothing to do with his murder."

"Assuming they were having an affair at all," Nora interjected. "We've inferred that from gossip, and from our conclusion that *Duet* was anchored in Queenstown harbor that night." She set her glass on the revolving bookcase, ice clinking. "But, Van, *Duet* might have been there because of *John* Howard. He sails well enough. Or maybe he and Lydia conspired in the killing." She shuddered. "Any way you cut it, John seems to have had strong motives for wanting Ted dead. My God, can't there be some other explanation?"

"There always can be alternative explanations." Van gazed into the fire as if seeking answers in a crystal ball. "Even if the facts are unassailable, one can always argue motive. In this case, the only solid fact we have is that someone wrote this letter. Based on Suzanne's statements—the statements of an admitted liar—we would presume the author to be Ted. But putting a blackmail demand in a signed letter is very risky, enormously arrogant, or foolish—or all of the above. The author could be Suzanne, or even some third party, framing Ted for blackmail and John for murder all in one fell swoop."

"A third party? That would be wonderful!"

Van continued, "Even if Ted was reckless enough to draft this letter, it is possible that John never received it. If Ted was killed before he mailed his ultimatum, John had no blackmail motive."

"Mmmmm. And maybe John never plagiarized anything. Maybe Ted made it up and was threatening John with a public lie. It would create an awful scandal. Even if John were quickly vindicated, the suspicion alone would knock him out of the Waldorf presidency."

"But would John—would anyone—really commit murder to prevent a temporary, unfounded embarrassment?"

Nora put her elbow on the arm of her chair and rested her forehead on her hand. Fatigue washed over her. "This makes my head hurt."

"Let it go. It is for the police to figure out who wrote this and whether it is related to Ted's murder. I only wish that Frank would return before the New Year."

Nora's head snapped up. "We can't possibly give this to Frank unless we determine that the plagiarism is true!"

"Now, Nora . . ."

"I mean it, Van. I *like* the Howards. I couldn't stand to heap more suspicion on them if they don't deserve it. I already mailed the log entries to Frank, and when he gets back we must explain the evidence that *Duet* was in Queenstown harbor that Friday night. That's bad enough." Nora jumped up and paced the short distance to the fireplace and back, wringing her hands, trying to control her anguish.

Van rose as well. He put his arms around her and patted her back, murmuring, "All right, all right. We will do nothing about the letter until we know whether John plagiarized his dissertation. We can check that out tomorrow." He put his hands on her shoulders and gently set her aside. "Then we will decide what to do."

"Thank you. I can't ask for more than that." His embrace had been comforting. She cleared her throat before continuing. "It's getting late. Let me wrap up that pie for your kids."

After Van left, Nora changed for bed, her thoughts circling around Ted Slater and the Howards. She curled up on her left side to encourage sleep, but instead examined all the alternatives she and Van had mentioned, and thought of others as well, each scenario more farfetched and convoluted than the last. What if Lydia did have an affair with Ted but it was because of his hold over John? Would John have turned a blind eye to an affair because of Ted's blackmail? Had Lydia conspired with Ted in the blackmail? Did she even know about it? Had she lured John to Ted's house intending that *John* should be murdered, and things had gone awry? At this, even Nora's imagination balked.

Her thoughts turned to Van and her affection for him. She seemed to have a talent for pulling his disapproval down around her ears. She rolled over and punched her pillow into a different configuration. Every time she needed him—like tonight, when she was so upset over the Howards—he immediately reached out to comfort her. But he seemed to have no difficulty keeping their relationship fraternal—which was exactly what she wanted, of course—what they had agreed to. She turned from the fetal position onto her back and lay full-length, a pillow under her knees, hands crossed on her breast like a corpse, and tried to focus on her breathing, tried to visualize a small dark circle growing and enveloping her consciousness. Eventually she gave it up, turned on the light and picked up *A Remarkable Woman: A Biography of Katharine Hepburn* by Anne Edwards. The time was 3:05 a.m.

229

Van's thoughts roiled with bits of Handel, the afterimage of his fingers on Nora's elbow, how the whisper of her breath on his cheek had made his heartbeat spike. But he could not silence the echo of her words about men and women living together. He had had similar doubts about marriage over the years, but hearing them expressed by Nora disturbed him. She'd sounded like someone uttering what she believed to be incontrovertible truth. He'd been torn between agreement and debate. Holding her in his arms, tenderness and his wish to take care of her—to protect her—nearly overwhelmed him, though his ability to mask those feelings pleased him. Besides, Nora was independent, stubborn, and spiky. She did not give way easily. She pushed the envelope of convention further than he liked. No doubt living with Nora would be half heaven and half hell—all of which was academic now.

He turned to the puzzle of Ted Slater's murder. He noticed the irony of finding thoughts of murder more relaxing than thoughts of his relationship with Nora, but did not deny that it was so. He focused on how John Howard might have plagiarized his dissertation and gone undetected all these years, on the ever-emerging evils of Ted Slater, and the various motives for his murder. The evidence they were withholding from the police weighed heavily on his conscience, and the knowledge that they would turn everything over when Frank returned from Philadelphia did not lighten the burden here and now. Although Nora's moral compass was ultimately sound, she had sometimes wavered over the line in this investigation. Once again his feelings for her had committed him to actions with which he was decidedly uncomfortable. When the clock chimed 3:00, he punched his pillow and turned his thoughts resolutely to the conjugation of irregular German verbs. He did not hear the clock chime the half-hour.

CHAPTER THIRTY-FOUR

Van dialed Nora's number. He'd called Duke University and the librarian had agreed to fax a copy of John Howard's dissertation. "I'd hoped for an electronic file, but John's dissertation is too old. She agreed to send it—finally—only because I pled an urgent need, the library is so dead during the holidays, the dissertation is so short, and I swore my undying gratitude. It is probably in my office now. How did you make out tracking down Smith?"

"I spent the whole blessed day on that search! And you, sir, are going to hear about it."

Van laughed. "If you are able to tease about it, I can only infer that ultimately you succeeded. But go ahead. Torture me with all the bloody details."

"Well, first I did the obvious, searched various indexes back from 1968. Half an hour into it, I offered a small prayer of thanks that he has such a weird first name. Have you any idea how many Smiths are published scholars? I tried Dissertation Abstracts, Mathematical Abstracts, Atlas Mathematical Conference Abstracts—I even considered that it might not be in English, but I figured that with a name like Smith . . . In the end, I just fell into it. I'd gone home for lunch, frustrated, and as I pushed my mail from one side of the table to the other, I found the most recent profile of college students, put out by NPEC—"

"NPEC?"

"The National Post-secondary Education Cooperative. I was on their steering committee for three years—and now I'm on their mailing list for life. That's when it hit me."

Van imagined Nora pacing as she talked, gesticulating with her free hand, and smiled at the image. "Of course," he said. "The connection between a profile of current college students and Smith's research more than thirty years ago is obvious."

"Well, maybe not obvious, but it is there, if one's thinking is convoluted enough. If you keep making wisecracks, this story could go on all night."

"My thoughts are my own," Van vowed.

"Promises, promises. Anyway, the connection is this. NPEC is tied in with the Department of Education, and they put tons of documents on-line, some of which aren't even available in paper any more. According to John's *curriculum vitae,* his dissertation had something to do with codes and things, and it dawned on me, who's more likely to be involved in that sort of work than government agencies? Now, because you are listening so quietly, I will reward you by skipping lightly over my afternoon's treks through websites for the CIA, the FBI, the various branches of the military, and the Pentagon. Suffice it to say, I finally landed at the National Security Agency website, and that's when I hit pay dirt!"

Nora told him about Executive Order 12958, which required the NSA to make available to the public thousands of documents previously designated Permanently Classified. "An hour ago, I downloaded an article by Smythe T. Smith titled *Decoding Apparent Randomness: The Utility of the Magee Elastic Model,*" she chortled. "Smith wrote other things, too, but this one seemed to hold the most promise. So, when shall we get together and compare our finds?"

Van's plans with his children would occupy that evening but he and Nora settled on 9:00 the next morning. He needed to study the dissertation. They might be getting John Howard into very deep trouble, and if so, he wanted to be sure of the ground on which he stood. When he got to the science building, the dissertation was there: ELASTIC MODELS IN THE ANALYSIS OF SECRET CODES. Only nineteen pages—typical of dissertations in mathematics.

He flipped through the pages, hoping the accusation was unfounded. Academic honor and honesty made up so much of his being that he could not get his mind around the idea that the president of his college had stolen intellectual property, certainly not a piece of work central to his academic credentials. He shoved the dissertation into his briefcase.

Dark Harbor

Two of his children awaited his arrival at home. Upset as he was, he felt grateful. Their presence would help him through the evening.

Van slept better than he had expected, but adrenaline started pumping before he even left his bed. He still had to examine the dissertation. While Kenyan blend dripped aromatically into the pot, he read the *Summary* and *Conclusions* sections of the dissertation. At a quarter before nine, he scribbled, "I'm at Professor Perry's house. Home for lunch. Dad," and left the half sheet of yellow paper on the kitchen table.

Nora opened the door with mug in hand. "Would you like some coffee?"

"Thank you, but no. I spent the early hours of the morning studying this." He gestured with the dissertation. "While I was at it, I consumed a whole pot. My stomach feels it."

"Did you eat breakfast?" Van shook his head. "Well, then, how about some toast and jam? It might settle your stomach."

Van grinned. "For a woman who chose to have no children, you give a convincing imitation of the Great Earth Mother. Is there any ailment, physical or mental, that you do not think would be improved by judicious dosing with food or drink?"

Nora laughed. "I'll take that as a yes."

Between bites, Van read the Smith article while Nora skimmed the dissertation. She laid it aside. "I've made no attempt to unravel the mathematical formulae, but my first impression is that the substance of John's dissertation mirrors the Smith article."

Her doleful expression told Van how much she had wanted the accusation to be false. Not more than he wished the same. He clenched his jaw and swallowed hard. "It does." He drew in all the air his lungs would hold and then forgot to breathe. "Damn it all, anyway!" The words exploded from his center, flying out on pent-up breath. "Damn it," he said again, more quietly, his hurt as deep as if he had been the object of personal injury. The ivory tower was not the ideal he had believed.

"You're sure."

"Quite sure." He pushed aside the remnants of his toast and pulled his chair closer to Nora. They leafed through the Smith article together,

Van ticking off points of comparison. "The dissertation has a different literature review—written more than thirty years later, after all—but the meat of it—the arguments, proofs, and conclusions—everything is plagiarized." Intellectually, he accepted the evidence. Emotional acceptance felt impossible.

"Do you suppose Lydia knew about this? That they conspired in his professional fraud?" The pain in Nora's voice reflected Van's own.

"God only knows." Their conversation twisted through issues and alternatives before coming to rest on the fact that plagiarism topped the list of academic crimes, and that, therefore, they were honor bound to act. Nora gazed at the river as if wishing for escape. Van spoke to her profile. "I will call President Howard and arrange an appointment."

He dropped the telephone receiver back onto its cradle. "John will see us at 3:00. He was curious, of course, and I think a bit put out that I would not tell him the reason for this meeting." He ran long fingers through his hair. "Damn it, Nora. I know we must do this, for the sake of the college—our colleagues—all of us. But . . ." Van's thoughts roiled. A relatively new member of the faculty, accusing his president of a violation of academic honor—of fraud—what retaliation might he face? Could there possibly be a perfectly reasonable explanation? He felt exposed. As a faculty leader, with more security and a lot more influence, Nora carried a certain immunity. Worry about himself and his future embarrassed him. This was not a Van he liked. Self-censure lent a note of bitterness to his voice when he said, "Does it strike you as ironic that we are going to confront John Howard for his academic deception and that in the process of doing so, we will be perpetrating a deception of our own?" Nora looked puzzled. "We will be lying to John—and Lydia—at least by omission. Talking only about plagiarism, not mentioning blackmail, the false log entries, Ted Slater's murder."

"I know you would prefer to be open about everything, but that isn't prudent. Remember what you said about questioning Ray? No private citizen with any semblance of good sense would confront a potential murderer in his own home, lay out the evidence, and wait to see what happens. Not that I really believe John is a murderer. Or Lydia, either. But, Frank would have our heads if we revealed all of that. Just think how he reacted when we talked to Suzanne and Ray."

A question popped into Van's mind: just how often did Nora consider Frank Pierce when determining a course of action? Instead of asking it, he said, "I know. And I agree. But if John demands to know how we came to spend our Christmas holidays ferreting out his plagiarism—well, it will be damned awkward, that's all." He and Nora agreed to meet at Nora's office at 2:30 and parted uneasily.

Alone with the tick of the grandfather clock, Nora felt her own sorrow, mourning the loss of respect for her friend. She liked John. And Lydia. But she often had to set aside personal feelings when evaluating the performance of a student or a colleague. She tried always to be humane but never to compromise principles. Usually she succeeded. If John killed Ted because of blackmail—well, the legal system would sort that out. But if John's plagiarism had nothing to do with Ted's murder, what course would be both just and humane? John would have to leave academic life, of course. There was no way around that. But would public exposure really serve a positive end? An end worth the pain it would cause? Nora brooded on such matters the rest of the morning and through lunch.

CHAPTER THIRTY-FIVE

Nora awaited Van's arrival, swiveling from bookcase to window, frustrated that her small office precluded pacing. Fifteen minutes late—not at all like Van. When she saw him approaching the building, she snatched up her shoulder bag briefcase and intercepted him on the sidewalk. "You're late. What happened?"

"I reviewed the evidence one more time." He shook his head. "Only plagiarism can explain the commonalities."

Sympathy for his low mood washed over Nora. "I wish it weren't so, too. But we both know that talking to John is the right thing—the only thing—to do." As they walked, she said, "Look, you have a better grasp of the mathematical substance of the work than I. You take the lead in discussing the evidence." Van took several steps before nodding his agreement. Nora continued, "We must give John an opportunity to explain. And let's try not to be too heavy-handed or moralistic."

Van said, "I should certainly hope not," in a tone that made Nora want to defend her comment, but she stifled the impulse. They walked the rest of the way to Ozmon House in silence.

John Howard took a seat facing Nora. "So, tell me, what's so important that it couldn't wait till after the New Year? It must be either very good or very bad." John's tone was light, his eyes watchful. "From the seriousness of your expressions, my guess is the latter."

Nora shifted her gaze from the intricate pattern of the Persian carpet to John's face. "I'm afraid it's very bad indeed."

Van handed the two documents to the president. John's eyes flicked across the pages. "Oh, my God." His body seemed to collapse into itself. The blood drained from his face.

"Did you knowingly—*willfully*—plagiarize the substance of your dissertation?" Van asked. His words fell into the silence like hammer blows. Nora flinched. But there really was no gentle way he could have asked that question.

John looked from Van to Nora and back again, a pulse visible in his neck. He inhaled deeply, and said, "I did."

The ready admission surprised Nora. She saw the jagged edges of pain in his eyes and spoke gently. "John, why?"

In the pause that followed Nora's question, Lydia came into the room. "I thought I heard the doorbell," she said cheerfully. No one spoke. She cast a questioning look at her husband.

John sat straighter, seeming to control his voice with effort. "My dear, I think you had better join us. I was just about to tell Nora and Van how I came to plagiarize my dissertation."

Lydia said, "*What?*" Then a mask of downcast eyes and silence dropped into place.

John began. "In my first two years in graduate school, I was the confidential assistant to the chair of the department. Among other duties, I maintained the departmental files for current and prospective graduate students. I never read any of the materials for other students—never. But one day I had the poor judgment to read my own." A note of relief seeped into his voice. "I learned that the professor I intended to ask to supervise my dissertation had a very low opinion of my scholarly potential. I remember his letter still: 'John is bright and highly motivated, but entirely without creativity.' If Lydia had not insisted that I complete my degree, I would have quit." Nora saw Lydia studying John, but he did not meet her eyes.

"That fall, I had to find a dissertation director and a thesis topic. I worked with Professor Ernst Webber, a German who immigrated to the United States at the beginning of World War II. He'd been in German intelligence and he agreed, as an unwritten condition of his naturalization, to work as a cryptoanalyst in our own intelligence effort. When the National Security Agency was founded in the early 1950's, Webber was one of the first faculty to get involved in NSA's Mathematical Sabbatical Program."

John leaned forward, elbows on knees, his eyes on his clasped hands. "Webber encouraged me, but I was paralyzed by fear of failure. When Lydia got pregnant, it felt like disaster. We couldn't live on a graduate student stipend and I couldn't let her parents support us. I had to finish my degree quickly." John looked from one silent listener to the other. "Not that that excuses what I did."

"Professor Webber said files of his past projects might suggest possibilities. I came across a report from his time at the NSA, by Smythe T. Smith, marked 'Permanently Classified.' It was in a banker's box of project files, stapled to the back of another document. My first impulse was to call Webber, but it was a Friday night, and I decided to wait till Monday." John paused. Nora could almost feel the silence in the room before he resumed. "But I was curious. Over the weekend, I read it. I started thinking it could be my dissertation. I even told myself that it would be a service to the profession, making public information to which researchers were entitled." Nora marveled that he spoke so candidly. "When I returned everything else to Webber, I kept the Smith manuscript. I reviewed the literature and found that nothing like it had been published. A mathematician named Smythe T. Smith had died in the late '40s, and how many of them could there be? When I discussed the concepts with Webber, he gave no indication that he recognized any of it. To make a long story shorter, I felt safe presenting the work as my own. It was accepted and the university awarded my doctoral degree." John massaged his forehead. "Since then, every time a search committee or review panel examined my credentials, I've feared discovery. When the NSA declassified 1.3 million pages of materials produced between the two world wars, I nearly had a nervous breakdown. But no one ever knew—till now." John straightened his shoulders. "So there you have it. Over the years, my anxiety about possible discovery abated but I've lived with the guilt every day of my life."

Lydia's voice was thick and her eyes brimmed with tears when she whispered, "Oh, John. If only you had told me . . ."

For a moment, neither Nora nor Van spoke. Watching a fundamentally good man as his world collapsed around him pained Nora. Van looked as miserable as she felt. They should have decided ahead of time how to end the interview. But she, at least, had not entirely accepted the truth until John confessed. She said, "I think we'd better be going. We'll talk later about what's to be done about this."

Van picked up the manuscripts from the coffee table in front of John. As he returned them to the folder, a copy of Ted Slater's letter slipped out and settled on the floor by John's foot. He held it out to Van, but his own name seemed to catch his eye. "What's this?" Van glanced at Nora. She lifted one shoulder a fraction of an inch. Van said, "A copy of the letter Ted Slater wrote to you. How did he learn about the plagiarism?"

Now it was really going to hit the fan. Nora heard Lydia's sudden intake of breath as John frowned and asked, "Ted? What do you mean?"

Nora gestured toward the letter in his hand. "That letter, threatening to expose your plagiarism if you did not meet his terms."

Lydia whimpered. John skimmed the letter and crumpled it into a ball, crossing his legs and arms as if protecting himself. "I received no such letter." He looked from Nora to Van. "Good God! You think . . . Surely you don't think I *killed* him!" The blood again drained from John's face and the knuckles of his clenched fists showed white as bleached bone. "I was *here* that Friday night, at home. I've already told that to Frank Pierce." At the mention of Frank's name, the enormity of what they were doing hit Nora. She searched frantically for a way to backpedal, but to no avail.

Van said, "Your whereabouts that Friday night is police business, President Howard, not ours. But we felt honor bound to speak to you before we go public with the plagiarism."

Nora turned to Lydia. Frank would have their heads anyway. No point holding back now. "And . . ." She cleared her throat. "And we will have to tell Frank that you were anchored in Queenstown harbor the night Ted was killed."

"But I wasn't! I was in Swan Creek."

"Lydia, please. Don't make this harder for all of us. My anchor light has a Fresnel lens—probably the only Fresnel lens on the Bay—and Ted's neighbor recognized it that night." Lydia seemed about to offer further denials but Nora raised her hand, her tone taking on the hard, impatient edge that could intimidate both students and colleagues. "Even if one were to argue a second Fresnel lens, your log entry about Swan Creek is clearly bogus. The sunken skiff is visible only at ebb tide and the hour you claim to have seen it that evening was near maximum flood." Disappointment and disillusion tasted bitter in her mouth. "If you had paid attention to the tide tables, we might never have known you copied from my log entry."

Lydia grimaced, her words hot with self-disgust. "I knew it. I knew that bloody log would be my undoing." She faced Nora. "I was desperate to get it back. I searched everywhere, but it just wasn't *there*."

Lydia's words echoed in Nora's head: *it just wasn't there*. Her pulse quickened as images flashed in her mind's eye—her rifled desk, books strewn on the floor, a kaleidoscope of broken glass. "You. *You* ransacked my house!"

Lydia bowed her head, trembling, the remorse in her voice almost palpable. "I'm sorry—so sorry—but I thought if I could get the log . . . I had to make it look like something else. I didn't do it to hurt you." Nora sat, cold and unmoved. Lydia looked beseechingly at John, squared her shoulders, a woman facing judgment without flinching. "Okay. I *was* there—outside. But as I walked from the dock to the house, I saw a man's silhouette on the curtains—definitely not Ted's—so I didn't go in. When I heard a car drive away, I went in and . . . and I found his body. He was already dead. I panicked. I just wanted to get away as fast as I could. I hoped no one would ever know I'd been there. That no one would ever know about . . . us."

The words were plausible enough. Once again, Nora and Van exchanged glances. This time it was Van who stepped into the confrontation. "We must tell the police what we know—about Lydia's presence in Queenstown harbor and about the blackmail letter. If that casts suspicion on both of you . . ." Van's tone conveyed both helplessness and resignation.

Every line of John's body revealed weariness. He said, "I swear to you, I never received that letter. I had no idea that Ted knew." He rubbed his forehead, as if finally grasping a complex concept. "He made an appointment with me for the next week—the week after he was murdered. He must have intended to confront me then."

Lydia leaped to her feet, wringing her hands like Lady Macbeth. "No! Please. Listen. Don't do this to us. I'll tell you the truth! Ted and I had planned to spend the weekend together." Her voice grew steadier, but her hands remained clenched. "We—we were drinking. And he became abusive, calling me names, twisting my arm." Her voice faltered. "It had happened before, recently, but this time was worse. He hit me. I feared for my life. I simply . . . defended myself."

John said, "Lydia! Don't."

She looked at him, eyes like a frightened doe, but continued. "But then—as I said—I panicked and tried to cover it up—tried to cover everything up. John . . . John knew nothing of this, not until this very minute. He wasn't there. No one else was there." Her tearful face tugged at Nora's sympathies. "Please. John's dissertation had nothing to do with anything. I *know* it. If I tell Frank what really happened, can't you . . . ? Must you expose something so painful? It would be a needless humiliation—and what good could come of it?"

Van spoke quietly, but Nora knew he was implacable. "Lydia, you do not understand the seriousness of his offense—of his *crime*. He stole another man's intellectual property! There is no place in education for a plagiarist—most especially not as the head of an academic institution!"

Lydia's tone was beseeching. "But you don't have to make it *public*—a mistake that's decades old—possibly creating confusion and doubt about a straightforward case of self-defense." She cast a frantic look at her husband. "John will resign and pledge never to seek an academic appointment again. Wouldn't that be punishment enough? To lose his career and have his wife's betrayal dragged before the public? Isn't that justice enough?"

Nora heard the echo of her own thoughts from earlier in the day. Van started to demur but Nora interjected, "John, would you agree to that? To resign from West and withdraw from academic life?"

"Of course." He paused before adding, "It would be very painful to our sons and families—if the plagiarism becomes public. Also, such a revelation could be detrimental to the college. I cannot ask it, but if you could remain silent about the plagiarism, it would be a great kindness."

Nora sought Van's reaction. He dipped his chin. She turned to Lydia. "We must tell Frank about the faked log and the Fresnel lens. But as for the plagiarism . . ." She shifted her gaze to John. "If Frank finds out about that on his own, well, it's out of our hands, isn't it? But we won't mention it, provided that you announce your resignation before the January Board meeting. Of course, if you ever take another academic job, we will come forward."

CHAPTER THIRTY-SIX

Lydia collapsed on the sofa, too stunned to show Nora and Van out. The door clicked shut behind them like the closing of a cell. When John returned, he took her hand in both of his. He spoke, every syllable black and blue with pain: "Lydia, darling, you shouldn't have confessed to protect me." All the color had drained from his face.

She spoke quietly, trying to smother his objections. "I did it for *us*, John." She lifted his hand, brushed her lips lightly across his knuckles. "Frank already knows about the affair and soon he'll know about the log and the anchor light. I am a suspect, no matter what. I had to do what I could to protect you. You are my life. Besides being a betrayed husband, that letter would be seen as another motive. There's no way to prove Ted hadn't actually blackmailed you." Seeing the despair on his face, she squeezed his hand. "Confessing was the only thing to do. And it was the *right* thing to do." She drew an unsteady breath. "It really was my fault. All of it. I would never intentionally betray you, John. You must believe that. But . . . Ted found out about the plagiarism because of me."

John turned disbelieving eyes on her. "You didn't even know."

"I didn't know, but I did betray your secret." That evening came into her mind as if she were living it now—reclining on the bed in the cheap motel room, Ted giving her a foot rub. Her thoughts flew like caged sparrows. What did John need to know? What would be hurtful to no purpose? She said, "It was last spring, when you and Liz were on the West Coast. We went to a motel on the Delaware shore. We had a great deal to drink. Somehow we got into a discussion of human nature. Ted praised consistency and said that the best people are consistent. I said no one is really consistent."

Ted didn't like to be contradicted. He twisted her foot sharply and she yelped in pain and surprise. He said, "Sorry." But there was flint in his tone when he said, "You have no evidence to support such a claim."

"Of course I have evidence." The gin made her bold. "Maybe I can't guarantee the inconsistency of every member of the human race, but I certainly have a basis for my opinion." Lydia propped herself up on her elbows, the better to see his face. "John is a perfect example. He's a mathematician, for God's sake, extremely consistent. But about a year ago, for no reason whatsoever, he did a complete about face on an issue dear to his heart for decades." Ted listened, every line of his face expressing skepticism. "It's true. His dissertation director was a man who had some sort of connection to the National Security Agency and he—John—used to go on and on about classified research being a crime against the free exchange of ideas, hamstringing young researchers and stifling new discoveries. He was trying to find a dissertation topic and floundering something awful. Back then, he said reports of classified research ought to be 'liberated.' But a while back, when the NSA declassified over a million pages of documents, John nearly went apoplectic." Lydia tried to sit up but Ted still held her foot. She continued, more loudly. "I mean it. All of a sudden, he was going on about confidentiality and the public trust, how people ought to be able to believe what their government tells them, saying anything designated 'forever classified' ought to be classified forever, damn it. It was a complete about-face. And if that isn't inconsistency, I don't know what is!"

"Well, now, don't exercise yourself. You've convinced me—not that you are right, only that you have some basis for your views." He resumed rubbing her foot, gently, almost absent-mindedly. They made love again before drifting into sleep.

Weeks later, when John and Liz were fundraising in Florida, Ted invited her to dinner at his house. The table had candles and flowers. The food was good, their conversation light and amusing. When he served dessert, he laid a manila folder by her wine glass. She looked at him questioningly. "It's a surprise, love. Open it."

Lydia found a photocopy of a document. "I don't have my glasses. And I can't see a thing in this light. I'll read it later," she said, pushing it aside.

"No, no. I insist. This is too good to delay." He retrieved reading glasses from her handbag and adjusted the rheostat. The document was a copy of John's dissertation. She frowned. Ted grinned. "Keep going, love. Keep going." Under the dissertation was another document, by Smythe T. Smith, National Security Agency, dated 1952. Ted laughed. "You don't get it, do you? Your perfect, precious husband—our president, the keeper of all that's right and honorable at West College— plagiarized his dissertation from Smith! His day of reckoning is at hand. And you, love, are the one who made it all possible."

"That's a lie. John would never plagiarize anything."

Ted laughed again. "You don't have to take my word for it. The proof is right in front of you."

The certainty on his face made her weak. "Oh, Ted, you can't tell. You mustn't! It would ruin John's chances for another presidency."

"If I tell, another presidency will be the least of John's worries. He'll be drummed out of higher education altogether! It might even be legally actionable." He burst out laughing. "If you could see your face!"

Lydia leaned toward him across the candles. "Ted, don't do this to me. Please. I beg you!"

Slater looked at her, a half smile on his lips. "Just how prettily can you beg? Come over here and show me."

Over the next six months, he brought up John's plagiarism repeatedly, tormenting and dominating her, but always ended up assuring her that John's secret was safe.

Sometimes, during long sleepless nights, she'd been tempted to confess everything to John. But what good would that do? Ted would still be able to blackmail them, and John would know of her betrayal— her double betrayal. Lydia had stifled her guilt, told herself that Ted's love for her kept him silent, refused to acknowledge the reversal in their balance of power.

When John and Liz planned the New England trip, Ted again invited her to his house. He insisted. So Lydia borrowed Nora's boat, her sail an excuse for being out of town for a few days.

She stowed her duffle on the V-berth and removed the bottle of Booth's gin nestled among the soft black folds of nightgown and underwear. Ted found black silk arousing and she wanted whatever edge she could muster. Their sex was always orgasmic, so she focused resolutely on anticipation, submerging anxiety.

Lydia made her first log entry: Wednesday, October 22, 13:12 hrs, clear, wind SW at 7 K.

The gentle sail freed Lydia's concentration. Her thoughts turned mostly to Ted. Physical attraction was only part of what had drawn her to him. They both chaffed at the limitations of a small college in a small town, and suffered fools with silent humor. She seemed to have found a kindred spirit.

But the last six months had been shadowed by Ted's darker side, his behavior increasingly unpredictable. He took pleasure in her tears, and followed them with warm displays of affection culminating in sex. The juxtaposition of her pain and his pleasure frightened her. She thought about ending the relationship, but in some dark corner, never brought to consciousness, hid an awareness that ending the affair was no longer her choice. She clung to the surety that eventually Ted would tire of her, or John would get another presidency, and the affair would end.

She anchored in Grays Inn Creek at 16:04 hrs. With an hour of good daylight left, she went topside with the log, a tall gin, and a folder of materials on Waldorf College. The oranges and pinks of a Chesapeake sunset painted the western sky. Lydia pulled up her collar against the twilight air. The weight of her need for John to move to another institution pressed upon her. She willed herself to concentrate on the materials at hand. When they went to Waldorf for the final round of interviews, her performance must be flawless. She went below, and poured more gin over ice.

Lydia rummaged in the dry locker for the plastic cased anchor light but found a brass one instead. She carried it topside. Swaying unsteadily, gulping the cold night air, she made her way forward and clipped the lantern to the bowstay. It hung almost motionless, the bright bluish light piercing the dark. She inched aft holding onto the lifeline and dropped heavily onto the port cushion. She found the Big Dipper and Polaris. The night sky swirled and soon she was retching over the gunwale, her stomach heaving long after it was empty. Inclined upon the cushion, her last thoughts before she fell into oblivion were of John and Liz.

At 4:00 in the morning, she woke with a jerk, *Duet* rolling from side to side. Damp had settled on her skin, swelling the cotton fibers of her shirt and pants, chilling her to the bone. The radio still played. The cabin light spread incandescent yellow across the bunks. Turning off the lights, she prayed the battery hadn't been drained too much. She stumbled to the V-berth and dropped limply onto the bunk.

She looked like hell the next morning but felt better than she had any right to. The battery did not fail her, and she proceeded under power long enough to boost the charge before hoisting sails. Sailing was balm to her body and her spirit. The familiar routines were a comfort: demands on her attention kept troubling thoughts at bay, and physical labor under the autumn sun renewed her.

Lydia made another log entry: "Anchored, Gibson I., 16:55 hrs. Distance of 23.1 m. Average speed, 3.2 K. Sunset, 17:05 hrs. Clear." She was happy, released from the ever-present scrutiny that was the lot of the president's wife. The information about Waldorf made more sense than it had the night before. Even her thoughts about Ted were optimistic. She ate with gusto and drank with restraint and went early to bed.

The slow start to Friday was a luxury she could rarely manage at the president's house. Dressed only in a large T-shirt, she carried a bowl of cereal and a banana topside to enjoy the fall air and watch the occasional cloud drift by. She could be in Queenstown harbor just at dusk, no problem. Sailing conditions were perfect. It felt like a good omen.

As she left the little bight under power, Lydia's glance fell on the cell phone. She hadn't checked for messages since leaving Centreville. The only message was from John, on Thursday morning: "Hello, my dear. I just wanted you to know that I'm home. Liz called last night to say two of our three appointments were cancelled, so we're rescheduling the trip. I hope you're having a good sail. See you Sunday." Panic coursed through her. She disconnected quickly, as if by that act she could make the contents of the message go away.

"Damn." Lydia gnawed on her lower lip, weighing options. John hadn't said he wanted her home and Ted would be really pissed if she cancelled their weekend. John wouldn't know she'd heard the message.

She'd proceed as planned, and consider what to tell him. She pushed anxiety aside and tended to *Duet*.

She anchored short of Salthouse Cove as daylight faded. She flew the anchor light from the bowstay, gathered her duffle, and closed the hatches. She saw Ted's lighted patio doors as she climbed down the stern ladder into the dink. The wail of a jazz trumpet floated on the night air as she hurried up the path.

Ted met her on the patio. "Hello, love." He kissed her soundly. He smelled of the aftershave she had given him and tasted faintly of gin. "Have some of this. It's just what you need. I'll have one for you in a minute." He wore black silk pajama bottoms and a short black kimono embroidered with stylized birds and flowers.

She took a long swallow of gin and tonic and handed the glass back to him. "Thanks. That would be lovely. But first I'd like a shower."

She dropped her sailing clothes on the bedroom floor and retrieved a long silk kimono from the closet. Ted joined her in the black and white marble shower. Lovemaking carried them from the shower to the bed. She mounted him, moving rhythmically. With one hand Ted squeezed and tugged at her nipple and with the other he traced the crack of her buttocks and teased the flesh with feathery hints of touches. Lydia clutched the headboard with both hands and moaned. They reached orgasm together.

By the time dinner was over, Lydia felt mellow. They relaxed by the fire sipping nightcaps and talking intermittently. It was the best time they had spent together in months. She was flipping through Ted's CDs when the doorbell rang. She blanched and for one nightmare instant her heart stopped, overcome by the irrational fear that it might be John. She froze, facing the glass doors to the patio. She could neither see the caller nor distinguish the words, but her heart hammered painful blows against her ribs.

Ted closed the door and joined Lydia. "You look ready to faint."

She laughed weakly. "I feel that way, too. Who was that anyway?"

"What would you say if I told you it was John?" He smiled as he spoke.

She squinted at him. "I'd say you are lying."

He shrugged. "In that case, it was nobody you need to worry about." And then he said, "By the way, love, I think it only gentlemanly to show this to you before I mail it." He took a letter from a folder on his desk and handed it to her.

"What's this?" She scanned the contents, blanched, and read it again more slowly. "I know you have no intention of blackmailing John. You wouldn't do that to me. But your teasing is getting tiresome." She threw the letter into the fireplace and it flamed into ash.

His voice was quiet, gentle. "I'm not teasing, love. If John gets the Waldorf presidency—as you've so often assured me he will—this is my main chance. If I act now, I can get what I want regardless of what happens to darling John—or to you."

Lydia swayed, and gripped the mantel for support. "He'll never stand still for blackmail. John has too much integrity for that."

"Integrity? That's a joke!" Ted laughed.

Lydia whispered, "He'll wonder how you knew. He might suspect."

"Well, yes, I suppose he might." Ted finished his drink. "Then again, I might tell him."

"Please, Ted. Please! Think about me." She blushed at the plaintive wail, but she knew from recent experience that her only hope of avoiding disaster lay in begging. "Think what this will do to me. If John is nothing, I'll be less than nothing. Surely you can't—you don't want to destroy someone you love."

Ted's eyes glinted. "Do you really think I give a shit?" His voice was sharp and hard, a sword unsheathed. "Do you think I'd even look at you twice if you weren't the wife of the president?" The words hammered her. "Every time you moaned and begged for it—every time I drove it home—I thought, 'Fuck you, John Howard.'" He turned toward the coffee table. "The only difference is, now he'll know he's being screwed."

Lydia leaped forward. She slapped him, one stinging blow across the cheek, before he fended her off, slapping her hard in return, grabbing her shoulders. "And don't get all teary. It doesn't amuse me any more," he said, thrusting her away.

Lydia ran into the bathroom, slamming the door and turning on the water to mask her sobs. She sank to the floor, mumbling, "It's over. Everything's over." Darkness overcame her. As consciousness slowly re-emerged, the same thought kept circling: even if he doesn't send the letter to John now, he would always have that leverage. Suddenly she was furious that he had made such a fool of her—that he had used her. She scrambled up, scrubbed her face with a towel, and stormed back into the living room, fury bubbling over. She'd cared for that sonofabitch. She'd thought they were kindred spirits—that he loved her! She stopped short, bewildered. The room was empty.

Then she saw him, on the floor between the coffee table and the fireplace, his body curled as if he'd been tackled carrying a football. "God damn you! Get up!" She rushed forward—but stopped when she stepped in the blood and spilled gin pooling around his head. Ice cubes lay scattered. He didn't move, didn't make a sound, and belatedly she knew. "Oh, my God." She heard the faint echo of a car engine.

Lydia stumbled to the sofa, her senses overloaded: pain in a stubbed toe, warm blood on her foot, a CD playing in the background. She clutched her elbows tight to her body and bent double, locking down the keening wail that tore at her throat.

She stared at the body, a distant observer of a scene strangely uncoupled from herself, blood splatters everywhere, muscles twitching before stillness set in. Panic surged as the surreal scene gave way to the real. "My God. He meant it when he said it was John at the door. What did he see? He must have . . ." Her rage drowned in fear. Her thoughts catapulted over each other. "Call a doctor. An ambulance. Oh, my God." She reached for the telephone, hand shaking, then faltered. "Don't be stupid. He's dead. And John . . ." She closed her eyes. "This can't be real."

She rocked back and forth like an autistic child. Blood soaked the hem of the kimono and stained the slippers. She struggled for control. "Think! You've got to clean up. Think!"

She closed the patio curtains, even though no other boats were in the harbor. What she had to do demanded to be hidden, even from the eyes of night.

She gathered rubber gloves, over-sized trash bags, and towels from the kitchen. The bloody slippers were Slater's and ill fitting, but she kept them on. She mustn't leave footprints. She mustn't leave fingerprints. She mustn't leave evidence of any sort. She put three garbage bags, one inside the other for strength, then took off the bloody kimono and stuffed it in. All of the windows were curtained now but her nakedness made her feel exposed. She wanted to run headlong into the covering dark, but willed herself to wipe every surface she could remember touching. Still wearing Ted's slippers, she got out the vacuum cleaner and ran it over the place where her duffle and sailing clothes had lain.

She stripped the bed and re-made it. She showered, washing away traces of tears along with Ted's blood, and redressed in her sailing clothes. She cleaned the shower, removed hair from the drain trap, then poured bleach down both drains just for good measure. She put out clean towels and bathmat. She stuffed the wet towels and sheets into the king sized pillowcases, the pillowcases into the garbage bag, tamping down the load. She retrieved the bloody poker and the wine bottle, adding them to the bag. She slipped into her shoes at the patio doors and left, opening the curtains and wiping the curtain pulls and door handles as she went.

The rage she felt when she slapped him had given way to lingering anger that precluded remorse but not fear. She scurried through the dark, tripped on the dock and fell forward. Pain shot through her knee and a dull thunk echoed over the water. "The neighbors . . ." She darted furtive glances all around. Nothing seemed amiss, but thoughts of secret watchers made her heart pound and left her gasping for breath. "Oh, God." She fumbled with the plastic bag, with the oarlock. She dipped the oars into the water as quietly as she could, rowing first along the shore, praying the trees and tall grasses would hide her passage. When *Duet* was fifty feet away, she turned toward the boat.

On board, she looked back at the house, reviewing her actions, persuading herself she had overlooked nothing. The wind was calm, the sky starry, the air chilly. Lydia felt intensely aware of her body: the painful throbbing of her skinned knee, cold fingers, blood pounding in her ears. Clasping her hands, she found her palms slick with sweat. Kneeling on the foredeck, she scrubbed her hands on her pant legs before grabbing the rode to haul the anchor on board. She turned off the anchor light but left it clipped to the bowstay. Every fiber of her being screamed that she must get away from this place.

The noise of the engine rolled across the harbor, beating upon the sleeping houses. Lydia's labored breathing left her faint. *Duet* slid through the darkness. The waning moon gave enough light to see the pilings of the abandoned ferry dock off the port beam. The boat was her friend, a stealthy shadow gliding through the night. From the red flasher she turned right, following the channel to the Chester River.

Her breathing eased. Approaching the R-12 flasher, she turned on the running lights and advanced the throttle.

Two thoughts possessed her: get rid of the plastic bag and come up with an alibi. She needed time to think. From R-12 she set a course of 320. A little less than two miles away was deep water just south of Overton Point on Eastern Neck. She could anchor in the protected bight of the wild life refuge with little chance of discovery in the off season.

Safely anchored, Lydia went below. Another wave of anxiety engulfed her. She reviewed again where she had been in the house. Satisfied that she had done everything possible to eliminate evidence of her presence, a partial ease comforted her.

"I'm well out of the river's flow, in eight feet of black water." Having decided to sink the evidence, Lydia searched for something to keep it on the bottom. Remembering Nora's junk box, she pulled the companionway steps aside and fished around for the bin of old engine parts and miscellaneous bits and pieces that "might be useful someday." She shoved several items into the bag, tied the whole into a compact bundle, and stabbed it a few times with a galley knife. She lowered the bundle over the side and watched as it sank into oblivion. Exhausted, she returned below.

She sank onto the starboard bunk, elbows on knees, head resting in her hands. "How long before I come to know this stranger in my body? The Lydia I've lived with all my life could not have done any of this. But John . . . we've got to survive. We will survive." Desperate not to be alone with her thoughts, she abandoned the option of staying out till Sunday and turned her mind to fabricating an alibi.

She picked up the log, cursing her stupidity in entering the trip from Gibson Island to Queenstown. Even if Ted were alive, that trip should never have been public. But the entries had become so habitual . . . Wielding the razor knife from the tool bag, she carefully cut out the incriminating page, the telltale edge nearly invisible in the book's binding.

She spread charts 3 and 4 on the fold-down table and considered where she could have spent the night, finally settling on Swan Creek. She had not anchored in Swan Creek in three or four years. She couldn't remember enough details. But it was one of Nora's habitual gunkholes. Lydia riffled the pages of the log. "Yes!" Nora had been there just a couple of weeks ago. She wrote carefully, altering the specifics a bit here and there.

With the college dock little more than six miles from her anchorage, and an alibi that required an arrival time around noon, she should not get underway before 10:30 or so. She had a long night to get through. At midnight she went topside, carrying her drink. The evidence was gone. Her alibi was complete. She dared to hope that no hint of the affair would ever come to light.

Her head on John's shoulder, Lydia had drifted into thought, the silence stretching to cover everything, smothering words before they could emerge. Reliving the nightmare, Lydia hadn't noticed the winter evening turn to cold night and miserable dawn. She looked at John. "Where has the night gone?" she asked. "I don't know whether I was sleeping or dreaming or—or just remembering." She tried not to telegraph her fright. "Did I say anything?"

"Not after you told me about how Ted knew about my plagiarism. You've been silent for hours. I was afraid to leave you." John sounded anxious but truculent.

Lydia struggled to breathe. "Ted had threatened me with your exposure for months." She gripped John's hand so hard that her engagement ring cut into her finger. With effort, she loosened her grip. "If the police knew that, they'd never believe that you didn't know, that you didn't cancel your trip in order to murder Ted. You see that, don't you?"

John pulled his hand away, a muscle working along his jaw, and spoke through clenched teeth. "Yes. I see that. And I see that all of this happened because of your unfounded jealousy and alcohol!" John grabbed her shoulders so hard that she winced. "Why the hell didn't you *talk* to me? Ask me about Liz? Or the plagiarism? At the very least, tell me that you put our entire lives in the hands of a blackmailing womanizer!"

Lydia gasped. "You're hurting me!"

John dropped his hands, muttered, "Sorry."

What had John suffered through the long hours of the night? Lydia said, "If you'd told me you plagiarized your dissertation, I would have guarded your secret with my life. Or if I'd known you knew about Ted . . .

I could only do what I thought was best. I love you, John. No matter what, I'll always love you."

Her words seemed to defuse his anger and leave him weary. "And I love you. God help me, but nothing you've done can change that." John drew her into the circle of his arms and kissed her hairline. "Is there anything else I need to know?"

Lydia hesitated, his last angry words about not confiding in him still in her ear. The silence stretched. Their conspiracy had been unspoken—unacknowledged—long enough. "Oh, John—when I came out of the bathroom and found him . . . I couldn't believe what you'd done."

"What are you talking about?"

Tears streamed down her cheeks. "I understand why you did it. And it's okay. I'll do anything I can to protect you."

"Are you saying you didn't kill him? You think *I* killed him?"

"Didn't you? You were there!"

"No. I was here. All night."

Lydia tried to clear her head. "But—but Ted said it was you at the door. And you said you knew I was there."

"I did. And I was trying to protect you. That's why I didn't mention the phone call." Confusion washed over Lydia. John said, "That Friday night. A man's muffled voice, saying he'd seen you with Ted, had seen what you did. So I knew you were there, and then when Ted's body was found, I assumed . . ."

"You got a phone call the night he was killed? Who?"

"The voice was disguised, but I'm virtually certain it was Ray Martin."

"Oh, Lord."

"I don't think he intends to tell. He'd have done so by now. Not that it matters, now that you've confessed to Van and Nora."

Lydia's voice went up an octave. "But I didn't really do it! If Ray saw me, he might have seen the killer! I've got to call Van and Nora— before they do anything—before they talk to Frank." She jumped up and ran to the hall phone.

CHAPTER THIRTY-SEVEN

Frank stomped back and forth beside Nora's patio doors, fists clenched, trying to keep from hitting something. "What the hell did you think you were doing? Confronting a murderer, not even telling anyone what you knew!"

Nora looked belligerent but she spoke patiently. "I told you. We didn't go to confront a murderer. We went to confront a plag—to talk to the president about an academic matter." Frank stifled his retort and Nora continued. "All the other stuff—just sort of slipped out." Nora flicked a beseeching glance at Van. Her words came in a torrent. "And then Lydia admitted she'd been at Ted's and . . . We were going to tell you about my anchor light and Lydia's log when you returned from Philadelphia anyway. But then it all spilled out, and as soon as we left the Howards, I called your parents' house. I left messages. I got in touch with you as soon as I possibly could!" Frank snorted. Nora's tone shifted from defensive to irritated. "I didn't know you'd come back till you called me!"

Frank hadn't known about Nora's calls to Philadelphia until his mother phoned at 6:30 that morning. Mama said she'd been tempted not to give him the message at all. Why did she persist in believing that Nora was after him, married or not? The near miss had brought a thin sheen of perspiration to Frank's forehead. Nora wouldn't leave messages with his mother if it weren't important. He'd called immediately.

Nora was still in bed, groggily surprised to learn that Frank was in Centreville. She'd said, "I need to talk to you about the Fresnel lens and Lydia's log and . . . It's really too complicated for a phone call. Can you give me half an hour?"

When Frank arrived at 7:10, Van sat at Nora's oak table, a glass of orange juice in hand. Frank felt his whole body turn to wood. He said, "I like to do interviews one-on-one. Go home. I'll stop by when I'm finished here." Van started to rise, but Nora jumped in, saying they'd been together the whole time, there was no point in going over it twice, and besides, she'd invited Van for breakfast. Frank couldn't think of a way to insist and still get their cooperation. And so together they told him everything.

Remembering the early morning calls, Frank fought to be fair: the overnight delay was not Nora's fault. But before that! What were they thinking? *Were* they thinking?

Van spoke soothingly. "In any event, Captain, you now know everything we know about the Fresnel lens, the faked log, and what Lydia said about self-defense."

Frank couldn't hide his disgust. "You just don't get it, do you? Amateurs have no business confronting murder suspects. A person kills once, and nine times out of ten, it's easier the second time." He scowled at Nora. "It was a dangerous, stupid thing to do." She tried to object but Frank talked over her. "Not only that, but now Lydia knows exactly what the evidence against her is! When I talk to her, all the cards are already on the table, no chance of surprise. At best, I'll get a rehearsed version of her statement. She might even change her story altogether!"

"Look, we're sorry. Okay?" Nora spoke over her shoulder as she went into the kitchen to answer the phone. "We didn't cause problems on purpose. And we aren't dead!"

Frank leaned against the mantel. A radio tuned to *Morning Edition* broadcast background for the rumble of his empty stomach. Nora returned and stopped in the middle of the floor, looking dazed.

"What is it?" Van and Frank spoke in unison.

"That was Lydia. She said she lied to us. She didn't kill Ted; she just cleaned up the crime scene. She wants us not to tell the police that she confessed."

Van said, "*What?*" as Frank said, "Jesus, Mary and Joseph! When is anybody going to talk to the *cops* about this murder?" He turned his fury on Nora. "Here you go again, jumping into the middle of things."

"I'm not jumping in! *She* called *me*! She said—"

"I knew this was gonna happen. I knew it." Frank strode around the room, too angry to be still. "You tell a suspect all the evidence and what do you expect? Sure as you're born, she's gonna come up with some song and dance to try to get out of it." He'd stopped not more than two feet from Nora, glaring, yelling in her face.

Van started toward them but Nora motioned him away. She was pale, but looked Frank in the eye. "What she said was, that given the evidence—the clean-up and all—" she glanced at Van. "That given the evidence, a confession that she did it in self-defense was the best she could think of to . . . to protect herself. But Ray Martin saw her there and she thinks he must have seen the killer as well."

Frank backed up a step. "How does she know Martin saw her? And why the hell didn't she mention it before?" The questions carried all the belligerence he felt.

"I didn't cross-examine her! All I know is that she said something about Ray seeing her at Ted's that night and calling John. She was sort of babbling."

Frank moaned. "You should have let me talk to her."

"I didn't know you'd want her to know you were here!" Nora's voice cracked. "Honestly, I'm damned if I do and damned if I don't."

"Hold it. Just hold on a minute and let me think." Frank slumped into a chair by the table and dropped his head into his hands. Finally he said, "I'm going to talk to Ray Martin. You—both of you—are going to do nothing. You are not going to talk to Ray Martin; you are not going to talk to Lydia or John Howard. You are not going to talk to *anyone*. If Lydia calls here again, don't answer. I'll talk to her after I talk to Ray. I don't want her—or John—to have a chance to get to him first."

Ray Martin wasn't in his office at 8:35. He didn't answer his home phone. Frank drove to his apartment and pounded on the door. Nothing. Inside, the TV blared. Frank pounded again. "Ray? Are you in there?" He thought he heard Ray's voice and turned the doorknob.

Ray was hunched over the kitchen table, two bottles of bourbon in front of him, one nearly empty and the other unopened. Tears dripped off his chin. Frank sat down across from him, wondering whether Ray was in any shape to tell him what he needed to know. "What is it, Ray?"

Ray blinked, unfocused. "She's dead. My mama's dead." He shook his head. "What the hell were those nursing home people doing anyway? What were they doing when Mama fell?"

"Ray. I'm sorry about your mother. Really sorry, man."

Ray slumped in the wooden chair, eyes squeezed shut, his whole body shaking with muffled sobs. "Just when things were about to turn around. Just when I was getting out from under." Ray turned brimming eyes toward Frank. "I would've had her outta there soon. Everything was coming together." Ray poured another drink, clinking the neck of the bottle against his glass. "I was doing it for her. An' now it's all for nothing." Ray buried his face in his folded arms, weeping.

"I know you're grieving, Ray, but you've got to get a hold of yourself. I have to talk to you. About the night Ted Slater was killed. This is really important, Ray. I need your help. I need to know what you saw."

"It doesn't matter. Nothing matters anymore. My mama's dead." Ray stood up jerkily, his chair scraping across the linoleum, and lurched toward the sink, slopping bourbon out of his glass as he went. Frank thought he might be going to throw up but he rummaged in the drawer beside the sink. "Now she's gone, I got nothing to live for." When he turned back toward Frank, a .22 pistol wavered in his right hand.

Frank sucked in his breath. Not the most destructive weapon, but able to do serious damage. He spoke quietly, trying to put comfort in his tone. "That's no way to talk, Ray. Maybe living doesn't matter to you but it matters to a lot of other people. Why don't you just give the gun to me?" Frank started to stand.

Ray waved the gun. "Stay where you are! Nobody's telling Ray Martin what to do any more."

"Sure, Ray. Sure. Just don't point that gun at anybody. Please." Frank sank back in his chair. "I need you to tell me about the night Ted Slater was killed. If you don't tell me what you saw, Lydia Howard's going to be arrested for Ted's murder and she says she didn't do it. That would matter to me, Ray, an innocent person going to jail." While he talked, Frank eyed the gun. The chances were good that he could take the gun away from Ray without either of them being seriously hurt, but that would surely end his chances of getting any information from Ray now. And he needed it *now*.

Ray squinted at Frank. "You know about the Howards? How'd you find out about them?"

"That isn't important now. I just need to know—"

"I didn't mean to cause trouble, you know. I wasn't really gonna tell anybody she was there." Ray's tears welled again and he gestured with the gun. "You gotta believe that. When I made that call, I wasn't trying to hurt anybody."

Frank leaned forward. "Ray, listen to me. I believe you. I believe you didn't mean to harm the Howards. But that is what is going to happen, Ray, if you don't tell me about that night." Frank's voice was low but intense. "Who did you see, Ray?"

"Lydia Howard."

"Yes, but who *else*, Ray?"

Ray seemed surprised by the question. "Nobody else."

Frank felt his face settle into grim lines. "So, did you actually see Lydia kill Ted?"

Ray jerked sideways, nearly losing his balance. "Hell no. She didn't kill the sonofabitch. *I* did."

"Tell me."

Ray seemed momentarily more sober and spoke disdainfully. "It isn't all that complicated. I went to his house Friday night to give it one more shot—to get him to lay off demanding money. He wouldn't let me in, said he was busy, all that shit. But I saw *her* reflected in the patio door, clear as a mirror." He fell silent, remembering. Frank waited. Ray downed a slug of bourbon, the glass in his left hand steadier than the gun in his right. He continued, "I went back to my car, thinking about her being there, and then I thought, 'Hey, if I can see her in the patio door, the curtains must be open. Maybe I could see something worth seeing.' When I got around back, she was reading something—a letter, I think. I couldn't hear anything, but I could see she was pretty upset. Then they started to argue, I guess, 'cause she slapped him and then he slapped her back and she ran out of the room." Ray fell silent, seeming content just to lean against the counter and nurse his drink.

Frank said, "Come on, Ray. Tell me everything."

"When she ran out, he saw me. I never knew what that sonofabitch was gonna do next. He waved for me to come in." Ray shook his head.

"And I did. And he said, 'Did you enjoy that, Ray? I hope so, because this is one peep show that's really gonna cost you.' I said he knew damned well that I didn't have any money, that I needed every penny I had to keep Mama in that nursing home." Ray's eyes teared and his voice cracked and Frank figured that's how it had been that Friday, too.

"That fucker says, 'Well, now, maybe that's a problem for you, Ray, but it's no concern of mine.' I begged him, but he just laughed. He said that Mama was a hopeless loony so it didn't much matter where she was. And then he turned to fix another drink. He said, 'If loonies weren't so damned funny, I'd say they all ought to be lined up and shot.' And he laughed like he thought that was funny." Ray's tears dripped onto his shirt. "I couldn't stand it, that bastard laughing at my mama. I didn't even think about it. It was like an instinct or something. I just picked up the poker and swung it as hard as I could. He folded like a dropped towel. No moaning. Nothing. I hit him again—a few more times. Every time I swung the poker, his blood and brains splattered all to hell and gone." Ray looked hard at Frank. "Did you ever taste blood? I mean, not your own? It was all warm and salty. I thought I was gonna be sick. I dropped the poker and headed for the bathroom but then I remembered Mrs. Howard." Ray's eyes never left Frank's. "I thought maybe I should kill her, too, but I didn't have the stomach for it—not for, you know, doing it on purpose, to somebody who never did anything to me. I figured I'd better get the hell outta there. And now I figure it's time to get the hell outta here." Ray put the barrel of the pistol under his chin.

"No!" Frank sprang up.

"Sit down! Or I'll do it right now. I swear I'll do it."

"Okay, okay. I'm sitting." Ray was leaning a little forward and Frank noticed how his sparse hair was sticking up, fine as a baby's. "Ray, listen to me. I need you. I need you to tell me exactly what you did." Ray looked puzzled. "Start with when you remembered Mrs. Howard was in the house."

"Oh." Ray moved his hand a few inches and the pistol rested against his shoulder. Frank wondered how long before the weight of the gun got too heavy for him and what he'd do when it did. "I went back out the patio door and around front to my car. I had blood all over me. My suitcase for Atlantic City was in the trunk, so I took off all the bloody stuff and put on clean clothes."

"Right there by the car?"

"Sure. Why not? It was dark, and nobody was gonna see anything through the trees." He paused. "Except I didn't have clean shoes. I tried to wipe the blood off but it was no use. I keep a pair in my office, so I went there. By then I had the shakes so bad I could hardly unlock the door, so I had a little drink—just to steady my nerves, you know. Maybe a couple."

"What happened to the clothes?"

"I took 'em with me, threw 'em in a dumpster near the casino. My best damn shoes," he added, his tone woeful.

"What about the phone call? Tell me about that." Ray stared at Frank, saying nothing. "Tell me about calling President Howard. Why did you do that?"

Ray didn't seem to remember that he hadn't mentioned the call. "I was going over everything in my head while I drank my bourbon and I was feeling pretty good about it. I figured there was no way in hell anyone was gonna know I was ever there." He shook his head. "I dunno. It's kinda mixed up. Partly I thought he should know she was two-timing him and partly I wanted to warn her—you know, that somebody knew she'd been there and she should be careful. I didn't mean to frame her for what I'd done. I'd never get anybody in trouble with the cops if I could help it."

"What did you say to John Howard?"

Ray squinted and didn't say anything for several seconds. "Something like, 'I saw your wife tonight. With Ted Slater. I saw what she did. If she's not careful, she's gonna be in a shitload of trouble.' Something like that."

"What did he say?"

"He said, 'Who is this? Who is this?' and I hung up."

"Have you told this to anybody else?"

"Hell, no. I wouldn't be telling you now if I wasn't about to check outta here." Ray waved the gun.

Frank had to keep him talking. "You didn't say anything more to the Howards?"

"Why the hell would I do that?" Ray wouldn't meet his eye. Frank waited, saying nothing. Ray shifted. "I'm not saying I didn't think about it. I did. Come Christmas, I knew I had to do something to get Mama out of that fuckin' nursing home, and that meant getting my hands on some money. I wasn't really gonna tell anybody, though," he whined. "It's just, they've got more money than they'll ever spend and I thought maybe I'd just threaten to tell. I needed some of that money to help Mama. And now there's nothing I can do for her, not ever again." Ray drained his glass. "I just wish I'd killed that bastard years ago, when it might've made things better for Mama. Now she'll never even know I was keeping my promise. I was gonna get her outta that hole."

Frank said, "Ray, you're going to need a lawyer. I'm going to have to take you in." Ray's tears gushed anew and he wiped at them with his shirtsleeve, to no noticeable effect. His voice was muffled by his arm. "Do you think I give a shit what happens to me now? My mama is dead." He wiped his eyes again.

Frank lunged forward, grabbing Ray's wrist. The gun went off, blowing a hole in the microwave. Ray struggled to keep hold of the pistol. It exploded again. And again. Frank fell backwards, pain searing his armpit, blood spreading across the floor.

CHAPTER THIRTY-EIGHT

Van dropped the mooring line. "There was a time in the middle of the semester when I was sure that May would never come."

Nora said, "I once had a professor who said, at the first class meeting each term, 'Will this semester never end?'" She laughed. "I know the feeling. But here we are, starting another sailing season. Life is good. Or it will be if *Duet* is well and truly repaired. I checked out a few things when I brought her up from Marsh Point last week. The marina seems to have done a great job on the engine. And the new gauges are beauties. But this weekend will be the real shake-down."

She took *Duet* down the Corsica under power, making about four and a half knots without strain. Along the way, Van recalibrated the knot meter. Approaching the Chester River, Nora headed into the wind and Van set the sails. She cut the engine, savoring the silence. Van said, "This is the life. Wind in our sails, the afternoon sun skipping across gray-blue waves, a breeze dancing over sea grasses along the shore. It doesn't get better than this."

Suddenly, images of blood and lightning strikes slashed through Nora's consciousness. Thoughts of their last sail spiked her heart rate until she willed herself to breathe slowly and stay in the moment. Shadows of cumulus clouds drifted by, stealing the water's sparkle and the air's warmth, making her glad she'd worn the sweater Van gave her for Christmas. Van wore its twin, a coincidence he must have noticed, too. Neither of them mentioned it. Nora had trod carefully the last few months. She'd worked hard to avoid triggering the sort of conflicts they'd endured during the murder investigation, striving to hold on to their friendship.

Approaching the mouth of the Corsica, Van said, "If we turn into the Chester, we might spy some Russian wildlife." The Russian Embassy owned a big house on Corsica Neck where diplomats came to relax, swimming naked with no apparent regard for local protocol. The Russians did not welcome visitors, so she stayed well off shore.

"We're too far off for a good view," she wailed in mock distress.

Van studied her face. "Are you sure you want to head for Queenstown harbor? That you are ready to lay the ghosts to rest?"

"I refuse to give up forever one of the prettiest nearby anchorages. So today is as good as any other to exorcise bad memories. We could be anchored by quarter to four, maybe row ashore and take a walk. What do you think?"

"Sounds like a plan to me."

The teasing response still felt affectionate. Nora gazed at the shoreline, willing her face not to reveal feelings she was unable either to quell or to acknowledge.

They furled the main near R-2 at the mouth of the harbor and sailed in with the genoa, anchoring near the spot they had come to think of as belonging to *Duet*. The light was soft, the air gentle, the surface of the water almost flat. Nora entered their position, time, anchorage, weather, and water information in her ship's log.

"The scene of the crime." Van said.

Nora looking shoreward. "Yes. The scene of the crime. Do you suppose anyone will notice my anchor light tonight?"

"It is certainly possible." He scanned the houses along the harbor. "If your friend had not been your friend, had not been from Maine, had not given you an anchor light with a Fresnel lens—if MacPhee hadn't been an optics expert or lived elsewhere or had gone out that night—if any one of a dozen antecedents had been different, we would not have known that Lydia was in the harbor that night. The Howards would have suffered even fewer consequences than they have."

Something about Van's casual attributions to chance prickled Nora. "I doubt that. We read the blackmail letter and uncovered the plagiarism, so John would have become a suspect. As soon as that happened, Lydia would've tried to protect him by confessing, pleading self-defense as she did with us. No matter what else, John would have had to leave academic life, so the outcome would have been the same."

"Perhaps. But for a plagiarist and an adulteress, they came out of it relatively unscathed. And let's not forget that they both were willing to cover-up murder. Their undoing hinged on Suzanne giving you that disk. And it is fortunate that Ray confessed. Although the evidence put him in Atlantic City at such a late hour that he could do the murder first, he might have had little serious attention. There were so many other people with motive and opportunity."

Nora stifled an urge to insist that Ray would have been found out, noted that she was feeling especially contrary. If she wasn't careful, she could ruin their sail. She said, "Poor Ray. He isn't a hardened criminal—just a smart man who fell to booze and gambling and got ground down."

"He is a thief and a murderer."

"I know. But I can't help feeling sorry for him." Her gaze moved from the bright green leaves of spring to the reflections of trees in the still water. "And I can't help feeling responsible for Frank rushing over there like that, no back-up or anything. He's still going for rehab. And he may not even get a guilty verdict. Yesterday I heard Ray's attorney is going to try to get the confession thrown out because Frank didn't read Ray his rights."

"Does that apply before someone is arrested? He was not under arrest. Besides, Ray was the one with a gun."

"Right. But the argument is that at some point, Frank should have Mirandized him. If that argument fails, they might claim diminished capacity—because he was both drunk and grieving."

"That is ludicrous. His confession was not coerced. *And* he shot an officer of the law. He should not get away with anything." Van coiled the starboard line and looped it over the winch. "What disgusts me is that even if the confession is admitted, they are preparing to argue that sometimes innocent people do confess. I have been subpoenaed by the defense to testify that Lydia also confessed to the murder."

Nora nodded. "Me, too. But don't worry. Frank will make his case." She thought of insights she'd had about Frank over the years—starting with his parents' standards and how hard he had worked to live up to them. Being black in a mostly white environment probably pushed him to excel, too. Even his careful grooming reflected a drive toward perfection. What she said was, "Did you know that as an undergraduate his nickname was The Matador? Mostly that was because of his grace and daring on the basketball court. But there's something else, too. For a real matador, the important contest isn't between the man and the bull. It's always between the man and himself. That's Frank all over. He always comes through in the end." She noticed that her tone was a little defensive—and that praising Frank did not seem to please Van any more now that it had five months ago.

"I hope you are right. But even the most capable people stumble upon occasion." Van scowled. "Even in hindsight, his anger that we talked with the Howards seems excessive."

"Tell it like it is: when we told him we had talked with the Howards, I thought he might burst a blood vessel." Nora grimaced. "He didn't enjoy that meeting any more than we did." She spoke with the authority of long understanding. "This case nearly drove him crazy."

Van looked at her. "Yes, and he's not the only one."

Nora turned aside. "We haven't checked out the boat yet. Let's get to it."

Van examined the new turnbuckles on the shrouds. Nora set the companionway ladder aside to admire again the repaired engine—new hoses, distributor, alternator, and starter motor. She said, "Looks good." Glancing at Van, she added, "John certainly performed well, given the excruciating circumstances." She wished she could take back the words. What ever possessed her to bring up the Howards again?

"That is the general opinion, I believe." Van was looking at the tiller where it hooked into the rudder post, fingering the stainless steel cotter pin Sid had installed to keep the key from coming loose again. "His public statement resigning from West and withdrawing his candidacy at Waldorf, standing by his wife, enduring hateful letters from outraged alumni and a mixed vote by the trustees, all combined to paint a picture of a beleaguered man who, in his downfall, earned admiration for sticking to principles of decency. Too practiced by half if you ask me."

Nora raised an eyebrow. "You sound bitter."

"John handled the scandal—the whole mess—in a way that actually earned him respect in some quarters. But as far as I am concerned, neither of them has a fit moral compass. I regret agreeing to sweep his plagiarism under the rug. Others have paid more dearly for much less wrongdoing."

"But you did agree. For better or for worse, you are bound." Van grimaced but said nothing more. Nora wondered whether Van was thinking about the scandal that followed his own wife's desertion. Her determination to deflect Van's obsession with the Howards' sins put a full stop to their conversation for some minutes. Eventually she said. "It's hard to believe that five months have passed."

"Do not remind me. The only day in my life worse than confronting the Howards was the day I learned my wife had left." His declaration confirmed her earlier suspicion. She busied herself testing the fathometer while Van examined the VHF radio and the new electrical panel.

They sat topside for happy hour, letting the evening bring serenity and a return to a lighter mood. The evergreens turned from hunter green to black as day eased into night. Light from a window ashore made a silver ribbon across the placid water. Was that the Sasser's house? Nora wondered whether their marriage was as bad as it had been. No light from Ted's house.

Van's thoughts seemed to have circled in the same direction, for he said, "I heard that Suzanne had art and antique dealers in to appraise things—that she's planning an auction."

"I'd guess that the house and everything in it are part of a past she wants to put behind her. Maybe the house will be bought by someone who loves to sail and will bring good karma."

By the time they had grilled chicken breasts and made a vegetable stew, working together had restored their ease. They laughed a lot as they finished the galley clean up.

Nora insisted that Van use the sleeping bag she handed him. He removed his boat shoes and climbed in without protest, stretching out on the port cushion, flat on his back. Nora hesitated in the companionway, then kissed him lightly on the cheek, saying, "Good night, dear friend," as she withdrew below.

She crawled into the V-berth and poked her head out of the forward hatch, smelling the cool air that crossed the bow. Their talk about the murder had reminded her of visiting Frank in the hospital, of his cold anger and polite acceptance of the flowers she brought. She hadn't talked to him since. Nora sighed. She'd hate to lose his friendship. She pushed that thought into the same box as thoughts of lost loves, failures, fears, and murder, and turned the mental key. Everything would work out in the end. Settling into her sleeping bag, she heard the halyard clinking against the mast and Van moving restlessly topside. Before long she slept, the chilly night air on her face, her sleeping bag a shroud of warm comfort.

Van whispered, "Good night," to the place where Nora had been and pondered the four words of her leave-taking. Over the past several months, his love for Nora had gown and bloomed beyond his intention or control. So far, his insistence on linking love, sex, and marriage had brought nothing but frustration. Perhaps he was being too cautious. Too old fashioned. Too inflexible. He settled into a more comfortable position. Thoughts of when and how he would join her in the V-berth carried him to sleep.